FORGOTTEN REALMS®

SIEGE OF DARKNESS

THE LEGEND OF DRIZZT BOOK IX

R. A. SALVATORE

Wizards
OF THE COAST
™

THE LEGEND OF DRIZZT
BOOK IX
SIEGE OF DARKNESS

©1994 TSR, Inc.
©2006 Wizards of the Coast, Inc.

Published by Wizards of the Coast, Inc. FORGOTTEN REALMS, WIZARDS OF THE COAST, and their respective logos are trademarks of Wizards of the Coast, Inc., in the U.S.A. and other countries.

Printed in the U.S.A.

Cover art by Todd Lockwood
This Edition First Printing: November 2006
Original Hardcover Edition First Printing: August 1994

9 8 7 6 5 4 3 2 1

ISBN-10: 0-7869-4021-2
ISBN-13: 978-0-7869-4021-9
620-95549720-001-EN

U.S., CANADA,
ASIA, PACIFIC, & LATIN AMERICA
Wizards of the Coast, Inc.
P.O. Box 707
Renton, WA 98057-0707
+1-800-324-6496

EUROPEAN HEADQUARTERS
Hasbro UK Ltd
Caswell Way
Newport, Gwent NP9 0YH
GREAT BRITAIN
Save this address for your records.

Visit our web site at www.wizards.com

THE SELLSWORDS
Servant of the Shard
Promise of the Witch-King
Road of the Patriarch

THE LEGEND OF DRIZZT
Homeland
Exile
Sojourn
The Crystal Shard
Streams of Silver
The Halfling's Gem
The Legacy
Starless Night
Siege of Darkness
Passage to Dawn
The Silent Blade
The Spine of the World
Sea of Swords

THE HUNTER'S BLADES TRILOGY
The Thousand Orcs
The Lone Drow
The Two Swords

THE CLERIC QUINTET
Canticle
In Sylvan Shadows
Night Masks
The Fallen Fortress
The Chaos Curse

I first encountered the works of R.A. Salvatore as an illustrator for Wizards of the Coast, when I had to come up with a new design for Drizzt as part of the Third Edition rebuild of DUNGEONS & DRAGONS.

I realized quickly that Bob wrote excellent action sequences, which is a rare gift and hard to come by in fantasy anymore. I love a good action painting, so it felt like a natural fit from the beginning. The cover for *The Thousand Orcs* was my first opportunity to paint a cover for one of Bob's books the way I thought it should look. The Hunter's Blades Trilogy is one of my favorite series to date. Those that followed presented many opportunities to see Drizzt in action, doing what he does best: kicking ass.

INTRODUCTION

Bob is an illustrator's dream author; he gives just enough description to evoke something, and then he gets back to the action. It leaves plenty of room for a guy like me to invent something cool, to build on the seed of an idea and realize something bigger than the words alone. Invention is one of the joys of illustration, and Bob's work provides plenty of inspiration—in just the right amount.

One thing that struck me about Bob's stories were his characters' names. Some of them are classic and very cool, like Drizzt Do'Urden; unusual and evocative, like Cattie-Brie; or stolid and regal like Bruenor.

Other times they're silly beyond words, like the Bouldershoulder brothers, or the Fishsquishers. I like a comic touch—I really do—so I thought I might suggest some other names to Bob, in a similar vein, in case he's ever short of ideas:

Skidz McStainy
Waffy Thunderslippers
Slappy Flipperbutt
Barfle Muffinstuffer
Shady Undergarments
Stanky McFlapjacks
Dinky Swizzleblister
Boffo Spankybottom
Dweebil McFeeble

Honestly, Bob: they're all yours! Use them wisely.

And long may you write!

—Todd Lockwood
July 7, 2006

Alustriel
One of the fabled Seven Sisters, Chosen of Mystra.

Auro'pol Dyrr
Matron mother of House Agrach Dyrr.

DRAMATIS PERSONAE

Bella don DelRoy Harpell
A beautiful young sorceress.

Belwar Disengulp
The Most Honored Burrow Warden of
Blingdenstone.

Berg'inyon Baenre
Leader of the House Baenre lizard riders.

Berkthgar the Bold
Chieftain of Settlestone.

Besnell
An elf from Silverymoon.

Bidderdoo Harpell
A wizard, partially transformed into a dog.

Bladen'Kerst
The second daughter of Matron Baenre.

Bruenor Battlehammer
The Eighth King of Mithral Hall.

Buster Bracer
The finest armorer in Mithral Hall.

Catti-brie
The adopted daughter of Bruenor Battlehammer and
a powerful fighter.

Cobble
A dwarf priest.

Dantrag Baenre
The late drow weapons master of House Baenre.

Deudermont
Captain of the pirate hunter *Sea Sprite*.

Dinin Do'Urden
Drizzt Do'Urden's brother.

Dracos Icingdeath
A terrifying white dragon, killed by Wulfgar.

Drizzt Do'Urden
A drow ranger, living in self-imposed exile from the
Underdark city of Menzoberranzan.

Entemoch
A earth elemental prince.

Errtu
A balor demon banished from the Prime Material
Plane by Drizzt.

Fini'they
Second daughter of House Faen Tlabbar.

Firble
A deep gnome from Blingdenstone.

Fredegar "Fret" Rockcrusher
A dwarf bard, advisor to Lady Alustriel.

Gandalug Battlehammer
Ancient founder of Mithral Hall.

General Dagna
A hero of Mithral Hall.

Ghenni'tiroth Tlabbar
Matron mother of House Faen Tlabbar.

Gromph Baenre
Archmage of Menzoberranzan, the city's most powerful wizard.

Guenhwyvar
Drizzt's panther companion.

Harbromme
Dwarf king of Citadel Adbar.

Harkle Harpell
A wizard from the famous Harpell clan.

Jarlaxle
Drow leader of the Bregan D'aerthe mercenary company.

Jerbollah
A dwarf priest.

K'yorl Odran
Matron mother of House Oblodra.

Matron Baenre
The First Matron of Menzoberranzan.

Methil
A mind flayer, also known as El-Viddenvelp.

Mez'Barris Armgo
Matron mother of House Barrison del'Armgo.

M'tarl
A Bregan D'aerthe lieutenant.

Ogremoch
Entemoch's evil twin.

Quethel Baenre
A priestess, favored of Lolth.

Regis
Drizzt's halfling friend.

Regweld Harpell
A mage of some note.

Schnicktick
King of the svirfneblin.

Sos'Umptu
Daughter of Matron Baenre, caretaker of the
House chapel.

Stumpet Rackingclaw
A dwarf priestess.

Suntunavick
A svirfneblin priest.

Terrien
Half-elf leader of the Knights of Silver.

Thibbledorf Pwent
Dwarf battlerager, leader of the Gutbuster Brigade.

Triel Baenre
Ambitious daughter of Matron Baenre.

Uthegental
Weapons master of House Barrison del'Armgo.

Vendes Baenre
One of Matron Baenre's wicked daughters.

Wulfgar
A mighty barbarian, fallen in battle.

Zaknafein
Drizzt's father.

Zeerith Q'Xorlarrin
Matron mother of House Xorlarrin.

To Lucy Scaramuzzi
The truest of teachers,
who taught me how to make a book—
even though all of my ideas
back in her second-grade classroom
were stolen from Snoopy!

B y all appearances, she was too fair a creature to be walking through the swirling sludge of this smoky layer of the Abyss. Too beautiful, her features were sculpted fine and delicate, her shining ebony skin giving her the appearance of animated artwork, an obsidian sculpture come to life.

The monstrous things around her, crawling slugs and bat-winged denizens, moni-

PROLOGUE

tored her every move, watched her carefully, cautiously. Even the largest and strongest of them, gigantic fiends that could sack a fair-sized city, kept a safe distance, for appearances could be deceiving. While this fine-featured female seemed delicate, even frail by the standards of the gruesome monsters of the Abyss, she could easily destroy any one, any ten, any fifty, of the fiends now watching her.

They knew it, too, and her passage was unhindered. She was Lolth, the Spider Queen, goddess of the drow, the dark elves. She was chaos incarnate, an instrument of destruction, a monster beneath a delicate facade.

Lolth calmly strolled into a region of tall, thick mushrooms clustered on small islands amid the grimy swirl. She walked from island to island without concern, stepping so lightly about the slurping sludge that not even the bottoms of her delicate black slippers were soiled. She found many of this level's strongest inhabitants, even true tanar'ri fiends, sleeping amid those mushroom groves, and rudely roused them. Inevitably, the irritable creatures came awake snarling and promising eternal torture, and just as inevitably, they were much relieved when Lolth demanded of them only a single answer to a single question.

"Where is he?" she asked each time, and though none of the monsters knew of the great fiend's exact location, their answers led Lolth on, guided her until at last she found the beast she was looking for, a huge bipedal tanar'ri with a canine maw, the horns of a bull, and tremendous, leathery wings folded behind its huge body. Looking quite bored, it sat in a chair it had carved from one of the mushrooms, its grotesque head resting on the upraised palm of one hand. Dirty, curved claws scratched rhythmically against its pallid cheek. In its other hand the beast held a many-tongued whip and every so often, snapped it around, lashing at the side of the mushroom chair, where crouched the unfortunate lesser creature it had selected for torture during this point of eternity.

The smaller denizen yelped and whined pitifully, and that drew another stinging crack of the merciless fiend's whip.

The seated beast grunted suddenly, head coming up alert, red eyes peering intently into the smoky veil swirling all around the mushroom throne. Something was about, it knew, something powerful.

Lolth walked into view, not slowing in the least as she regarded this monster, the greatest of this area.

A guttural growl escaped the tanar'ri's lips, lips that curled into an evil smile, then turned down into a frown as it considered the pretty morsel walking into its lair. At first, the fiend thought Lolth a gift, a lost, wandering dark elf far from the Material Plane and her home. It

didn't take the fiend long to recognize the truth of this
one, though.

It sat up straight in its chair. Then, with incredible speed and fluidity for one its size, it brought itself
to its full height, twelve feet, and towered over the
intruder.

"Sit, Errtu," Lolth bade it, waving her hand impatiently. "I have not come to destroy you."

A second growl issued from the proud tanar'ri, but
Errtu made no move for Lolth, understanding that
she could easily do what she had just claimed she had
not come here to do. Just to salvage a bit of his pride,
Errtu remained standing.

"Sit!" Lolth said suddenly, fiercely, and Errtu, before
he registered the movement, found himself back on the
mushroom throne. Frustrated, he took up his whip and
battered the sniveling beast that groveled at his side.

"Why are you here, drow?" Errtu grumbled, his
deep voice breaking into higher, crackling whines, like
fingernails on slate.

"You have heard the rumblings of the pantheon?"
Lolth asked.

Errtu considered the question for a long moment. Of
course he had heard that the gods of the Realms were
quarreling, stepping over each other in intrigue-laden
power grabs and using intelligent lesser creatures as
pawns in their private games. In the Abyss, this meant
that the denizens, even greater tanar'ri such as Errtu,
were often caught up in unwanted political intrigue.

Which was exactly what Errtu figured, and feared,
was happening here.

"A time of great strife is approaching," Lolth explained. "A time when the gods will pay for their foolishness."

Errtu chuckled, a grating, terrible sound. Lolth's red-glowing gaze fell over him scornfully.

"Why would such an event displease you, Lady of Chaos?" the fiend asked.

"This trouble will be beyond me," Lolth explained, deadly serious, "beyond us all. I will enjoy watching the fools of the pantheon jostled about, stripped of their false pride, some perhaps even slain, but any worshipped being who is not cautious will find herself caught in the trouble."

"Lolth was never known for caution," Errtu put in dryly.

"Lolth was never a fool," the Spider Queen quickly replied.

Errtu nodded but sat quietly for a moment on his mushroom throne, digesting it all. "What has this to do with me?" he asked finally, for tanar'ri were not worshipped, and thus, Errtu did not draw his powers from the prayers of any faithful.

"Menzoberranzan," Lolth replied, naming the fabled city of drow, the largest base of her worshippers in all the Realms.

Errtu cocked his grotesque head.

"The city is in chaos already," Lolth explained.

"As you would have it," Errtu put in, and he snickered. "As you have arranged it."

Lolth didn't refute that. "But there is danger," the beautiful drow went on. "If I am caught in the troubles of the pantheon, the prayers of my priestesses will go unanswered."

"Am I expected to answer them?" Errtu asked incredulously.

"The faithful will need protection."

"I cannot go to Menzoberranzan!" Errtu roared suddenly, his outrage, the outrage of years of banishment, spilling over. Menzoberranzan was a city of Faerûn's Underdark, the great labyrinth beneath the world's surface. but though it was separated from the region of sunlight by miles of thick rock, it was still a place of the Material Plane. Years ago, Errtu had been on that plane, at the call of a minor wizard, and had stayed there in search of Crenshinibon, the Crystal Shard, a mighty artifact, relic of a past and greater age of sorcery. The great tanar'ri had been so close to the relic! He had entered the tower it had created in its image, and had worked with its possessor, a pitiful human who would have died soon enough, leaving the fiend to his coveted treasure. But then Errtu had met a dark elf, a renegade from Lolth's own flock, from Menzoberranzan, the city she now apparently wanted him to protect!

Drizzt Do'Urden had defeated Errtu and to a tanar'ri, a defeat on the Material Plane meant a hundred years of banishment in the Abyss.

Now Errtu trembled visibly with rage, and Lolth took a step backward, preparing herself in case the beast attacked before she could explain her offer. "You cannot go," she agreed, "but your minions can. I will see that a gate is kept open, if all the priestesses of my domain must tend it continually."

Errtu's thunderous roar drowned out the words.

Lolth understood the source of that agony. A fiend's greatest pleasure was to walk loose on the Prime Material Plane, to challenge the weak souls and weaker bodies of the various races. Lolth understood, but she did not sympathize. Evil Lolth never sympathized with any creature.

"I cannot deny you!" Errtu admitted, and his great, bulbous, bloodshot eyes narrowed wickedly.

His statement was true enough. Lolth could enlist his aid simply by offering him his very existence in return. The Spider Queen was smarter than that, however. If she enslaved Errtu and was, indeed, as she expected, caught up in the coming storm, Errtu might escape her capture or, worse, find a way to strike back at her. Lolth was malicious and merciless in the extreme, but she was, above all else, intelligent. She had in her possession honey for this fly.

"This is no threat," she said honestly to the fiend. "This is an offer."

Errtu did not interrupt, still, the bored and outraged fiend trembled on the edge of catastrophe.

"I have a gift, Errtu," she purred, "a gift that will allow you to end the banishment Drizzt Do'Urden has placed on you."

The tanar'ri did not seem convinced. "No gift," he rumbled. "No magic can break the terms of banishment. Only he who banished me can end the indenture."

Lolth nodded her agreement. Not even a goddess had the power to go against that rule. "But that is exactly the point!" the Spider Queen exclaimed. "This gift will make Drizzt Do'Urden want you back on his plane of existence, back within his reach."

Errtu did not seem convinced.

In response, Lolth lifted one arm and clamped her fist tightly, and a signal, a burst of multicolored sparks and a rocking blast of thunder, shook the swirling sludge and momentarily stole the perpetual gray of the dismal level.

Forlorn and beaten, head down—for it did not take one such as Lolth very long to sunder the pride—he walked from the fog. Errtu did not know him, but understood the significance of this gift.

Lolth clamped her fist tight again, another explosive signal sounded, and her captive fell back into the veil of smoke.

Errtu eyed the Spider Queen suspiciously. The tanar'ri was more than a little interested, of course, but he realized that most everyone who had ever trusted the diabolical Lolth had paid greatly for their foolishness. Still, this bait was too great for Errtu to resist. His canine maw turned up into a grotesque, wicked smile.

"Look upon Menzoberranzan," Lolth said, and she waved her arm before the thick stalk of a nearby mushroom. The plant's fibers became glassy, reflecting the smoke, and a moment later, Lolth and the fiend saw the city of drow. "Your role in this will be small, I assure you," Lolth said, "but vital. Do not fail me, great Errtu!"

It was as much a threat as a plea, the fiend knew.

"The gift?" he asked.

"When things are put aright."

Again a suspicious look crossed Errtu's huge face.

"Drizzt Do'Urden is a pittance," Lolth said. "Daermon N'a'shezbaernon, his family, is no more, so he means nothing to me. Still, it would please me to watch great and evil Errtu pay back the renegade for all the inconveniences he has caused."

Errtu was not stupid, far from it. What Lolth was saying made perfect sense, yet he could not ignore the fact that it was Lolth, the Spider Queen, the Lady of Chaos, who was making these tempting offers.

Neither could he ignore the fact that her gift promised him relief from the interminable boredom. He could beat a thousand minor fiends a day, every day, torture them and send them crawling pitifully into the muck. But if he did that for a million days, it would not equal the pleasure of a single hour on the Material Plane, walking among the weak, tormenting those who did not deserve his vengeance.

The great tanar'ri agreed.

PART ONE

I watched the preparations unfolding at Mithral Hall, preparations for war, for, though we, especially Catti-brie, had dealt House Baenre a stinging defeat back in Menzoberranzan, none of us doubted that the dark elves might come our way once more. Above all else, Matron Baenre was likely angry, and having spent my youth in Menzoberranzan, I knew it was not a good thing to make an enemy of the first matron mother.

RUMBLES OF DISCORD

Still, I liked what I was seeing here in the dwarven stronghold. Most of all, I enjoyed the spectacle of Bruenor Battlehammer.

Bruenor! My dearest friend. The dwarf I had fought beside since my days in Icewind Dale—days that seemed very long ago indeed! I had feared Bruenor's spirit forever broken when Wulfgar fell, that the fire that had guided this most stubborn of dwarves through seemingly insurmountable obstacles in his quest to reclaim his lost homeland had been forever doused. Not so, I learned in those days of preparation. Bruenor's physical scars were deeper now—his left eye was lost, and a bluish line ran diagonally across his face, from forehead to jawbone—but the flames of spirit had been rekindled, burning bright behind his good eye.

Bruenor directed the preparations, from agreeing to the fortification designs being constructed in the lowest tunnels to sending out emissaries to the neighboring settlements in search of allies. He asked for no help in the decision-making, and needed none, for this was Bruenor, Eighth King of Mithral Hall, a veteran of so many adventures, a dwarf who had earned his title.

His grief was gone, and he was king again, to the joy of his friends and subjects. "Let the damned drow come!" Bruenor growled quite often, and always he nodded in my direction if I was about, as if to remind me that he meant no personal insult.

In truth, that determined war cry from Bruenor Battlehammer was among the sweetest things I had ever heard.

What was it, I wondered, that had brought the grieving dwarf from his despair? And it wasn't just Bruenor. All around me I saw an excitement, in the dwarves, in Catti-brie, even in Regis, the halfling known more for preparing for lunch and nap than for war. I felt it, too. That tingling anticipation, that camaraderie that had me and all the others patting each other on the back, offering praises for the simplest of additions to the common defense, and raising our voices together in cheer whenever good news was announced.

What was it? It was more than shared fear, more than giving thanks for what we had while realizing that it might soon be stolen away. I didn't understand it then, in that time of frenzy, in that euphoria of frantic preparations. Now, looking back, it is an easy thing to recognize.

It was hope.

To any intelligent being, there is no emotion more important than hope. Individually or collectively, we must hope that the future will be better than the past, that our offspring, and theirs after them, will be a bit closer to an ideal society, whatever our perception of that might be. Certainly a warrior barbarian's hope for the future might differ from the ideal fostered in the imagination of a peaceful farmer. And a dwarf would not strive to live in a world that resembled an elf's ideal! But the hope itself is not so different. It is at those times when we feel we are contributing to that ultimate end, as it was in Mithral Hall when we believed the battle with Menzoberranzan would soon come—that we would defeat the dark elves and end, once and for all, the threat from the Underdark city—we feel true elation.

Hope is the key. The future will be better than the past, or the present. Without this belief, there is only the self-indulgent, ultimately empty striving of the present, as in drow society, or simple despair, the time of life wasted in waiting for death.

Bruenor had found a cause—we all had—and never have I been more alive than in those days of preparation in Mithral Hall.
                                    —Drizzt Do'Urden

DIPLOMACY

Her thick auburn hair bouncing below her shoulders, Catti-brie worked furiously to keep the drow's whirling scimitars at bay. She was a solidly built woman, a hundred and thirty pounds of muscles finely toned from living her life with Bruenor's dwarven clan. Catti-brie was no stranger to the forge or the sledge.

Or the sword, and this new blade, its white-metal pommel sculpted in the likeness of a unicorn's head, was by far the most balanced weapon she had ever swung. Still, Catti-brie was hard-pressed, indeed, overmatched, by her opponent this day. Few in the Realms could match blades with Drizzt Do'Urden, the drow ranger.

He was no larger than Catti-brie, a few pounds heavier perhaps, with his tight-muscled frame. His white hair hung as low as Catti-brie's mane and was equally thick, and his ebony skin glistened with streaks of sweat, a testament to the young woman's prowess.

Drizzt's two scimitars crossed in front of him—one of them glowing a fierce blue even through the protective padding that covered it—then went back out wide, inviting Catti-brie to thrust straight between.

She knew better than to make the attempt. Drizzt was too quick, and could strike her blade near its tip with one scimitar, while the other alternately parried low, batting the opposite way near the hilt. With a single step diagonally to the side, following his closer-parrying blade, Drizzt would have her beaten.

Catti-brie stepped back instead, and presented her sword in front of her. Her deep blue eyes peeked out around the blade, which had been thickened with heavy material, and she locked stares with the drow's lavender orbs.

"An opportunity missed?" Drizzt teased.

"A trap avoided," Catti-brie was quick to reply.

Drizzt came ahead in a rush, his blades crossing, going wide, and cutting across, one high and one low. Catti-brie dropped her left foot behind her and fell into a crouch, turning her sword to parry the low-rushing blade, dipping her head to avoid the high.

She needn't have bothered, for the cross came too soon, before Drizzt's feet had caught up to the move, and both his scimitars swished through the air, short of the mark.

Catti-brie didn't miss the opening, and darted ahead, sword thrusting.

Back snapped Drizzt's blades, impossibly fast, slamming the sword on both its sides. But Drizzt's feet weren't positioned correctly for him to follow the move, to go diagonally ahead and take advantage of Catti-brie's turned sword.

The young woman went ahead and to the side instead, sliding her weapon free of the clinch and executing the real attack, the slash at Drizzt's hip.

Drizzt's backhand caught her short, drove her sword harmlessly high.

They broke apart again, eyeing each other, Catti-brie wearing a sly smile. In all their months of training, she had never come so close to scoring a hit on the agile and skilled drow.

Drizzt's expression stole her glory, though, and the drow dipped the tips of his scimitars toward the floor, shaking his head in frustration.

"The bracers?" Catti-brie asked, referring to the magical wrist bands, wide pieces of black material lined with gleaming mithral rings. Drizzt had taken them from Dantrag Baenre, the deposed weapons master of Menzoberranzan's First House, after defeating Dantrag in mortal combat. Rumors said those marvelous bracers allowed Dantrag's hands to move incredibly fast, giving him the advantage in combat.

Upon battling the lightning-quick Baenre, Drizzt had come to believe those rumors, and after wearing the bracers in sparring for the last few tendays, he had confirmed their abilities. But Drizzt wasn't convinced that the bracers were a good thing. In the fight with Dantrag, he had turned Dantrag's supposed advantage against the drow, for the weapons master's hands moved too quickly for Dantrag to alter any started move, too quickly for Dantrag to improvise if his opponent made an unexpected turn. Now, in these sparring exercises, Drizzt was learning that the bracers held another disadvantage.

His feet couldn't keep up with his hands.

"Ye'll learn them," Catti-brie assured.

Drizzt wasn't so certain. "Fighting is an art of balance and movement," he explained.

"And faster ye are!" Catti-brie replied.

Drizzt shook his head. "Faster are my hands," he said. "A warrior does not win with his hands. He wins with his feet, by positioning himself to best strike the openings in his opponent's defenses."

"The feet'll catch up," Catti-brie replied. "Dantrag was the best Menzoberranzan had to offer, and ye said yerself that the bracers were the reason."

Drizzt couldn't disagree that the bracers greatly aided Dantrag, but he wondered how much they would benefit one of his skill, or one of Zaknafein's, his father's, skill. It could be, Drizzt realized, that the bracers would aid a lesser fighter, one who needed to depend on the sheer speed of his weapons. But the complete fighter, the master who had found harmony between all his muscles, would be put off balance. Or perhaps the bracers would aid someone wielding a heavier weapon, a mighty warhammer, such as Aegis-fang. Drizzt's scimitars, slender blades of no more than two pounds of metal, perfectly balanced by both workmanship and enchantment, weaved effortlessly, and even without the bracers, his hands were quicker than his feet.

"Come on then," Catti-brie scolded, waving her sword in front of her, her wide blue eyes narrowing intently, her shapely hips swiveling as she fell into a low balance.

She sensed her chance, Drizzt realized. She knew he was fighting at a disadvantage and finally sensed her chance to pay back one of the many stinging hits he had given her in their sparring.

Drizzt took a deep breath and lifted the blades. He owed it to Catti-brie to oblige, but he meant to make her earn it!

He came forward slowly, playing defensively. Her sword shot out, and he hit it twice before it ever got close, on its left side with his right hand, and on its left side again, bringing his left hand right over the presented blade and batting it with a downward parry.

Catti-brie fell with the momentum of the double block, spinning a complete circle, rotating away from her adversary. When she came around, predictably, Drizzt was in close, scimitars weaving.

Still the patient drow measured his attack, did not come too fast and strong. His blades crossed and went out wide, teasing the young woman.

Catti-brie growled and threw her sword straight out again, determined to find that elusive hole. And in came the scimitars, striking in rapid succession, again both hitting the left side of Catti-brie's sword. As before, Catti-brie spun to the right, but this time Drizzt came in hard.

Down went the young woman in a low crouch, her rear grazing the floor, and she skittered back. Both of Drizzt's blades swooshed through the air above and before her, for again his cuts came before his feet could rightly respond and position him.

Drizzt was amazed to find that Catti-brie was no longer in front of him.

He called the move the "Ghost Step," and had taught it to Catti-brie only a tenday earlier. The trick was to use the opponent's swinging weapon as an optical shield, to move within the vision-blocked area so perfectly and quickly that your opponent would not know you had come forward and to the side, that you had, in fact, stepped behind his leading hip.

Reflexively, the drow snapped his leading scimitar straight back, blade pointed low, for Catti-brie had gone past in a crouch. He beat the sword to the mark, too quickly, and the momentum of his scimitar sent it sailing futilely in front of the coming attack.

Drizzt winced as the unicorn-handled sword slapped hard against his hip.

For Catti-brie, the moment was one of pure delight. She knew, of course, that the bracers were hindering Drizzt, causing him to make mistakes of balance—mistakes that Drizzt Do'Urden hadn't made since his earliest days of fighting—but even with the uncomfortable bracers, the drow was a powerful adversary, and could likely defeat most swordsmen.

How delicious it was, then, when Catti-brie found her new sword slicing in unhindered!

Her joy was stolen momentarily by an urge to sink the blade deeper, a sudden, inexplicable anger focused directly on Drizzt.

"Touch!" Drizzt called, the signal that he had been hit, and when Catti-brie straightened and sorted out the scene, she found the drow standing a few feet away, rubbing his sore hip.

"Sorry," she apologized, realizing she had struck far too hard.

"Not to worry," Drizzt replied slyly. "Surely your one hit does not equal the combined pains my scimitars have caused you." The dark elf's lips curled up into a mischievous smile. "Or the pains I will surely inflict on you in return!"

"Me thinking's that I'm catching ye, Drizzt Do'Urden," Catti-brie answered calmly, confidently. "Ye'll get yer hits, but ye'll take yer hits as well!"

They both laughed at that, and Catti-brie moved to the side of the room and began to remove her practice gear.

Drizzt slid the padding from one of his scimitars and considered those last words. Catti-brie was indeed improving, he agreed. She had a warrior's heart, tempered by a poet's philosophy, a deadly combination indeed. Catti-brie, like Drizzt, would rather talk her way out of a battle than wage it, but when the avenues of diplomacy were exhausted, when the fight became a matter of survival, then the young woman would fight with conscience clear and passion heated. All her heart and all her skill would come to bear, and in Catti-brie, both of those ingredients were considerable.

And she was barely into her twenties! In Menzoberranzan, had she been a drow, she would be in Arach-Tinilith now, the school of Lolth, her strong morals being assaulted daily by the lies of the Spider Queen's priestesses. Drizzt shook that thought away. He didn't even want to think of Catti-brie in that awful place. Suppose she had gone to the drow school of fighters, Melee-Magthere, instead, he mused. How would she fare against the likes of young drow?

Well, Drizzt decided, Catti-brie would be near the top of her class, certainly among the top ten or fifteen percent, and her passion and dedication would get her there. How much could she improve under his tutelage? Drizzt wondered, and his expression soured as he considered the limitations of Catti-brie's heritage. He was in his sixties, barely more than a child by drow standards, for they could live to see seven centuries, but when Catti-brie reached his tender age, she would be old, too old to fight well.

That notion pained Drizzt greatly. Unless the blade of an enemy or the claws of a monster shortened his life, he would watch Catti-brie grow old, would watch her pass from this life.

Drizzt looked at her now as she removed the padded baldric and unclasped the metal collar guard. Under the padding above the waist, she wore only a simple shirt of light material. It was wet with perspiration now and clung to her.

She was a warrior, Drizzt agreed, but she was also a beautiful young woman, shapely and strong, with the spirit of a foal first learning to run and a heart filled with passion.

The sound of distant furnaces, the sudden, increased ringing of hammer on steel, should have alerted Drizzt that the room's door had opened, but it simply didn't register in the distracted drow's consciousness.

"Hey!" came a roar from the side of the chamber, and Drizzt turned to see Bruenor storm into the room. He half expected the dwarf, Catti-brie's adoptive, overprotective, father, to demand what in the Nine Hells Drizzt was looking at, and Drizzt's sigh was one of pure relief when Bruenor, his fiery red beard foamed with spittle, instead took up a tirade about Settlestone, the barbarian settlement south of Mithral Hall.

Still, the drow figured he was blushing—and hoped that his ebon-hued skin would hide it—as he shook his head, ran his fingers through his white hair to brush it back from his face, and likewise began to remove the practice gear.

Catti-brie walked over, shaking her thick auburn mane to get the droplets out. "Berkthgar is being difficult?" she reasoned, referring to Berkthgar the Bold, Settlestone's new chieftain.

Bruenor snorted. "Berkthgar can't be anything but difficult!"

Drizzt looked up at beautiful Catti-brie. He didn't want to picture her growing old, though he knew she would do it with more grace than most.

"He's a proud one," Catti-brie replied to her father, "and afraid."

"Bah!" Bruenor retorted. "What's he got to be afraid of? Got a couple hunnerd strong men around him and not an enemy in sight."

"He is afraid he will not stand well against the shadow of his predecessor," Drizzt explained, and Catti-brie nodded.

Bruenor stopped in midbluster and considered the drow's words. Berkthgar was living in Wulfgar's shadow, in the shadow of the greatest hero the barbarian tribes of faraway Icewind Dale had ever known. The man who had killed Dracos Icingdeath, the white dragon; the man who, at the tender age of twenty, had united the fierce tribes and shown them a better way of living.

Bruenor didn't believe any human could shine through the spectacle of Wulfgar's shadow, and his resigned nod showed that he agreed with, and ultimately accepted, the truth of the reasoning. A great sadness edged his expression and rimmed his steel-gray eyes, as well, for Bruenor could not think of Wulfgar, the human who had been a son to him, without that sadness.

"On what point is he being difficult?" Drizzt asked, trying to push past the difficult moment.

"On the whole damned alliance," Bruenor huffed.

Drizzt and Catti-brie exchanged curious expressions. It made no sense, of course. The barbarians of Settlestone and the dwarves of Mithral Hall already were allies, working hand in hand, with Bruenor's people mining the precious mithral and shaping it into valuable artifacts, and the barbarians doing the bargaining with merchants from nearby towns, such as Nesmé on the Trollmoors, or Silverymoon to the east. The two peoples, Bruenor's and Wulfgar's, had fought together to clear Mithral Hall of evil gray dwarves, the duergar, and the barbarians had come down from their homes in faraway Icewind Dale, resolved to stay, only because of this solid friendship and alliance with Bruenor's clan. It made no sense that Berkthgar was being difficult, not with the prospect of a drow attack hanging over their heads.

"He wants the hammer," Bruenor explained, recognizing Drizzt and Catti-brie's doubts.

That explained everything. The hammer was Wulfgar's hammer, mighty Aegis-fang, which Bruenor himself had forged as a gift for Wulfgar during the years the young man had been indentured to the red-bearded dwarf. During those years, Bruenor, Drizzt, and Catti-brie had taught the fierce young barbarian a better way.

Of course Berkthgar would want Aegis-fang, Drizzt realized. The war-hammer had become more than a weapon, had become a symbol to the hearty men and women of Settlestone. Aegis-fang symbolized the memory of Wulfgar, and if Berkthgar could convince Bruenor to let him wield it, his stature among his people would increase tenfold.

It was perfectly logical, but Drizzt knew Berkthgar would never, ever convince Bruenor to give him the hammer.

The dwarf was looking at Catti-brie then, and Drizzt, in regarding her as well, wondered if she was thinking that giving the hammer to the new barbarian leader might be a good thing. How many emotions must be swirling in the young woman's thoughts! Drizzt knew. She and Wulfgar were to have been wed. They had grown into adulthood together and had learned many of life's lessons side by side. Could Catti-brie now get beyond that, beyond her own grief, and follow a logical course to seal the alliance?

"No," she said finally, resolutely. "The hammer he cannot have."

Drizzt nodded his agreement, and was glad that Catti-brie would not let go of her memories of Wulfgar, of her love for the man. He, too, had loved Wulfgar, as a brother, and he could not picture anyone else, neither Berkthgar nor the god Tempus himself, carrying Aegis-fang.

"Never thought to give it to him," Bruenor agreed. He wagged an angry fist in the air, the muscles of his arm straining with the obvious tension. "But if that half-son of a reindeer asks again, I'll give him something else, don't ye doubt!"

Drizzt saw a serious problem brewing. Berkthgar wanted the hammer, that was understandable, even expected, but the young, ambitious barbarian leader apparently did not appreciate the depth of his request. This situation could get much worse than a strain on necessary allies, Drizzt knew. This could lead to open fighting between the peoples, for Drizzt did not doubt Bruenor's claim for a moment. If Berkthgar demanded the hammer as ransom for what he should give unconditionally, he'd be lucky to get back into the sunshine with his limbs attached.

"Me and Drizzt'll go to Settlestone," Catti-brie offered. "We'll get Berkthgar's word and give him nothing in return."

"The boy's a fool!" Bruenor huffed.

"But his people are not foolish," Catti-brie added. "He's wanting the hammer to make himself more the leader. We'll teach him that asking for something he cannot have will make him less the leader."

Strong, and passionate, and so wise, Drizzt mused, watching the young woman. She would indeed accomplish what she had claimed. He and Catti-brie would go to Settlestone and return with everything Catti-brie had just promised her father.

The drow blew a long, low sigh as Bruenor and Catti-brie moved off, the young woman going to retrieve her belongings from the side of the room. He watched the renewed hop in Bruenor's step, the life returned to the fiery dwarf. How many years would King Bruenor Battlehammer rule? Drizzt wondered. A hundred? Two hundred?

Unless the blade of an enemy or the claws of a monster shortened his life, the dwarf, too, would watch Catti-brie grow old and pass away.

It was an image that Drizzt, watching the light step of this spirited young foal, could not bear to entertain.

⚔ ⚔ ⚔ ⚔ ⚔

Khazid'hea, or Cutter, rested patiently on Catti-brie's hip, its moment of anger passed. The sentient sword was pleased by the young woman's progress as a fighter. She was able, no doubt, but still Khazid'hea wanted more, wanted to be wielded by the very finest warrior.

Right now, that warrior seemed to be Drizzt Do'Urden.

The sword had gone after Drizzt when the drow renegade had killed its former wielder, Dantrag Baenre. Khazid'hea had altered its pommel, as it usually did, from the sculpted head of a fiend—which had lured Dantrag—

to one of a unicorn, knowing that was the symbol of Drizzt Do'Urden's goddess. Still, the drow ranger had bade Catti-brie take the sword, for he favored the scimitar.

Favored the scimitar!

How Khazid'hea wished that it might alter its blade as it could the pommel! If the weapon could curve its blade, shorten and thicken it . . .

But Khazid'hea could not, and Drizzt would not wield a sword. The woman was good, though, and getting better. She was human, and would not likely live long enough to attain as great a proficiency as Drizzt, but if the sword could compel her to slay the drow . . .

There were many ways to become the best.

⚔ ⚔ ⚔ ⚔ ⚔

Matron Baenre, withered and too old to be alive, even for a drow, stood in the great chapel of Menzoberranzan's First House, her House, watching the slow progress as her slave workers tried to extract the fallen stalactite from the roof of the dome-shaped structure. The place would soon be repaired, she knew. The rubble on the floor had already been cleared away, and the bloodstains of the dozen drow killed in the tragedy had long ago been scoured clean.

But the pain of that moment, of Matron Baenre's supreme embarrassment in front of every important matron mother of Menzoberranzan, in the very moment of the first matron mother's pinnacle of power, lingered. The spearlike stalactite had cut into the roof, but it might as well have torn Matron Baenre's own heart. She had forged an alliance between the warlike Houses of the drow city, a joining solidified by the promise of new glory when the drow army conquered Mithral Hall.

New glory for the Spider Queen. New glory for Matron Baenre.

Shattered by the point of a stalactite, by the escape of that renegade Drizzt Do'Urden. To Drizzt she had lost her eldest son, Dantrag, perhaps the finest weapons master in Menzoberranzan. To Drizzt she had lost her daughter, wicked Vendes. And most painful of all to the old wretch, she had lost to Drizzt and his friends the alliance, the promise of greater glory. For when the matron mothers, the rulers of Menzoberranzan and priestesses all, had watched the stalactite pierce the roof of this chapel, this most sacred place of Lolth, at the time of high ritual, their confidence that the goddess had sanctioned both this alliance and the coming war had crumbled. They had left House Baenre in a rush, back to their own houses, where they sealed their gates and tried to discern the will of Lolth.

Matron Baenre's status had suffered greatly.

Even with all that had happened, though, the first matron mother was confident she could restore the alliance. On a necklace around her neck she kept a ring carved from the tooth of an ancient dwarven king, one Gandalug Battlehammer, patron of Clan Battlehammer, founder of Mithral Hall. Matron Baenre owned Gandalug's spirit and could exact answers from it about the ways of the dwarven mines. Despite Drizzt's escape, the dark elves could go to Mithral Hall, could punish Drizzt and his friends.

She could restore the alliance, but for some reason that Matron Baenre did not understand, Lolth, the Spider Queen herself, held her in check. The yochlol, the handmaidens of Lolth, had come to Baenre and warned her to forego the alliance and instead focus her attention on her family, to secure her House defenses. It was a demand no priestess of the Spider Queen would dare disobey.

She heard the harsh clicking of hard boots on the floor behind her and the jingle of ample jewelry, and she didn't have to turn around to know that Jarlaxle had entered.

"You have done as I asked?" she questioned, still looking at the continuing work on the domed ceiling.

"Greetings to you as well, First Matron Mother," the always sarcastic male replied. That turned Baenre to face him, and she scowled, as she and so many other of Menzoberranzan's ruling females scowled when they looked at the mercenary.

He was swaggering—there was no other word to describe him. The dark elves of Menzoberranzan, particularly the lowly males, normally donned quiet, practical clothes, dark-hued robes adorned with spiders or webs, or plain black jerkins beneath supple chain mail armor, and almost always,

both male and female drow wore camouflaging *piwafwis*, dark cloaks that could hide them from the probing eyes of their many enemies.

Not so with Jarlaxle. His head was shaven and always capped by an outrageous wide-brimmed hat feathering the gigantic plume of a diatryma bird. In lieu of a cloak or robe, he wore a shimmering cape that flickered through every color of the spectrum, both in light and under the scrutiny of heat-sensing eyes looking in the infrared range. His sleeveless vest was cut high to show the tight muscles of his stomach, and he carried an assortment of rings and necklaces, bracelets, even anklets, that chimed gratingly—but only when the mercenary wanted them to. Like his boots, which had sounded so clearly on the hard chapel floor, the jewelry could be silenced completely.

Matron Baenre noted that the mercenary's customary eye patch was over his left eye this day, but what, if anything, that signified, she could not tell.

For who knew what magic was in that patch, or in those jewels and those boots, or in the two wands he wore tucked under his belt, and the fine sword he kept beside them? Half those items, even one of the wands, Matron Baenre believed, were likely fakes, with little or no magical properties other than, perhaps, the ability to fall silent. Half of everything Jarlaxle did was a bluff, but half of it was devious and ultimately deadly.

That was why the swaggering mercenary was so dangerous.

That was why Matron Baenre hated Jarlaxle so, and why she needed him so. He was the leader of Bregan D'aerthe, a network of spies, thieves, and killers, mostly rogue males made Houseless when their families had been wiped out in one of the many interhouse wars. As mysterious as their dangerous leader, Bregan D'aerthe's members were not known, but they were indeed very powerful—as powerful as most of the city's established Houses—and very effective.

"What have you learned?" Matron Baenre asked bluntly.

"It would take me centuries to spew it all," the cocky rogue replied.

Baenre's red-glowing eyes narrowed, and Jarlaxle realized she was not in the mood for his flippancy. She was scared, he knew, and considering the catastrophe at the high ritual, rightly so.

"I find no conspiracy," the mercenary honestly admitted.

Matron Baenre's eyes widened, and she swayed back on her heels, surprised by the straightforward answer. She had enacted spells that would allow her to detect any outright lies the mercenary spoke, of course. And of course, Jarlaxle would know that. Those spells never seemed to bother the crafty mercenary leader, who could dance around the perimeters of any question, never quite telling the truth, but never overtly lying.

This time, though, he had answered bluntly, and right to the heart of the obvious question. And as far as Matron Baenre could tell, he was telling the truth.

Baenre could not accept it. Perhaps her spell was not functioning as intended. Perhaps Lolth had indeed abandoned her for her failure, and was thus deceiving her now concerning Jarlaxle's sincerity.

"Matron Mez'Barris Armgo," Jarlaxle went on, referring to the matron mother of Barrison del'Armgo, the city's Second House, "remains loyal to you, and to your cause, despite the . . ." He fished around for the correct word. "The disturbance," he said at length, "to the high ritual. Matron Mez'Barris is even ordering her garrison to keep on the ready in case the march to Mithral Hall is resumed. And they are more than eager to go, I can assure you, especially with . . ." The mercenary paused and sighed with mock sadness, and Matron Baenre understood his reasoning.

Logically, Mez'Barris would be eager to go to Mithral Hall, for with Dantrag Baenre dead, her own weapons master, mighty Uthegental, was indisputably the greatest in the city. If Uthegental could get the rogue Do'Urden, what glories House Barrison del'Armgo might know!

Yet that very logic, and Jarlaxle's apparently honest claim, flew in the face of Matron Baenre's fears, for without the assistance of Barrison del'Armgo, no combination of Houses in Menzoberranzan could threaten House Baenre.

"The minor shuffling among your surviving children has commenced, of course," Jarlaxle went on. "But they have had little contact, and if any of them plan to move against you, it will be without the aid of Triel, who has been kept busy in the Academy since the escape of the rogue."

Matron Baenre did well to hide her relief at that statement. If Triel, the most powerful of her daughters, and certainly the one most in Lolth's

favor, was not planning to rise against her, a coup from within seemed unlikely.

"It is expected that you will soon name Berg'inyon as weapons master, and Gromph will not oppose," Jarlaxle remarked.

Matron Baenre nodded her agreement. Gromph was her elderboy, and as Archmage of Menzoberranzan, he held more power than any male in the city—except for, perhaps, sly Jarlaxle. Gromph would not disapprove of Berg'inyon as weapons master of House Baenre. The ranking of Baenre's daughters seemed secure as well, she had to admit. Triel was in place as Mistress Mother of Arach-Tinilith in the Academy, and though those remaining in the House might squabble over the duties and powers left vacant by the loss of Vendes, it didn't seem likely to concern her.

Matron Baenre looked back to the spike Drizzt and his companions had put through the ceiling, and was not satisfied. In cruel and merciless Menzoberranzan, satisfaction and the smugness that inevitably accompanied it too often led to an untimely demise.

2

THE GUTBUSTER BRIGADE

W e're thinking we'll need the thing?" Catti-brie asked as she and Drizzt made their way along the lower levels of Mithral Hall. They moved along a corridor that opened wide to their left, into the great tiered cavern housing the famed dwarven Undercity.

Drizzt paused and regarded her, then went to the left, drawing Catti-brie behind him. He stepped through the opening, emerging on the second tier up from the huge cavern's floor.

The place was bustling, with dwarves running every which way, shouting to be heard over the continual hum of great pumping bellows and the determined ring of hammer on mithral. This was the heart of Mithral Hall, a huge, open cavern cut into gigantic steps on both its east and west walls, so that the whole place resembled an inverted pyramid. The widest floor area was the lowest level, between the gigantic steps, housing the huge furnaces. Strong dwarves pulled carts laden with ore along prescribed routes, while others worked the many levers of the intricate ovens, and still others tugged smaller carts of finished metals up to the tiers. There the various craftsman pounded the ore into useful items. Normally, a great variety of goods would be produced here—fine silverware, gem-studded chalices, and ornate helmets—gorgeous but of little practical use. Now, though, with war hanging over their heads, the dwarves focused on weapons and true defensive armor. Twenty feet to the side of Drizzt and Catti-brie, a dwarf

so soot-covered that the color of his beard was not distinguishable leaned another iron-shafted, mithral-tipped ballista bolt against the wall. The dwarf couldn't even reach the top of the eight-foot spear, but he regarded its barbed and many-edged tip and chuckled. No doubt he enjoyed a fantasy concerning its flight and little drow elves all standing in a row.

On one of the arcing bridges spanning the tiers, perhaps a hundred and fifty feet up from the two friends, a substantial argument broke out. Drizzt and Catti-brie could not make out the words above the general din, but they realized that it had to do with plans for dropping that bridge, and most of the other bridges, forcing any invading dark elves along certain routes if they intended to reach the complex's higher levels.

None of them, not Drizzt, Catti-brie, or any of Bruenor's people, hoped it would ever come to that.

The two friends exchanged knowing looks. Rarely in the long history of Mithral Hall had the Undercity seen this kind of excitement. It bordered on frenzy. Two thousand dwarves rushed around, shouting, pounding their hammers, or hauling loads that a mule wouldn't pull.

All of this because they feared the drow were coming.

Catti-brie understood then why Drizzt had detoured into this place, why he had insisted on finding the halfling Regis before going to Settlestone, as Bruenor had bade them.

"Let's go find the sneaky one," she said to Drizzt, having to yell to be heard. Drizzt nodded and followed her back into the relative quiet of the dim corridors. They moved away from the Undercity then, toward the remote chambers where Bruenor had told them they could find the halfling. Silently they moved along—and Drizzt was impressed with how quietly Catti-brie had learned to move. Like him, she wore a fine mesh armor suit of thin but incredibly strong mithral rings, custom fitted to her by Buster Bracer, the finest armorer in Mithral Hall. Catti-brie's armor did little to diminish the dwarf's reputation, for it was so perfectly crafted and supple that it bent with her movements as easily as a thick shirt.

Like Drizzt's, Catti-brie's boots were thin and well worn but to the drow's sharp ears, few humans, even so attired, could move so silently. Drizzt subtly eyed her in the dim, flickering light of the widely spaced torches. He noted that she was stepping like a drow, the ball of her foot touching down first, instead of the more common human heel-toe method. Her time in the Underdark, chasing Drizzt to Menzoberranzan, had served her well.

The drow nodded his approval but made no comment. Catti-brie had already earned her pride points this day, he figured. No sense in puffing up her ego any more.

The corridors were empty and growing increasingly dark. Drizzt did not miss this point. He even let his vision slip into the infrared spectrum, where the varying heat of objects showed him their general shapes. Human Catti-brie did not possess such Underdark vision, of course, but around her head she wore a thin silver chain, set in its front with a green gemstone streaked by a single line of black: a cat's eye agate. It had been given to her by Lady Alustriel herself, enchanted so that its wearer could see, even in the darkest, deepest tunnels, as though she were standing in an open field under a starry sky.

The two friends had no trouble navigating in the darkness, but still, they were not comfortable with it. Why weren't the torches burning? they each wondered. Both had their hands close to weapon hilts. Catti-brie wished she had brought Taulmaril the Heartseeker, her magical bow, with her.

A tremendous crash sounded, and the floor trembled under their feet. Both were down in a crouch, and Drizzt's scimitars appeared in his hands so quickly that Catti-brie didn't even register the movement. At first the young woman thought the impossibly fast maneuver the result of the magical bracers, but in glancing at Drizzt, she realized he wasn't even wearing them. She likewise drew her sword and took a deep breath, privately scolding herself for thinking she was getting close in fighting skill to the incredible ranger. Catti-brie shook the thought aside—no time for it now—and concentrated on the winding corridor ahead. Side by side, she and Drizzt slowly advanced, looking for shadows where enemies might hide and for lines in the wall that would indicate cunning secret doors to side passages. Such ways were common in the dwarven complex, for most dwarves could make them, and most dwarves, greedy by nature, kept personal treasures hidden away. Catti-brie did not know this little-used section of Mithral Hall very well. Neither did Drizzt.

Another crash came, and the floor trembled again, more than before, and the friends knew they were getting closer. Catti-brie was glad she had been training so hard, and gladder still that Drizzt Do'Urden was by her side.

She stopped moving, and Drizzt did likewise, turning to regard her.

"Guenhwyvar?" she silently mouthed, referring to Drizzt's feline friend, a loyal panther that the drow could summon from the Astral Plane.

Drizzt considered the suggestion for a moment. He tried not to summon Guenhwyvar too often now, knowing there might soon be a time when the panther would be needed often. There were limits on the magic. Guenhwyvar could only remain on the Prime Material Plane for half a day out of every two.

Not yet, Drizzt decided. Bruenor had not indicated what Regis might be doing down here, but the dwarf had given no hint that there might be danger. The drow shook his head slightly, and the two moved on, silent and sure.

A third crash came, followed by a groan.

"Yer head, ye durned fool!" came a sharp scolding. "Ye gots to use yer stinkin' head!"

Drizzt and Catti-brie straightened immediately and relaxed their grips on their weapons. "Pwent," they said together, referring to Thibbledorf Pwent, the outrageous battlerager, the most obnoxious and bad-smelling dwarf south of the Spine of the World—and probably north of it, as well.

"Next ye'll be wantin' to wear a stinkin' helmet!" the tirade continued.

Around the next bend, the two companions came to a fork in the corridor. To the left, Pwent continued roaring in outrage, and to the right was a door with torchlight showing through its many cracks. Drizzt cocked his head, catching a slight and familiar chuckle that way.

He motioned for Catti-brie to follow and went through the door without knocking. Regis stood alone inside, leaning on a crank near the left-hand wall. The halfling's smile lit up when he saw his friends, and he waved one hand high to them—relatively high, for Regis was small, even by halfling standards, his curly brown hair barely topping three feet. He had an ample belly, though it seemed to be shrinking of late, as even the lazy halfling took seriously the threat to this place that had become his home.

He put a finger over pursed lips as Drizzt and Catti-brie approached, and he pointed to the "door" before him. It didn't take either of the companions long to understand what was transpiring. The crank next to Regis operated a sheet of heavy metal that ran along runners above and to the side of the door. The wood of the door could hardly be seen now, for the plate was in place right before it.

"Go!" came a thunderous command from the other side, followed by charging footsteps and a grunting roar, then a tremendous explosion as the barreling dwarf hit, and of course bounced off, the barricaded portal.

"Battlerager training," Regis calmly explained.

Catti-brie gave Drizzt a sour look, remembering what her father had told her of Pwent's plans. "The Gutbuster Brigade," she remarked, and Drizzt nodded, for Bruenor had told him, too, that Thibbledorf Pwent meant to train a group of dwarves in the not-so-subtle art of battleraging, his personal Gutbuster Brigade, highly motivated, skilled in frenzy, and not too smart.

Another dwarf hit the barricaded door, probably headfirst, and Drizzt understood how Pwent meant to facilitate the third of his three requirements for his soldiers.

Catti-brie shook her head and sighed. She did not doubt the military value of the brigade—Pwent could outfight anyone in Mithral Hall, except for Drizzt and maybe Bruenor, but the notion of a bunch of little Thibbledorf Pwents running around surely turned her stomach!

Behind the door, Pwent was thoroughly scolding his troops, calling them every dwarven curse name, more than a few that Catti-brie, who had lived among the clan for more than a score of years, had never heard, and more than a few that Pwent seemed to be making up on the spot, such as "mule-kissin', flea-sniffin', water-drinkin', who-thinks-ye-squeeze-the-durned-cow-to-get-the-durned-milk, lumps o' sandstone."

"We are off to Settlestone," Drizzt explained to Regis, the drow suddenly anxious to be out of there. "Berkthgar is being difficult."

Regis nodded. "I was there when he told Bruenor he wanted the warhammer." The halfling's cherubic face turned up into one of his common, wistful smiles. "I truly believed Bruenor would cleave him down the middle!"

"We're needing Berkthgar," Catti-brie reminded the halfling.

Regis pooh-poohed that thought away. "Bluffing," he insisted. "Berkthgar needs us, and his people would not take kindly to his turning his back on the dwarves who have been so good to his folk."

"Bruenor would not really kill him," Drizzt said, somewhat unconvincingly. All three friends paused and looked to each other, each considering the tough dwarf king, the old and fiery Bruenor returned. They thought of Aegis-fang, the most beautiful of weapons, the flanks of its gleaming mithral head inscribed with the sacred runes of the dwarven gods. One side was cut with the hammer and anvil of Moradin the Soulforger, the other with the crossed axes of Clanggedon, dwarven god of battle, and both were covered perfectly by the carving of the gem within the mountain, the symbol of Dumathoin, the Keeper of Secrets. Bruenor had been among the best of the dwarven smiths, but after Aegis-fang, that pinnacle of creative triumph, he had rarely bothered to return to his forge.

They thought of Aegis-fang, and they thought of Wulfgar, who had been like Bruenor's son, the tall, fair-haired youth for whom Bruenor had made the mighty hammer.

"Bruenor *would* really kill him," Catti-brie said, echoing the thoughts of all three.

Drizzt started to speak, but Regis stopped him by holding up a finger.

" . . . now get yer head lower!" Pwent was barking on the other side of the door. Regis nodded and smiled and motioned for Drizzt to continue.

"We thought you might—"

Another crash sounded, then another groan, followed by the flapping of dwarven lips as the fallen would-be battlerager shook his head vigorously.

"Good recovery!" Pwent congratulated.

"We thought you might accompany us," Drizzt said, ignoring Catti-brie's sigh of disgust.

Regis thought about it for a moment. The halfling would have liked to get out of the mines and stretch in the sunshine once more, though the summer was all but over and the autumn chill already began to nip the air.

"I have to stay," the unusually dedicated halfling remarked. "I've much to do."

Both Drizzt and Catti-brie nodded. Regis had changed over the last few months, during the time of crisis. When Drizzt and Catti-brie had gone to Menzoberranzan—Drizzt to end the threat to Mithral Hall, Catti-brie to find Drizzt—Regis had taken command to spur grieving Bruenor into preparing for war. Regis, who had spent most of his life finding the softest couch to lie upon, had impressed even the toughest dwarf generals, even Thibbledorf Pwent, with his fire and energy. Now the halfling would have loved to go, both of them knew, but he remained true to his mission.

Drizzt looked hard at Regis, trying to find the best way to make his request. To his surprise, the halfling saw it coming, and immediately Regis's hands went to the chain around his neck. He lifted the ruby pendant over his head and casually tossed it to Drizzt.

Another testament to the halfling's growth, Drizzt knew, as he stared down at the sparkling ruby affixed to the chain. This was the halfling's most precious possession, a powerful charm Regis had stolen from his old guild master in far-off Calimport. The halfling had guarded it, coveted it, like a mother lion with a single cub, at least until this point.

Drizzt continued to look at the ruby, felt himself drawn by its multiple facets, spiraling down to depths that promised . . .

The drow shook his head and forced himself to look away. Even without one to command it, the enchanted ruby had reached out for him! Never had he witnessed such a powerful charm. And yet, Jarlaxle, the mercenary, had given it back to him, had willingly swapped it when they had met in the tunnels outside Menzoberranzan after Drizzt's escape. It was unexpected and important that Jarlaxle had given it back to Drizzt, but what the significance might be, Drizzt had not yet discerned.

"You should be careful before using that on Berkthgar," Regis said, drawing Drizzt from his thoughts. "He is proud, and if he figures out that sorcery was used against him, the alliance may indeed be dissolved."

"True enough," Catti-brie agreed. She looked to Drizzt.

"Only if we need it," the drow remarked, looping the chain around his neck. The pendant settled near his breast and the ivory unicorn head, symbol of his goddess, that rested there.

Another dwarf hit the door and bounced off, then lay groaning on the floor.

"Bah!" they heard Pwent snort. "Ye're a bunch o' elf-lickin' pixies! I'll show ye how it's done!"

Regis nodded—that was his cue—and immediately began to turn the crank, drawing the metal plate out from behind the portal.

"Watch out," he warned his two companions, for they stood in the general direction of where Pwent would make his door-busting entrance.

"I'm for leaving," Catti-brie said, starting for the other, normal, door. The young woman had no desire to see Pwent. Likely, he would pinch her cheek with his grubby fingers and tell her to "work on that beard" so that she might be a beautiful woman.

Drizzt didn't take much convincing. He held up the ruby, nodded a silent thanks to Regis, and rushed out into the hall after Catti-brie.

They hadn't gone a dozen steps when they heard the training door explode, followed by Pwent's hysterical laughter and the admiring "oohs" and "aahs" of the naive Gutbuster Brigade.

"We should send the lot of them to Menzoberranzan," Catti-brie said dryly. "Pwent'd chase the whole city to the ends of the world!"

Drizzt—who had grown up among the unbelievably powerful drow Houses and had seen the wrath of the high priestesses and magical feats beyond anything he had witnessed in his years on the surface—did not disagree.

✕ ✕ ✕ ✕ ✕

Councilor Firble ran a wrinkled hand over his nearly bald pate, feeling uncomfortable in the torchlight. Firble was a svirfneblin, a deep gnome, eighty pounds of wiry muscles packed into a three-and-a-half-foot frame. Few races of the Underdark could get along as well as the svirfnebli, and no race, except perhaps the rare pech, understood the ways of the deep stone so well.

Still, Firble was more than a bit afraid now, out in the—hopefully—empty corridors beyond the borders of Blingdenstone, the city that was his home. He hated the torchlight, hated any light, but the orders from King Schnicktick were final and unarguable: no gnome was to traverse the corridors without a burning torch in his hand.

No gnome except for one. Firble's companion this day carried no torch, for he possessed no hands. Belwar Dissengulp, Most Honored Burrow Warden of Blingdenstone, had lost his hands to drow, to Drizzt Do'Urden's brother Dinin, many years before. Unlike so many other Underdark races, though, the svirfnebli were not without compassion, and their artisans had fashioned marvelous replacements of pure, enchanted mithral: a block-headed hammer capping Belwar's right arm and a two-headed pickaxe on his left.

"Completed the circuit, we have," Firble remarked. "And back to Bling-denstone we go!"

"Not so!" Belwar grumbled. His voice was deeper and stronger than those of most svirfnebli, and was fitting, considering his stout, barrel-chested build.

"There are no drow in the tunnels," Firble insisted. "Not a fight in three tendays!"

It was true enough. After months of battling drow from Menzoberran-zan in the tunnels near Blingdenstone, the corridors had gone strangely quiet. Belwar understood that Drizzt Do'Urden, his friend, had somehow played a part in this change, and he feared that Drizzt had been captured or killed.

"Quiet, it is," Firble said more softly, as if he had just realized the danger of his own volume. A shudder coursed the smaller svirfneblin's spine. Belwar had forced him out here—it was his turn in the rotation, but normally one as experienced and venerable as Firble would have been excused from scouting duties. Belwar had insisted, though, and for some reason Firble did not understand, King Schnicktick had agreed with the most honored burrow warden.

Not that Firble was unaccustomed to the tunnels. Quite the contrary. He was the only gnome of Blingdenstone with actual contacts in Menzo-berranzan, and was more acquainted with the tunnels near the drow city than any other deep gnome. That dubious distinction was causing Firble fits these days, particularly from Belwar. When a disguised Catti-brie had been captured by the svirfnebli, and subsequently recognized as no enemy, Firble, at great personal risk, had been the one to show her quicker, secret ways into Menzoberranzan.

Now Belwar wasn't worried about any drow in the tunnels, Firble knew. The tunnels were quiet. The gnome patrols and other secret allies could find no hint that any drow were about at all, not even along the dark elves' normal routes closer to Menzoberranzan. Something important had happened in the drow city, that much was obvious, and it seemed obvious, too, that Drizzt and that troublesome Catti-brie were somehow involved. That was the real reason Belwar had forced Firble out here, Firble knew, and he shuddered again to think that was why King Schnicktick had so readily agreed with Belwar.

"Something has happened," Belwar said, unexpectedly playing his cards, as though he understood Firble's line of silent reasoning. "Something in Menzoberranzan."

Firble eyed the most honored burrow warden suspiciously. He knew what would soon be asked of him, knew that he would soon be dealing with that trickster Jarlaxle again.

"The stones themselves are uneasy," Belwar went on.

"As if the drow will soon march," Firble interjected dryly.

"*Cosim camman denoctusd,*" Belwar agreed, in an ancient svirfneblin saying that translated roughly into "the settled ground before the earthquake," or, as it was more commonly known to surface dwellers, "the calm before the storm."

"That I meet with my drow informant, King Schnicktick desires," Firble reasoned, seeing no sense in holding back the guess any longer. He knew he would not be suggesting something that Belwar wasn't about to suggest to him.

"*Cosim camman denoctusd,*" Belwar said again, with increased determination. Belwar, Schnicktick, and many others in Blingdenstone were convinced that the drow would soon march in force. Though the most direct tunnels to the surface, to where Drizzt Do'Urden called home, were east of Blingdenstone, beyond Menzoberranzan, the drow first would have to set out west, and would come uncomfortably close to the gnome city. So unsettling was that thought that King Schnicktick had ordered scouting parties far to the east and south, as far from home and Menzoberranzan as the svirfnebli had ever roamed. There were whispers of deserting Blingdenstone altogether, if the rumors proved likely and a new location could be found. No gnome wanted that, Belwar and Firble perhaps least of all. Both were old, nearing their second full century, and both were tied, heart and soul, to this city called Blingdenstone.

But among all the svirfnebli, these two understood the power of a drow march, understood that if Menzoberranzan's army came to Blingdenstone, the gnomes would be obliterated.

"Set up the meeting, I will," Firble said with a resigned sigh. "He will tell me little, I do not doubt. Never does he, and high always is the price!"

Belwar said nothing, and sympathized little for the cost of such a meeting with the greedy drow informant. The most honored burrow warden understood that the price of ignorance would be much higher. He also realized that Firble understood, as well, and that the councilor's apparent resignation was just a part of Firble's bluster. Belwar had come to know Firble well, and found that he liked the oft-complaining gnome.

Now Belwar, and every other svirfneblin in Blingdenstone, desperately needed Firble and his contacts.

3

AT PLAY

Drizzt and Catti-brie skipped down the rocky trails, weaving in and out of boulder tumbles as effortlessly and spiritedly as two children at play. Their trek became an impromptu race as each hopped breaks in the stone, leaped to catch low branches, then swung down as far as the small mountain trees would carry them. They came onto one low, level spot together, where each leaped a small pool—though Catti-brie didn't quite clear it—and split up as they approached a slab of rock taller than either of them. Catti-brie went right and Drizzt started left, then changed his mind and headed up the side of the barrier instead.

Catti-brie skidded around the slab, pleased to see that she was first to the other side.

"My lead!" she cried, but even as she spoke she saw her companion's dark, graceful form sail over her head.

"Not so!" Drizzt corrected, touching down so lightly that it seemed as if he had never been off the ground. Catti-brie groaned and kicked into a run again, but pulled up short, seeing that Drizzt had stopped.

"Too fine a day," the dark elf remarked. Indeed, it was as fine a day as the southern spur of the Spine of the World ever offered once the autumn winds began to blow. The air was crisp, the breeze cool, and puffy white clouds—gigantic snowballs, they seemed—raced across the deep blue sky on swift mountain winds.

"Too fine for arguing with Berkthgar," Catti-brie added, thinking that was the direction of the drow's statement. She bent a bit and put her hands to her thighs for support, then turned her head back and up, trying to catch her breath.

"Too fine to leave Guenhwyvar out of it!" Drizzt clarified happily.

Catti-brie's smile was wide when she looked down to see Drizzt take the onyx panther figurine out of his backpack. It was among the most beautiful of artworks Catti-brie had ever seen, perfectly detailed to show the muscled flanks and the true, insightful expression of the great cat. As perfect as it was, though, the figurine paled beside the magnificent creature that it allowed Drizzt to summon.

The drow reverently placed the item on the ground before him. "Come to me, Guenhwyvar," he called softly. Apparently the panther was eager to return, for a gray mist swirled around the item almost immediately, gradually taking shape and solidifying.

Guenhwyvar came to the Material Plane with ears straight up, relaxed, as though the cat understood from the inflections of Drizzt's call that there was no emergency, that she was being summoned merely for companionship.

"We are racing to Settlestone," Drizzt explained. "Do you think you can keep pace?"

The panther understood. A single spring from powerful hind legs sent Guenhwyvar soaring over Catti-brie's head, across the twenty-foot expanse to the top of the rock slab she and Drizzt had just crossed. The cat hit the rock's flat top, backpedaled, and spun to face the duo. Then for no other reason than to give praise to the day, Guenhwyvar reared and stood tall in the air, a sight that sent her friends' hearts racing. Guenhwyvar was six hundred pounds, twice the size of an ordinary panther, with a head almost as wide as Drizzt's shoulders, a paw that could cover a man's face, and spectacular, shining green eyes that revealed an intelligence far beyond what an animal should possess. Guenhwyvar was the most loyal of companions, an unjudging friend, and every time Drizzt, Catti-brie, Bruenor, or Regis, looked at the cat, their lives were made just a bit warmer.

"Me thinking's that we should get a head start," Catti-brie whispered mischievously.

Drizzt gave a slight, inconspicuous nod, and they broke together, running full-out down the trail. A few seconds later they heard Guenhwyvar roar behind them, still from atop the slab of rock. The trail was relatively clear and Drizzt sprinted out ahead of Catti-brie, though the woman, young and strong, with a heart that would have been more appropriate in the chest of a sturdy dwarf, could not be shaken.

"Ye're not to beat me!" she cried, to which Drizzt laughed. His mirth disappeared as he rounded a bend to find that stubborn and daring Catti-brie had taken a somewhat treacherous shortcut, light-skipping over a patch of broken and uneven stones, to take an unexpected lead.

Suddenly this was more than a friendly competition. Drizzt lowered his head and ran full-out, careening down the uneven ground so recklessly that he was barely able to avoid smacking face first into a tree. Catti-brie paced him, step for step, and kept her lead.

Guenhwyvar roared again, and they knew they were being mocked.

Sure enough, barely a few seconds later, a black streak rebounded off a wall of stone to Drizzt's side, crossing level with the drow's head. Guenhwyvar cut back across the trail between the two companions, and passed Catti-brie so quickly and so silently that she hardly realized she was no longer leading.

Sometime later, Guenhwyvar let her get ahead again, then Drizzt took a treacherous shortcut and slipped into the front—only to be passed again by the panther. So it went, with competitive Drizzt and Catti-brie working hard, and Guenhwyvar merely hard at play.

The three were exhausted—at least Drizzt and Catti-brie were; Guenhwyvar wasn't even breathing hard—when they broke for lunch on a small clearing, protected from the wind by a high wall on the north and east, and dropping off fast in a sheer cliff to the south. Several rocks dotted the clearing, perfect stools for the tired companions. A grouping of stones was set in the middle as a fire pit, for this was a usual campsite of the oft-wandering drow.

Catti-brie relaxed while Drizzt brought up a small fire. Far below she could see the gray plumes of smoke rising lazily into the clear air from the houses of Settlestone. It was a sobering sight, for it reminded the young woman, who had spent the morning at such a pace, of the gravity of her mission and of the situation. How many runs might she, Drizzt, and Guenhwyvar share if the dark elves came calling?

Those plumes of smoke also reminded Catti-brie of the man who had brought the tough barbarians to this place from Icewind Dale, the man who was to have been her husband. Wulfgar had died trying to save her, had died in the grasp of a yochlol, a handmaiden of evil Lolth. Both Catti-brie and Drizzt had to bear some responsibility for that loss, yet it wasn't guilt that pained the young woman now, or that pained Drizzt. He, too, had noticed the smoke and had taken a break from his fire-tending to watch and contemplate.

The companions did not smile now, for simple loss, because they had taken so many runs just like this one, except that Wulfgar had raced beside them, his long strides making up for the fact that he could not squeeze through breaks that his two smaller companions could pass at full speed.

"I wish . . . " Catti-brie said, and the words resonated in the ears of the similarly wishing dark elf.

"Our war, if it comes, would be better fought with Wulfgar, son of Beornegar, leading the men of Settlestone," Drizzt agreed, and what both he and Catti-brie silently thought was that all their lives would be better if Wulfgar were alive.

There. Drizzt had said it openly, and there was no more to say. They ate their lunch silently. Even Guenhwyvar lay very still and made not a sound.

Catti-brie's mind drifted from her friends, back to Icewind Dale, to the rocky mountain, Kelvin's Cairn, dotting the otherwise flat tundra. It was so similar to this very place. Colder, perhaps, but the air held the same crispness, the same clear, vital texture. How far she and her friends, Drizzt and Guenhwyvar, Bruenor and Regis, and of course, Wulfgar, had come from that place! And in so short a time! A frenzy of adventures, a lifetime of excitement and thrills and good deeds. Together they were an unbeatable force.

So they had thought.

Catti-brie had seen the emotions of a lifetime, indeed, and she was barely into her twenties. She had run fast through life, like her run down the mountain trails, free and high-spirited, skipping without care, feeling immortal.

Almost.

At the Seams

A *conspiracy?*" the drow's fingers flashed, using the silent hand code of the dark elves, its movements so intricate and varied that nearly every connotation of every word in the drow language could be represented.

Jarlaxle replied with a slight shake of his head. He sighed and seemed sincerely perplexed—a sight not often seen—and motioned for his cohort to follow him to a more secure area.

They crossed the wide, winding avenues of Menzoberranzan, flat, clear areas between the towering stalagmite mounds that served as homes to the various drow families. Those mounds, and a fair number of long stalactites leering down from the huge cavern's ceiling, were hollowed out and sculpted with sweeping balconies and walkways. The clusters within each family compound were often joined by high bridges, most shaped to resemble spiderwebs. And on all the houses, especially those of the older and more established families, the most wondrous designs were highlighted by glowing faerie fire, purple and blue, sometimes outlined in red and not so often, in green. Menzoberranzan was the most spectacular of cities, breathtaking, surreal, and an ignorant visitor—who would not be ignorant, or likely even alive, for long!—would never guess that the artisans of such beauty were among the most malicious of Toril's races.

Jarlaxle moved without a whisper down the darker, tighter avenues surrounding the lesser Houses. His focus was ahead and to the sides, his keen

eye—and his eye patch was over his right eye at the time—discerning the slightest of movements in the most distant shadows.

The mercenary leader's surprise was complete when he glanced back at his companion and found, not M'tarl, the lieutenant of Bregan D'aerthe he had set out with, but another, very powerful, drow.

Jarlaxle was rarely without a quick response, but the specter of Gromph Baenre, Matron Baenre's elderboy, the archmage of Menzoberranzan, standing so unexpectedly beside him, surely stole his wit.

"I trust that M'tarl will be returned to me when you are finished," Jarlaxle said, quickly regaining his seldom-lost composure.

Without a word, the archmage waved his arm, and a shimmering green globe appeared in the air, several feet from the floor. A thin silver cord hung down from it, its visible end barely brushing the stone floor.

Jarlaxle shrugged and took up the cord, and as soon as he touched it, he was drawn upward into the globe, into the extradimensional space beyond the shimmering portal.

The casting was impressive, Jarlaxle decided, for he found within not the usual empty space created by such an evocation, but a lushly furnished sitting room, complete with a zombielike servant that offered him a drink of fine wine before he ever sat down. Jarlaxle took a moment to allow his vision to shift into the normal spectrum of light, for the place was bathed in a soft blue glow. This was not unusual for wizards, even drow wizards accustomed to the lightless ways of the Underdark, for one could not read scrolls or spellbooks without light!

"He will be returned if he can survive where I put him long enough for us to complete our conversation," Gromph replied. The wizard seemed not too concerned, as he, too, came into the extradimensional pocket. The mighty Baenre closed his eyes and whispered a word, and his *piwafwi* cloak and other unremarkable attire transformed. Now he looked the part of his prestigious station. His flowing robe showed many pockets and was emblazoned with sigils and runes of power. As with the House structures, faerie fire highlighted these runes, though the archmage could darken the runes with a thought, and his robe would be more concealing than the finest of *piwafwis*. Two brooches, one a black-legged, red-bodied spider, the other a shining green emerald, adorned the magnificent robe, though Jarlaxle could hardly see them, for the old wizard's long white hair hung down the side of his head and in front of his shoulders and chest.

With his interest in things magical, Jarlaxle had seen the brooches on the city's previous archmage, though Gromph had held the position longer than most of Menzoberranzan's drow had been alive. The spider brooch allowed the archmage to cast the lingering heat enchantment into Narbondel, the pillar clock of Menzoberranzan. The heat would rise to the tip of the clock over a twelve-hour period, then diminish back toward the base in a like amount of time, until the stone was again cool, a very obvious and effective clock for heat-sensing drow eyes.

The other brooch gave Gromph perpetual youth. By Jarlaxle's estimation, this one had seen the birth and death of seven centuries, yet so young did he appear that it seemed he might be ready to begin his training at the drow Academy!

Not so, Jarlaxle silently recanted in studying the wizard. There was an aura of power and dignity about Gromph, reflected clearly in his eyes, which showed the wisdom of long and often bitter experience. This one was cunning and devious, able to scrutinize any situation immediately, and in truth, Jarlaxle felt more uncomfortable and more vulnerable standing before Gromph than before Matron Baenre herself.

"A conspiracy?" Gromph asked again, this time aloud. "Have the other Houses finally become fed up with my mother and banded together against House Baenre?"

"I have already given a full accounting to Matron—"

"I heard every word," Gromph interrupted, snarling impatiently. "Now I wish to know the truth."

"An interesting concept," Jarlaxle said, smiling wryly at the realization that Gromph was truly nervous. "Truth."

"A rare thing," Gromph agreed, regaining his composure and resting back in his chair, his slender fingers tapping together before him. "But a thing that sometimes keeps meddling fools alive."

Jarlaxle's smile vanished. He studied Gromph intently, surprised at so bold a threat. Gromph was powerful—by all measures of Menzoberranzan, the old wretch was as powerful as any male could become. But Jarlaxle did not operate by any of Menzoberranzan's measures, and for the wizard to take such a risk as to threaten Jarlaxle . . .

Jarlaxle was even more surprised when he realized that Gromph, mighty Gromph Baenre, was beyond nervous. He was truly scared.

"I will not even bother to remind you of the value of this 'meddling fool,' " Jarlaxle said.

"Do spare me."

Jarlaxle laughed in his face.

Gromph brought his hands to his hips, his outer robes opening in front with the movement and revealing a pair of wands set under his belt, one on each hip.

"No conspiracy," Jarlaxle said suddenly, firmly.

"The truth," Gromph remarked in dangerous, low tones.

"The truth," Jarlaxle replied as straightforwardly as he had ever spoken. "I have as much invested in House Baenre as do you, Archmage. If the lesser Houses were banding against Baenre, or if Baenre's daughters plotted her demise, Bregan D'aerthe would stand beside her, at least to the point of giving her fair notice of the coming coup."

Gromph's expression became very serious. What Jarlaxle noted most was that the elderboy of House Baenre had taken no apparent notice of his obvious—and intentional—slip in referring to Matron Baenre as merely "Baenre." Errors such as that often cost drow, particularly male drow, their lives.

"What is it then?" Gromph asked, and the very tone of the question, almost an outright plea, caught Jarlaxle off his guard. Never before had he seen the archmage, or heard of the archmage, in so desperate a state.

"You sense it!" Gromph snapped. "There is something wrong about the very air we breathe!"

For centuries untold, Jarlaxle silently added, a notion he knew he would be wise to keep to himself. To Gromph he offered only, "The chapel was damaged."

The archmage nodded, his expression turning sour. The great domed chapel of House Baenre was the holiest place in the entire city, the ultimate shrine to Lolth. In perhaps the most terrible slap in the face the Spider Queen had ever experienced, the renegade Do'Urden and his friends had, upon their escape, dropped a stalactite from the cavern's roof that punctured the treasured dome like a gigantic spear.

"The Spider Queen is angered," Gromph remarked.

"I would be," Jarlaxle agreed.

Gromph snapped an angry glare over the smug mercenary. Not for any insult he had given Lolth, Jarlaxle understood, but simply because of his flippant attitude.

When that glare had no more effect than to bring a smile to Jarlaxle's lips, Gromph sprang from his chair and paced like a caged displacer beast. The zombie host, unthinking and purely programmed, rushed over, drinks in hand.

Gromph growled and held his palm upraised, a ball of flame suddenly appearing atop it. With his other hand Gromph placed something small and red—it looked like a scale—into the flame and began an ominous chant.

Jarlaxle watched patiently as Gromph played out his frustration, the mercenary preferring that the wizard aim that retort at the zombie and not at him.

A lick of flame shot out from Gromph's hand. Lazily, determinedly, like a snake that had already immobilized its prey with poison, the flame wound around the zombie, which, of course, neither moved nor complained. In mere seconds, the zombie was engulfed by this serpent of fire. When Gromph casually sat again, the burning thing followed its predetermined course back to stand impassively. It made it back to its station, but soon crumbled, one of its legs consumed.

"The smell . . . " Jarlaxle began, putting a hand over his nose.

"Is of power!" Gromph finished, his red eyes narrowing, the nostrils of his thin nose flaring. The wizard took a deep breath and basked in the stench.

"It is not Lolth who fosters the wrongness of the air," Jarlaxle said suddenly, wanting to steal the obviously frustrated wizard's bluster and be done with Gromph and out of this reeking place.

"What do you know?" Gromph demanded, suddenly very anxious once more.

"No more than you," Jarlaxle replied. "Lolth is likely angry at Drizzt's escape, and at the damage to the chapel. You above all can appreciate the importance of that chapel." Jarlaxle's sly tone sent Gromph's nostrils flaring once more. The mercenary knew he had hit a sore spot, a weakness in the archmage's armored robes. Gromph had created the pinnacle of the Baenre chapel, a gigantic, shimmering illusion hovering over the central altar. It continually shifted form, going from a beautiful drow female to a huge spider and back again. It was no secret in Menzoberranzan that Gromph was not the most devout of Lolth's followers, no secret that the creation of the magnificent illusion had spared him his mother's unmerciful wrath.

"But there are too many things happening for Lolth to be the sole cause," Jarlaxle went on after savoring the minor victory for a moment. "And too many of them adversely affect Lolth's own base of power."

"A rival deity?" Gromph asked, revealing more intrigue than he intended. "Or an underground revolt?" The wizard sat back suddenly, thinking he had hit upon something, thinking that any underground revolt would certainly fall into the domain of a certain rogue mercenary leader.

But Jarlaxle was in no way cornered, for if either of Gromph's suspicions had any basis, Jarlaxle did not know of it.

"Something," was all the mercenary replied. "Something perhaps very dangerous to us all. For more than a score of years, one House or another has, for some reason, overestimated the worth of capturing the renegade Do'Urden, and their very zeal has elevated his stature and multiplied the troubles he has caused."

"So you believe all of this is tied to Drizzt's escape," Gromph reasoned.

"I believe many matron mothers will believe that," Jarlaxle was quick to reply. "And, thus, Drizzt's escape will indeed play a role in what is to come. But I have not said, and do not believe, that what you sense is amiss is the result of the renegade's flight from House Baenre."

Gromph closed his eyes and let the logic settle. Jarlaxle was right, of course. Menzoberranzan was a place so wound up in its own intrigue that truth mattered less than suspicion, that suspicion often became a self—fulfilling prophecy, and thus, often created truth.

"I may wish to speak with you again, mercenary," the archmage said quietly, and Jarlaxle noticed a door near where he had entered the extradimensional pocket. Beside it the zombie still burned, now just a crumpled, blackened ball of almost bare bone.

Jarlaxle started for the door.

"Alas," Gromph said dramatically, and Jarlaxle paused. "M'tarl did not survive."

"A pity for M'tarl," Jarlaxle added, not wanting Gromph to think that the loss would in any way wound Bregan D'aerthe.

Jarlaxle went out the door, down the cord, and slipped away silently into the shadows of the city, trying to digest all that had occurred. Rarely had he spoken to Gromph, and even more rarely had Gromph requested, in his own convoluted way, the audience. That fact was significant, Jarlaxle realized. Something very strange was happening here, a slight tingle in the air. Jarlaxle, a lover of chaos—mostly because, within the swirl of chaos, he always seemed to come out ahead—was intrigued. What was even more intriguing was that Gromph, despite his fears and all that he had to lose, was also intrigued!

The archmage's mention of a possible second deity proved that, showed his entire hand. For Gromph was an old wretch, despite the fact that he had come as far in life as any male drow in Menzoberranzan could hope to climb.

No, not despite that fact, Jarlaxle silently corrected himself. Because of that fact. Gromph was bitter, and had been so for centuries, because, in his lofty view of his own worth, he saw even the position of archmage as pointless, as a limit imposed by an accident of gender.

The greatest weakness in Menzoberranzan was not the rivalry of the various Houses, Jarlaxle knew, but the strict matriarchal system imposed by Lolth's followers. Half the drow population was subjugated merely because they had been born male.

That was a weakness.

And subjugation inevitably bred bitterness, even—especially!—in one who had gone as far as Gromph. Because from his lofty perch, the archmage

could clearly see how much farther he might possibly go if he had been born with a different set of genitals.

Gromph had indicated he might wish to speak with Jarlaxle again, and Jarlaxle had the feeling he and the bitter mage would indeed meet, perhaps quite often. He spent the next twenty steps of his walk back across Menzoberranzan wondering what information Gromph might extract from poor M'tarl, for of course the lieutenant was not dead—though he might soon wish he were.

Jarlaxle laughed at his own foolishness. He had spoken truly to Gromph, of course, and so M'tarl couldn't reveal anything incriminating. The mercenary sighed. He wasn't used to speaking truthfully, wasn't used to walking where there were no webs.

That notion dismissed, Jarlaxle turned his attention to the city. Something was brewing. Jarlaxle, the ultimate survivor, could sense it, and so could Gromph. Something important would occur all too soon, and what the mercenary needed to do was figure out how he might profit from it, whatever it might be.

5

CATTI-BRIE'S CHAMPION

D rizzt called Guenhwyvar to his side when the companions came down to the lower trails. The panther sat quietly, expecting what was to come.

"Ye should bring the cat in," Catti-brie suggested, understanding Drizzt's intent. The barbarians, though they had come far from their tundra homes and their secluded ways, remained somewhat distrustful of magic, and the sight of the panther always unnerved more than a few of Berkthgar's people, and didn't sit so well with Berkthgar himself.

"It is enough for them that I will enter their settlement," Drizzt replied.

Catti-brie had to nod in agreement. The sight of Drizzt, of a dark elf, one of a race noted for magic and evil, was perhaps even more unnerving to the Northmen than the panther. "Still, it'd teach Berkthgar good if ye had the cat sit on him for a while," she remarked.

Drizzt chuckled as he conjured an image of Guenhwyvar stretching comfortably on the back of the large, wriggling man. "The folk of Settlestone will grow accustomed to the panther as they did to my own presence," the drow replied. "Think of how many years it took Bruenor to become comfortable around Guenhwyvar."

The panther gave a low growl, as if she understood their every word.

"It wasn't the years," Catti-brie returned. "It was the number of times Guen pulled me stubborn father's backside out of a hot fire!"

When Guenhwyvar growled again, both Drizzt and Catti-brie had a good laugh at surly Bruenor's expense. The mirth subsided as Drizzt took out the figurine and bade Guenhwyvar farewell, promising to call the panther back as soon as he and Catti-brie were on the trails once more, heading back to Mithral Hall.

The formidable panther, growling low, walked in circles around the figurine. Gradually those growls diminished as Guenhwyvar faded into gray mist, then into nothing at all.

Drizzt scooped up the figurine and looked to the plumes of smoke rising from nearby Settlestone. "Are you ready?" he asked his companion.

"He'll be a stubborn one," Catti-brie admitted.

"We just have to get Berkthgar to understand the depth of Bruenor's distress," Drizzt offered, starting off again for the town.

"We just have to get Berkthgar to imagine Bruenor's axe sweeping in for the bridge of his nose," Catti-brie muttered. "Right between the eyes."

Settlestone was a rocky, windswept cluster of stone houses set in a vale and protected on three sides by the climbing, broken sides of the towering mountains known as the Spine of the World. The rock structures, resembling houses of cards against the backdrop of the gigantic mountains, had been built by the dwarves of Mithral Hall, by Bruenor's ancestors, hundreds of years before, when the place had been called Dwarvendarrow. It had been used as a trading post by Bruenor's people and was the only place for merchants to peek at the wonders that came from Mithral Hall, for the dwarves did not wish to entertain foreigners in their secret mines.

Even one who did not know the history of Dwarvendarrow would reason that this place had been constructed by the bearded folk. Only dwarves could have imbued the rocks with such strength, for, though the settlement had been uninhabited for centuries, and though the wind sweeping down the channel of the tall mountain walls was unrelenting, the structures had remained. In setting the place up for their own use, Wulfgar's people had no more a task than to brace an occasional wall, sweep out the tons of pebbles that had half buried some of the houses, and flush out the animals that had come to live there.

So it was a trading post again, looking much as it had in the heyday of Mithral Hall, but now called Settlestone and now used by humans working as agents for the busy dwarves. The agreement seemed sound and profitable to both parties, but Berkthgar had no idea of how tentative things had suddenly become. If he did not relent on his demand to carry Aegis-fang, both Drizzt and Catti-brie knew, Bruenor would likely order the barbarian and his people off the land.

The proud barbarians would never follow such a command, of course. The land had been granted, not loaned.

The prospect of war, of Bruenor's people coming down from the mountains and driving the barbarians away, was not so outlandish.

All because of Aegis-fang.

"Wulfgar would not be so glad to know the source of the arguing," Catti-brie remarked as she and Drizzt neared the settlement. "'Twas he who bringed them all together. Seems a pity indeed that it's his memory threatening to tear them apart."

A pity and a terrible irony, Drizzt silently agreed. His steps became more determined. Put in that light, this diplomatic mission took on even greater significance. Suddenly Drizzt was marching to Settlestone for much more than a petty squabble between two unyielding rulers. The drow was going for Wulfgar's honor.

As they came down to the valley floor, they heard chanting, a rhythmic, solemn recitation of the deeds of a legendary warrior. They crossed into the empty ways, past the open house doors that the hearty folk never bothered to secure. Both knew where the chanting was coming from, and both knew where they would find the men, women, and children of Settlestone.

The only addition the barbarian settlers had made to the town was a large structure that could fit all four hundred people of Settlestone and a like number of visitors. Hengorot, "the Mead Hall," it was called. It was a solemn place of worship, of valor recalled, and ultimately of sharing food and drink.

Hengorot wasn't finished. Half its long, low walls were of stone, but the rest was enclosed by deerskin canopies. That fact seemed fitting to Drizzt, seemed to reflect how far Wulfgar's people had come, and how far they had to go. When they had lived on the tundra of Icewind Dale, they had been nomadic, following the reindeer herd, so all their houses had been of skin, which could be packed up and taken with the wandering tribe.

No longer were the hearty folk nomads; no longer was their existence dependent on the reindeer herd. It was an unreliable source that often led to warring between the various tribes, or with the folk of Ten-Towns, on the three lakes, the only non-barbarians in Icewind Dale.

Drizzt was glad to see the level of peace and harmony that the northmen had attained, but still it pained him to look at the uncompleted part of Hengorot, to view the skins and remember, too, the sacrifices these people had made. Their way of life, which had survived for thousands of years, was no more. Looking at this construction of Hengorot, a mere shade of the glories the mead hall had known, looking at the stone that now enclosed this proud people, the drow could not help but wonder if this way was indeed "progress."

Catti-brie, who had lived most of her young life in Icewind Dale, and who had heard countless tales of the nomadic barbarians, had understood the loss all along. In coming to Settlestone, the barbarians had given away a measure of their freedom and more than a bit of their heritage. They were richer now, far richer than they could have ever dreamt, and no longer would a harsh winter threaten their very existence. But there had been a price. Like the stars. The stars were different here beside the mountains. They didn't come down to the flat horizon, drawing a person's soul into the heavens.

With a resigned sigh, a bit of her own homesickness for Icewind Dale, Catti-brie reminded herself of the pressing situation. She knew that Berkthgar was being stubborn, but knew, too, how pained the barbarian leader was over Wulfgar's fall, and how pained he must be to think that a dwarf held the key to the warhammer that had become the most honored weapon in his tribe's history.

Never mind that the dwarf had been the one to forge that weapon; never mind that the man who had carried it to such glory had, in fact, been like that dwarf's son. To Berkthgar, Catti-brie knew, the lost hero was not the son of Bruenor, but was Wulfgar, son of Beornegar, of the Tribe of the Elk.

Wulfgar of Icewind Dale, not of Mithral Hall. Wulfgar, who epitomized all that had been respected and treasured among the barbarian people. Perhaps most of all, Catti-brie appreciated the gravity of the task before them.

Two tall, broad-shouldered guards flanked the skin flap of the mead hall's opening, their beards and breath smelling more than a little of thick mead. They bristled at first, then moved hastily aside when they recognized the visitors. One rushed to the closest end of the long table set in the hall's center to announce Drizzt and Catti-brie, listing their known feats and their heritage—Catti-brie's at least, for Drizzt's heritage would not be a source of glory in Settlestone.

Drizzt and Catti-brie waited patiently at the door with the other man, who easily outweighed the two of them put together. Both of them focused on Berkthgar, seated halfway down the table's right-hand side, and he inevitably looked past the man announcing the visitors to stare back at them.

Catti-brie thought the man a fool in his argument with Bruenor, but neither she nor Drizzt could help but be impressed by the giant barbarian. He was nearly as tall as Wulfgar, fully six and a half towering feet, with broad shoulders and hardened arms the size of a fat dwarf's thighs. His brown hair was shaggy, hanging low over his shoulders, and he was beginning a beard for winter, the thick tufts on his neck and cheeks making him appear all the more fierce and imposing. Settlestone's leaders were picked in contests of strength, in matches of fierce battle, as the barbarians had selected their leaders through their history. No man in Settlestone could defeat Berkthgar—Berkthgar the Bold, he was called—and yet, because of that fact, he lived, more than any of the others, in the shadow of a dead man who had become legend.

"Pray, join us!" Berkthgar greeted warmly, but the set of his expression told the two companions that he had been expecting this visit, and was not so thrilled to see them. The chieftain focused particularly on Drizzt, and Catti-brie read both eagerness and trepidation in the large man's sky-blue eyes.

Stools were offered to Drizzt and Catti-brie—a high honor for Catti-brie, for no other woman was seated at the table, unless upon the lap of a suitor. In Hengorot, and in all this society, the women and children, save for the

older male children, were servants. They hustled now, placing mugs of mead before the newest guests.

Both Drizzt and Catti-brie eyed the drinks suspiciously, knowing they had to keep their heads perfectly clear, but when Berkthgar offered a toast to them and held his own mug high, custom demanded they likewise salute. And in Hengorot, one simply did not sip mead!

Both friends downed their mugs to rousing cheers, and both looked to each other despairingly as another full mug quickly replaced the emptied one.

Unexpectedly, Drizzt rose and deftly hopped up on the long table.

"My greetings to the men and women of Settlestone, to the people of Berkthgar the Bold!" he began, and a chorus of deafening cheers went up, roars for Berkthgar, the focus of the town's pride. The huge, shaggy-haired man got slapped on the back a hundred times in the next minute, but not once did he blink, and not once did he take his suspicious gaze from the dark elf.

Catti-brie understood what was going on here. The barbarians had come to grudgingly accept Drizzt, but still he was a scrawny elf, and a dark elf on top of it all! The paradox was more than a little uncomfortable for them. They saw Drizzt as weak—probably no stronger than some of their hearty womenfolk—and yet they realized that not one of them could defeat the drow in combat. Berkthgar was the most uncomfortable of all, for he knew why Drizzt and Catti-brie had come, and he suspected this issue about the hammer would be settled between him and Drizzt.

"Truly we are grateful, nay, thrilled, at your hospitality. None in all the Realms can set a table more inviting!" Again the cheers. Drizzt was playing them well, and it didn't hurt that more than half of them were falling-down drunk.

"But we cannot remain for long," Drizzt said, his voice suddenly solemn. The effect on those seated near the drow was stunning, as they seemed to sober immediately, seemed to suddenly grasp the weight of the drow's visit.

Catti-brie saw the sparkle of the ruby pendant hanging around Drizzt's neck, and she understood that though Drizzt wasn't actively using the enchanting gem, its mere presence was as intoxicating as any amount of thick mead.

"The heavy sword of war hangs over us all," Drizzt went on gravely. "This is the time of allian—"

Berkthgar abruptly ended the drow's speech by slamming his mug on the table so brutally that it shattered, splattering those nearby with golden-brown mead and glass fragments. Still holding the mug's handle, the barbarian leader unsteadily clambered atop the table to tower over the dark elf.

In the blink of an eye, Hengorot hushed.

"You come here claiming alliance," the barbarian leader began slowly. "You come asking for alliance." He paused and looked around at his anxious people for dramatic effect. "And yet you hold prisoner the weapon that has become a symbol of my people, a weapon brought to glory by Wulfgar, son of Beornegar!"

Thunderous cheers erupted, and Catti-brie looked up to Drizzt and shrugged helplessly. She always hated it when the barbarians referred to Wulfgar by his legacy, as the son of Beornegar. For them to do so was an item of pride, and pride alone never sat well with the pragmatic woman.

Besides, Wulfgar needed no claim of lineage to heighten his short life's achievements. His children, had he sired any, would have been the ones to rightfully speak of their father.

"We are friends of the dwarf king you serve, dark elf," Berkthgar went on, his booming voice resonating off the stone sections of Hengorot's walls. "And we ask the same of Bruenor Battlehammer, son of Bangor, son of Garumn. You shall have your alliance, but not until Aegis-fang is delivered to me.

"I am Berkthgar!" the barbarian leader bellowed.

"Berkthgar the Bold!" several of the man's advisors quickly piped in, and another chorus went up, a toast of mugs lifted high to the mighty chieftain of Settlestone.

"Bruenor would sooner deliver his own axe," Drizzt replied, thoroughly fed up with Berkthgar's glories. The drow understood then that he and Catti-brie had been expected in Settlestone, for Berkthgar's little speech, and the reaction to it, had been carefully planned, even rehearsed.

"And I do not think you would enjoy the way he would deliver that axe," the drow finished quietly, when the roaring had died away. Again came the hush of expectation, for the drow's words could be taken as a challenge, and Berkthgar, blue eyes squinting dangerously, seemed more than ready to pick up the gauntlet.

"But Bruenor is not here," the barbarian leader said evenly. "Will Drizzt Do'Urden champion his cause?"

Drizzt straightened, trying to decide the best course.

Catti-brie's mind, too, was working fast. She held little doubt that Drizzt would accept the challenge and put Berkthgar down at once, and the men of Settlestone surely would not tolerate that kind of embarrassment.

"Wulfgar was to be my husband!" she yelled, rising from her chair just as Drizzt was about to respond. "And I am the daughter of Bruenor—by rights, the princess of Mithral Hall. If anyone here is to champion my father's cause—"

"You will name him," Berkthgar reasoned.

"I will *be . . . her*," Catti-brie replied grimly.

Roars went up again, all around the mead hall, and more than a few women at the back of the room tittered and nodded hopefully.

Drizzt didn't seem so pleased, and the look he put over Catti-brie was purely plaintive, begging her to calm this situation before things got fully out of hand. He didn't want a fight at all. Neither did Catti-brie, but the room was in a frenzy then, with more than half the voices crying for Berkthgar to "Fight the woman!" as though Catti-brie's challenge had already been launched.

The look that Berkthgar put over Catti-brie was one of pure outrage.

She understood and sympathized with his predicament. She had meant to go on and explain that she would be Bruenor's only champion, if there was to be a champion, but that she had not come here to fight. Events had swept her past that point, however.

"Never!" Berkthgar roared above the din, and the room calmed somewhat, eager cries dying away to whispers. "Never have I battled a woman!"

That's an attitude Berkthgar had better overcome soon, Drizzt thought, for if the dark elves were indeed marching to Mithral Hall, there would be little room for such inhibitions. Females were typically the strongest of drow warriors, both magically and with weapons.

"Fight her!" cried one man, obviously very drunk, and he was laughing as he called, and so, too, were his fellows around him.

Berkthgar looked from the man to Catti-brie, his huge chest heaving as he tried to take in deep breaths to calm his rage.

He could not win, Catti-brie realized. If they fought, he could not win, even if he battered her. To the hearty men of Settlestone, even lifting a weapon against her would be considered cowardly.

Catti-brie climbed onto the table and gave a slight nod as she passed in front of Drizzt. Hands on hips—and her hip out to the side to accentuate her feminine figure—she gave a wistful smile to the barbarian leader. "Not with weapons, perhaps," she said. "But there are other ways a man and woman might compete."

All the room exploded at that comment. Mugs were lifted so forcefully in toast that little mead remained in them as they came back down to the eager mouths of the men. Several in the back end of Hengorot took up a lewd song, clapping each other on the back at every crescendo.

Drizzt's lavender eyes grew so wide that they seemed as if they would simply roll out of their sockets. When Catti-brie took the moment to regard him, she feared he would draw his weapons and kill everyone in the room. For an instant, she was flattered, but that quickly passed, replaced by disappointment that the drow would think so little of her.

She gave him a look that said just that as she turned and jumped down from the table. A man nearby reached out to catch her, but she slapped his hands away and strode defiantly for the door.

"There's fire in that one!" she heard behind her.

"Alas for poor Berkthgar!" came another rowdy cry.

On the table, the stunned barbarian leader turned this way and that, purposely avoiding the dark elf's gaze. Berkthgar was at a loss. Bruenor's daughter, though a famed adventurer, was not known for such antics. But Berkthgar was also more than a little intrigued. Every man in Settlestone considered Catti-brie, the princess of Mithral Hall, the fairest prize in all the region.

"Aegis-fang will be mine!" Berkthgar finally cried, and the roar behind him, and all around him, was deafening.

The barbarian leader was relieved to see that Drizzt was no longer facing him, was no longer anywhere in sight, when he turned back. One great leap had taken the dark elf from the table, and he strode eagerly for the door.

Outside Hengorot, in a quiet spot near an empty house, Drizzt took Catti-brie by the arm and turned her to face him. She expected him to shout at her, even expected him to slap her.

He laughed at her instead.

"Clever," Drizzt congratulated. "But can you take him?"

"How do ye know that I did not mean what I said?" Catti-brie snapped in reply.

"Because you have more respect for yourself than that," Drizzt answered without hesitation.

It was the perfect answer, the one Catti-brie needed to hear from her friend, and she did not press the point further.

"But can you take him?" the drow asked again, seriously. Catti-brie was good, and getting better with every lesson, but Berkthgar was huge and tremendously strong.

"He's drunk," Catti-brie replied. "And he's slow, like Wulfgar was before ye showed him the better way o' fighting." Her blue eyes, rich as the sky just before the dawn, sparkled. "Like ye showed me."

Drizzt patted her on the shoulder lightly, understanding then that this fight would be as important to her as it was to Berkthgar. The barbarian came storming out of the tent then, leaving a horde of sputtering comrades leering out of the open flap.

"Taking him won't be half the trouble as figuring out how to let him keep his honor," Catti-brie whispered.

Drizzt nodded and patted her shoulder again, then walked away, going in a wide circuit around Berkthgar and back toward the tent. Catti-brie had taken things into hand, he decided, and he owed her the respect to let her see this through.

The barbarians fell back as the drow came into the tent and pointedly closed the flap, taking one last look at Catti-brie as he did, to see her walking side by side with Berkthgar—and he so resembled huge Wulfgar from the back!—down the windswept lane.

For Drizzt Do'Urden, the image was not a pleasant one.

"Ye're not surprised?" Catti-brie asked as she removed the practice padding from her backpack and began sliding it over the fine edge of her sword. She felt a twinge of emotion as she did so, a sudden feeling of disappointment, even anger, which she did not understand.

"I did not believe for a moment that you had brought me out here for the reason you hinted at," Berkthgar replied casually. "Though if you had—"

"Shut yer mouth," Catti-brie sharply interrupted.

Berkthgar's jaw went firm. He was not accustomed to being talked to in that manner, particularly not from a woman. "We of Settlestone do not cover our blades when we fight," he said boastfully.

Catti-brie returned the barbarian leader's determined look, and as she did, she slid the sword back out from its protective sheath. A sudden rush of elation washed over her. As with the earlier feeling, she did not understand it, and so she thought that perhaps her anger toward Berkthgar was more profound than she had dared to admit to herself.

Berkthgar walked away then, to his house, and soon returned wearing a smug smile and a sheath strapped across his back. Above his right shoulder Catti-brie could see the hilt and crosspiece of his sword—a crosspiece nearly as long as her entire blade!—and the bottom portion of the sheath poked out below Berkthgar's left hip, extending almost to the ground.

Catti-brie watched, awestruck, wondering what she had gotten herself into, as Berkthgar solemnly drew the sword to the extent of his arm. The sheath had been cut along its upper side after a foot of leather so that the barbarian could then extract the gigantic blade.

And gigantic indeed was Berkthgar's flamberge! Its wavy blade extended over four feet, and after that came an eight-inch ricasso between the formal crosspiece and a second, smaller one of edged steel.

With one arm, muscles standing taut in ironlike cords, Berkthgar began spinning the blade, creating a great "whooshing" sound in the air above his head. Then he brought its tip to the ground before him and rested his arm on the crosspiece, which was about shoulder height to his six-and-a-half-foot frame.

"Ye meaning to fight with that, or kill fatted cows?" Catti-brie asked, trying hard to steal some of the man's mounting pride.

"I would still allow you to choose the other contest," Berkthgar replied calmly.

Catti-brie's sword snapped out in front of her, at the ready, and she went down in a low, defensive crouch.

The barbarian hooted and went into a similar pose, but then straightened, looking perplexed. "I cannot," Berkthgar began. "If I were to strike you even a glancing blow, King Battlehammer's heart would break as surely as would your skull."

Catti-brie came forward suddenly, jabbing at Berkthgar's shoulder and tearing a line in his furred jerkin.

He looked down at the cut, then his eyes came slowly back to regard Catti-brie, but other than that, he made no move.

"Ye're just afraid because ye're knowing that ye can't move that cow-killer fast enough," the young woman taunted.

Berkthgar blinked very slowly, exaggerated the movement as if to show how boring he thought this whole affair was. "I will show you the mantle where Bankenfuere is kept," he said. "And I will show you the bedding before the mantle."

"The thing's better for a mantle than a swordsman's hands!" Catti-brie growled, tired of this one's juvenile sexual references. She sprang ahead again and slapped the flat of her blade hard against Berkthgar's cheek, then jumped back, still snarling. "If ye're afraid, then admit it!"

Berkthgar's hand went immediately to his wound, and when it came away, the barbarian saw that his fingers were red with blood. Catti-brie winced at that, for she hadn't meant to hit him quite so hard.

Subtle were the intrusions of Khazid'hea.

"I am out of patience with you, foolish woman," snarled the barbarian, and up came the tip of tremendous Bankenfuere, the Northern Fury.

Berkthgar growled and leaped ahead, both hands on the hilt this time as he swung the huge blade across in front of him. He attacked with the flat of his blade, as had Catti-brie, but the young woman realized that would hardly matter. Getting hit by the flat of that tremendous flamberge would still reduce her bones to mush!

Catti-brie wasn't anywhere near Berkthgar at that point, the woman in fast retreat—and wondering again if she was in over her head—as soon as the sword went up. The flamberge curled in an arc back over, left to right, then came across a second time, this cut angling down. Faster than Catti-brie expected, Berkthgar reversed the flow, the blade swishing horizontally again, this time left to right, then settled back at the ready beside the barbarian's muscular shoulder.

An impressive display indeed, but Catti-brie had watched the routine carefully, no longer through awestruck eyes, and she noticed more than a few holes in the barbarian's defenses.

Of course, she had to be perfect in her timing. One slip, and Bankenfuere would turn her into worm food.

On came Berkthgar, with another horizontal cut, a predictable attack, for there were only so many ways one could maneuver such a weapon! Catti-brie fell back a step, then an extra step just to make sure, and darted in behind the lumbering sweep of the blade, looking to score a hit on the barbarian's arm. Berkthgar was quicker than that, though, and he had the blade coming around and over so fast that Catti-brie had to abort the attack and scramble hard just to get out of the way.

Still, she had won that pass, she figured, for now she had a better measure of Berkthgar's reach. And by her thinking, every passing moment favored her, for she saw the sweat beading on the drunken barbarian's forehead, his great chest heaving just a bit more than before.

"If ye do other things as poorly as ye fight, then suren I'm glad I chose this contest," Catti-brie said, a taunt that sent proud Berkthgar into another wild-swinging tirade.

Catti-brie dodged and scrambled as Bankenfuere came across in several titanic, and ultimately futile, swipes. Across it came again, the barbarian's fury far from played out, and Catti-brie leaped back. Around and over went

the blade, Berkthgar charging ahead, and Catti-brie went far out to the side, just ahead as the great sword came whipping down and across.

"I shall catch up to you soon enough!" Berkthgar promised, turning square to the young woman and whipping his mighty blade left to right once more, bringing it to the ready beside his right shoulder.

Catti-brie started in behind the cut, taking a long stride with her right foot, extending her sword arm toward Berkthgar's exposed hip. She dug her left foot in solidly, though, and had no intention of continuing the move. As soon as Bankenfuere came across to intercept, Catti-brie leaped back, pivoted on her anchor leg, and rushed in behind the blade, going for Berkthgar's right hip instead, and scored a nasty, stinging hit.

The barbarian growled and spun so forcefully that he nearly overbalanced.

Catti-brie stood a few feet away, crouched low, ready. There was no doubt that swinging the heavy weapon was beginning to take a toll on the man, especially after his generous swallows of mead.

"A few more passes," Catti-brie whispered, forcing herself to be patient.

And so she played on as the minutes passed, as Berkthgar's breathing came as loudly as the moaning wind. Through each attack, Catti-brie confirmed her final routine, one that took advantage of the fact that Berkthgar's huge blade and thick arms made a perfect optical barricade.

✕ ✕ ✕ ✕ ✕

Drizzt suffered through the half-hour of rude comments.

"Never has he lasted this long!" offered one barbarian.

"Berkthgar the Brauzen!" cried another, the barbarian word for stamina.

"Brauzen!" all the rowdy men shouted together, lifting their mugs in cheer. Some of the women in the back of Hengorot tittered at the bawdy display, but most wore sour expressions.

"Brauzen," the drow whispered, and Drizzt thought the word perfectly fitting for describing his own patience during those insufferably long minutes. As angry as he was at the rude jokes at Catti-brie's expense, he was more fearful that Berkthgar would harm her, perhaps defeat her in battle and take her in other ways.

Drizzt worked hard to keep his imagination at bay. For all his boasting, for all of his people's boasting, Berkthgar was an honorable man. But he was drunk . . .

I will kill him, Drizzt decided, and if anything the drow feared had come to pass, he indeed would cut mighty Berkthgar down.

It never got to that point, though, for Berkthgar and Catti-brie walked back into the tent, looking a bit ruffled, the barbarian's stubbly beard darkened in one area with some dried blood, but otherwise seeming okay.

Catti-brie winked subtly as she passed the drow.

Hengorot fell into a hush, the drunken men no doubt expecting some lewd tales of their leader's exploits.

Berkthgar looked to Catti-brie, and she wouldn't blink.

"I will not carry Aegis-fang," the barbarian leader announced.

Moans and hoots erupted, as did speculation about who won the "contest."

Berkthgar blushed, and Drizzt feared there would be trouble.

Catti-brie went up on the table. "Not a better man in Settlestone!" she insisted.

Several barbarians rushed forward to the table's edge, willing to take up that challenge.

"Not a better man!" Catti-brie growled at them, her fury driving them back.

"I'll not carry the warhammer, in honor of Wulfgar," Berkthgar explained. "And for the honor of Catti-brie."

Blank stares came back at him.

"If I am to properly suit the daughter of King Bruenor, our friend and ally," the barbarian leader went on, and Drizzt smiled at that reference, "then it is my own weapon, Bankenfuere, that must become legend." He held high the huge flamberge, and the crowd roared with glee.

The issue was ended, the alliance sealed, and more mead was passed around before Catti-brie even got down from the table, heading for Drizzt.

She stopped as she walked beside the barbarian leader, and gave him a sly look.

"If ye ever openly lie," she whispered, taking care that no one could hear, "or if ye ever even hint that ye bedded me, then be knowin' that I'll come back and cut ye down in front o' all yer people."

Berkthgar's expression grew somber at that, and even more somber as he turned to watch Catti-brie depart, to see her deadly drow friend standing easily, hands on scimitar hilts, his lavender eyes telling the barbarian in no uncertain terms his feelings for Catti-brie. Berkthgar didn't want to tangle with Catti-brie again, but he would rather battle her a hundred times than fight the drow ranger.

"You'll come back and cut him down?" Drizzt asked as they exited the town, revealing to Catti-brie that his keen ears had caught her parting words with the barbarian.

"Not a promise I'd ever want to try," Catti-brie replied, shaking her head. "Fighting that one when he's not so full o' mead would be about the same as walking into the cave of a restless bear."

Drizzt stopped abruptly, and Catti-brie, after taking a couple more steps, turned around to regard him.

He stood pointing at her, smiling widely. "I have done that!" he remarked, and so Drizzt had yet another tale to recount as the two—and three, for Drizzt was quick to recall Guenhwyvar—made their way along the trails, back into the mountains.

Later, as the stars twinkled brightly and the campfire burned low, Drizzt sat watching Catti-brie's prone form, her rhythmic breathing telling the drow that she was fast asleep.

"You know I love her," the drow said to Guenhwyvar.

The panther blinked her shining green eyes, but otherwise did not move.

"Yet, how could I?" Drizzt asked. "And not for the memory of Wulfgar," he quickly added, and he nodded as he heard himself speak the words, knowing that Wulfgar, who loved Drizzt as Drizzt loved him, would not disapprove.

"How could I ever?" the drow reiterated, his voice barely a whisper.

Guenhwyvar issued a long, low growl, but if it had any meaning, other than to convey that the panther was interested in what the drow was saying, it was lost on Drizzt.

"She will not live so long," Drizzt went on quietly. "I will still be a young drow when she is gone." Drizzt looked from Catti-brie to the panther, and a new insight occurred to him. "You must understand such things, my eternal friend," the drow said. "Where will I fall in the span of your life? How many others have you kept as you keep me, my Guenhwyvar, and how many more shall there be?"

Drizzt rested his back against the mountain wall and looked to Catti-brie, then up to the stars. Sad were his thoughts, and yet, in many ways, they were comforting, like an eternal play, like emotions shared, like memories of Wulfgar. Drizzt sent those thoughts skyward, into the heavenly canopy, letting them break apart on the ceaseless and mournful wind.

His dreams were full of images of friends, of Zaknafein, his father, of Belwar, the svirfneblin gnome, of Captain Deudermont, of the good ship *Sea Sprite*, of Regis and Bruenor, of Wulfgar, and most of all, of Catti-brie.

It was as calm and pleasant a sleep as Drizzt Do'Urden had ever known.

Guenhwyvar watched the drow for some time, then rested her great feline head on wide paws and closed her green eyes. Drizzt's comments had hit the mark, except, of course, his intimation that her memory of him would be inconsequential in the centuries ahead. Guenhwyvar had indeed come to the call of many masters, most goodly, some wicked, in the past millennium, and even beyond that. Some the panther remembered, some not, but Drizzt . . .

Forever would Guenhwyvar remember the renegade dark elf, whose heart was so strong and so good and whose loyalty was no less than the panther's own.

PART TWO

F orever after, the bards of the Realms called it the Time of Troubles, the time when the gods were kicked out of the heavens, their avatars walking among the mortals. The time when the Tablets of Fate were stolen, invoking the wrath of Ao, Overlord of the Gods, when magic went awry, and when, as a consequence, social and religious hierarchies, so often based on magical strength, fell into chaos.

THE ONSET OF CHAOS

I have heard many tales from fanatical priests of their encounters with their particular avatars, frenzied stories from men and women who claim to have looked upon their deities. So many others came to convert to a religion during this troubled time, likewise claiming they had seen the light and the truth, however convoluted it might be.

I do not disagree with the claims, and would not openly attack the premise of their encounters. I am glad for those who have found enrichment amidst the chaos; I am glad whenever another person finds the contentment of spiritual guidance.

But what of faith?

What of fidelity and loyalty? Complete trust? Faith is not granted by tangible proof. It comes from the heart and the soul. If a person needs proof of a god's existence, then the very notion of spirituality is diminished into sensuality and we have reduced what is holy into what is logical.

I have touched the unicorn, so rare and so precious, the symbol of the goddess Mielikki, who holds my heart and soul. This was before the onset of the Time of Troubles, yet were I of a like mind to those who make the claims of viewing avatars, I could say the same. I could say that I have touched Mielikki, that she came to me in a magical glade in the mountains near Dead Orc Pass.

The unicorn was not Mielikki, and yet it was, as is the sunrise and the seasons, as are the birds and the squirrels, and the strength of a tree that has lived through the dawn and death of centuries. As are the leaves, blowing on autumn winds and the snow piling deep in cold mountain vales. As are the smell of a crisp night, the twinkle of the starry canopy, and the howl of a distant wolf.

No, I'll not argue openly against one who has claimed to have seen an avatar, because that person will not understand that the mere presence of such a being undermines the very purpose of, and value of, faith. Because if the true gods were so tangible and so accessible, then we would no longer be independent creatures set on a journey to find the truth, but merely a herd of sheep needing the guidance of a shepherd and his dogs, unthinking and without the essence of faith.

The guidance is there, I know. Not in such a tangible form, but in what we know to be good and just. It is our own reactions to the acts of others that show us the value of our own actions, and if we have fallen so far as to need an avatar, an undeniable manifestation of a god, to show us our way, then we are pitiful creatures indeed.

The Time of Troubles? Yes. And even more so if we are to believe the suggestion of avatars, because truth is singular and cannot, by definition, support so many varied, even opposing manifestations.

The unicorn was not Mielikki, and yet it was, for I have touched Mielikki. Not as an avatar, or as a unicorn, but as a way of viewing my place in the world. Mielikki is my heart. I follow her precepts because, were I to write precepts based on my own conscience, they would be the same. I follow Mielikki because she represents what I call truth.

Such is the case for most of the followers of most of the various gods, and if we looked more closely at the pantheon of the Realms, we would realize that the precepts of the "goodly" gods are not so different. It is the worldly interpretations of those precepts that vary from faith to faith.

As for the other gods, the gods of strife and chaos, such as Lolth, the Spider Queen, who possesses the hearts of those priestesses who rule Menzoberranzan . . .

They are not worth mentioning. There is no truth, only worldly gain, and any religion based on such principles is, in fact, no more than a practice of self-indulgence and in no way a measure of spirituality. In worldly terms, the priestesses of the Spider Queen are quite formidable; in spiritual terms, they are empty. Thus, their lives are without love and without joy.

So tell me not of avatars. Show me not your proof that yours is the true god. I grant you your beliefs without question and without judgment, but if you grant me what is in my heart, then such tangible evidence is irrelevant.

                                        −Drizzt Do'Urden

WHEN MAGIC WENT AWRY

B erg'inyon Baenre, weapons master of the First House of Menzoberran-zan, put his twin swords through a dizzying routine, blades spinning circuits in the air between him and his opponent, an insubordinate drow common soldier.

A crowd of the Baenre House guard, highly trained though mostly males, formed a semicircle around the pair, while other dark elves watched from high perches, tightly saddled astride sticky-footed, huge subterranean lizards, the beasts casually standing along the vertical slopes of nearby stalactites or towering stalagmite mounds.

Though few thought him as good a swordsman as his brother Dantrag had been, the soldiers cheered every time Berg'inyon scored a minor hit or parried a fast-flying counter.

Berg'inyon noticed a reluctance in ther praise, though, and knew the source. He had been the leader of the Baenre lizard riders, the most elite grouping of the male House guards, for many years. But with Dantrag slain, he had become the House weapons master as well. Berg'inyon felt the intense pressure of his dual stations, felt his mother's scrutinizing gaze on his every movement and every decision. He did not doubt that his own actions had intensified as a result. How many fights had he begun, how many punishments had he exacted on his subordinates, since Dantrag's death?

The common drow came ahead with a weak thrust that almost slipped

past distracted Berg'inyon's defenses. A sword came up and around at the last moment to drive the enemy's blade aside.

Berg'inyon heard the sudden hush behind him at the near miss, understood that several of the soldiers back there—perhaps all of them—hoped his enemy's next thrust would be quicker, too quick.

The weapons master growled low and came ahead in a flurry, spurred on by the hatred of those around him, of those under his command. Let them hate him! he decided. But while they did, they must also respect him—no, not respect, Berg'inyon decided. They must fear him.

He came forward one step, then a second, his swords snapping alternately, left and right, and each being cleanly picked off. The give and take had become common, with Berg'inyon coming ahead two steps, then retreating. This time, though, the Baenre did not retreat. He shuffled forward two more steps, his swords snapping as his opponent's blades rushed for the parry.

Berg'inyon had the lesser drow up on his heels, so the young Baenre rushed ahead again. His opponent was quick enough with his swords to turn the expected thrusts, but he could not retreat properly, and Berg'inyon was up against him in a clinch, their blades joined to either side, down low, by the hilt.

There was no real danger here—it was more like a break in the battle—but Berg'inyon realized something his opponent apparently did not. With a growl, the young Baenre heaved his off-balance opponent away. The drow skidded back a couple of steps, brought his swords up immediately to fend off any pursuit.

None came; it seemed a simple break of the clinch.

Then the backpedaling drow bumped into the House Baenre fence.

In the city of Menzoberranzan, there was perhaps nothing as spectacular as the twenty-foot-high, web-designed fence ringing House Baenre, anchored on the various stalagmite mounds that ringed the compound. Its silvery metallic cords, thick as a dark elf's leg, were wound into beautiful, symmetrical designs, as intricate as the work of any spider. No weapon could cut through it, no magic, save a single item that Matron Baenre possessed, could get one over it, and the simplest touch or brush against one of those enchanted strands would hold fast a titan.

Berg'inyon's opponent hit the fence hard with the flat of his back. His eyes went wide as he suddenly realized the young Baenre's tactics, as he saw the faces of those gathered brighten in approval of the vicious trick, as he saw devious and wicked Berg'inyon calmly approach.

The drow fell away from the fence and rushed out to meet the weapons master's advance.

The two went through a fast series of attacks and parries, with stunned Berg'inyon on the defensive. Only through his years of superior training was the drow noble able to bring himself back even against his surprising opponent.

Surprising indeed, as every drow face, and all the whispers, confirmed.

"You brushed the fence," Berg'inyon said.

The drow soldier did not disagree. The tips of his weapons drooped as Berg'inyon's drooped, and he glanced over his shoulder to confirm what he, and all the others, knew could not be.

"You hit the fence," Berg'inyon said again, skeptically, as the drow turned back to face him.

"Across the back," he agreed.

Berg'inyon's swords went into their respective scabbards and the young Baenre stormed past his opponent, to stand right before the enchanted web. His opponent and all the other dark elves followed closely, too intrigued to even think of continuing the fight.

Berg'inyon motioned to a nearby female. "Rest your sword against it," he bade her.

The female drew her blade and laid it across one of the thick strands. She looked to Berg'inyon and around to all the others, then easily lifted the blade from the fence.

Another drow farther down the line dared to place his hand on the web. Those around him looked at him incredulously, thinking him dangerously daring, but he had no trouble removing himself from the metal.

Panic rushed through Berg'inyon. The fence, it was said, had been a gift from Lolth herself in millennia past. If it was no longer functioning, it might well mean that House Baenre had fallen out of the Spider Queen's favor. It might well mean that Lolth had dropped House Baenre's defense to allow for a conspiracy of lower Houses.

"To your posts, all of you!" the young Baenre shouted, and the gathered dark elves, sharing Berg'inyon's reasoning and his fears, did not have to be told twice.

Berg'inyon headed for the compound's great central mound to find his mother. He crossed paths with the drow he had just been fighting, and the commoner's eyes widened in sudden fear. Normally Berg'inyon, honorable only by the low standards of dark elves, would have snapped his sword out and through the drow, ending the conflict. Caught up in the excitement of the fence's failure, the commoner was off his guard. He knew it, too, and he expected to be killed.

"To your post," Berg'inyon said to him, for if the young Baenre's suspicions proved correct, that a conspiracy had been launched against House Baenre and Lolth had deserted them, he would need every one of the House's twenty-five hundred soldiers.

✕ ✕ ✕ ✕ ✕

King Bruenor Battlehammer had spent the morning in the upper chapel of Mithral Hall, trying to sort out the new hierarchy of priests within the complex. His dear friend Cobble had been the reigning priest, a dwarf of powerful magic and deep wisdom.

That wisdom hadn't gotten poor Cobble out of the way of a nasty drow spell, though, and the cleric had been squashed by a falling wall of iron.

There were more than a dozen remaining acolytes in Mithral Hall. They formed two lines, one on each side of Bruenor's audience chair. Each priest was anxious to impress his—or, in the case of Stumpet Rakingclaw, her—king.

Bruenor nodded to the dwarf at the head of the line to his left. As he did, he lifted a mug of mead, the holy water this particular priest had concocted. Bruenor sipped, then drained the surprisingly refreshing mead in a single swallow as the cleric stepped forward.

"A burst of light in honor of King Bruenor!" the would-be head priest cried, and he waved his arms and began a chanting prayer to Moradin, the Soulforger, god of the dwarves.

"Clean and fresh, and just the slightest twinge of bitterness," Bruenor remarked, running a finger along the rim of the emptied mug and sucking on it, that he might savor the last drop. The scribe directly behind the throne noted every word. "A hearty bouquet, properly curling nose hairs," Bruenor added. "Seven."

The eleven other clerics groaned. Seven on a scale of ten was the highest grade Bruenor had given any of the five samples of holy water he had already taste-tested.

If Jerbollah, the dwarf now in a frenzy of spellcasting, could perform as well with magic, he would be difficult to beat for the coveted position.

"And the light shall be," Jerbollah cried, the climax of his spell, "red!"

There came a tremendous popping noise, as if a hundred dwarves had just yanked their fingers from puckered mouths. And . . . nothing.

"Red!" Jerbollah cried in delight.

"What?" demanded Bruenor, who, like those dwarves beside him, saw nothing different about the lighting in the chapel.

"Red!" Jerbollah said again, and when he turned around, Bruenor and the others understood. Jerbollah's face was glowing a bright red—literally, the confused cleric was seeing the world through a rose-colored veil.

Frustrated Bruenor dropped his head into his palm and groaned.

"Makes a good batch o' holy water, though," one of the dwarves nearby remarked, to a chorus of snickers.

Poor Jerbollah, who thought his spell had worked brilliantly, did not understand what was so funny.

Stumpet Rakingclaw leaped forward, seizing the moment. She handed her mug of holy water to Bruenor and rushed out before the throne.

"I had planned something different," she explained quickly, as Bruenor sipped, then swallowed the mead—and the dwarf king's face brightened once more as he declared this batch a nine. "But a cleric of Moradin, of Clanggedon, who knows battle best of all, must be ready to improvise!"

"Do tell us, O Strumpet!" one of the other dwarves roared, and even Bruenor cracked a smile as the laughter exploded around him.

Stumpet, who was used to the nickname and wore it like a badge of honor, took no offense. "Jerbollah called for red," she explained, "so red it shall be!"

"It already *is* red," insisted Jerbollah, who earned a slap on the head from the dwarf behind him for his foolishness.

The fiery young Stumpet ruffled her short red beard and went into a series of movements so exaggerated that it seemed as if she had fallen into convulsions.

"Move it, Strumpet," a dwarf near the throne whispered, to renewed laughter.

Bruenor held up the mug and tapped it with his finger. "Nine," he reminded the wise-cracking dwarf. Stumpet was in the clear lead. If she pulled off her spell where Jerbollah had failed, she would be almost impossible to beat, which would make her the wisecracking dwarf's superior.

The dwarf behind the humbled jokester slapped him on the back of the head.

"Red!" Stumpet cried with all her might.

Nothing happened.

A few snickers came from the line, but in truth, the gathered dwarves were more curious than amused. Stumpet was a powerful spellcaster and should have been able to throw some light, whatever color, into the room. The feeling began to wash over them all—except Jerbollah, who insisted that his spell had worked perfectly—that something might be wrong.

Stumpet turned back to the throne, confused and embarrassed. She started to say something, to apologize, when a tremendous explosion rocked the ground so violently that she and half the other dwarves in the room were knocked from their feet.

Stumpet rolled and turned, looking back to the empty area of the chapel. A ball of blue sparks appeared from nowhere, hovered in the air, then shot straight for a very surprised Bruenor. The dwarf king ducked and thrust his arm up to block, and the mug that held Stumpet's batch of holy water shattered, sheared off at the handle. A blue storm of raging sparks burst from the impact, sending dwarves scurrying for cover.

More sparking bursts ignited across the room, glowing balls zipping this way and that, thunderlike booms shaking the floor and walls.

"What in the Nine Hells did ye do?" the dwarf king, a little curled-up ball on his great chair, screamed at poor Stumpet.

The female dwarf tried to respond, tried to disclaim responsibility for this unexpected turn, but a small tube appeared in midair, generally pointed her way, and fired multicolored balls that sent Stumpet scrambling away.

It went on for several long, frightening minutes, dwarves diving every which way, sparks seeming to follow them wherever they hid, burning their backsides and singeing their beards. Then it was over, as suddenly as it had begun, leaving the chapel perfectly quiet and smelling of sulphur.

Gradually Bruenor straightened in his chair and tried to regain some of his lost dignity.

"What in the Nine Hells did ye do?" he demanded again, to which poor Stumpet merely shrugged. A couple of dwarves managed a slight laugh at that.

"At least it's still red," Jerbollah remarked under his breath, but loud enough to be heard. Again he was slapped by the dwarf behind him.

Bruenor shook his head in disgust, then froze in place as two eyeballs appeared in the air before him, scrutinizing him ominously.

Then they dropped to the floor and rolled around haphazardly, coming to rest several feet apart.

Bruenor looked on in disbelief as a spectral hand came out of the air and herded the eyeballs close together and turned them so that they were both facing the dwarf king once more.

"Well, that's never happened before," said a disembodied voice.

Bruenor jumped in fright, then settled and groaned yet again. He hadn't heard that voice in a long time, but never would he forget it. And it explained so much about what was going on in the chapel.

"Harkle Harpell," Bruenor said, and whispers ignited all around him, for most of the other dwarves had heard Bruenor's tales of Longsaddle, a town to the west of Mithral Hall, home of the legendary, eccentric wizard clan, the Harpells. Bruenor and his companions had passed through Longsaddle, had toured the Ivy Mansion, on their way to find Mithral Hall. It was a place the dwarf, no fan of wizardly magic, would never forget, and never remember fondly.

"My greetings, King Bruenor," said the voice, emanating from the floor right below the steadied eyeballs.

"Are ye really here?" the dwarf king asked.

"Hmmm," groaned the floor. "I can hear both you and those who are around me at the Fuzzy Quarterstaff," Harkle replied, referring to the tavern at the Ivy Mansion, back in Longsaddle. "Just a moment, if you please."

The floor "Hmmmm'd" several more times, and the eyeballs blinked once or twice, perhaps the most curious sight Bruenor had ever seen, as an eyelid appeared from nowhere, covered the ball momentarily, then disappeared once more.

"It seems that I'm in both places," Harkle tried to explain. "I'm quite blind back here—of course, my eyes are there. I wonder if I might get them back . . ." The spectral hand appeared again, groping for the eyeballs. It tried to grasp one of them securely, but only wound up turning the ball around on the floor.

"Whoa!" shouted a distressed Harkle. "So that is how a lizard sees the world! I must note it . . ."

"Harkle!" Bruenor roared in frustration.

"Oh, yes, yes, of course," replied Harkle, coming to what little senses he possessed. "Please excuse my distraction, King Bruenor. This has never happened before."

"Well it's happened now," Bruenor said dryly.

"My eyes are there," Harkle said, as though trying to sort things out aloud. "But, of course, I will be there as well, quite soon. Actually, I had hoped to be there now, but didn't get through. Curious indeed. I could try again, or could ask one of my brothers to try—"

"No!" Bruenor bellowed, cringing at the thought that other Harpell body parts might soon rain down on him.

"Of course," Harkle agreed after a moment. "Too dangerous. Too curious. Very well, then. I come in answer to your call, friend dwarf king!"

Bruenor dropped his head into his palm and sighed. He had feared those very words for more than two tendays now. He had sent an emissary to Longsaddle for help in the potential war only because Drizzt had insisted.

To Bruenor, having the Harpells as allies might eliminate the need for enemies.

"A tenday," Harkle's disembodied voice said. "I will arrive in a tenday!"

There came a long pause. "Err, umm, could you be so kind as to keep my eyeballs safe?"

Bruenor nodded to the side, and several dwarves scrambled ahead, curious and no longer afraid of the exotic items. They battled to scoop up the eyes and finally sorted them out, with two different dwarves each holding one—and each taking obvious pleasure in making faces at the eye.

Bruenor shouted for them to quit playing even before Harkle's voice screamed in horror.

"Please!" pleaded the somewhat absent mage. "Only one dwarf to hold both eyes." Immediately the two dwarves clutched their prizes more tightly.

"Give 'em to Stumpet!" Bruenor roared. "She started this whole thing!"

Reluctantly, but not daring to go against an order from their king, the dwarves handed the eyeballs over.

"And do please keep them moist," Harkle requested, to which, Stumpet immediately tossed one of the orbs into her mouth.

"Not like that!" screamed the voice. "Oh, not like that!"

"I should get them," protested Jerbollah. "My spell worked!" The dwarf behind Jerbollah slapped him on the head.

Bruenor slumped low in his chair, shaking his head. It was going to be a long time in putting his clerical order back together, and longer still would be the preparations for war when the Harpells arrived.

Across the room, Stumpet, who, despite her antics, was the most level-headed of dwarves, was not so lighthearted. Harkle's unexpected presence had deflected the other apparent problems, perhaps, but the weird arrival of the wizard from Longsaddle did not explain the happenings here. Stumpet, several of the other clerics, and even the scribe realized that something was very wrong.

⚔ ⚔ ⚔ ⚔ ⚔

Guenhwyvar was tired by the time she, Drizzt, and Catti-brie came to the high pass leading to Mithral Hall's eastern door. Drizzt had kept the panther on the Material Plane longer than usual, and though it was taxing,

Guenhwyvar was glad for the stay. With all the preparations going on in the deep tunnels below the dwarven complex, Drizzt did not get outside much, and consequently, neither did Guenhwyvar.

For a long, long time, the panther figurine had been in the hands of various drow in Menzoberranzan, and thus, the panther had gone centuries without seeing the out-of-doors on the Material Plane. Still, the out-of-doors was where Guenhwyvar was most at home, where natural panthers lived, and where the panther's first companions on the Material Plane had lived.

Guenhwyvar had indeed enjoyed this romp along mountain trails with Drizzt and Catti-brie, but now was the time to go home, to rest again on the Astral Plane. For all their love of companionship, neither the drow nor the panther could afford that luxury now, with so great a danger looming, an impending war in which Drizzt and Guenhwyvar would likely play a major role, fighting side by side.

The panther paced around the figurine, gradually diminished, and faded to an insubstantial gray mist.

✕ ✕ ✕ ✕ ✕

Gone from the material world, Guenhwyvar entered a long, low, winding tunnel, the silvery path that would take her back to the Astral Plane. The panther loped easily, not eager to be gone and too tired to run full out. The journey was not so long anyway, and always uneventful.

Guenhwyvar skidded to a stop as she rounded one long bend, her ears falling flat.

The tunnel ahead was ablaze.

Diabolical forms, fiendish manifestations that seemed unconcerned with the approaching cat, leaped from those flames. Guenhwyvar padded ahead a few short strides. She could feel the intense heat, could see the fiery fiends, and could hear their laughter as they continued to consume the circular tunnel's walls.

A rush of air told Guenhwyvar that the tunnel had been ruptured, some-where in the emptiness between the planes of existence. Fiery fiends were pulled into elongated shapes then sucked out. The remaining flames danced wildly, leaping and flickering, seeming to go out altogether, then rising together in a sudden and violent surge. The wind came strong at Guenhwyvar's back, compelling the panther to go forward, compelling everything in the tunnel to fly out through the breach, into nothingness.

Guenhwyvar knew instinctively that if she succumbed to that force, there would be no turning back, that she would become a lost thing, helpless, wandering between the planes.

The panther dug in her claws and backpedaled slowly, fighting the fierce wind every inch of the way. Her black coat ruffled up, sleek fur turning the wrong way.

One step back.

The tunnel was smooth and hard, and there was little for panther claws to dig against. Guenhwyvar's paws pedaled more frantically, but inevitably the cat began to slide forward toward the flames and the breach.

⚔ ⚔ ⚔ ⚔ ⚔

"What is it?" Catti-brie asked, seeing Drizzt's confusion as he picked up the figurine.

"Warm," Drizzt replied. "The figurine is warm."

Catti-brie's expression likewise crinkled with confusion. She had a feeling of sheer dread then, a feeling she could not understand. "Call Guen back," she prompted.

Drizzt, equally fearful, was already doing exactly that. He placed the figurine on the ground and called out to the panther.

⚔ ⚔ ⚔ ⚔ ⚔

Guenhwyvar heard the call, and wanted desperately to answer it, but now the cat was close to the breach. Wild flames danced high, singeing the panther's face. The wind was stronger than ever, and there was nothing, nothing at all, for Guenhwyvar to hold on to.

The panther knew fear, and the panther knew grief. Never again would she come to Drizzt's call; never again would she hunt beside the ranger in

the forests near Mithral Hall or race down a mountain with Drizzt and Catti-brie.

Guenhwyvar had known grief before, when some of her previous masters had died. This time, though, there could be no replacement for Drizzt. And none for Catti-brie or Regis, or even Bruenor, that most frustrating of creatures, whose love and hate relationship with Guenhwyvar had provided the panther with many hours of teasing enjoyment.

Guenhwyvar remembered the time Drizzt had bade her lie atop sleeping Bruenor and nap. How the dwarf had roared!

Flames bit at Guenhwyvar's face. She could see through the breach now, see the emptiness that awaited her.

Somewhere far off, beyond the shield of the screeching wind, came Drizzt's call, a call the cat could not answer.

BAENRE'S FAULT

Uthegental Armgo, the patron and weapons master of Barrison del'Armgo, Second House of Menzoberranzan, was not Jarlaxle's favorite drow. In fact, Jarlaxle wasn't certain that this one was truly a drow at all. Standing near six feet, with a muscled torso that weighed close to two hundred pounds, Uthegental was the largest dark elf in Menzoberranzan, one of the largest of the normally slender race ever seen in the Underdark. More than size distinguished the fierce weapons master, though. While Jarlaxle was considered eccentric, Uthegental was simply frightening. He cropped his white hair short and spiked it with the thick, gelatinous extract gained by boiling rothé udders. A mithral ring was stuck through Uthegental's angular nose, and a golden pin protruded through each cheek.

His weapon was a trident, black like the fine-fitting mail of jointed plates he wore, and a net—magical, so it was said—hung on his belt, within easy reach.

Jarlaxle was glad that at least Uthegental wasn't wearing his war paint this day, zigzagging streaks of some dye the mercenary did not know that showed yellow and red in both the normal and infrared spectrums. It was common knowledge in Menzoberranzan that Uthegental, in addition to being patron to Matron Mother Mez'Barris, was the consort of many Barrison del'Armgo females. The Second House considered him breeding

stock, and the thought of dozens of little Uthegentals running around brought a sour expression to Jarlaxle's face.

"The magic is wild, yet I remain strong!" the exotic weapons master growled, his perpetually furrowed brow making him even more imposing. He held one iron-muscled arm to the side and tightened his biceps as he crooked his elbow, the rock-hard muscles of his arm standing high and proud.

Jarlaxle took a moment to remind himself where he was, in the midst of his own encampment, in his own room and seated behind his own desk, secretly surrounded by a dozen highly skilled and undeniably loyal soldiers of Bregan D'aerthe. Even without the concealed allies, Jarlaxle's desk was equipped with more than a few deadly traps for troublesome guests. and of course, Jarlaxle was no minor warrior himself. A small part of him—a *very* small part of him—wondered how he might measure up in battle against Uthegental.

Few warriors, drow or otherwise, could intimidate the mercenary leader, but he allowed himself a bit of humility in the face of this maniac.

"*Ultrin Sargtlin!*" Uthegental went on, the drow term for "Supreme Warrior," a claim that seemed secure within the city with Dantrag Baenre dead. Jarlaxle often imagined the battle that most of Menzoberranzan's dark elves thought would one day be waged by bitter rivals Uthegental and Dantrag.

Dantrag had been the quicker—quicker than anyone—but with his sheer strength and size, Uthegental had rated as Jarlaxle's favorite in such a contest. It was said that when he went into his battle rage, Uthegental possessed the strength of a giant, and this fearsome weapons master was so tough that when he battled lesser creatures, such as goblin slaves, he always allowed his opponent to swing first, and never tried to parry the attack, accepting the vicious hit, reveling in the pain, before tearing his enemy limb from limb and having the choicest body parts prepared for his supper.

Jarlaxle shuddered at the notion, then put the image from his mind, reminding himself that he and Uthegental had more important business.

"There is no weapons master, no drow at all, in Menzoberranzan to stand against me," Uthegental continued his boasting, for no reason that Jarlaxle could discern beyond the savage's overblown sense of pride.

He went on and on, as was his way, and while Jarlaxle wanted to ask him if there was a point to it all, he kept silent, confident that the emissary from the Second House would eventually get around to a serious discussion.

Uthegental stopped his mounting tirade suddenly, and his hand shot out, snatching from the top of the desk a gem that the mercenary used as a paperweight. Uthegental muttered some word that Jarlaxle did not catch, but the mercenary's keen eye did note a slight flicker in the huge drow's brooch, the House emblem of Barrison del'Armgo. Uthegental then held the gem aloft and squeezed it with all his strength. The muscles in his sculpted arm strained and bulged, but the gem held firm.

"I should be able to crush this," Uthegental growled. "Such is the power, the magic, that I have been Lolth-blessed with!"

"The gem would not be worth as much when reduced to powder," Jarlaxle replied dryly. What was Uthegental's point? he wondered. Of course, something strange was going on with magic all over the city. Now Jarlaxle better understood Uthegental's earlier boasting. The exotic weapons master was indeed still strong, but not *as* strong, a fact that apparently worried Uthegental more than a little.

"Magic is failing," the weapons master said, "failing everywhere. The priestesses kneel in prayer, sacrifice drow after drow, and still nothing they do brings Lolth or her handmaidens to them. Magic is failing, and it is Matron Baenre's fault!"

Jarlaxle took note of the way Uthegental seemed to repeat things. Probably to remind himself of what he was talking about, the mercenary mused, and his sour expression aptly reflected his opinion of Uthegental's intellect. Of course, Uthegental would never catch the subtle indication.

"You cannot know that," the mercenary replied. Uthegental's accusation no doubt came from Matron Mez'Barris herself. Many things were coming clear to the mercenary now, mostly the fact that Mez'Barris had sent Uthegental to feel out Bregan D'aerthe, to see if the time was ripe for a coup against Baenre. Uthegental's words could certainly be considered damning, but not against Barrison del'Armgo, for their weapons master was always running off at the mouth, and never with anything complimentary to anyone but himself.

"It was Matron Baenre who allowed the rogue Do'Urden to escape," Uthegental bellowed. "It was she who presided over the failed high ritual! Failed, as magic is failing."

Say it again, Jarlaxle thought, but wisely kept that derisive reply silent. The mercenary's frustration at that moment wasn't simply with the ignorance revealed by Uthegental. It was with the fact that Uthegental's reasoning was common all over the city. To Jarlaxle's thinking, the dark elves of Menzoberranzan continually limited themselves by their blind insistence that everything was symptomatic of a deeper meaning, that the Spider Queen had some grand design behind their every movement. In the eyes of the priestesses, if Drizzt Do'Urden denied Lolth and ran away, it was only because Lolth wanted House Do'Urden to fall and wanted the challenge of recapturing him presented to the other ambitious Houses of the city.

It was a limiting philosophy, one that denied free will. Certainly Lolth might play a hand in the hunt for Drizzt. Certainly she might be angered by the disruption of the high ritual, if she even bothered to take note of the event! But the reasoning that what was happening now was completely tied to that one event—ultimately a minor one in the five-thousand year history of Menzoberranzan—was a view of foolish pride, wherein the dwellers of Menzoberranzan seemed to think that all the multiverse revolved around them.

"Why then is all magic failing every House?" Jarlaxle asked Uthegental. "Why not just House Baenre?"

Uthegental briskly shook his head, not even willing to consider the reasoning. "We have failed Lolth and are being punished," he declared. "If only *I* had met the rogue instead of pitiful Dantrag Baenre!"

Now that was a sight Jarlaxle would wish to see! Drizzt Do'Urden battling Uthegental. The mere thought of it sent a tingle down the mercenary's spine.

"You cannot deny that Dantrag was in Lolth's favor," Jarlaxle reasoned, "while Drizzt Do'Urden most certainly was not. How, then, did Drizzt win?"

Uthegental's brow furrowed so fiercely that his red-glowing eyes nearly disappeared entirely, and Jarlaxle quickly reassessed the prudence of pushing the brute along that line of reasoning. It was one thing to back Matron Baenre; it was another to shake the foundation for one religion-blinded slave's entire world.

"It will sort itself out properly," Jarlaxle assured. "In all of Arach-Tinil-ith, in all of the Academy, and in every chapel of every House, prayers are being offered to Lolth."

"Their prayers are not being answered," Uthegental promptly reminded. "Lolth is angry with us and will not speak with us until we have punished those who have wronged her."

Their prayers were not being answered, or their prayers were not even being heard, Jarlaxle thought. Unlike most of the other typically xenopho-bic drow in Menzoberranzan, the mercenary was in touch with the outside world. He knew from his contacts that Blingdenstone's svirfneblin priests were having equal difficulty in their communion, that the deep gnomes' magic had also gone awry. Something had happened to the pantheon itself, Jarlaxle believed, and to the very fabric of magic.

"It is not Lolth," he said boldly, to which Uthegental's eyes went wide. Understanding exactly what was at stake here, the entire hierarchy of the city and perhaps the lives of half of Menzoberranzan's drow, Jarlaxle pressed ahead. "Rather, it is not *solely* Lolth. When you go back into the city, consider Narbondel," he said, referring to the stone pillar clock of Menzoberranzan. "Even now, in what should be the cool dark of night, it glows brighter and hotter than ever before, so hot that its glow can even be viewed without the heat-sensing vision, so hot that any drow near the pillar cannot even allow their vision to slip into the heat-sensing spectrum, lest they be blinded.

"Yet Narbondel is enchanted by a wizard, and not a priestess," Jarlaxle went on, hoping that dim Uthegental would follow the reasoning.

"You doubt that Lolth could affect the clock?" the weapons master growled.

"I doubt she would!" Jarlaxle countered vehemently. "The magic of Nar-bondel is separate from Lolth, has always been separate from Lolth. Before Gromph Baenre, some of the previous archmages of Menzoberranzan were not even followers of Lolth!" He almost added that Gromph wasn't so devout, either, but decided to keep that bit of information back. No sense in giving

the desperate Second House additional reasons to think that House Baenre was even more out of the Spider Queen's favor.

"And consider the faerie fires highlighting every structure," Jarlaxle continued. He could tell by the angle of Uthegental's furrowed brow that the brute was suddenly more curious than outraged—not a common sight. "Blinking on and off, or winking out altogether. Wizard's faerie fire, not the magic of a priestess, and decorating every House, not just House Baenre. Events are beyond us, I say, and beyond the high ritual. Tell Matron Mez'Barris, with all my respect, that I do not believe Matron Baenre can be blamed for this, and I do not believe the solution will be found in a war against the First House. Not unless Lolth herself sends us a clear directive."

Uthegental's expression soon returned to its normal scowl. Of course this one was frustrated, Jarlaxle realized. The most intelligent drow of Menzoberranzan, the most intelligent svirfnebli of Blingdenstone, were frustrated, and nothing Jarlaxle might say would change Uthegental's mind, or the war-loving savage's desire to attack House Baenre. But Jarlaxle knew he didn't have to convince Uthegental. He just had to make Uthegental say the right things upon his return to House Barrison del'Armgo. The mere fact that Mez'Barris sent so prominent an emissary, her own patron and weapons master, told Jarlaxle she would not lead a conspiracy against Baenre without the aid of, or at least the approval of, Bregan D'aerthe.

"I go," Uthegental declared, the most welcome words Jarlaxle had heard since the brute had entered his encampment.

Jarlaxle removed his wide-brimmed hat and ran his hands over his bald pate as he slipped back comfortably in his chair. He could not begin to guess the extent of the events. Perhaps within the apparent chaos of the fabric of reality, Lolth herself had been destroyed. Not such a bad thing, Jarlaxle supposed.

Still, he hoped things would sort themselves out soon, and properly, as he had indicated to Uthegental, for he knew this request—and it was a request—to go to war would come again, and again after that, and each time, it would be backed by increasing desperation. Sooner or later, House Baenre would be attacked.

Jarlaxle thought of the encounter he had witnessed between Matron

Baenre and K'yorl Odran, matron mother of House Oblodra, the city's third, and perhaps most dangerous House, when Baenre had first begun to put together the alliance to send a conquering army to Mithral Hall. Baenre had dealt from a position of power then, fully in Lolth's favor. She had openly insulted K'yorl and the Third House and forced the unpredictable matron mother into her alliance with bare threats.

K'yorl would never forget that, Jarlaxle knew, and she could possibly be pushing Mez'Barris Armgo in the direction of a war against House Baenre.

Jarlaxle loved chaos, thrived amidst confusion, but this scenario was beginning to worry him more than a little.

⚔ ⚔ ⚔ ⚔ ⚔

Contrary to the usually correct mercenary's belief, K'yorl Odran was not nudging Matron Mez'Barris into a war against House Baenre. Quite the opposite, K'yorl was working hard to prevent such a conflict, meeting secretly with the matron mothers of the six other ruling Houses ranked below House Baenre—except for Ghenni'tiroth Tlabbar, Matron of House Faen Tlabbar, the Fourth House, whom K'yorl could not stand and would not trust. It wasn't that K'yorl had forgiven Matron Baenre for the insult, and it wasn't that K'yorl was afraid of the strange events. Far from it.

If it hadn't been for their extensive scouting network beyond House Oblodra and the obvious signs such as Narbondel and the winking faerie fire, the members of the Third House wouldn't even have known that anything was amiss. For the powers of House Oblodra came not from wizardly magic, nor from the clerical prayers to the Spider Queen. The Oblodrans were psionicists. Their powers were formed by internal forces of the mind, and thus far, the Time of Troubles had not affected them.

K'yorl couldn't let the rest of the city know that. She had the score of priestesses under her command hard at work, forcing the psionic equivalent of faerie fire highlighting her house to blink, as were the other houses. And to Mez'Barris and the other matron mothers, she seemed as agitated and nervous as they.

She had to keep a lid on things; she had to keep the conspiracy talk quieted. For when K'yorl could be certain that the loss of magic was not a devious trick, her family would strike—alone. She might pay House Faen Tlabbar back first, for all the years she had spent watching their every ambitious move, or she might strike directly against wretched Baenre.

Either way, the wicked matron mother meant to strike alone.

⚔ ⚔ ⚔ ⚔ ⚔

Matron Baenre sat stiffly in a chair on the raised and torch-lit central dais in the great chapel of her house. Her daughter Sos'Umptu, who served as caretaker to this most holy of drow places, sat to her left, and Triel, the eldest Baenre daughter and matron mistress of the drow Academy, was on her right. All three stared upward, to the illusionary image Gromph had put there, and it seemed strangely fitting that the image did not continue its shape-shifting, from drow to arachnid and back again, but rather, had been caught somewhere in the middle of the transformation and suspended there, like the powers that had elevated House Baenre to its preeminent position.

Not far away, goblin and minotaur slaves continued their work in repairing the dome, but Matron Baenre had lost all hope that putting her chapel back together would right the strange and terrible events in Menzoberranzan. She had come to believe Jarlaxle's reasoning that something larger than a failed high ritual and the escape of a single rogue was involved here. She had come to believe that what was happening in Menzoberranzan might be symptomatic of the whole world, of the whole multiverse, and that it was quite beyond her understanding or her control.

That didn't make things easier for Matron Baenre. If the other Houses didn't share those beliefs, they would try to use her as a sacrifice to put things aright. She glanced briefly at both her daughters. Sos'Umptu was among the least ambitious drow females she had ever known, and Baenre didn't fear much from that one. Triel, on the other hand, might be more dangerous. Though she always seemed content with her life as matron mistress of the Academy, a position of no minor importance, it was widely accepted that Triel, the eldest daughter, would one day rule the First House.

Triel was a patient one, like her mother, but like her mother, she was also calculating. If she became convinced that it was necessary to remove her mother from the throne of House Baenre, that such an act would restore the Baenre name and reputation, then she would do so mercilessly.

That is why Matron Baenre had recalled her from the Academy to a meeting and had located that meeting within the chapel. This was Sos'Umptu's place, Lolth's place, and Triel would not dare strike out at her mother here.

"I plan to issue a call from the Academy that no House shall use this troubled time to war against another," Triel offered, breaking the virtual silence—for none of the Baenres had taken note of the hammering and groaning from the slaves working on the curving roof a mere hundred feet away. None of them took note even when a minotaur casually tossed a goblin to its death, for no better reason than enjoyment.

Matron Baenre took a deep breath and considered the words, and the meaning behind the words. Of course Triel would issue such a plea. The Academy was perhaps the most stabilizing force in Menzoberranzan. But why had Triel chosen this moment to tell her mother? Why not just wait until the plea was presented openly and to all?

Was Triel trying to reassure her? Matron Baenre wondered. Or was she merely trying to put her off her guard?

The thoughts circled in Matron Baenre's mind, ran around and collided with one another, leaving her in a trembling, paranoid fit. Rationally, she understood the self-destructive nature of trying to read things into every word, of trying to outguess those who might be less than enemies, who might even be allies. But Matron Baenre was growing desperate. A few tendays before, she had been at the pinnacle of her power, had brought the city together beneath her in readiness for a massive strike at the dwarven complex of Mithral Hall, near the surface.

How fast it had been taken away, as fast as the fall of a stalactite from the ceiling of the cavern above her treasured chapel.

She wasn't done yet, though. Matron Baenre had not lived through more than two thousand years to give up now. Damn Triel, if she was indeed plotting to take the throne. Damn them all!

The matron mother clapped her hands together sharply, and both her daughters started with surprise as a bipedal, man-sized monstrosity popped into view, standing right before them, draped in tremendous flowing crimson robes. The creature's purplish head resembled that of an octopus, except that only four skinny tentacles waved from the perimeter of its round, many-toothed orifice, and its eyes were pupilless and milky white.

The illithid, or mind flayer, was not unknown to the Baenre daughters. Far from it, El-Viddenvelp, or Methil, as he was commonly called, was Matron Baenre's advisor and had been at her side for many years. Recovered from their startlement, both Sos'Umptu and Triel turned curious stares to their surprising mother.

My greetings to you Triel, the illithid imparted telepathically. and *of course, to you, Sos'Umptu, in this, your place.*

Both daughters nodded and conjured similar mental replies, knowing that Methil would catch the thoughts as clearly as if they had spoken them aloud.

"Fools!" Matron Baenre shouted at both of them. She leaped from her chair and spun around, her withered features fierce. "How are we to survive this time if two of my principle commanders and closest advisors are such fools?"

Sos'Umptu was beside herself with shame, wrought of confusion. She even went so far as to cover her face with the wide sleeve of her thick purple-and-black robe.

Triel, more worldly-wise than her younger sister, initially felt the same shock, but quickly came to understand her mother's point. "The illithid has not lost its powers," she stated, and Sos'Umptu peeked curiously from above her arm.

"Not at all," Matron Baenre agreed, and her tone was not happy.

"But then we have an advantage," Sos'Umptu dared to speak. "For Methil is loyal enough," she said bluntly. There was no use in masking her true feelings behind words of half-truth, for the illithid would read her mind anyway. "And he is the only one of his kind in Menzoberranzan."

"But not the only one who uses such powers!" Matron Baenre roared at her, causing her to shrink back in her chair once more.

"K'yorl," Triel gasped. "If Methil has use of his powers . . ."

"Then so do the Oblodrans," Baenre finished grimly.

They exercise their powers continually, Methil telepathically confirmed to all three. *The highlights of House Oblodra would not be winking were it not for the mental commands of K'yorl's coven.*

"Can we be certain of this?" Triel asked, for there seemed no definite patterns in the failing of magic, just a chaotic mess. Perhaps Methil had not yet been affected, or did not even know that he had been affected. And perhaps Oblodra's faerie fire highlights, though different in creation than the fires glowing around the other houses, were caught in the same chaos.

Psionic powers can be sensed by psionic creatures, Methil assured her. *The Third House teems with energy.*

"And K'yorl gives the appearance that this is not so," Matron Baenre added in a nasty tone.

"She wishes to attack by surprise," Triel reasoned.

Matron Baenre nodded grimly.

"What of Methil?" Sos'Umptu offered hopefully. "His powers are great."

"Methil is more than a match for K'yorl," Matron Baenre assured her daughter, though Methil was silently doing the same thing, imparting a sense of undeniable confidence. "But K'yorl is not alone among the Oblodrans with her psionic powers."

"How many?" Triel wanted to know, to which Matron Baenre merely shrugged.

Many, Methil's thoughts answered.

Triel was thinking it, so she knew that Methil was hearing it, and so she said it aloud, suspiciously. "And if the Oblodrans do come against us, which side will Methil take?"

Matron Baenre was, for an instant, shocked by her daughter's boldness, but she understood that Triel had little choice in divulging her suspicions.

"And will he bring in his allies from the illithid cavern not far away?" Triel pressed. "Surely if a hundred illithids came to our side in this, our time of need . . ."

There was nothing from Methil, not a hint of telepathic communication, and that was answer enough for the Baenres.

"Our problems are not the problems of the mind flayers," Matron Baenre said. It was true enough, and she knew so. She had tried to enlist the illithids in the raid on Mithral Hall, promising them riches and a secure alliance, but the motivations of the otherworldly, octopus-headed creatures were not the same as those of the dark elves, or of any race in all the Underdark. Those motivations remained beyond Matron Baenre's understanding, despite her years of dealing with Methil. The most she could get from the illithids for her important raid was Methil and two others agreeing to go along in exchange for a hundred kobolds and a score of drow males, to be used as slaves by the illithid community in their small cavern city.

There was little else to say. The House guards were positioned at full readiness. Every spare drow was in prayer for help from the Spider Queen. House Baenre was doing everything it could to avert disaster, and yet, Matron Baenre did not believe they would succeed. K'yorl had come to her unannounced on several occasions, had gotten past her magical fence and past the many magical wards set around the complex. The matron mother of House Oblodra had done so only to taunt Baenre, and in truth, had little power remaining to do anything more than that by the time her image was revealed to Baenre. But what might K'yorl accomplish with those magical guards down? Baenre had to wonder. How could Matron Baenre resist the psionicist without countering magic of her own?

Her only defense seemed to be Methil, a creature she neither trusted nor understood.

She did not like the odds.

8
MAGICAL MANIFESTATIONS

Guenhwyvar knew pain, knew agony beyond anything the panther had ever felt. But more than that, the panther knew despair, true despair. Guenhwyvar was a creature formed of magic, the manifestation of the life-force of the animal known on Toril as the panther. The very spark of existence within the great panther depended on magic, as did the conduit that allowed Drizzt and the others before him to bring Guenhwyvar to the Prime Material Plane.

Magic having unraveled; the fabric that wove the universal Weave into a mystical and predictable pattern was torn.

The panther knew despair.

Guenhwyvar heard Drizzt's continued calling, begging. The drow knew the cat was in trouble, and his voice reflected that desperation. In his heart, so connected with his panther companion, Drizzt Do'Urden understood that Guenhwyvar would soon be lost to him forever.

The chilling thought gave the panther a moment of renewed hope and determination. Guenhwyvar focused on Drizzt, conjured an image of the pain she would feel if she could never again return to her beloved master. Growling low in sheer defiance, the panther scraped her back legs so forcefully that more than one claw hooked on the smooth, hard surface and was subsequently yanked out.

The pain did not stop the panther, not when Guenhwyvar measured it against the reality of slipping forward into those flames, of falling out of the tunnel, the only connection to the material world and Drizzt Do'Urden.

The struggle went on for more time than any creature should have resisted. But though Guenhwyvar had not slid any closer to the breach, neither had the panther earned back any ground toward her pleading master.

Finally, exhausted, Guenhwyvar gave a forlorn, helpless look over her shoulder. Her muscles trembled, then gave way.

The panther was swept to the fiery breach.

✕ ✕ ✕ ✕ ✕

Matron Baenre paced the small room nervously, expecting a guard to run in at any moment with news that the compound had been overrun, that the entire city had risen against her House, blaming her for the troubles that had befallen them.

Not so long ago, Baenre had dreamt of conquest, had aspired to the pinnacle of power. Mithral Hall had been within her grasp, and even more than that, the city seemed ready to fall into step behind her lead.

Now she believed she could not hold on to even her own House, to the Baenre empire that had stood for five thousand years.

"Mithral Hall," the wicked drow growled in a damning curse, as though that distant place had been the cause of it all. Her slight chest heaving with forced gasps of air, Baenre reached with both hands to her neck and tore free the chain that lay there.

"Mithral Hall!" she shouted into the ring-shaped pendant, fashioned from the tooth of Gandalug Battlehammer, the patron of Bruenor's clan, the real link to that surface world. Every drow, even those closest to Matron Baenre, thought Drizzt Do'Urden was the catalyst for the invasion, the excuse that allowed Lolth to give her blessing to the dangerous attempt at a conquest so near the surface.

Drizzt was but a part of the puzzle, and a small part, for this little ring was the true impetus. Sealed within it was the tormented spirit of Gandalug, who knew the ways of Mithral Hall and the ways of Clan Battlehammer.

Matron Baenre had taken the dwarf king herself centuries before, and it was only blind fate that had brought a renegade from Menzoberranzan in contact with Bruenor's clan, blind fate that had provided an excuse for the conquest Matron Baenre had desired for many, many decades.

With a shout of outrage, Baenre hurled the tooth across the room, then fell back in shock as the item exploded.

Baenre stared blankly into the room's corner as the smoke cleared away, at the naked dwarf kneeling there. The matron mother pulled herself to her feet, shaking her head in disbelief, for this was no summoned spirit, but Gandalug's physical body!

"You dare to come forth?" Baenre screamed, but her anger masked her fear. When she had previously called Gandalug's physical form forth from the extradimensional prison, he was never truly whole, never corporeal—and never naked. Looking at him now, Baenre knew Gandalug's prison was gone, that Gandalug was returned exactly as he had been the moment Baenre had captured him, except for his clothes.

The battered old dwarf looked up at his captor, his tormentor. Baenre had spoken in the drow tongue, and of course, Gandalug hadn't understood a word. That hardly mattered, though, for the old dwarf wasn't listening. He was, in fact, beyond words.

Struggling, growling, with every pained movement, Gandalug forced his back to straighten, then put one, then the other, leg under him and rose determinedly. He understood that something was different. After centuries of torment and mostly emptiness, a fugue state in a gray void, Gandalug Battlehammer felt somehow different, felt whole and real. Since his capture, the old dwarf had lived a surreal existence, had lived a dream, surrounded by vivid, frightening images whenever this old wretch had called him forth, encompassed by interminable periods of nothingness, where place and time and thought were one long emptiness.

But now . . . now Gandalug felt different, felt even the creaks and pains of his old bones. And how wonderful those sensations were!

"Go back!" Baenre ordered, this time in the tongue of the surface, the language she always used to communicate with the old dwarf. "Back to your prison until I call you forth!"

Gandalug looked around, to the chain lying on the floor, the tooth ring nowhere in sight.

"I'm not fer tinkin' so," the old dwarf remarked in his heavy, ancient dialect, and he advanced a step.

Baenre's eyes narrowed dangerously. "You dare?" she whispered, drawing forth a slender wand. She knew how dangerous this one could be, and thus she wasted no time in pointing the item and reciting an arcane phrase, meaning to call forth a stream of webbing that would engulf the dwarf and hold him fast.

Nothing happened.

Gandalug took another step, growling like a hungry animal with every inch.

Baenre's steely-eyed gaze fell away, revealing her sudden fear. She was a creature weaned on magic, who relied on magic to protect her and to vanquish her enemies. With the items she possessed—which she carried with her at all times—and her mighty spell repertoire, she could fend off nearly any enemy, could likely crush a battalion of toughened dwarven fighters. But without those items, and with no spells coming to her call, Matron Baenre was a pitiful, bluffing thing, withered and frail.

It wouldn't have mattered to Gandalug had a titan been standing before him. For some reason he could not understand, he was free of the prison, free and in his own body, a sensation he had not felt in two thousand years.

Baenre had other tricks to try, and in truth, some of them, like the pouch that carried a horde of spiders that would rush to her call, had not yet fallen into the chaotic and magical web that was the Time of Troubles. She couldn't chance it, though. Not now, not when she was so very vulnerable.

She turned and ran for the door.

The corded muscles of Gandalug's mighty legs tightened, and the dwarf sprang, clearing the fifteen feet to get to the door before his tormentor.

A fist slammed Baenre's chest, stealing her breath, and before she could respond, she was up in the air, twirling around over the enraged dwarf's head.

Then she was flying, to crash and crumple against the wall across the room.

"I'm to be rippin' yer head off," Gandalug promised as he steadily advanced.

The door burst open, and Berg'inyon rushed into the room. Gandalug spun to face him as Berg'inyon drew his twin blades. Startled by the sight—how had a dwarf come into Menzoberranzan, into his own mother's private chambers?—Berg'inyon got the blades up just as Gandalug grabbed them, one in each hand.

Had the enchantment still been upon the weapons master's fine blades, they would have cut cleanly through the tough dwarven flesh. Even without the enchantment, the magic lost in the swirl of chaos, the swords dug deeply.

Gandalug hardly cared. He heaved Berg'inyon's arms out wide, the slender drow no match for his sheer strength. The dwarf whipped his head forward, crashing it into Berg'inyon's supple armor, slender rings that also relied on enchantment for their strength.

Gandalug repeated the movement over and over, and Berg'inyon's grunts fast became breathless gasps. Soon the young Baenre was out on his feet, hardly conscious as Gandalug yanked the swords from his hands. The dwarf's head came in one more time, and Berg'inyon, no longer connected to, and thus supported by, the dwarf, fell away.

Still ignoring the deep cuts on his hands, Gandalug threw one of Berg'inyon's swords to the side of the room, took the other properly in hand, and turned on Matron Baenre, who was still sitting against the wall, trying to clear her thoughts.

"Where's yer smile?" the dwarf taunted, stalking in. "I'm wantin' a smile on yer stinkin' face when I hold yer head up in me hand fer all t'see!"

The next step was the dwarf king's last, as an octopus-headed monstrosity materialized before him, its grotesque tentacles waving his way.

A stunning blast of mental energy rolled Gandalug over, and he nearly dropped the sword. He shook his head fiercely to keep his wits about him.

He continued to growl, to shake his hairy head, as a second blast, then a third, assaulted his sensibilities. Had he held that wall of rage, Gandalug might have withstood even these, and even the two subsequent attacks from

Methil. But that rage melted into confusion, which was not a powerful enough feeling to defeat the mighty illithid's intrusions.

Gandalug didn't hear the drow-made sword fall to the stone, didn't hear Matron Baenre call out for Methil and for the recovering Berg'inyon, as she instructed the pair not to kill the dwarf.

Baenre was scared, scared by these shifts in magic that she could not understand. But that fear did not prevent her from remembering her wicked self. For some unexplained reason, Gandalug had become alive again, in his own body and free of the apparently disintegrated ring.

That mystery would not prevent Baenre from paying this one back for the attack and the insult. Baenre was a master at torturing a spirit, but even her prowess in that fine art paled beside her abilities to torture a living creature.

✕ ✕ ✕ ✕ ✕

"Guenhwyvar!" The figurine was wickedly hot now, but Drizzt held on stubbornly, pressed it close to his chest, his heart, though wisps of smoke were running up from the edge of his cloak and the flesh of his hands was beginning to blister.

He knew, and he would not let go. He knew that Guenhwyvar would be gone from him forever, and like a friend hugging close a dying comrade, Drizzt would not let go, would be there to the end.

His desperate calls began to lessen, not from resignation, but simply because his voice could not get past the lump of grief in his throat. Now his fingers, too, were burning, but he would not let go.

Catti-brie did it for him. On a sudden, desperate impulse, the young woman, herself torn with the pain of grief, grabbed roughly at Drizzt's arm and slapped hard the figurine, knocking it to the ground.

Drizzt's startled expression turned to one of outrage and denial, like the final burst of rage from a mother as she watched her child's casket lowered into the grave. For the moment the figurine hit the ground, Catti-brie drew Khazid'hea from its sheath and leaped to the spot. Up went the sword, over her head, its fine edge still showing the red line of its enchantment.

"No!" Drizzt cried, lunging for her.

He was too late. Tears rimming her blue eyes, her thoughts jumbled, Catti-brie found the courage for a last, desperate try, and she brought the mighty blade to bear. Khazid'hea could cut through stone, and so it did now, at the very instant that Guenhwyvar went through the breach.

There came a flash, and a throbbing pain, a pulsating magic, shot up Catti-brie's arm, hurling her backward and to the ground. Drizzt skidded, pivoted, and ducked low, shielding his head as the figurine's head fell free, loosing a line of raging fire far out into the air.

The flames blew out a moment later and a thick gray smoke poured from the body of the broken figurine. Gradually Drizzt straightened from his defensive crouch and Catti-brie came back to her senses, both to find a haggard-looking Guenhwyvar, the panther's thick coat still smoking, standing before them.

Drizzt dived to his knees and fell over the panther, wrapping Guenhwyvar in a great hug. They both crawled their way to Catti-brie, who was still sitting on the ground, laughing and sobbing though she was weak from the impact of the magic.

"What have you done?" Drizzt asked her.

She had no immediate answers. She did not know how to explain what had happened when Khazid'hea struck the enchanted figurine. She looked to the blade now, lying quiet at her side, its edge no longer glowing and a burr showing along its previously unblemished length.

"I think I've ruined me sword," Catti-brie replied softly.

ꓘ ꓘ ꓘ ꓘ ꓘ

Later that same day, Drizzt lounged on the bed in his room in the upper levels of Mithral Hall, looking worriedly at his panther companion. Guenhwyvar was back, and that was a better thing, he supposed, than what his instincts had told him would have happened had Catti-brie not cut the figurine.

A better thing, but not a good thing. The panther was weary, resting by the hearth across the small room, head down and eyes closed. That nap would not suffice, Drizzt knew. Guenhwyvar was a creature of the Astral

Plane and could truly rejuvenate only among the stars. On several occasions necessity had prompted Drizzt to keep Guenhwyvar on the Material Plane for extended periods, but even a single day beyond the half the cat usually stayed left Guen exhausted.

Even now the artisans of Mithral Hall, dwarves of no small skill, were inspecting the cut figurine, and Bruenor had sent an emissary out to Silverymoon, seeking help from Lady Alustriel, as skilled as any this side of the great desert Anauroch in the ways of magic.

How long would it take? Drizzt wondered, unsure if any of them could repair the figurine. How long could Guenhwyvar survive?

Unannounced, Catti-brie burst through the door. One look at her tear-streaked face told Drizzt that something was amiss. He rolled from the bed to his feet and stepped toward the mantle, where his twin scimitars hung.

Catti-brie intercepted him before he had completed the step and wrapped him in a powerful hug that knocked them both to the bed.

"All I ever wanted," she said urgently, squeezing tight.

Drizzt likewise held on, confused and overwhelmed. He managed to turn his head so he could look into the young woman's eyes, trying to read some clues.

"I was made for ye, Drizzt Do'Urden," Catti-brie said between sobs. "Ye're all that's been in me thoughts since the day we met."

It was too crazy. Drizzt tried to extract himself, but he didn't want to hurt Catti-brie and her hold was simply too strong and desperate.

"Look at me," she sobbed. "Tell me ye feel the same!"

Drizzt did look at Catti-brie, as deeply as he had ever studied the beautiful young woman. He did care for her—of course he did. He did love her, and had even allowed himself a fantasy or two about this very situation.

But now it seemed simply too weird, too unexpected and with no introduction. He got the distinct feeling that something was out of sorts with the woman, something crazy, like the magic all around them.

"What of Wulfgar?" Drizzt managed to say, though the name got muffled as Catti-brie pressed tightly, her hair thick against Drizzt's face. The poor drow could not deny the woman's allure, the sweet scent of Catti-brie's hair, the warmth of her toned body.

Catti-brie's head snapped as if he had hit her. "Who?"

It was Drizzt's turn to feel as if he had been slapped.

"Take me," Catti-brie implored.

Drizzt's eyes couldn't have gone any wider without falling out of their sockets.

"Wield me!" she cried.

"Wield me?" Drizzt echoed under his breath.

"Make me the instrument of your dance," she went on. "Oh, I beg! It is all I was made for, all I desire." She stopped suddenly and pushed back to arm's length, staring wide-eyed at Drizzt as though some new angle had just popped into her head. "I am better than the others," she promised slyly.

What others? Drizzt wanted to scream, but by this point, the drow couldn't get any words out of his slack-jawed mouth.

"As are yerself," Catti-brie went on. "Better than that woman, I'm now knowing!"

Drizzt had almost found his center again, had almost regained control enough to reply, when the weight of that last statement buried him. Damn the subtlety! the drow determined, and he twisted and pulled free, rolling from the bed and springing to his feet.

Catti-brie dived right behind, wrapped herself around one of his legs, and held on with all her strength.

"Oh, do not deny me, me love!" she screamed, so urgently that Guen-hwyvar lifted her head from the hearth and gave a low growl. "Wield me, I'm begging! Only in yer hands might I be whole!"

Drizzt reached down with both hands, meaning to extract his leg from the tight grip. He noticed something then, on Catti-brie's hip, that gave him pause, that stunned him and explained everything all at once.

He noticed the sword Catti-brie had picked up in the Underdark, the sword that had a pommel shaped into the head of a unicorn. Only it was no longer a unicorn.

It was Catti-brie's face.

In one swift movement, Drizzt drew the sword out of its sheath and tugged free, hopping back two steps. Khazid'hea's red line, that enchanted edge, had returned in full and beamed now more brightly than ever before.

Drizzt slid back another step, expecting to be tackled again.

There was no pursuit. The young woman remained in place, half sitting, half kneeling on the floor. She threw her head back as if in ecstacy. "Oh, yes!" she cried.

Drizzt stared down at the pommel, watched in blank amazement as it shifted from the image of Catti-brie's face back into a unicorn. He felt an overwhelming warmth from the weapon, a connection as intimate as that of a lover.

Panting for breath, the drow looked back to Catti-brie, who was sitting straighter now, looking around curiously.

"What're ye doing with me sword?" she asked quietly. Again she looked around the room, Drizzt's room, seeming totally confused. She would have asked, "And what am I doing here?" Drizzt realized, except that the question was already obvious from the expression on her beautiful face.

"We have to talk," Drizzt said to her.

9
IMPLICATIONS

I t was rare that both Gromph and Triel Baenre would be in audience with their mother at the same time, rarer still that they would be joined by Berg'inyon, Sos'Umptu, and the two other notable Baenre daughters, Bladen'Kerst and Quenthel. Six of the seven sat in comfortable chairs around the dais in the chapel. Not Bladen'Kerst, though. Ever seeming the caged animal, the most sadistic drow in the First House paced in circles, her brow furrowed and thin lips pursed. She was the second oldest daughter behind Triel and should have been out of the house by this time, perhaps as a matron in the Academy, or even more likely, as a matron mother of her own, lesser, House. Matron Baenre had not allowed that, however, fearing that her daughter's simple lack of civility, even by drow standards, would disgrace House Baenre.

Triel looked up and shook her head disdainfully at Bladen'Kerst every time she passed. She rarely gave Bladen'Kerst any thought. Like Vendes Baenre, her younger sister who had been killed by Drizzt Do'Urden during the escape, Bladen'Kerst was an instrument of her mother's torture and nothing more. She was a buffoon, a showpiece, and no real threat to anyone in House Baenre above the rank of common soldier.

Quenthel was quite a different matter, and in the long interludes between Bladen'Kerst's passing, Triel's stern and scrutinizing gaze never left that one.

And Quenthel returned the look with open hostility. She had risen to the rank of high priestess in record time and was reputed to be in Lolth's highest favor. Quenthel held no illusions about her tentative position. Had it not been for that fact of favor, Triel would have obliterated her long ago. For Quenthel had made no secret of her ambitions, which included the stepping stone as matron mistress of Arach-Tinilith, a position Triel had no intention of abandoning.

"Sit down!" Matron Baenre snapped finally at the annoying Bladen'Kerst. One of Baenre's eyes was swollen shut and the side of her face still showed the welt where she had collided with the wall. She was not used to carrying such scars, nor were others used to seeing her that way. Normally a spell of healing would have cleaned up her face, but these were not normal times.

Bladen'Kerst stopped and stared hard at her mother, focusing on those wounds. They carried a double-edged signal. First, they showed that Baenre's powers were not as they should be, that the matron mother, that all of them, might be very vulnerable. Second, coupled with the scowl that perpetually clouded the worried matron mother's features, those wounds reflected anger.

Anger overweighed the perceived, and likely temporary, vulnerability, Bladen'Kerst wisely decided, and sat down in her appointed chair. Her hard boot, unusual for drow, but effective for kicking males, tapped hard and urgently on the floor.

No one paid her any attention, though. All of them followed Matron Baenre's predictable, dangerous gaze to Quenthel.

"Now is not the time for personal ambitions," Matron Baenre said calmly, seriously.

Quenthel's eyes widened as though she had been caught completely off guard.

"I warn you," Matron Baenre pressed, not the least deterred by the innocent expression.

"As do I!" Triel quickly and determinedly interjected. She wouldn't usually interrupt her mother, knew better than that, but she figured that this matter had to be put down once and for all, and that Baenre would appreciate the assistance. "You have relied on Lolth's favor to protect you these years. But

Lolth is away from us now, for some reason that we do not understand. You are vulnerable, my sister, more vulnerable than any of us."

Quenthel came forward in her seat, even managed a smile. "Would you chance that Lolth will return to us, as we both know she shall?" the younger Baenre hissed. "And what might it be that drove the Spider Queen from us?" As she asked the last question, her gaze fell over her mother, as daring as anyone had ever been in the face of Matron Baenre.

"Not what you assume!" Triel snapped. She had expected Quenthel to try to lay blame on Matron Baenre's lap. The removal of the matron mother could only benefit ambitious Quenthel and might indeed restore some prestige to the fast-falling House. In truth, even Triel had considered that course, but she had subsequently dismissed it, no longer believing that Matron Baenre's recent failures had anything to do with the strangeness going on around them. "Lolth has fled every House."

"This goes beyond Lolth," Gromph, the wizard whose magic came from no god or goddess, added pointedly.

"Enough," said Baenre, looking around alternately, her stare calming her children. "We cannot know what has brought about the events. What we must consider is how those events will affect our position."

"The city desires a *pera'dene*," Quenthel reasoned, the drow word for scapegoat. Her unblinking stare at Baenre told the matron mother who she had in mind.

"Fool!" Baenre snapped into the face of that glare. "Do you think they would stop with *my* heart?"

That blunt statement caught Quenthel off guard.

"For some of the lesser Houses, there never has been and never will be a better opportunity to unseat this House," Matron Baenre went on, speaking to all of them. "If you think to unseat me, then do so, but know that it will do little to change the rebellion that is rising against us." She huffed and threw her arms up helplessly. "Indeed, you would only be aiding our enemies. I am your tie to Bregan D'aerthe, and know that our enemies have also courted Jarlaxle. And *I* am Baenre! Not Triel, and not Quenthel. Without me, you all would fall to chaos, fighting for control, each with your own factions within the House guard. Where will you be when K'yorl Oblodra enters the compound?"

It was a sobering thought. Matron Baenre had passed word to each of them that the Oblodrans had not lost their powers, and all the Baenres knew the hatred the Third House held for them.

"Now is not the time for personal ambitions," Matron Baenre reiterated. "Now is the time for us to hold together and hold our position."

The nods around her were sincere, Baenre knew, though Quenthel was not nodding. "You should hope that Lolth does not come back to me before she returns to you," the ambitious sister said boldly, aiming the remark squarely at Triel.

Triel seemed unimpressed. "You should hope that Lolth comes back at all," she replied casually, "else I will tear off your head and have Gromph place it atop Narbondel, that your eyes may glow when the day is full."

Quenthel went to reply, but Gromph beat her to it.

"A pleasure, my dear sister," he said to Triel. There was no love lost between the two, but while Gromph was ambivalent toward Triel, he perfectly hated Quenthel and her dangerous ambitions. If House Baenre fell, so, too, would Gromph.

The implied alliance between the two elder Baenre children worked wonders in calming the upstart younger sister, and Quenthel said not another word the rest of the meeting.

"May we speak now of K'yorl, and the danger to us all?" Matron Baenre asked.

When no dissenting voices came forth—and if there had been, Baenre likely would have run out of patience and had the speaker put to a slow death—the matron mother took up the issue of House defense. She explained that Jarlaxle and his band could still be trusted, but warned that the mercenary would be one to change sides if the battle was going badly for House Baenre. Triel assured them all that the Academy remained loyal, and Berg'inyon's report of the readiness of the House guard was beaming.

Despite the promising news and the well-earned reputation of the Baenre garrison, the conversation ultimately came down to the only apparent way to fully fend off K'yorl and her psionic family. Berg'inyon, who had taken part in the fight with the dwarf Gandalug, voiced it first.

"What of Methil?" he asked. "And the hundred illithids he represents? If they stand with us, the threat from House Oblodra seems minor."

The others nodded their agreement with the assessment, but Matron Baenre knew that such friends as mind flayers could not be counted on. "Methil remains at our side because he and his people know we are the keystone of security for his people. The illithids do not number one one-hundredth the drow in Menzoberranzan. That is the extent of their loyalty. If Methil comes to believe that House Oblodra is the stronger, he will not stand beside us." Baenre gave an ironic, seemingly helpless chuckle.

"The other illithids might even side with K'yorl," she reasoned. "The wretch is akin to them with her powers of the mind. Perhaps they understand one another."

"Should we speak so bluntly?" Sos'Umptu asked. She looked about the dais, concerned, and the others understood that she feared Methil might even be among them, invisibly, hearing every word, reading their every thought.

"It does not matter," Matron Baenre replied casually. "Methil already knows my fears. One cannot hide from an illithid."

"Then what are we to do?" Triel asked.

"We are to muster our strength," Baenre replied determinedly. "We are to show no fear and no weakness. And we are not to do anything that might push Lolth further from us." She aimed that last remark at the rivals, Quenthel and Triel, particularly at Triel, who seemed more than ready to use this Lolth-absent time to be rid of her troublesome sister.

"We must show the illithids we remain the power in Menzoberranzan," Baenre went on. "If they know this, then they will side with us, not wanting House Baenre to be weakened by K'yorl's advances."

"I go to Sorcere," said Gromph, the archmage.

"And I to Arach-Tinilith," added a determined Triel.

"I make no illusions about friendship among my rivals," Gromph added. "But a few promises of repayment when issues sort themselves out will go far in finding allies."

"The students have been allowed no contact outside the school," Triel put in. "They know of the problems in general, of course, but they know nothing of the threat to House Baenre. In their ignorance, they remain loyal."

Matron Baenre nodded to both of them. "And you will meet with the lower Houses that we have established," she said to Quenthel, a most important assignment. A large portion of House Baenre's power lay in the dozen minor Houses that former Baenre nobles had come to head. So obviously a favorite of Lolth's, Quenthel was the perfect choice for such an assignment.

Her expression revealed that she had been won over—more by Triel and Gromph's threats, no doubt, than by the tidbit that had just been thrown her way.

The most important ingredient in squashing the rivalries, Baenre knew, was to allow both Triel and Quenthel to save face and feel important. Thus, this meeting had been a success and all the power of House Baenre would be coordinated into a single defensive force.

Baenre's smile remained a meager one, though. She knew what Methil could do, and suspected that K'yorl was not so much weaker. All of House Baenre would be ready, but without the Lolth-given clerical magic and Gromph's wizardly prowess, would that be enough?

╳ ╳ ╳ ╳ ╳

Just off Bruenor's audience hall on the top level of Mithral Hall was a small room that the dwarf king had set aside for the artisans working on repairing the panther figurine. Inside was a small forge and delicate tools, along with dozens of beakers and flasks containing various ingredients and salves.

Drizzt was eager indeed when he was summoned to that room. He'd gone there a dozen times a day, of course, but without invitation, and every time to find dwarves huddled over the still-broken artifact and shaking their bearded heads. A tenday had passed since the incident, and Guenhwyvar was so exhausted that she could no longer stand, could barely lift her head from her paws as she lay in front of the hearth in Drizzt's room.

The waiting was the worst part.

Now, though, Drizzt had been called into the room. He knew that an emissary had arrived that morning from Silverymoon. He could only hope that Alustriel had some positive solutions to offer.

Bruenor was watching his approach through the open door of the audience chamber. The red-bearded dwarf nodded and poked his head to the side, and Drizzt cut the sharp corner, pushing open the door without bothering to knock.

It was among the most curious of sights that Drizzt Do'Urden had ever witnessed. The broken—still broken!—figurine was on a small, round table. Regis stood beside it, working furiously with a mortar and pestle, mushing some blackish substance.

Across the table from Drizzt stood a short, stout dwarf, Buster Bracer, the noted armorer, the one, in fact, who had forged Drizzt's own supple chain mail, back in Icewind Dale. Drizzt didn't dare greet the dwarf now, fearing to upset his obvious concentration. Buster stood with his feet wide apart. Every so often, he took an exaggerated breath, then held perfectly steady, for in his hands, wrapped in wetted cloth of the finest material, he held . . . eyeballs.

Drizzt had no idea of what was going on until a voice, a familiar, bubbly voice, startled him from his shock.

"Greetings, O One of the Midnight Skin!" the disembodied wizard said happily.

"Harkle Harpell?" Drizzt asked.

"Could it be anyone else?" Regis remarked dryly.

Drizzt conceded the point. "What is this about?" he asked, pointedly looking toward the halfling, for he knew that any answer from Harkle would likely shed more dimness on the blurry situation.

Regis lifted the mixing bowl a bit. "A poultice from Silverymoon," he explained hopefully. "Harkle has overseen its mixing."

"Overseen," the absent mage joked, "which means they held my eyes over the bowl!"

Drizzt didn't manage a smile, not with the head of the all-important figurine still lying at the sculpted body's feet.

Regis snickered, more in disdain than humor. "It should be ready," he explained. "But I wanted you to apply it."

"Drow fingers are so dexterous!" Harkle piped in.

"Where are you?" Drizzt demanded, impatient and unnerved by the outrageous arrangement.

Harkle blinked, those eyelids appearing from thin air. "In Nesmé," he mage replied. "We will be passing north of the Trollmoors soon."

"And to Mithral Hall, where you will be reunited with your eyes," Drizzt said.

"I am *looking* forward to it!" Harkle roared, but again he laughed alone.

"He keeps that up and I'm throwin' the damned eyes into me forge," Buster Bracer growled.

Regis placed the bowl on the table and retrieved a tiny metal tool. "You'll not need much of the poultice," the halfling said as he handed the delicate instrument to Drizzt. "And Harkle has warned us to try to keep the mixture on the outside of the joined pieces."

"It is only a glue," the mage's voice added. "The magic of the figurine will be the force that truly makes the item whole. The poultice will have to be scraped away in a few day's time. If it works as planned, the figurine will be . . ." He paused, searching for the word. "Will be healed," he finished.

"If it works," Drizzt echoed. He took a moment to feel the delicate instrument in his hands, making sure that the burns he had received when the figurine's magic had gone awry were healed, making sure that he could feel the item perfectly.

"It will work," Regis assured.

Drizzt took a deep, steadying breath and picked up the panther head. He stared into the sculpted eyes, so much like Guenhwyvar's own knowing orbs. With all the care of a parent tending its child, Drizzt placed the head against the body and began the painstaking task of spreading the gluelike poultice around its perimeter.

More than two hours passed before Drizzt and Regis exited the room, moving into the audience hall where Bruenor was still meeting with Lady Alustriel's emissary and several other dwarves.

Bruenor did not appear happy, but Drizzt noted he seemed more at ease than he had since the onset of this strange time.

"It ain't a trick o' the drow," the dwarf king said as soon as Drizzt and Regis approached. "Or the damned drow are more powerful than anyone ever thought! It's all the world, so says Alustriel."

"Lady Alustriel," corrected the emissary, a very tidy-looking dwarf dressed in flowing white robes and with a short and neatly trimmed beard.

"My greetings, Fredegar," Drizzt said, recognizing Fredegar Rockcrusher, better known as Fret, Lady Alustriel's favored bard and advisor. "So at last you have found the opportunity to see the wonders of Mithral Hall."

"Would that the times were better," Fret answered glumly. "Pray tell me, how fares Catti-brie?"

"She is well," Drizzt answered. He smiled as he thought of the young woman, who had returned to Settlestone to convey some information from Bruenor.

"It ain't a trick o' the drow," Bruenor said again, more emphatically, making it clear that he didn't consider this the proper time and place for such light and meaningless conversation.

Drizzt nodded his agreement—he had been assuring Bruenor that his people were not involved all along. "Whatever has happened, it has rendered Regis's ruby useless," the drow said. He reached over and lifted the pendant from the halfling's chest. "Now it is but a plain, though undeniably beautiful, stone. And the unknown force has affected Guenhwyvar, and reached all the way to the Harpells. No magic of the drow is this powerful, else they would have long ago conquered the surface world."

"Something new?" Bruenor asked.

"The effects have been felt for several tendays now," Fret interjected. "Though only in the last couple of tendays has magic become so totally unpredictable and dangerous."

Bruenor, never one to care much for magic, snorted loudly.

"It's a good thing, then!" he decided. "The damned drow're more needin' magic than are me own folk, or the men o' Settlestone! Let all the magic drain away, I'm sayin', and let the drow come on and play!"

Thibbledorf Pwent nearly jumped out of his boots at that thought. He leaped over to stand before Bruenor and Fret, and slapped one of his dirty, smelly hands across the tidy dwarf's back. Few things could calm an excited battlerager, but Fret's horrified, then outraged, look did just that, surprising Pwent completely.

"What?" the battlerager demanded.

"If you ever touch me again, I will crush your skull," Fret, who wasn't half the size of powerful Pwent, promised in an even tone, and for some inexplicable reason, Pwent believed him and backed off a step.

Drizzt, who knew tidy Fret quite well from his many visits to Silverymoon, understood that Fret couldn't stand ten seconds in a fight against Pwent—unless the confrontation centered around dirt. In that instance, with Pwent messing up Fret's meticulous grooming, Drizzt would put all of his coin on Fret, as sure a bet as the drow would ever know.

It wasn't an issue, though, for Pwent, boisterous as he was, would never do anything against Bruenor, and Bruenor obviously wanted no trouble with an emissary, particularly a dwarven emissary from friendly Silverymoon. Indeed, all in the room had a good laugh at the confrontation, and all seemed more relaxed at the realization that these strange events were not connected to the mysterious dark elves.

All except for Drizzt Do'Urden. Drizzt would not relax until the figurine was repaired, its magic restored, and poor Guenhwyvar could return to her home on the Astral Plane.

THE THIRD HOUSE

It wasn't that Jarlaxle, who always thought ahead of others, hadn't been expecting the visit, it was simply the ease with which K'yorl Odran entered his camp, slipped past his guards and walked right through the wall of his private chambers, that so unnerved him. He saw her ghostly outline enter and fought hard to compose himself as she became more substantial and more threatening.

"I had expected you would come many days ago," Jarlaxle said calmly.

"Is this the proper greeting for a matron mother?" K'yorl asked.

Jarlaxle almost laughed, until he considered the female's stance. Too at ease, he decided, too ready to punish, even to kill. K'yorl did not understand the value of Bregan D'aerthe, apparently, and that left Jarlaxle, the master of bluff and the player of intrigue, at somewhat of a disadvantage.

He came up from his comfortable chair, stepped out from behind his desk, and gave a low bow, pulling his wide-brimmed and outrageously plumed hat from his head and sweeping it across the floor. "My greetings, K'yorl Odran, Matron Mother of House Oblodra, Third House of Menzoberranzan. Not often has my humble home been so graced . . ."

"Enough," K'yorl spat, and Jarlaxle came up and replaced the hat. Never taking his gaze from the female, never blinking, the mercenary went back to his chair and flopped down comfortably, putting both his boots atop his desk with a resounding slam.

It was then Jarlaxle felt the intrusion into his mind, a deeply unsettling probe into his thoughts. He quickly dismissed his many curses at the failure of conventional magic—usually his enchanted eye patch would have protected him from such a mental intrusion—and used his wits instead. He focused his gaze on K'yorl, pictured her with her clothes off, and filled his mind with thoughts so base that the matron mother, in the midst of serious business, lost all patience.

"I could have the skin flailed from your bones for such thoughts," K'yorl informed him.

"Such thoughts?" Jarlaxle said as though he had been wounded. "Surely you are not intruding on my mind, Matron K'yorl! Though I am but a male, such practices are surely frowned on. Lolth would not be pleased."

"Damn Lolth," K'yorl growled, and Jarlaxle was stunned that she had put it so clearly, so bluntly. Of course everyone knew that House Oblodra was not the most religious of drow Houses, but the Oblodrans had always kept at least the pretense of piety.

K'yorl tapped her temple, her features stern. "If Lolth was worthy of my praise, then she would have recognized the truth of power," the matron mother explained. "It is the mind that separates us from our lessers, the mind that should determine order."

Jarlaxle offered no response. He had no desire to get into this argument with so dangerous and unpredictable a foe.

K'yorl did not press the point, but simply waved her hand as if throwing it all away. She was frustrated, Jarlaxle could see, and in this one frustration equated with danger.

"It is beyond the Spider Queen now," K'yorl said. "I am beyond Lolth. And it begins this day."

Jarlaxle allowed a look of surprise to cross his features.

"You expected it," K'yorl said accusingly.

That was true enough—Jarlaxle had wondered why the Oblodrans had waited this long with all the other Houses so vulnerable—but he would not concede the point.

"Where in this does Bregan D'aerthe stand?" K'yorl demanded.

Jarlaxle got the feeling that any answer he gave would be moot, since

K'yorl was probably going to tell *him* exactly where Bregan D'aerthe stood. "With the victors," he said cryptically and casually.

K'yorl smiled in salute to his cleverness. "I will be the victor," she assured him. "It will be over quickly, this very day, and with few drow dead."

Jarlaxle doubted that. House Oblodra had never shown any regard for life, be it drow or otherwise. The drow numbers within the Third House were small mainly because the wild clan members killed as often as they bred. They were renowned for a game that they played, a challenge of the highest stakes called *Khaless*—ironically, the drow word for trust. A globe of darkness and magical silence would be hung in the air above the deepest point in the chasm called the Clawrift. The competing dark elves would then levitate into the globe and there, unable to see or hear, it would become a challenge of simple and pure courage.

The first one to come out of the globe and back to secure footing was the loser, so the trick was to remain in the globe until the very last second of the levitation enchantment.

More often than not, both stubborn competitors would wait too long and would plunge to their demise.

Now K'yorl, merciless and ultimately wicked, was trying to assure Jarlaxle that the drow losses would be kept at a minimum. By whose standard? the mercenary wondered, and if the answer was K'yorl's, then likely half the city would be dead before the end of the day.

There was little Jarlaxle could do about that, he realized. He and Bregan D'aerthe were as dependent on magic as any other dark elf camps, and without it he couldn't even keep K'yorl out of his private chamber—even his private thoughts!

"This day," K'yorl said again, grimly. "And when it is done, I will call for you, and you will come."

Jarlaxle didn't nod, didn't answer at all. He didn't have to. He could feel the mental intrusion again, and knew that K'yorl understood him. He hated her, and hated what she was about to do, but Jarlaxle was ever pragmatic, and if things went as K'yorl predicted, then he would indeed go to her call.

She smiled again and faded away. Then, like a ghost, she simply walked through Jarlaxle's stone wall.

Jarlaxle rested back in his chair, his fingers tapping nervously together. He had never felt so vulnerable, or so caught in the middle of an uncontrollable situation. He could get word to Matron Baenre, of course, but to what gain? Even House Baenre, so vast and proud, could not stand against K'yorl when her magic worked and theirs did not. Likely, Matron Baenre would be dead soon, and all her family with her, and where would the mercenary hide?

He would not hide, of course. He would go to K'yorl's call.

Jarlaxle understood why K'yorl had paid him the visit and why it was important to her, who seemed to have everything in her favor, to enlist him in her court. He and his band were the only drow in Menzoberranzan with any true ties outside the city, a crucial factor for anyone aspiring to the position of first matron mother—not that anyone other than Matron Baenre had aspired to that coveted position in close to a thousand years.

Jarlaxle's fingers continued tapping. Perhaps it was time for a change, he thought. He quickly dismissed that hopeful notion, for even if he was right, this change did not seem for the better. Apparently, though, K'yorl believed that the situation with conventional magic was a temporary thing, else she would not have been so interested in enlisting Bregan D'aerthe.

Jarlaxle had to believe, had to pray, that she was right, especially if her coup succeeded—and the mercenary had no reason to believe it would not. He would not survive long, he realized, if First Matron Mother K'yorl, a drow he hated above all others, could enter his thoughts at will.

⚔ ⚔ ⚔ ⚔ ⚔

She was too beautiful to be drow, seemed the perfection of drow features to any, male or female, who looked at her. It was this beauty alone that held in check the deadly lances and crossbows of the House Baenre guard and made Berg'inyon Baenre, after one glance at her, bid her enter the compound.

The magical fence wasn't working and there were no conventional gates in the perimeter of the Baenre household. Normally, the spiderweb of the fence would spiral out, opening a wide hole on command, but now Berg'inyon had to ask the drow to climb over.

She said not a word, but simply approached the fence. Spiral wide it did, one last gasp of magic before this creature, the avatar of the goddess who had created it.

Berg'inyon led the way, though he knew beyond doubt that this one needed no guidance. He understood that she was heading for the chapel—of course she would be heading for the chapel!—so he instructed some of his soldiers to find the matron mother.

Sos'Umptu met them at the door of the chapel, the place that was in her care. She protested for an instant, but just for an instant.

Berg'inyon had never seen his devoted sister so flustered, had never seen her jaw go slack for lack of strength. She fell away from them, to her knees.

The beautiful drow walked past her without a word. She turned sharply—Sos'Umptu gasped—and put her glare over Berg'inyon as he continued to follow.

"You are just a male," Sos'Umptu whispered in explanation. "Be gone from this holy place."

Berg'inyon was too stricken to reply, to even sort out how he felt at that moment. He never turned his back, just gave a series of ridiculous bows, and verily fell through the chapel's door, back out into the courtyard.

Both Bladen'Kerst and Quenthel were out there, but the rest of the group that had gathered in response to the whispered rumors had wisely been dispersed by the sisters.

"Go back to your post," Bladen'Kerst snarled at Berg'inyon. "Nothing has happened!" It wasn't so much a statement as a command.

"Nothing has happened," Berg'inyon echoed, and that became the order of the day, and a wise one, Berg'inyon immediately realized. This was Lolth herself, or some close minion. He knew this in his heart.

He knew it, and the soldiers would whisper it, but their enemies must not learn of this!

Berg'inyon scrambled across the courtyard, passed the word, the command that "nothing had happened." He took up a post that allowed him an overview of the chapel and was surprised to see that his ambitious sisters dared not enter, but rather paced around the main entrance nervously.

Sos'Umptu came out as well and joined their parade. No words were openly exchanged—Berg'inyon didn't even notice any flashes of the silent hand code—as Matron Baenre hustled across the courtyard. She passed by her daughters and scurried into the chapel, and the pacing outside began anew.

For Matron Baenre it was the answer to her prayers and the realization of her nightmares all at once. She knew immediately who and what it was that sat before her on the central dais. She knew, and she believed.

"If I am the offending person, then I offer myself . . ." she began humbly, falling to her knees as she spoke.

"*Wael!*" the avatar snapped at her, the drow word for fool, and Baenre hid her face in her hands with shame.

"*Usstan'sargh wael!*" the beautiful drow went on, calling Matron Baenre an arrogant fool. Baenre trembled at the verbal attack, thought for a moment that she had sunk lower than her worst fears, that her goddess had come personally for no better reason than to shame her to death. Images of her tortured body being dragged through the winding avenues of Menzoberranzan flashed in her mind, thoughts of herself as the epitome of a fallen drow leader.

Yet thoughts such as that were exactly what this creature who was more than a drow had just berated her about, Matron Baenre suddenly realized. She dared look up.

"Do not place so much importance on yourself," the avatar said calmly.

Matron Baenre allowed herself to breathe a sigh of relief. Then this wasn't about her, she understood. All of this, the failure of magic and prayer, was beyond her, beyond all the mortal realms.

"K'yorl has erred," the avatar went on, reminding Baenre that while these catastrophic events might be above her, their ramifications most certainly were not.

"She has dared to believe that she can win without your favor," Matron Baenre reasoned, and her surprise was total when the avatar scoffed at the notion.

"She could destroy you with a thought."

Matron Baenre shuddered and lowered her head once more.

"But she has erred on the side of caution," the avatar went on. "She delayed her attack, and now, when she decided that the advantage was indeed hers to hold, she has allowed a personal feud to delay her most important strike even longer."

"Then the powers have returned!" Baenre gasped. "You are returned."

"*Wael!*" the frustrated avatar screamed. "Did you think I would not return?" Matron Baenre fell flat to the floor and groveled with all her heart.

"The Time of Troubles will end," the avatar said a moment later, calm once more. "And you will know what you must do when all is as it should be."

Baenre looked up just long enough to see the avatar's narrow-eyed glare full upon her. "Do you think I am so resourceless?" the beautiful drow asked.

A horrified expression, purely sincere, crossed Baenre's face, and she began to numbly shake her head back and forth, denying she had ever lost faith.

Again, she lay flat out, groveling, and stopped her prayers only when something hard hit the floor beside her head. She dared to look up, to find a lump of yellow stone, sulphur, lying beside her.

"You must fend off K'yorl for a short while," the avatar explained. "Go join the matron mothers and your eldest daughter and son in the meeting room. Stoke the flames and allow those I have enlisted to come through to your side. Together we will teach K'yorl the truth of power!"

A bright smile erupted on Baenre's face with the realization that she was not out of Lolth's favor, that her goddess had called on her to play a crucial role in this crucial hour. The fact that Lolth had all but admitted she was still rather impotent did not matter. The Spider Queen would return, and Baenre would shine again in her devious eyes.

By the time Matron Baenre mustered the courage to come off the floor, the beautiful drow had already exited the chapel. She crossed the compound without interference, walked through the fence as she had done at her arrival, and disappeared into the shadows of the city.

As soon as she heard the awful rumor that House Oblodra's strange psionic powers had not been too adversely affected by whatever was happening to other magic, Ghenni'tiroth Tlabbar, the matron mother of Faen Tlabbar, Menzoberranzan's Fourth House, knew she was in dire trouble. K'yorl Odran hated the tall, slender Ghenni'tiroth above all others, for Ghenni'tiroth had made no secret of the fact that she believed Faen Tlabbar, and not Oblodra, should rank as Menzoberranzan's Third House.

With almost eight hundred drow soldiers, Faen Tlabbar's number nearly doubled that of House Oblodra, and only the little understood powers of K'yorl and her minions had kept Faen Tlabbar back.

How much greater those powers loomed now, with all conventional magic rendered unpredictable at best!

Throughout it all, Ghenni'tiroth remained in the House chapel, a relatively small room near the summit of her compound's central stalagmite mound. A single candle burned upon the altar, shedding minimal light by surface standards, but serving as a beacon to the dark elves whose eyes were more accustomed to blackness. A second source of illumination came from the room's west-facing window, for even from halfway across the city, the wild glow of Narbondel could be clearly seen.

Ghenni'tiroth showed little concern for the pillar clock, other than the significance it now held as an indicator of their troubles. She was among the most fanatical of Lolth's priestesses, a drow female who had survived more than six centuries in unquestioning servitude to the Spider Queen. But she was in trouble now, and Lolth, for some reason she could not understand, would not come to her call.

She reminded herself constantly to keep fast her faith as she knelt and huddled over a platinum platter, the famed Faen Tlabbar Communing Plate. The heart of the latest sacrifice, a not-so-insignificant drow male, sat atop it, an offering to the goddess who would not answer Ghenni'tiroth's desperate prayers.

Ghenni'tiroth straightened suddenly as the heart rose from the bloody platter, came up several inches and hovered in midair.

"The sacrifice is not sufficient," came a voice behind her, a voice she had dreaded hearing since the advent of the Time of Troubles.

She did not turn to face K'yorl Odran.

"There is war in the compound," Ghenni'tiroth stated more than asked.

K'yorl scoffed at the notion. A wave of her hand sent the sacrificial organ flying across the room.

Ghenni'tiroth spun around, eyes wide with outrage. She started to scream out the drow word for sacrilege, but stopped, the sound caught in her throat, as another heart floated in the air, from K'yorl toward her.

"The sacrifice was not sufficient," K'yorl said calmly. "Use this heart, the heart of Fini'they."

Ghenni'tiroth slumped back at the mention of the obviously dead priestess, her second in the House. Ghenni'tiroth had taken in Fini'they as her own daughter when Fini'they's family, a lower-ranking and insignificant House, had been destroyed by a rival House. Insignificant indeed had been Fini'they's House—Ghenni'tiroth could not even remember its proper name—but Fini'they had not been so. She was a powerful priestess, and ultimately loyal, even loving, to her adopted mother.

Ghenni'tiroth leaned back further, horrified, as her daughter's heart floated past and settled with a sickening wet sound on the platinum platter.

"Pray to Lolth," K'yorl ordered.

Ghenni'tiroth did just that. Perhaps K'yorl had erred, she thought. Perhaps in death Fini'they would prove most helpful, would prove a suitable sacrifice to bring the Spider Queen to the aid of House Faen Tlabbar.

After a long and uneventful moment, Ghenni'tiroth became aware of K'yorl's laughter.

"Perhaps we are in need of a greater sacrifice," the wicked matron mother of House Oblodra said slyly.

It wasn't difficult for Ghenni'tiroth, the only figure in House Faen Tlabbar greater than Fini'they, to figure out who K'yorl was talking about.

Secretly, barely moving her fingers, Ghenni'tiroth brought her deadly, poisoned dagger out of its sheath under the concealing folds of her spider-emblazoned robes. "Scrag-tooth," the dagger was called, and it had gotten a younger Ghenni'tiroth out of many situations much like this.

Of course, on those occasions, magic had been predictable, reliable, and those opponents had not been as formidable as K'yorl. Even as Ghenni'tiroth locked gazes with the Oblodran, kept K'yorl distracted while she subtly shifted her hand, K'yorl read her thoughts and expected the attack.

Ghenni'tiroth shouted a command word, and the dagger's magic functioned, sending the missile shooting out from under her robes directly at the heart of her adversary.

The magic functioned! Ghenni'tiroth silently cheered. But her elation faded quickly when the blade passed right through the specter of K'yorl Odran to embed itself uselessly in the fabric of a tapestry adorning the room's opposite wall.

"I do so hope the poison does not ruin the pattern," K'yorl, standing far to the left of her image, remarked.

Ghenni'tiroth shifted about and turned a steely-eyed gaze at the taunting creature.

"You cannot outfight me, you cannot outthink me," K'yorl said evenly. "You cannot even hide your thoughts from me. The war is ended before it ever began."

Ghenni'tiroth wanted to scream out a denial, but found herself as silent as Fini'they, whose heart lay on the platter before her.

"How much killing need there be?" K'yorl asked, catching Ghenni'tiroth off her guard. The matron of Faen Tlabbar turned a suspicious, but ultimately curious, expression toward her adversary.

"My House is small," K'yorl remarked, and that was true enough, unless one counted the thousands of kobold slaves said to be running around the tunnels along the edges of the Clawrift, just below House Oblodra. "And I am in need of allies if I wish to depose that wretch Baenre and her bloated family."

Ghenni'tiroth wasn't even conscious of the movement as her tongue came out and licked her thin lips. There was a flicker of hope.

"You cannot beat me," K'yorl said with all confidence. "Perhaps I will accept a surrender."

That word didn't sit well with the proud leader of the Third House.

"An alliance then, if that is what you must call it," K'yorl clarified, recognizing the look. "It is no secret that I am not on the best of terms with the Spider Queen."

Ghenni'tiroth rocked back on her legs, considering the implications. If she helped K'yorl, who was not in Lolth's favor, overcome Baenre, then what would be the implications to her House if and when everything was sorted out?

"All of this is Baenre's fault," K'yorl remarked, reading Ghenni'tiroth's every thought. "Baenre brought about the Spider Queen's abandonment," K'yorl scoffed. "She could not even hold a single prisoner, could not even conduct a proper high ritual."

The words rang true, painfully true, to Ghenni'tiroth, who vastly preferred Matron Baenre to K'yorl Odran. She wanted to deny them, and yet, that surely meant her death and the death of her House, since K'yorl held so obvious an advantage.

"Perhaps I will accept a surren—" K'yorl chuckled wickedly and caught herself in midsentence. "Perhaps an alliance would benefit us both," she said instead.

Ghenni'tiroth licked her lips again, not knowing where to turn. A glance at Fini'they's heart did much to convince her, though. "Perhaps it would," she said.

K'yorl nodded and smiled again that devious and infamous grin that was known throughout Menzoberranzan as an indication that K'yorl was lying.

Ghenni'tiroth returned the grin—until she remembered who it was she was dealing with, until she forced herself, through the temptation of the teasing bait that K'yorl had offered, to remember the reputation of this most wicked drow.

"Perhaps not," K'yorl said calmly, and Ghenni'tiroth was knocked backward suddenly by an unseen force, a physical though invisible manifestation of K'yorl's powerful will.

The matron of Faen Tlabbar jerked and twisted, heard the crack of one of her ribs. She tried to call out against K'yorl, to cry out to Lolth in one final, desperate prayer, but found her words garbled as an invisible hand grasped tightly on her throat, cutting off her air.

Ghenni'tiroth jerked again, violently, and again, and more cracking sounds came from her chest, from intense pressure within her torso. She rocked backward and would have fallen to the floor except that K'yorl's will held her slender form fast.

"I am sorry Fini'they was not enough to bring in your impotent Spider Queen," K'yorl taunted, brazenly blasphemous.

Ghenni'tiroth's eyes bulged and seemed as if they would pop from their sockets. Her back arched weirdly, agonizingly, and gurgling sounds continued to stream from her throat. She tore at the flesh of her own neck, trying to grasp the unseen hand, but only drew lines of her own bright blood.

Then there came a final crackle, a loud snapping, and Ghenni'tiroth resisted no more. The pressure was gone from her throat, for what good that did her. K'yorl's unseen hand grabbed her hair and yanked her head forward so that she looked down at the unusual bulge in her chest, beside her left breast.

Ghenni'tiroth's eyes widened in horror as her robes parted and her skin erupted. A great gout of blood and gore poured from the wound, and Ghenni'tiroth fell limply, lying sidelong to the platinum plate.

She watched the last beat of her own heart on that sacrificial platter.

"Perhaps Lolth will hear this call," K'yorl remarked, but Ghenni'tiroth could no longer understand the words.

K'yorl went to the body and retrieved the potion bottle that Ghenni'tiroth carried, that all House Faen Tlabbar females carried. The mixture, a concoction that forced passionate servitude of drow males, was a potent one—or would be, if conventional magic returned. This bottle was likely the most potent, and K'yorl marked it well for a certain mercenary leader.

K'yorl went to the wall and claimed Scrag-tooth as her own.

To the victor . . .

With a final look to the dead matron mother, K'yorl called on her psionic powers and became less than substantial, became a ghost that could walk through the walls and past the guards of the well-defended compound. Her smile was supreme, as was her confidence, but as Lolth's avatar had told Baenre, Odran had indeed erred. She had followed a personal vengeance, had struck out first against a lesser foe.

Even as K'yorl drifted past the structures of House Faen Tlabbar, gloating over the death of her most hated enemy, Matrons Baenre and Mez'Barris

Armgo, along with Triel and Gromph Baenre and the matron mothers of Menzoberranzan's fifth through eighth Houses, were gathered in a private chamber at the back of the Qu'ellarz'orl, the raised plateau within the huge cavern that held some of the more important drow Houses, including House Baenre. The eight of them huddled, each to a leg, around the spider-shaped brazier set upon the small room's single table. Each had brought their most valuable of flammable items, and Matron Baenre carried the lump of sulphur that the avatar had given her.

None of them mentioned, but all of them knew, that this might be their only chance.

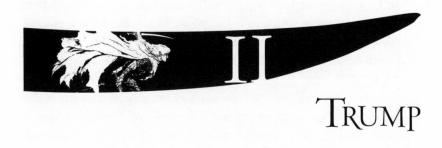

TRUMP

Normally it pleased Jarlaxle to be in the middle of such a conflict, to be the object of wooing tactics by both sides in a dispute. This time, though, Jarlaxle was uneasy with the position. He didn't like dealing with K'yorl Odran on any account, as friends, and especially not as enemies, and he was uneasy with House Baenre being so desperately involved in any struggle. Jarlaxle simply had too much invested with Matron Baenre. The wary mercenary leader usually didn't count on anything, but he had fully expected House Baenre to rule in Menzoberranzan until at least the end of his life, as it had ruled since the beginning of his life and for millennia before that.

It wasn't that Jarlaxle held any special feelings toward the city's First House. It was just that Baenre offered him an anchor point, a measure of permanence in the continually shifting power struggles of Menzoberranzan.

It would last forever, so he had thought, but after talking with K'yorl—how he hated that one!—Jarlaxle wasn't so sure.

K'yorl wanted to enlist him, most likely wanted Bregan D'aerthe to serve as her connection with the world beyond Menzoberranzan. They could do that, and do it well, but Jarlaxle doubted that he, who always had a private agenda, could remain in K'yorl's favor for long. At some point, sooner or later, she would read the truth in his mind, and she would dispatch and replace him.

That was the way of the drow.

⚔ ⚔ ⚔ ⚔ ⚔

The fiend was gargantuan, a gigantic, bipedal, doglike creature with four muscled arms, two of which ended in powerful pincers. How it entered Jarlaxle's private cave, along the sheer facing of the Clawrift, some hundred yards below and behind the compound of House Oblodra, none of the drow guards knew.

"*Tanar'ri!*" The warning word, the name of the greatest creatures of the Abyss, known in all the languages of the Realms, was passed in whispers and silent hand signals all through the complex, and the reaction to it was uniformly one of horror.

Pity the two drow guards who first encountered the towering, fifteen-foot monster. Loyal to Bregan D'aerthe, courageous in the belief that others would back their actions, they commanded the great beast to halt, and when it did not, the drow guards attacked.

Had their weapons held their previous enchantment, they might have hurt the beast somewhat. But magic had not returned to the Material Plane in any predictable or reliable manner. Thus, the tanar'ri, too, was deprived of its considerable spell repertoire, but the beast, four thousand pounds of muscle and physical hazards, hardly needed magical assistance.

The two drow were summarily dismembered, and the tanar'ri walked on, seeking Jarlaxle, as Errtu had bade it.

It found the mercenary leader, along with a score of his finest soldiers, around the first bend. Several drow leaped forward to the defense, but Jarlaxle, better understanding the power of this beast, held them at bay, was not so willing to throw away drow lives.

"Glabrezu," he said with all respect, recognizing the beast.

Glabrezu's canine maw curled up in a snarl, and its eyes narrowed as it scrutinized Jarlaxle, privately confirming that it had found the correct dark elf.

"*Baenre cok diemrey nochtero,*" the tanar'ri said in a growl, and without waiting for a response, the gigantic beast lumbered about and waddled away, crouching low so that its head did not scrape the corridor's high ceiling.

Again, several brave, stupid drow moved as if to pursue, and again Jarlaxle, smiling now more widely than he had in many tendays, held them back. The tanar'ri had spoken in the language of the lower planes, a language that Jarlaxle understood perfectly, and it had spoken the words Jarlaxle had longed to hear.

The question was clear on the expressions of all the unnerved drow standing beside him. They did not understand the language and wanted desperately to know what the tanar'ri had said.

"*Baenre cok diemrey nochtero,*" Jarlaxle explained to them. "House Baenre will prevail."

His wry smile, filled with hope, and the eager way he clenched his fists, told his soldiers that such a prediction was a good thing.

✕ ✕ ✕ ✕ ✕

Zeerith Q'Xorlarrin, matron mother of the Fifth House, understood the significance of the makeup of the gathering. Triel and Gromph Baenre attended primarily to fill the two vacant spots at the spider-shaped brazier. One of those places rightfully belonged to K'yorl, and since they were gathered to fend off K'yorl, as the avatar of the Spider Queen had bade them, she hadn't been invited.

The other vacant place, the one filled by Gromph, was normally reserved for Zeerith's closest drow friend, Matron Mother Ghenni'tiroth Tlabbar. None had said it aloud, but Zeerith understood the significance of the Baenre son's presence and of the matron mother's failure to appear.

K'yorl hated Ghenni'tiroth—that was no secret—and so Ghenni'tiroth had been left open as a sacrifice to delay the intrusions of House Oblodra. These other supposed allies and the goddess they all served had allowed Zeerith's best friend to perish.

That thought bothered the matron mother for a short while, until she came to realize that she was the third highest-ranking drow in the meeting chamber. If the summoning was successful, if K'yorl and House Oblodra were beaten back, then the hierarchy of the ruling Houses would surely shift. Oblodra would fall, leaving vacant the third place, and since Faen Tlabbar was suddenly without a proper matron mother, it was feasible that House Xorlarrin could leap past it into that coveted spot.

Ghenni'tiroth had been given as a sacrifice. Zeerith Q'Xorlarrin smiled widely.

Such were the ways of the drow.

Into the brazier went Gromph's prized spider mask, a most magical item, the only one in all of Menzoberranzan that could get someone over the House Baenre web fence. The flames shot into the air, orange and angry green.

Mez'Barris nodded to Baenre, and the withered old matron mother tossed in the lump of sulphur that the avatar had given her.

If a hundred excited dwarves had pumped a huge bellows, their fire would not have been more furious. The flames shot straight up in a multicolored column that held the eight watchers fast with its unholy glory.

"What is this?" came a question from the front of the room, near the only door. "You dare hold a meeting of council without informing House Oblodra?"

Matron Baenre, at the head of the table and thus, with her back directly to K'yorl, held up her hand to calm the others gathered around the spider brazier. Slowly she turned to face that most hated drow, and the two promptly locked vicious stares.

"The executioner does not invite her victim to the block," Baenre said evenly. "She takes her there, or lures her in."

Baenre's blunt words made more than a few of the gathered drow uneasy. If K'yorl had been handled more tactfully, some of them might have escaped with their lives.

Matron Baenre knew better, though. Their only hope, her only hope, was to trust the Spider Queen, to believe with all their hearts that the avatar had not steered them wrongly.

When K'yorl's first wave of mental energy rolled over Baenre, she, too, began to foster some doubts. She held her ground for some seconds, a remarkable display of will, but then K'yorl overwhelmed her, pushed her back against the table. Baenre felt her feet coming from the floor, felt as if a gigantic, unseen hand had reached out and grabbed her and was now edging her toward the flames.

"How much grander the call to Lolth will be," K'yorl shrieked happily, "when Matron Baenre is added to the flames!"

The others in the room, particularly the other five matron mothers, did not know how to react. Mez'Barris put her head down and quietly began muttering the words of a spell, praying that Lolth would hear her and grant her this.

Zeerith and the others watched the flames. The avatar had told them to do this, but why hadn't an ally, a tanar'ri or some other fiend, come through?

In the sludge-filled Abyss, perched atop his mushroom throne, Errtu greatly enjoyed the chaotic scene. Even through the scrying device Lolth had prepared for him, the great tanar'ri could feel the fears of the gathered worshippers and could taste the bitter hatred on the lips of K'yorl Odran.

He liked K'yorl, Errtu decided. Here was one of his own heart, purely and deliciously wicked, a murderess who killed for pleasure, a player of intrigue for no better reason than the fun of the game. The great tanar'ri wanted to watch K'yorl push her adversary into the pillar of flame.

But Lolth's instructions had been explicit, and her bartered goods too tempting for the fiend to pass up. Amazingly, given the state of magic at the time, the gate was opening, and opening wide.

Errtu had already sent one tanar'ri, a giant glabrezu, through a smaller gate to act as messenger, but that gate, brought about by the avatar herself, had been tenuous and open for only a fraction of a moment. Errtu had not believed the feat could be duplicated, not now.

The notion of magical chaos gave the fiend a sudden inspiration. Perhaps the old rules of banishment no longer applied. Perhaps he himself might walk through this opening gate, onto the Material Plane once more. Then he would not need to serve as Lolth's lackey; then he might find the renegade Do'Urden on his own, and after punishing the drow, he could return to the frozen Northland, where the precious Crenshinibon, the legendary Crystal Shard, lay buried!

The gate was opened. Errtu stepped in.

And was summarily rejected, pushed back into the Abyss, the place of his hundred-year banishment.

Several fiends stalked by the great tanar'ri, sensing the opening, heading for the gate, but snarling Errtu, enraged by the defeat, held them back.

Let this wicked drow, K'yorl, push Lolth's favored into the flames, the wretched Errtu decided. The gate would remain open with the sacrifice, might even open wider.

Errtu did not like the banishment, did not like being lackey to any being. Let Lolth suffer; let Baenre be consumed, and only then would he do as the Spider Queen had asked!

✕ ✕ ✕ ✕ ✕

The only thing that saved Baenre from exactly that fate was the unexpected intervention of Methil, the illithid. The glabrezu had gone to Methil after visiting Jarlaxle, bringing the same prediction that House Baenre would prevail, and Methil, serving as ambassador of his people, made it a point to remain on the winning side.

The illithid's psionic waves disrupted K'yorl's telepathic attack, and Matron Baenre slumped back to the side of the table.

K'yorl's eyes went wide, surprised by the defeat—until Methil, who had been standing invisibly and secretly at Matron Baenre's side, came into view.

Wait for this to end, K'yorl's thoughts screamed at the octopus-headed creature. *See who wins and decide where your alliances lie.*

Methil's assurance that he already knew the outcome did not disturb K'yorl half as much as the sight of the gigantic, batlike wing that suddenly extended from the pillar of flame: a tanar'ri—a true tanar'ri!

Another glabrezu hopped out of the fire to land on the floor between Baenre and her adversary. K'yorl hit it with a psionic barrage, but she was no match for such a creature, and she knew it.

She took note that the pillar was still dancing wildly, that another fiend was forming within the flames. Lolth was against her! she suddenly realized. All the Abyss seemed to be coming to Matron Baenre's call!

K'yorl did the only thing she could, became insubstantial once more and fled across the city, back to her house.

Fiends rushed through the open gate, a hundred of them, and still more. It went on for more than an hour, the minions of Errtu, and thus, the minions of Lolth, coming to the call of the desperate matron mothers, swooping across the city in frenzied glee to surround House Oblodra.

Smiles of satisfaction, even open cheers, were exchanged in the meeting room at the back of the Qu'ellarz'orl. The avatar had done as promised, and the future of Lolth's faithful seemed deliciously dark once more.

Of the eight gathered, only Gromph wore a grin that was less than sincere. Not that he wanted House Oblodra to win, of course, but the male held no joy at the thought that things might soon be as they had always been, that he, for all his power and devotion to the ways of magic, would, above all else, be a mere male once more.

He took some consolation, as the flames died away and the others began to exit, in noticing that several of the offered items, including his prized spider mask, had not been consumed by the magical flames. Gromph looked to the door, to the matron mothers and Triel, and they were so obsessed with the spectacle of the fiends that they took no notice of him at all.

Quietly and without attracting attention, the covetous drow wizard replaced his precious item under the folds of his robe, then added to his collection some of the most prized artifacts of Menzoberranzan's greatest Houses.

PART THREE

How I wanted to go to Catti-brie after I realized the dangers of her sword! How I wanted to stand by her and protect her! The item had possessed her, after all, and was imbued with a powerful and obviously sentient magic.

RESOLUTION

Catti-brie wanted me by her side—who wouldn't want the supportive shoulder of a friend with such a struggle looming?—and yet she did not want me there, could not have me there, for she knew this battle was hers to fight alone.

I had to respect her conclusion, and in those days when the Time of Troubles began to end and the magics of the world sorted themselves out once more, I came to learn that sometimes the most difficult battles are the ones we are forced not to fight.

I came to learn then why mothers and fathers seldom have fingernails and often carry an expression of forlorn resignation. What agony it must be for a parent in Silverymoon to be told by her offspring, no longer a child, that he or she has decided to head out to the west, to Waterdeep, to sail for adventure along the Sword Coast. Everything within that parent wants to yell out "Stay!" Every instinct within that parent wants to hug the child close, to protect that child forever. And yet, ultimately, those instincts are wrong.

In the heart, there is no sting greater than watching the struggles of one you love, knowing that only through such strife will that person grow and recognize the potential of his or her existence. Too many thieves in the Realms believe the formula for happiness lies in an unguarded treasure trove. Too many wizards seek to circumvent the years of study required for true power. They find a spell on a scroll or an enchanted item that is far beyond their understanding, yet they try it anyway, only to be consumed by the powerful magic. Too many priests in the Realms, and too many religious sects in general, ask of themselves and of their congregations only humble servitude.

All of them are doomed to fail in the true test of happiness. There is one ingredient missing in stumbling upon an unguarded treasure hoard; there is one element absent when a minor wizard lays his hands on an archmage's staff; there is one item unaccounted for in humble, unquestioning, and unambitious servitude.

A sense of accomplishment.

It is the most important ingredient in any rational being's formula of happiness. It is the element that builds confidence and allows us to go on to other, greater tasks. It is the item that promotes a sense of self-worth, that allows any person to believe there is value in life itself, that gives a sense of purpose to bolster us as we face life's unanswerable questions.

So it was with Catti-brie and her sword. This battle had found her, and she had determined to fight it. Had I followed my protective instincts, I would have refused to aid her in taking on this quest. My protective instincts told me to go to Bruenor, who would have surely ordered the sentient sword destroyed. By doing that, or taking any other course to prevent Catti-brie's battle, I would have, in effect, failed to trust in her, failed to respect her individual needs and her chosen destiny, and thus, I would have stolen a bit of her freedom. That had been Wulfgar's single failure. In his fears for the woman he so dearly loved, the brave and proud barbarian had tried to smother her in his protective hug.

I think he saw the truth of his error in the moments before his death. I think he remembered then the reasons he loved Catti-brie: her strength and independence. How ironic it is that our instincts often run exactly opposite from what we truly desire for those we love.

In the situation I earlier named, the parents would have to let their child go to Waterdeep and the Sword Coast. And so it was with Catti-brie. She chose to take her sword, chose to explore its sentient side, perhaps at great personal risk. The decision was hers to make, and once she had made it, I had to respect it, had to respect her. I didn't see her much over the next couple of tendays, as she waged her private battle.

But I thought of her and worried for her every waking moment, and even in my dreams.

–Drizzt Do'Urden

12
WORTH THE TROUBLES

I have tricked tanar'ri to go to your city, Menzoberranzan, and soon I must force them back," the great Errtu roared. "And I cannot even go to this place and join in their havoc, or even to retrieve them!" The balor sat on his mushroom throne, watching the scrying device that showed him the city of drow. Earlier, he was receiving fleeting images only, as this magic, too, struggled against the effects of the strange time. The images had been coming more strongly lately, though, and now the mirrorlike surface was uncloudy, showing a clear scene of House Oblodra, wedged between the fingers of the Clawrift. Fiends great and minor stalked and swooped around the walled compound, banging strong fists against the stone, hurling threats and missiles of rock. The Oblodrans had buttoned the place up tightly, for even with their psionic powers, and the fact that the fiends' magic fared no better than anyone else's, the otherworldly beasts were simply too physically strong, their minds too warped by evil to be much affected by telepathic barrages.

And they were backed by a united army of drow, lying in wait behind the fiendish lines. Hundreds of crossbows and javelins were pointed House Oblodra's way. Scores of drow riding sticky-footed subterranean lizards stalked the walls and ceiling near the doomed house. Any Oblodran that showed her face would be hit by a barrage from every angle.

"Those same fiends are preventing the Third House from being attacked," Errtu snarled at Lolth, reminding the Spider Queen whose army was in control here. "Your minions fear my minions, and rightly so!"

The beautiful drow, back in the Abyss once more, understood that Errtu's outburst was one part outrage and nine parts bluster. No tanar'ri ever had to be "tricked" into going to the Material Plane, where it might wreak havoc. That was their very nature, the most profound joy in their miserable existence.

"You ask much, Lady of Spiders," Errtu grumbled on.

"I give much in return," Lolth reminded him.

"We shall see."

Lolth's red-glowing eyes narrowed at the tanar'ri's continuing sarcasm. The payment she had offered Errtu, a gift that could potentially free the fiend from nearly a century more of banishment, was no small thing.

"The four glabrezu will be difficult to retrieve," Errtu went on, feigning exasperation, playing this out to the extreme. "They are always difficult!"

"No more so than a balor," Lolth said in blunt response. Errtu turned on her, his face a mask of hatred.

"The Time of Troubles nears its end," Lolth said calmly into that dangerous visage.

"It has been too long!" Errtu roared.

Lolth ignored the tone of the comment, understanding that Errtu had to act outraged and overburdened to prevent her from concluding that the tanar'ri owed her something more. "It has been longer to my eyes than to your own, fiend," the Spider Queen retorted.

Errtu muttered a curse under his smelly breath.

"But it nears its end," Lolth went on, quietly, calmly. Both she and Errtu looked to the image on the scrying surface just as a great winged tanar'ri soared up out of the Clawrift, clutching a small, wriggling creature in one of its great fists. The pitiful catch could not have been more than three feet tall and seemed less than that in the massive fiend's clutches. It wore a ragged vest that did not hide its rust-colored scales, a vest made even more ragged from the tearing of the tanar'ri's clawed grasp.

"A kobold," Errtu remarked.

"Known allies of House Oblodra," Lolth explained. "Thousands of the wretches run the tunnels along the chasm walls."

The flying tanar'ri gave a hoot, grasped the kobold with its other clawed hand as well, and ripped the squealing thing in half.

"One less ally of House Oblodra," Errtu whispered, and from the pleased look on the balor's face, Lolth understood Errtu's true feelings about this whole event. The great tanar'ri was living vicariously through his minions, was watching their destructive antics and feeding off the scene.

It crossed Lolth's mind to reconsider her offered gift. Why should she repay the fiend for doing something it so obviously wanted to do?

The Spider Queen, never a fool, shook the thoughts from her mind. She had nothing to lose in giving Errtu what she had promised. Her eyes were set on the conquest of Mithral Hall, on forcing Matron Baenre to extend her grasp so that the city of drow would be less secure, and more chaotic, more likely to see interhouse warfare. The renegade Do'Urden was nothing to her, though she surely wanted him dead.

Who better to do that than Errtu? Lolth wondered. Even if the renegade survived the coming war—and Lolth did not believe he would—Errtu could use her gift to force Drizzt to call him from his banishment, to allow him back to the Material Plane. Once there, the mighty balor's first goal would undoubtedly be to exact vengeance on the renegade. Drizzt had beaten Errtu once, but no one ever defeated a balor the second time around.

Lolth knew Errtu well enough to understand that Drizzt Do'Urden would be far luckier indeed if he died swiftly in the coming war.

She said no more about the payment for the fiend's aid, understanding that in giving it to Errtu, she was, in effect, giving herself a present. "When the Time of Troubles has passed, my priestesses will aid you in forcing the tanar'ri back to the Abyss," Lolth said.

Errtu did not hide his surprise well. He knew that Lolth had been planning some sort of campaign, and he assumed his monstrous minions would be sent along beside the drow army. Now that Lolth had clearly stated her intentions, though, the fiend recognized her reasoning. If a horde of tanar'ri marched beside the drow, all the Realms would rise against them, including goodly creatures of great power from the upper planes.

Also, both Lolth and Errtu knew well that the drow priestesses, powerful as they were, would not be able to control such a horde once the rampage of warfare had begun.

"All but one," Errtu corrected.

Lolth eyed him curiously.

"I will need an emissary to go to Drizzt Do'Urden," the fiend explained. "To tell the fool what I have, and what I require in exchange for it."

Lolth considered the words for a moment. She had to play this out carefully. She had to hold Errtu back, she knew, or risk complicating what should be a relatively straightforward conquest of the dwarven halls, but she could not let the fiend know her army's destination. If Errtu thought Lolth's minions would soon put Drizzt Do'Urden, the great fiend's only chance at getting back to the Material Plane anytime soon, in jeopardy, he would covertly oppose her.

"Not yet," the Spider Queen said. "Drizzt Do'Urden is out of the way, and there he shall stay until my city is back in order."

"Menzoberranzan is never in order," Errtu replied slyly.

"In relative order," Lolth corrected. "You will have your gift when I give it, and only then will you send your emissary."

"Lady of Spiders . . ." The balor growled threateningly.

"The Time of Troubles nears its end," Lolth snapped in Errtu's ugly face. "My powers return in full. Beware your threats, balor, else you shall find yourself in a more wretched place than this!"

Her purplish black robes flying furiously behind her, the Spider Queen spun around sharply and moved off, swiftly disappearing into the swirling mist. She smirked at the proper ending to the meeting. Diplomacy went only so far with chaotic fiends. After reaching a point, the time inevitably came for open threats.

Errtu slumped back on his mushroom throne in the realization that Lolth was in full command of this situation. She held the link for his minions to the Material Plane, and she held the gift that might allow Errtu to end his banishment. On top of all of that, Errtu did not doubt the Spider Queen's claims that the pantheon was at last sorting itself out. And if the Time of Troubles was indeed a passing period, and Lolth's powers returned in full, she was far beyond the balor.

Resignedly, Errtu looked back to the image on the scrying surface. Five more kobolds had been pulled up from the Clawrift. They huddled together in a tight group while a host of fiends circled around them, teasing them, tormenting them. The great balor could smell their fear, could taste this torturous kill as sweetly as if he were among those circling fiends.

Errtu's mood brightened immediately.

⚔ ⚔ ⚔ ⚔ ⚔

Belwar Dissengulp and a score of svirfnebli warriors sat on a ledge, overlooking a large chamber strewn with boulders and stalactites. Each held a rope—Belwar's was fastened through a loop on his belt and a mushroom-hide strap set over his pickaxe hand—that they might rappel quickly to the floor. For down below, the gnomish priests were at work, drawing runes of power on the floor with heated dyes and discussing the prior failures and the most effective ways they might combine their powers, both for the summoning, and in case the summoning, as had happened twice already, went bad.

The gnomish priests had heard the call of their god, Segojan, had sensed the returning of priestly magic. For the svirfnebli, no act could greater signify the end of this strange period, no act could better assure them that all was right once more, than the summoning of an elemental earth giant. This was their sphere, their life, and their love. They were attuned to the rock, at one with the stone and dirt that surrounded their dwellings. To call an elemental forth, to share in its friendship, would satisfy the priests that their god was well. Anything less would not suffice.

They had tried several times. The first summoning had brought forth nothing, not a even trembling in the ground. The second, third, and fourth had raised tall stone pillars, but they had shown no signs of animation. Three of the stalagmite mounds in this very chamber were testaments to those failures.

On the fifth try, an elemental had come forth, and the gnomish priests had rejoiced—until the monster turned on them in rage, killing a dozen gnomes before Belwar and his troupe had managed to break it apart. That failure was perhaps the very worst thing that could befall the gnomes, for

they came to believe not only that Segojan was out of their reach, but that, perhaps, he was angry with them. They had tried again—and again the elemental came forth only to attack them.

Belwar's defenses were better in place that sixth time, as they were now, and the stone-limbed monster was beaten back quickly, with no loss of svirfnebli.

After that second disaster, Belwar had asked that the priests wait a while before trying again, but they had refused, desperate to find Segojan's favor, desperate to know that their god was with them. Belwar was not without influence, though, and he had gone to King Schnicktick and forced a compromise.

Five days had passed since that sixth summoning, five days wherein the gnomish priests and all of Blingdenstone had prayed to Segojan, had begged him to no longer turn against them.

Unknown to the svirfnebli, those five days had also seen the end of the Time of Troubles, the realignment and correction of the pantheon.

Belwar watched now as the robed priests began their dance around the rune-emblazoned circle they had drawn on the ground. Each carried a stone, a small green gem previously enchanted. One by one, they placed a gem on the perimeter of the circle and crushed it with a huge mallet. When that was completed, the high priest walked into the circle, to its very center, placed his gem on the ground, and crying out a word of completion, smashed it under his mithral mallet.

For a moment there was only silence, then the ground began to tremble slightly. The high priest rushed out of the circle to join his huddling companions.

The trembling increased, multiplied. A large crack ran around the circumference of the enchanted area, separating that circle from the rest of the chamber. Inside the circle, rock split apart, and split again, rolling and roiling into a malleable mud.

Bubbles grew and blew apart with great popping sounds, and the whole chamber warmed.

A great head—a huge head!—poked up from the floor.

On the ledge, Belwar and his cohorts groaned. Never had they seen so tremendous an elemental! Suddenly, they were all plotting escape routes rather than attack routes.

The shoulders came forth from the floor, an arm on each side—an arm that could sweep the lot of the priests into oblivion with a single movement. Curious looks mixed with trepidation on the faces of priests and warriors alike. This creature was not like any elemental they had ever seen. Though its stone was smoother, with no cracks showing, it appeared more unfinished, less in the image of a bipedal creature. Yet, at the same time, it exuded an aura of sheer power and completion beyond anything the gnomes had ever known.

"The glory of Segojan are we witnessing!" one gnome near Belwar squealed in glee.

"Or the end of our people," Belwar added under his breath so that none would hear.

By the girth of the head and shoulders, the gnomes expected the monster to rise twenty feet or more, but when the trembling stopped and all was quiet again, the creature barely topped ten feet—not as tall as many of the elementals even single svirfneblin priests had previously summoned. Still, the gnomes had no doubt that this was a greater achievement, that this creature was more powerful than anything they had ever brought forth. The priests had their suspicions—so did Belwar, who had lived a long time and had listened carefully to the legends that gave his people their identity and their strength.

"Entemoch!" the most honored burrow warden gasped from his perch, and the name, the name of the Prince of Earth Elementals, was echoed from gnome to gnome.

Another name predictably followed, the name of Ogremoch, Entemoch's evil twin, and it was spoken sharply and with open fear. If this was Ogremoch and not Entemoch, then they all were doomed.

The priests fell to their knees, trembling, paying homage, hoping beyond hope that this was indeed Entemoch, who had always been their friend.

Belwar was the first down from the ledge, hitting the ground with a grunt and running off to stand before the summoned creature.

It regarded him from on high, made no move, and offered no sign as to its intentions.

"Entemoch!" Belwar shouted. Behind him, the priests lifted their faces. Some found the courage to stand and walk beside the brave burrow warden.

"Entemoch!" Belwar called again. "Answered our call, you have. Are we to take this as a sign that all is right with Segojan, that we are in his favor?"

The creature brought its huge hand to the floor, palm up, before Belwar. The burrow warden looked to the high priest standing at his right.

The priest nodded. "To trust in Segojan is our duty," he said, and he and Belwar stepped onto the hand together.

Up they rose, coming to a stop right before the behemoth's face. And they relaxed and were glad, for they saw compassion there, and friendship. This was indeed Entemoch, they both knew in their hearts, and not Ogremoch, and Segojan was with them.

The elemental prince lifted its hand above its head and melted back into the ground, leaving Belwar and the high priest in the center of the circle, perfectly reformed.

Cheers resounded through the chamber, and more than one rough-hewn svirfneblin face was streaked with tears. The priests patted themselves on the back, congratulated themselves and all the gnomes of Blingdenstone. They sang praises to King Schnicktick, whose guidance had led them to this pinnacle of svirfneblin achievement.

For at least one of them, Belwar, the celebration was short-lived. Their god was back with them, it seemed, and their magic was returning, but what did that mean for the drow of Menzoberranzan? the most honored burrow warden wondered. Was the Spider Queen, too, returned? And the powers of the drow wizards as well?

Before all of this had begun, the gnomes had come to believe, and not without reason, that the drow were planning for war. With the onset of this chaotic time, that war had not come, but that was reasonable, Belwar knew, since the drow were more dependent on magic than were the gnomes. If things were indeed aright once more, as the arrival of Entemoch seemed to indicate, then Blingdenstone might soon be threatened.

All around the most honored burrow warden, gnomish priests and warriors danced and cried out for joy. How soon, he wondered, might those cries be screams of pain or shrieks of grief?

REPAIRING THE DAMAGE

Delicately!" Fret whispered harshly, watching Drizzt's hands as the drow scraped and chipped away the dried salve around the neck of the panther figurine. "Oh, do be careful!"

Of course Drizzt was being careful! As careful as the drow had ever been in any task. As important as the figurine appeared to be to Fret, it was a hundred times more important to Drizzt, who treasured and loved his panther companion. Never had the drow taken on a more critical task, not with his wits or his weapons. Now he used the delicate tool Fret had given him, a slender silver rod with a flattened and slightly hooked end.

Another piece of salve fell away—almost a half inch along the side of the panther's neck was clear of the stuff. And clear of any crack, Drizzt noted hopefully. So perfectly had the salve bonded the onyx figurine that not a line could be seen where the break had been.

Drizzt sublimated his excitement, understanding that it would inevitably lead him to rush in his work. He had to take his time. The circumference of the figurine's neck was no more than a few inches, but Drizzt fully expected, and Fret had agreed with the estimate, that he would spend the entire morning at his work.

The drow ranger moved back from the figurine so that Fret could see the cleared area. The tidy dwarf nodded to Drizzt after viewing it, even smiled hopefully. Fret trusted in Lady Alustriel's magic and her ability to mend a tragedy.

With a pat on Drizzt's shoulder, the dwarf moved aside and Drizzt went back to work, slowly and delicately, one tiny fleck at a time.

By noon, the neck was clear of salve. Drizzt turned the figurine over in his hands, studying the area where the break had been, seeing no indication, neither a crack nor any residue from the salve, that the figurine had been damaged. He clasped the item by the head and after a deep, steadying breath, dared to hold it aloft, with all the pressure of its weight centered on the area of the cut.

It held fast. Drizzt shook his hand, daring it to break apart, but it did not.

"The bonding will be as strong as any other area on the item," Fret assured the drow. "Take heart that the figurine is whole once more."

"Agreed," Drizzt replied, "but what of its magic?"

Fret had no answer.

"The real challenge will be in sending Guenhwyvar home to the Astral Plane," the drow went on.

"Or in calling the panther back," Fret added.

That notion stung Drizzt. The tidy dwarf was right, he knew. He might be able to open a tunnel to allow Guenhwyvar to return home, only to have the panther lost to him forever. Still, Drizzt entertained no thoughts of keeping the cat beside him. Guenhwyvar's condition had stabilized—apparently the panther could indeed remain on the Material Plane indefinitely—but the great cat was not in good health or good spirits. While she seemed no longer in danger of dying, Guenhwyvar roamed around in a state of perpetual exhaustion, muscles slack along her once sleek sides, eyes often closed as the panther tried to find desperately needed sleep.

"Better to dismiss Guenhwyvar to her home," Drizzt said determinedly. "Surely my life will be diminished if I cannot recall Guenhwyvar, but better that than the life Guenhwyvar must now endure."

They went together, the figurine in hand, to Drizzt's room. As usual, Guenhwyvar lay on the rug in front of the hearth, absorbing the heat of the glowing embers. Drizzt didn't hesitate. He marched right up before the panther—who lifted her head sluggishly to regard him—and placed the figurine on the floor before her.

"Lady Alustriel, and good Fret here, have come to our aid, Guenhwyvar," Drizzt announced. His voice quivered a bit as he tried to continue, as the realization hit him that this might be the last time he ever saw the panther.

Guenhwyvar sensed that discomfort and with great effort, managed to sit up, putting her head in line with kneeling Drizzt's face.

"Go home, my friend," Drizzt whispered, "go home."

The panther hesitated, eyeing the drow intently, as if trying to discern the source of Drizzt's obvious unease. Guenhwyvar, too, got the feeling—from Drizzt and not from the figurine, which seemed whole to the panther once more—that this might be a final parting of dear friends.

But the cat had no control in the matter. In her exhausted state, Guenhwyvar could not have ignored the call of the magic if she tried. Shakily, the cat got to her feet and paced around the figurine.

Drizzt was both thrilled and scared when Guenhwyvar's form began to melt away into gray mist, then into nothing at all.

When the cat was gone, Drizzt scooped up the figurine, taking heart that he felt no warmth coming from it, that apparently whatever had gone wrong the last time he tried to send Guenhwyvar home was not happening again. He realized suddenly how foolish he had been, and looked at Fret, his violet orbs wide with shock.

"What is it?" the tidy dwarf asked.

"I have not Catti-brie's sword!" Drizzt whispered harshly. "If the path is not clear to the Astral Plane . . ."

"The magic is right once more," Fret replied at once, patting his hand soothingly in the air, "in the figurine and in all the world around us. The magic is right once more."

Drizzt held the figurine close. He had no idea of where Catti-brie might be, and knew she had her sword with her. All he could do, then, was sit tight, wait, and hope.

✕ ✕ ✕ ✕ ✕

Bruenor sat on his throne, Regis beside him, and the halfling looking much more excited than the dwarf king. Regis had already seen the guests that would soon be announced to Bruenor, and curious Regis was always happy to see the extraordinary Harpells of Longsaddle. Four of them had come to Mithral Hall, four wizards who might play an important role in defending the dwarven complex—if they didn't inadvertently take the place down instead.

Such were the risks of dealing with the Harpells.

The four stumbled into the throne room, nearly running down the poor dwarf who had first entered to announce them. There was Harkle, of course, wearing a bandage around his face, for his eyes were already in Mithral Hall. Guiding him was fat Regweld, who had ridden into the outer hall on a curious mount, the front of which resembled a horse and the back of which had hind legs and a back end more akin to a frog. Regweld had appropriately named the thing Puddlejumper.

The third Harpell Bruenor and Regis did not know, and the wizard did not offer his name. He merely growled low and nodded in their direction.

"I am Bella don DelRoy Harpell," announced the fourth, a short and quite beautiful young woman, except that her eyes did not look in the same direction. Both orbs were green, but one shined with a fierce inner light, while the other was dulled over and grayish. With Bella, though, that seemed to only add to her appearance, to give her fine features a somewhat exotic look.

Bruenor recognized one of the given names, and understood that Bella was probably the leader of this group. "Daughter of DelRoy, leader of Longsaddle?" the dwarf asked, to which the petite woman dipped low in a bow, so low that her bright blond mane nearly swept the floor.

"Greetings from Longsaddle, Eighth King of Mithral Hall," Bella said politely. "Your call was not unheeded."

A pity, Bruenor thought, but he remained tactfully quiet.

"With me are—"

"Harkle and Regweld," Regis interrupted, knowing the two quite well from a previous stay in Longsaddle. "Well met! And it is good to see that your experiments in crossbreeding a horse and a frog came to fruition."

"Puddlejumper!" the normally forlorn Regweld happily replied.

That name promised a sight that Regis would like to see!

"I am the daughter of DelRoy," Bella said rather sharply, eyeing the halfling squarely. "Please do not interrupt again, or I shall have to turn you into something Puddlejumper would enjoy eating."

The sparkle in her good green eye as she regarded Regis, and the similar glint in the halfling's gray orbs, told Regis that the threat was a hollow one. He heeded it anyway, suddenly anxious to keep on Bella's good side. She wasn't five feet tall, the halfling realized, and a bit on the heavy side, somewhat resembling a slightly larger version of Regis himself—except that there was no mistaking her feminine attributes. At least, not for Regis.

"My third companion is Bidderdoo," Bella went on.

The name sounded curiously familiar to both Bruenor and Regis, and came perfectly clear when Bidderdoo answered the introduction with a bark.

Bruenor groaned; Regis clapped and laughed aloud. When they had gone through Longsaddle, on their way to find Mithral Hall, Bidderdoo, through use of a bad potion, had played the role of the Harpell family dog.

"The transformation is not yet complete," Bella apologized, and she gave Bidderdoo a quick backhand on the shoulder, reminding him to put his tongue back in his mouth.

Harkle cleared his throat loudly and fidgeted about.

"Of course," Bruenor said immediately, taking the cue. The dwarf gave a sharp whistle, and one of his attendants came out of a side room, carrying the disembodied eyes, one in each hand. To his credit, the dwarf tried to keep them as steady as possible, and aimed them both in Harkle's direction.

"Oh, it is so good to see myself again!" the wizard exclaimed, and he spun around. Following what he could see, he started for himself, or for his eyes, or for the back wall, actually, and the door he and his companions had already come through. He cried out, "No, no!" and turned a complete circle, trying to get his bearing, which wasn't an easy thing while viewing himself from across the room.

Bruenor groaned again.

"It is so confusing!" an exasperated Harkle remarked as Regweld grabbed him and tried to turn him aright.

"Ah, yes," the wizard said, and turned back the wrong way once more, heading for the door.

"The other way!" frustrated Regweld cried.

Bruenor grabbed the dwarven attendant and took the eyes, turning them both to look directly into his own scowling visage.

Harkle screamed.

"Hey!" Bruenor roared. "Turn around."

Harkle calmed himself and did as instructed, his body facing Bruenor once more.

Bruenor looked to Regis, snickered, and tossed one of the eyes Harkle's way, then followed it a split second later with the other, snapping his wrist so the thing spun as it soared through the air.

Harkle screamed again and fainted.

Regweld caught one of the eyes; Bidderdoo went for the other with his mouth. Luckily, Bella cut him off. She missed though, and the eye bounced off her arm, fell to the floor, and rolled around.

"That was very naughty, King Dwarf!" the daughter of DelRoy scolded. "That was . . ." She couldn't maintain the facade, and was soon laughing, as were her companions—though Bidderdoo's chuckles sounded more like a growl. Regis joined in, and Bruenor, too, but only for a second. The dwarf king could not forget the fact that these bumbling wizards might be his only magical defense against an army of dark elves.

It was not a pleasant thought.

✕ ✕ ✕ ✕ ✕

Drizzt was out of Mithral Hall at dawn the next morning. He had seen a campfire on the side of the mountain the night before and knew it was Catti-brie's. He still had not tried calling Guenhwyvar back and resisted the urge now, reminding himself to take on one problem at a time.

The problem now was Catti-brie, or, more specifically, her sword.

He found the young woman as he came around a bend in the path, crossing into the shadow between two large boulders. She was almost directly below him, on a small, flat clearing overlooking the wide, rolling terrain east of Mithral Hall. With the rising sun breaking the horizon directly before her, Drizzt could make out only her silhouette. Her movements were graceful as she walked through a practice dance with her sword, waving it in slow, long lines before and above her. Drizzt rested and watched approvingly of both the grace and perfection of the woman's dance. He had shown her this, and as always, Catti-brie had learned well. She could have been his own shadow, Drizzt realized, so perfect and synchronous were her movements.

He let her continue, both because of the importance of this practice and because he enjoyed watching her.

Finally, after nearly twenty minutes, Catti-brie took a deep breath and held her arms out high and wide, reveling in the rising sun.

"Well done," Drizzt congratulated, walking down to her.

Catti-brie nearly jumped at the sound, and she spun around, a bit embarrassed and annoyed, to see the drow.

"Ye should warn a girl," she said.

"I came upon you quite by accident," Drizzt lied, "but fortunately it would seem."

"I seen the Harpells go into Mithral Hall yesterday," Catti-brie replied. "Have ye speaked with them?"

Drizzt shook his head. "They are not important right now," he explained. "I need only to speak with you."

It sounded serious. Catti-brie moved to slide her sword into its scabbard, but Drizzt's hand came out, motioning for her to stop.

"I have come for the sword," he explained.

"Khazid'hea?" Catti-brie asked, surprised.

"What?" asked the even more surprised drow.

"That is its name," Catti-brie explained, holding the fine blade before her, its razor-sharp edge glowing red once more. "Khazid'hea."

Drizzt knew the word, a drow word! It meant "to cut," or "cutter," and seemed an appropriate name indeed for a blade that could slice through solid stone. But how could Catti-brie know it? the drow wondered, and his face asked the question as plainly as words ever could.

"The sword told me!" Catti-brie answered.

Drizzt nodded and calmed. He shouldn't have been so surprised—he knew the sword was sentient, after all.

"Khazid'hea," the drow agreed. He drew Twinkle from its sheath, flipped it over in his hand, and presented it, hilt-first, to Catti-brie.

She stared at the offering blankly, not understanding.

"A fair exchange," Drizzt explained, "Twinkle for Khazid'hea."

"Ye favor the scimitar," Catti-brie said.

"I will learn to use a scimitar and sword in harmony," Drizzt replied. "Accept the exchange. Khazid'hea has begged that I be its wielder, and I will oblige. It is right that the blade and I are joined."

Catti-brie's look went from surprise to incredulity. She couldn't believe Drizzt would demand this of her! She had spent days—tendays!—alone in the mountains, practicing with this sword, connecting with its unnatural intelligence, trying to establish a bond.

"Have you forgotten our encounter?" Drizzt asked, somewhat cruelly. Catti-brie blushed a deep red. Indeed, she had not forgotten, and never would, and what a fool she felt when she realized how she—or at least how her sword, using her body—had thrown herself at Drizzt.

"Give me the sword," Drizzt said firmly, waving Twinkle's hilt before the stunned young woman. "It is right that we are joined."

Catti-brie clutched Khazid'hea defensively. She closed her eyes then, and seemed to sway, and Drizzt got the impression she was communing with the blade, hearing its feelings.

When she opened her eyes once more, Drizzt's free hand moved for the sword, and to the drow's surprise and satisfaction, the sword tip came up suddenly, nicking his hand and forcing him back.

"The sword does not want ye!" Catti-brie practically growled.

"You would strike me?" Drizzt asked, and his question calmed the young woman.

"Just a reaction," she stammered, trying to apologize.

Just a reaction, Drizzt silently echoed, but exactly the reaction he had hoped to see. The sword was willing to defend her right to wield it; the sword had rejected him in light of its rightful owner.

In the blink of an eye, Drizzt flipped Twinkle over and replaced it on his belt. His smile clued Catti-brie to the truth of the encounter.

"A test," she said. "Ye just gived me a test!"

"It was necessary."

"Ye never had any mind to take Khazid'hea," the woman went on, her volume rising with her ire. "Even if I'd taken yer offer . . ."

"I would have taken the sword," Drizzt answered honestly. "And I would have placed it on display in a secure place in the Hall of Dumathoin."

"And ye would have taken back Twinkle," Catti-brie huffed. "Ye lyin' drow!"

Drizzt considered the words, then shrugged and nodded his agreement with the reasoning.

Catti-brie gave an impertinent pout and tossed her head, which sent her auburn mane flying over her shoulder. "The sword just knows now that I'm the better fighter," she said, sounding sincere.

Drizzt laughed aloud.

"Draw yer blades, then!" Catti-brie huffed, falling back into a ready posture. "Let me show ye what me and me sword can do!"

Drizzt's smile was wide as his scimitars came into his hands. These would be the last and most crucial tests, he knew, to see if Catti-brie had truly taken control of the sword.

Metal rang out in the clear morning air, the two friends hopping about for position, their breath blowing clouds in the chill air. Soon after the sparring had begun, Drizzt's guard slipped, presenting Catti-brie with a perfect strike.

In came Khazid'hea, but it stopped far short, and the young woman jumped back. "Ye did that on purpose!" she accused, and she was right, and by not going for a vicious hit, she and her sword had passed the second test.

Only one test to go.

Drizzt said nothing as he went back into his crouch. He wasn't wearing the bracers, Catti-brie noticed, and so he wouldn't likely be off balance. She came on anyway, gladly and fiercely, and put up a fine fight as the sun broke clear of the horizon and began its slow climb into the eastern sky.

She couldn't match the drow, though, and in truth, hadn't seen Drizzt fight with this much vigor in a long time. When the sparring ended, Catti-brie was sitting on her rump, a scimitar resting easily atop each of her shoulders and her own sword lying on the ground several feet away.

Drizzt feared that the sentient sword would be outraged that its wielder had been so clearly beaten. He stepped away from Catti-brie and went to Khazid'hea first, bending low to scoop it up. The drow paused, though, his hand just an inch from the pommel.

No longer did Khazid'hea wear the pommel of a unicorn, nor even the fiendish visage it had taken when in the hands of Dantrag Baenre. That pommel resembled a sleek feline body now, something like Guenhwyvar running flat out, legs extended front and back. More important to Drizzt, though, there was a rune inscribed on the side of that feline, the twin mountains, symbol of Dumathoin, the dwarven god, Catti-brie's god, the Keeper of Secrets Under the Mountain.

Drizzt picked up Khazid'hea, and felt no enmity or any of the desire the sword had previously shown him. Catti-brie was beside him, then, smiling in regard to his obvious approval of her choice for a pommel.

Drizzt handed Khazid'hea back to its rightful owner.

THE WRATH OF LOLTH

B aenre felt strong again. Lolth was back, and Lolth was with her, and K'yorl Odran, that wretched K'yorl, had badly erred. Always before, the Spider Queen had kept House Oblodra in her favor, even though the so-called "priestesses" of the House were not pious and sometimes openly expressed their disdain for Lolth. These strange powers of the Oblodrans, this psionic strength, had intrigued Lolth as much as it had frightened the other Houses in Menzoberranzan. None of those Houses wanted a war against K'yorl and her clan, and Lolth hadn't demanded one. If Menzoberranzan was ever attacked from the outside, particularly from the illithids, whose cavern lair was not so far away, K'yorl and the Oblodrans would be of great help.

But no more. K'yorl had crossed over a very dangerous line. She had murdered a matron mother, and while that in itself was not uncommon, she had intended to usurp power from Lolth's priestesses, and not in the name of the Spider Queen.

Matron Baenre knew all of this, felt the will and strength of Lolth within her. "The Time of Troubles has passed," she announced to her family, to everyone gathered in her house, in the nearly repaired chapel.

Mez'Barris Armgo was there as well, in a seat of honor on the central dais, at Matron Baenre's personal invitation.

Matron Baenre took the seat next to the matron mother of the Second

House as the gathered crowd exploded in cheers, and led by Triel, in song to the Spider Queen.

Ended? Mez'Barris asked of Baenre, using the silent hand code, for they could not have been heard above the roar of two thousand Baenre soldiers.

The Time of Troubles has ended, Baenre's delicate fingers responded.

Except for House Oblodra, Mez'Barris reasoned, to which Baenre only chuckled wickedly. It was no secret in Menzoberranzan that House Oblodra was in serious trouble. No secret indeed, for the tanar'ri and other fiends continued to circle the Oblodran compound, plucking kobolds from the ledges along the Clawrift, even attacking with abandon any Oblodran who showed herself.

K'yorl will be forgiven? Mez'Barris asked, popping up her left thumb at the end of the code to indicate a question.

Matron Baenre shook her head once briskly, then pointedly looked away, to Triel, who was leading the gathering in rousing prayers to the Spider Queen.

Mez'Barris tapped a long, curving fingernail against her teeth nervously, wondering how Baenre could be so secure in this decision. Did Baenre plan to go after House Oblodra alone, or did she mean to call Barrison del'Armgo into yet another alliance? Mez'Barris did not doubt that her House and House Baenre could crush House Oblodra, but she wasn't thrilled at the prospect of tangling with K'yorl and those unexplored powers.

Methil, invisible and standing off to the side of the dais, read the visiting matron mother's thoughts easily, and in turn, imparted them to Matron Baenre.

"It is the will of Lolth," Matron Baenre said sharply, turning back to regard Mez'Barris. "K'yorl has denounced the Spider Queen, and thus, she will be punished."

"By the Academy, as is the custom?" Mez'Barris asked, and hoped.

A fiery sparkle erupted behind Matron Baenre's red-glowing eyes. "By me," she answered bluntly, and turned away again, indicating that Mez'Barris would garner no further information.

Mez'Barris was wise enough not to press the point. She slumped back in her chair, trying to sort out this surprising, disturbing information.

Matron Baenre had not declared that an alliance of Houses would attack Oblodra; she had declared a personal war. Did she truly believe she could defeat K'yorl? Or were those fiends, even the great tanar'ri, more fully under her control than Mez'Barris had been led to believe? That notion scared the matron mother of Barrison del'Armgo more than a little, for, if it were true, what other "punishments" might the angry and ambitious Matron Baenre hand out?

Mez'Barris sighed deeply and let the thoughts pass. There was little she could do now, sitting in the chapel of House Baenre, surrounded by two thousand Baenre soldiers. She had to trust in Baenre, she knew.

No, she silently corrected herself, not trust, never that. Mez'Barris had to hope Matron Baenre would think she was more valuable to the cause—whatever it might now be—alive than dead.

⚔ ⚔ ⚔ ⚔ ⚔

Seated atop a blue-glowing driftdisk, Matron Baenre herself led the procession from House Baenre, down from the Qu'ellarz'orl and across the city, her army singing Lolth's praises every step. The Baenre lizard riders, Berg'inyon in command, flanked the main body, sweeping in and around the other House compounds to ensure that no surprises would block the trail.

It was a necessary precaution whenever the first matron mother went out, but Matron Baenre did not fear any ambush, not now. With the exception of Mez'Barris Armgo, no others had been told of the Baenre march, and certainly the lesser Houses, either alone or in unison, would not dare to strike at the First House unless the attack had been perfectly coordinated.

From the opposite end of the great cavern came another procession, also led by a Baenre. Triel, Gromph, and the other mistresses and masters of the drow Academy came from their structures, leading their students, every one. Normally it was this very force, the powerful Academy, that exacted punishment on an individual House for crimes against Menzoberranzan, but this time Triel had informed her charges that they would come only to watch, to see the glory of Lolth revealed.

By the time the two groups joined the gathering already in place at the Clawrift, their numbers had swelled five times over. Nobles and soldiers from every House in the city turned out to watch the spectacle as soon as they came to understand that House Baenre and House Oblodra would finish this struggle once and for all.

When they arrived before the front gates of House Oblodra, the Baenre soldiers formed a defensive semicircle behind Matron Baenre, shielding her, not from K'yorl and the Odran family, but from the rest of the gathering. There was much whispering, drow hands flashed frantically in heated conversations, and the fiends, understanding that some calamity was about to come, whipped into a frenzy, swooping across the Oblodran compound, even exercising their returned magic with an occasional bolt of blue-white lightning or a fireball.

Matron Baenre let the display continue for several minutes, realizing the terror it caused within the doomed compound. She wanted to savor this moment above all others, wanted to bask in the smell of terror emanating from the compound of that most hated family.

Then it was time to begin—or to finish, actually. Baenre knew what she must do. She had seen it in a vision during the ceremony preceding the war, and despite the doubts of Mez'Barris when she had shared it with her, Baenre held faith in the Spider Queen, held faith that it was Lolth's will that House Oblodra be devoured.

She reached under her robes and produced a piece of sulphur, the same yellow lump the avatar had given her to allow the priestesses to open the gate to the Abyss in the small room at the back of the Qu'ellarz'orl. Baenre thrust her hand skyward, and up into the air she floated. There came a great crackling explosion, a rumble of thunder.

All was suddenly silent, all eyes turned to the specter of Matron Baenre, hovering twenty feet off the cavern floor.

Berg'inyon, responsible for his mother's security, looked to Sos'Umptu, his expression sour. He thought his mother was terribly vulnerable up there.

Sos'Umptu laughed at him. He was not a priestess; he could not understand that Matron Baenre was more protected at that moment than at any other time in her long life.

"K'yorl Odran!" Baenre called, and her voice seemed magnified, like the voice of a giant.

⚔ ⚔ ⚔ ⚔ ⚔

Locked in a room in the highest level of the tallest stalagmite mound within the Oblodran compound, K'yorl Odran heard Baenre's call, heard it clearly. Her hands gripped tight on her throne's carved marble arms. She squeezed her eyes shut, as she ordered herself to concentrate.

Now, above any other time, K'yorl needed her powers, and now, for the first time, she could not access them! Something was terribly wrong, she knew, and though she believed that Lolth must somehow be behind this, she sensed, as many of the Spider Queen's priestesses had sensed when the Time of Troubles had begun, that this trouble was beyond even Lolth.

The problems had begun soon after K'yorl had been chased back to her house by the loosed tanar'ri. She and her daughters had gathered to formulate an attack plan to drive off the fiends. As always with the efficient Oblodran meetings, the group shared its thoughts telepathically, the equivalent of holding several understandable conversations at once.

The defense plan was coming together well—K'yorl grew confident that the tanar'ri would be sent back to their own plane of existence, and when that was accomplished, she and her family could go and properly punish Matron Baenre and the others. Then something terrible had happened. One of the tanar'ri had thrown forth a blast of lightning, a searing, blinding bolt that sent a crack running along the outer wall of the Oblodran compound. That in itself was not so bad; the compound, like all the Houses of Menzoberranzan, could take a tremendous amount of punishment, but what the blast, what the return of magical powers, signified, was disastrous to the Oblodrans.

At that same moment, the telepathic conversation had abruptly ended, and try as they may, the nobles of the doomed House could not begin it anew.

K'yorl was as intelligent as any drow in Menzoberranzan. Her powers of concentration were unparalleled. She felt the psionic strength within her mind, the powers that allowed her to walk through walls or yank the beat-

ing heart from an enemy's chest. They were there, deep in her mind, but she could not bring them forth. She continued to blame herself, her lack of concentration in the face of disaster. She even punched herself on the side of the head, as if that physical jarring would knock out some magical manifestation.

Her efforts were futile. As the Time of Troubles had come to its end, as the tapestry of magic in the Realms had rewoven, many rippling side-effects had occurred. Throughout the Realms, dead magic zones had appeared, areas where no spells would function, or, even worse, where no spells would function as intended. Another of those side-effects involved psionic powers, the magiclike powers of the mind. The strength was still there, as K'yorl sensed, but bringing forth that strength required a different mental route than before.

The illithids, as Methil had informed Matron Baenre, had already discerned that route, and their powers were functioning nearly as completely as before. But they were an entire race of psionicists, and a race possessed of communal intelligence. The illithids had already made the necessary adjustments to accessing their psionic powers, but K'yorl Odran and her once powerful family had not.

So the matron of the Third House sat in the darkness, eyes squeezed tightly shut, concentrating. She heard Baenre's call, knew that if she did not go to Baenre, Baenre would soon come to her.

Given time, K'yorl would have sorted through the mental puzzle. Given a month, perhaps, she would have begun to bring forth her powers once more.

K'yorl didn't have a month; K'yorl didn't have an hour.

⚔ ⚔ ⚔ ⚔ ⚔

Matron Baenre felt the pulsing magic within the lump of sulphur, an inner heat, fast-building in intensity. She was amazed as her hand shifted, as the sulphur implored her to change the angle.

Baenre nodded. She understood then that some force from beyond the Material Plane, some creature of the Abyss, and perhaps even Lolth herself, was guiding the movement. Up went her hand, putting the pulsing lump in line with the top level of the highest tower in the Oblodran compound.

"Who are you?" she asked.

I am Errtu, came a reply in her mind. Baenre knew the name, knew the creature was a balor, the most terrible and powerful of all tanar'ri. Lolth had armed her well!

She felt the pure malice of the connected creature building within the sulphur, felt the energy growing to where she thought the lump would explode, probably bringing Errtu to her side.

That could not happen, of course, though she did not know it.

It was the power of the artifact itself she felt, that seemingly innocuous piece of sulphur, imbued with the magic of Lolth, wielded by the highest priestess of the Spider Queen in all of Menzoberranzan.

Purely on instinct, Baenre flattened her hand, and the sulphur sent forth a line of glowing, crackling yellow light. It struck the wall high on the Oblodran tower, the very wall between K'yorl and Baenre. Lines of light and energy encircled the stalagmite mound, crackling, biting into the stone, stealing the integrity of the place.

The sulphur went quiet again, its bolt of seemingly live energy freed, but Baenre did not lower her hand and did not take her awestruck stare from the tower wall.

Neither did the ten thousand dark elves that stood behind her. Neither did K'yorl Odran, who could suddenly see the yellow lines of destruction as they ate their way through the stone.

All in the city gasped as one as the tower's top exploded into dust and was blown away.

There sat K'yorl, still atop her black marble throne, suddenly in the open, staring down at the tremendous gathering.

Many winged tanar'ri swooped around the vulnerable matron mother, but they did not approach too closely, wisely fearing the wrath of Errtu should they steal even a moment of his fun.

K'yorl, always proud and strong, rose from her throne and walked to the edge of the tower. She surveyed the gathering, and so respectful were many drow, even matron mothers, of her strange powers, that they turned away when they felt her scrutinizing gaze on them, as though she, from on high, was deciding who she would punish for this attack.

Finally K'yorl's gaze settled on Matron Baenre, who did not flinch and did not turn away.

"You dare!" K'yorl roared down, but her voice seemed small.

"*You* dare!" Matron Baenre yelled back, the power of her voice echoing off the walls of the cavern. "You have forsaken the Spider Queen."

"To the Abyss with Lolth, where she rightly belongs!" stubborn K'yorl replied, the last words she ever spoke.

Baenre thrust her hand higher and felt the next manifestation of power, the opening of an interplanar gate. No yellow light came forth, no visible force at all, but K'yorl felt it keenly.

She tried to call out in protest, but could say nothing beyond a whimper and a gurgle as her features suddenly twisted, elongated. She tried to resist, dug her heels in, and concentrated once more on bringing forth her powers.

K'yorl felt her skin being pulled free of her bones, felt her entire form being stretched out of shape, elongated, as the sulphur pulled at her with undeniable strength. Stubbornly she held on through the incredible agony, through the horrible realization of her doom. She opened her mouth, wanting to utter one more damning curse, but all that came out was her tongue, pulled to its length and beyond.

K'yorl felt her entire body stretching down from the tower, reaching for the sulphur and the gate. She should have been dead already.

Matron Baenre held her hand steady, but could not help closing her eyes, as K'yorl's weirdly elongated form suddenly flew from the top of the broken tower, soaring straight for her.

Several drow, Berg'inyon included, screamed, others gasped again, and still others called to the glory of Lolth, as K'yorl, stretched and narrowed so that she resembled a living spear, entered the sulphur, the gate that would take her to the Abyss, to Errtu, Lolth's appointed agent of torture.

Behind K'yorl came the fiends, with a tremendous fanfare, roaring and loosing bolts of lightning against the Oblodran compound, igniting balls of exploding fire and other blinding displays of their power. Compelled by Errtu, they stretched and thinned and flew into the sulphur, and Matron Baenre held on against her terror, transforming it into a sensation of sheer power.

In a few moments, all the fiends, even the greatest tanar'ri, were gone. Matron Baenre felt their presence still, transformed somehow within the sulphur.

Suddenly, it was quiet once more. Many dark elves looked to each other, wondering if the punishment was complete, wondering if House Oblodra would be allowed to survive under a new leader. Nobles from several different Houses flashed signals to each other expressing their concern that Baenre would now put one of her own daughters in command of the Third House, further sealing her ultimate position within the city.

But Baenre had no such thoughts. This was a punishment demanded by Lolth, a complete punishment, as terrible as anything that had ever been exacted on a House in Menzoberranzan. Again heeding the telepathic instructions of Errtu, Matron Baenre hurled the throbbing piece of sulphur into the Clawrift, and when cheers went up around her, the dark elves thinking the ceremony complete, she raised her arms out wide and commanded them all to witness the wrath of Lolth.

They felt the first rumblings within the Clawrift beneath their feet. A few anxious moments passed, too quiet, too hushed.

One of K'yorl's daughters appeared on the open platform atop the broken tower. She ran to the edge, calling, pleading, to Matron Baenre. A moment later, when Baenre gave no response, she happened to glance to the side, to one of the fingerlike chasms of the great Clawrift.

Wide went her eyes, and her scream was as terrified as any drow had ever heard. From the higher vantage point offered by her levitation spell, Matron Baenre followed the gaze and was next to react, throwing her arms high and wide and crying out to her goddess in ecstasy. A moment later, the gathering understood.

A huge black tentacle snaked over the rim of the Clawrift, wriggling its way behind the Oblodran compound. Like a wave, dark elves fell back, stumbling all over each other, as the twenty-foot-thick monstrosity came around the back, along the side, and along the front wall, back toward the chasm.

"Baenre!" pleaded the desperate, doomed Oblodran.

"You have denied Lolth," the first matron mother replied calmly. "Feel her wrath!"

The ground beneath the cavern trembled slightly as the tentacle, the angry hand of Lolth, tightened its grasp on the Oblodran compound. The wall buckled and collapsed as the thing began its steady sweep.

K'yorl's daughter leaped from the tower as it, too, began to crumble. She cleared the tentacle, and was still alive, though broken, on the ground when a group of dark elves got to her. Uthegental Armgo was among that group, and the mighty weapons master pushed aside the others, preventing them from finishing the pitiful creature off. He hoisted the Odran in his powerful arms, and through bleary eyes, the battered female regarded him, even managed a faint smile, as though she expected he had come out to save her.

Uthegental laughed at her, lifted her above his head and ran forward, heaving her over the side of the tentacle, back into the rolling rubble that had been her house.

The cheers, the screams, were deafening, and so was the rumble as the tentacle swept all that had been House Oblodra, all the structures and all the drow, into the chasm.

15

GREED

The mercenary shook his bald head, as defiant an act as he had ever made against Matron Baenre. At this moment, so soon after the first matron mother's awesome display of power, and given the fact that she was obviously in the Spider Queen's highest favor, Jarlaxle's questioning of her plans seemed even more dangerous.

Triel Baenre sneered at Jarlaxle, and Berg'inyon closed his eyes. Neither of them really wanted to see the useful male beaten to death. Wicked Bladen'Kerst, though, licked her lips anxiously and gripped the five-headed tentacle whip tied on her hip, hoping that her mother would allow her the pleasure.

"I fear it is not the time," Jarlaxle said openly, bluntly.

"Lolth instructs me differently," Baenre replied, and she seemed quite cool and calm, given the defiance of a mere male.

"We cannot be certain that our magic will continue to work as we expect," Jarlaxle reasoned.

Baenre nodded, and the others then realized, to their absolute surprise, that their mother was glad the mercenary was taking a negative role. Jarlaxle's questions were pertinent, and he was, in fact, helping Baenre sort through the details of her proposed new alliance and the march to Mithral Hall.

Triel Baenre eyed her mother suspiciously as all of this sank in. If Matron Baenre had received her instructions directly from the Spider Queen, as she had openly stated, then why would she want, or even tolerate, defiance or questioning at all? Why would Matron Baenre need to have these most basic questions concerning the wisdom of the march answered?

"The magic is secure," Baenre replied.

Jarlaxle conceded the point. Everything he had heard, both within and beyond the drow city, seemed to back that claim. "You will have no trouble forming an alliance after the spectacle of House Oblodra's fall. Matron Mez'Barris Armgo has been supportive all along, and no matron mother would dare even hint that she fears to follow your lead."

"The Clawrift is large enough to hold the rubble of many Houses," Baenre said dryly.

Jarlaxle snickered. "Indeed," he said. "And indeed this is the time for alliance, for whatever purpose that alliance must be formed."

"It is time to march to Mithral Hall," Baenre interrupted, her tone one of finality, "time to rise up from despair and bring higher glories to the Spider Queen."

"We have suffered many losses," Jarlaxle dared to press. "House Oblodra and their kobold slaves were to lead the attack, dying in the dwarven traps set for drow."

"The kobolds will be brought up from their holes in the Clawrift," Baenre assured him.

Jarlaxle didn't disagree, but he knew the tunnels below the rim of the chasm better than anyone, now that all of House Oblodra was dead. Baenre would get some kobolds, several hundred perhaps, but House Oblodra could have provided many thousand.

"The city's hierarchy is in question," the mercenary went on. "The Third House is no more, and the fourth is without its matron mother. Your own family still has not recovered from the renegade's escape and the loss of Dantrag and Vendes."

Baenre suddenly sat forward in her throne. Jarlaxle didn't flinch, but many of the Baenre children did, fearing that their mother understood the truth of the mercenary's last statement, and that Baenre simply would not tolerate any bickering between her surviving children as they sorted out the responsibilities and opportunities left open by the loss of their brother and sister.

Baenre stopped as quickly as she had started, standing before the throne. She let her dangerous gaze linger over each of her gathered children, then dropped it fully over the impertinent mercenary. "Come with me," she commanded.

Jarlaxle stepped aside to let her pass, and obediently and wisely fell into step right behind her. Triel moved to follow, but Baenre spun around, stopping her daughter in her tracks. "Just him," she growled.

A black column centered the throne room, and a crack appeared along its seemingly perfect and unblemished side as Baenre and the mercenary approached. The crack widened as the cunning door slid open, allowing the two to enter the cylindrical chamber within.

Jarlaxle expected Baenre to yell at him, or to talk to him, even threaten him, once the door closed again, separating them from her family. But the matron mother said nothing, just calmly walked over to a hole in the floor. She stepped into the hole, but did not fall, rather floated down to the next lower level, the great Baenre mound's third level, on currents of magical energy. Jarlaxle followed as soon as the way was clear, but still, when he got to the third level, he had to hurry to keep up with the hustling matron mother, gliding through the floor once more, and again, and again, until she came to the dungeons beneath the great mound.

Still she offered not a word of explanation, and Jarlaxle began to wonder if he was to be imprisoned down here. Many drow, even drow nobles, had found that grim fate. It was rumored that several had been kept as Baenre prisoners for more than a century, endlessly tortured, then healed by the priestesses, that they might be tortured again.

A wave of Baenre's hand sent the two guards standing beside one cell door scrambling for cover.

Jarlaxle was as relieved as curious when he walked into the cell behind Baenre to find a curious, barrel-chested dwarf chained to the far wall. The mercenary looked back to Baenre, and only then did he realize she was not wearing one of her customary necklaces, the one fashioned of a dwarf's tooth.

"A recent catch?" Jarlaxle asked, though he suspected differently.

"Two thousand years," Baenre replied. "I give to you Gandalug Battlehammer, patron of Clan Battlehammer, founder of Mithral Hall."

Jarlaxle rocked back on his heels. He had heard the rumors, of course, that Baenre's tooth pendant contained the soul of an ancient dwarf king, but never had he suspected such a connection. He realized then, suddenly, that this entire foray to Mithral Hall was not about Drizzt Do'Urden, that the renegade was merely a connection, an excuse, for something Baenre had desired for a very long time.

Jarlaxle looked at Baenre suddenly, curiously. "Two thousand years?" he echoed aloud, while he silently wondered just how old this withered drow really was.

"I have kept his soul through the centuries," Baenre went on, eyeing the old dwarf directly. "During the time Lolth could not hear our call, the item was destroyed and Gandalug came forth, alive again." She walked over, put her snarling visage right up to the battered, naked dwarf's long, pointed nose, and put one hand on his round, solid shoulder. "Alive, but no more free than he was before."

Gandalug cleared his throat as if he meant to spit on Baenre. He stopped, though, when he realized that a spider had crawled out of the ring on her hand, onto his shoulder, and was now making its way along his neck.

Gandalug understood that Baenre would not kill him, that she needed him for her proposed conquest. He did not fear death, but would have preferred it to this torment and weighed against the realization that he might unwittingly aid in the fall of his own people. Baenre's gruesome mind flayer had already scoured Gandalug's thoughts more than once, taking information that no beatings could ever have extracted from the stubborn old dwarf.

Rationally, Gandalug had nothing to fear, but that did little to comfort him now. Gandalug hated spiders above all else, hated and feared them. As soon as he felt the hairy, crawly thing on his neck, he froze, eyes unblinking, sweat beading on his forehead.

Baenre walked away, leaving her pet spider on the dwarf's neck. She turned to Jarlaxle again, a supreme look on her face, as though Gandalug's presence should make all the difference in the world to the doubting mercenary.

It didn't. Jarlaxle never once doubted that Menzoberranzan could defeat Mithral Hall, never once doubted that the conquest would be successful. But what of the aftermath of that conquest? The drow city was in turmoil. There would soon be a fierce struggle, perhaps even an open war, to fill the vacancy left by both House Oblodra's demise and the death of Ghenni'tiroth Tlabbar. Living for centuries on the edge of disaster with his secretive band, the mercenary understood the perils of overextending his grab for power, understood that if one stretched his forces too far, they could simply collapse.

But Jarlaxle knew, too, that he would not convince Matron Baenre. So be it, he decided. Let Baenre march to Mithral Hall with no further questions from him. He would even encourage her. If things went as she planned, then all would be the better for it.

If not . . .

Jarlaxle didn't bother to entertain those possibilities. He knew where Gromph stood, knew the wizard's frustration and the frustrations of Bregan D'aerthe, a band almost exclusively male. Let Baenre go to Mithral Hall, and if she failed, then Jarlaxle would take Baenre's own advice and "rise up from despair."

Indeed.

16
OPEN HEARTS

Drizzt found her on the same east-facing plateau where she had practiced all those tendays, the very spot where she had at last gained control of her strong-willed sword. Long shadows rolled out from the mountains, the sun low in the sky behind them. The first stars shone clearly, twinkling above Silverymoon, and Sundabar to the east beyond that.

Catti-brie sat unmoving, legs bent and knees pulled in tightly to her chest. If she heard the approach of the almost silent drow, she gave no indication, just rocked gently back and forth, staring into the deepening gloom.

"The night is beautiful," Drizzt said, and when Catti-brie did not jump at the sound of his voice, he realized she had recognized his approach. "But the wind is chill."

"The winter's coming in full," Catti-brie replied softly, not taking her gaze from the darkened eastern sky.

Drizzt sought a reply, wanted to keep talking. He felt awkward here, strangely so, for never in the years he had known Catti-brie had there been such tension between them. The drow walked over and crouched beside Catti-brie, but did not look at her, as she did not look at him.

"I'll call Guenhwyvar this night," Drizzt remarked.

Catti-brie nodded.

Her continued silence caught the drow off guard. His calling of the panther, for the first time since the figurine was repaired, was no small thing. Would the figurine's magic work properly, enabling Guenhwyvar to return to his side? Fret had assured him it would, but Drizzt could not be certain, could not rest easily, until the task was completed and the panther, the healed panther, was back beside him.

It should have been important to Catti-brie as well. She should have cared as much as Drizzt cared, for she and Guenhwyvar were as close as any. Yet she didn't reply, and her silence made Drizzt, anger budding within him, turn to regard her more closely.

He saw tears rimming her blue eyes, tears that washed away Drizzt's anger, that told him that what had happened between himself and Catti-brie had apparently not been so deeply buried. The last time they had met, on this very spot, they had hidden the questions they both wanted to ask behind the energy of a sparring match. Catti-brie's concentration had to be complete on that occasion, and in the days before it, as she fought to master her sword, but now that task was completed. Now, like Drizzt, she had time to think, and in that time, Catti-brie had remembered.

"Ye're knowin' it was the sword?" she asked, almost pleaded.

Drizzt smiled, trying to comfort her. Of course it had been the sentient sword that had inspired her to throw herself at him. Fully the sword, only the sword. But a large part of Drizzt—and possibly of Catti-brie, he thought in looking at her—wished differently. There had been an undeniable tension between them for some time, a complicated situation, and even more so now, after the possession incident with Khazid'hea.

"Ye did right in pushing me away," Catti-brie said, and she snorted and cleared her throat, hiding a sniffle.

Drizzt paused for a long moment, realizing the potential weight of his reply. "I pushed you away only because I saw the pommel," he said, and that drew Catti-brie's attention from the eastern sky, made her look at the drow directly, her deep blue eyes locking with his violet orbs.

"It was the sword," Drizzt said quietly, "only the sword."

Catti-brie didn't blink, barely drew breath. She was thinking how noble this drow had been. So many other men would not have asked questions, would have taken advantage of the situation. And would that have been such a bad thing? the young woman had to ask herself now. Her feelings for Drizzt were deep and real, a bond of friendship and love. Would it have been such a bad thing if he had made love to her in that room?

Yes, she decided, for both of them, because, while it was her body that had been offered, it was Khazid'hea that was in control. Things were awkward enough between them now, but if Drizzt had relented to the feelings that Catti-brie knew he held for her, if he had not been so noble in that strange situation and had given in to the offered temptation, likely neither of them would have been able to look the other in the eye afterward.

Like they were doing now, on a quiet plateau high in the mountains, with a chill and crisp breeze and the stars glowing ever more brightly above them.

"Ye're a good man, Drizzt Do'Urden," the grateful woman said with a heartfelt smile.

"Hardly a man," Drizzt replied, chuckling, and glad for the relief of tension.

Only a temporary relief, though. The chuckle and the smile died away almost immediately, leaving them in the same place, the same awkward moment, caught somewhere between romance and fear.

Catti-brie looked back to the sky, and Drizzt did likewise.

"Ye know I loved him," the young woman said.

"You still do," Drizzt answered, and his smile was genuine when Catti-brie turned back again to regard him.

She turned away almost at once, looked back to the bright stars and thought of Wulfgar.

"You would have married him," Drizzt went on.

Catti-brie wasn't so sure of that. For all the true love she held for Wulfgar, the barbarian carried around the weight of his heritage and a society that valued women not as partners, but as servants. Wulfgar had climbed above many of the narrow-thinking ways of his tribal people, but as his wedding to Catti-brie approached, he had become more protective of her, to the point of being insulting. That, above anything else, proud and capable Catti-brie could not tolerate.

Her doubts were clear on her face, and Drizzt, who knew her better than anyone, read them easily.

"You would have married him," he said again, his firm tone forcing Catti-brie to look back to him.

"Wulfgar was no fool," Drizzt went on.

"Don't ye be blamin' it all on Entreri and the halfling's gem," Catti-brie warned. After the threat of the drow hunting party had been turned away, after Wulfgar's demise, Drizzt had explained to her, and to Bruenor, who perhaps more than anyone else needed to hear the justification, that Entreri, posing as Regis, had used the hypnotic powers of the ruby pendant on Wulfgar. Yet that theory could not fully explain the barbarian's outrageous behavior, because Wulfgar had started down that path long before Entreri had even arrived at Mithral Hall.

"Surely the gem pushed Wulfgar further," Drizzt countered.

"Pushed him where he wanted to go."

"No." The simple reply, spoken with absolute surety, almost caught Catti-brie off guard. She cocked her head to the side, her thick auburn hair cascading over one shoulder, waiting for the drow to elaborate.

"He was scared," Drizzt went on. "Nothing in the world frightened mighty Wulfgar more than the thought of losing his Catti-brie."

"*His* Catti-brie?" she echoed.

Drizzt laughed at her oversensitivity. "His Catti-brie, as he was your Wulfgar," he said, and Catti-brie's smirk fell away as fully as her trap of words.

"He loved you," Drizzt went on, "with all his heart." He paused, but Catti-brie had nothing to say, just sat very still, very quiet, hearing his every word. "He loved you, and that love made him feel vulnerable, and frightened him. Nothing anyone could do to Wulfgar, not torture, not battle, not even death, frightened him, but the slightest scratch on Catti-brie would burn like a hot dagger in his heart.

"So he acted the part of the fool for a short while before you were to be wed," Drizzt said. "The very next time you saw battle, your own strength and independence would have held a mirror up to Wulfgar, would have shown him his error. Unlike so many of his proud people, unlike Berkthgar, Wulfgar admitted his mistakes and never made them again."

As she listened to the words of her wise friend, Catti-brie remembered exactly that incident, the battle in which Wulfgar had been killed.

Those very fears for Catti-brie had played a large part in the barbarian's death, but before he was taken from her, he had looked into her eyes and had indeed realized what his foolishness had cost him, had cost them both.

Catti-brie had to believe that now, recalling the scene in light of the drow's words. She had to believe that her love for Wulfgar had been real, very real, and not misplaced, that he was all she had thought him to be.

Now she could. For the first time since Wulfgar's death, Catti-brie could remember him without the pangs of guilt, without the fears that, had he lived, she would not have married him. Because Drizzt was right; Wulfgar would have admitted the error despite his pride, and he would have grown, as he always had before. That was the finest quality of the man, an almost childlike quality, that viewed the world and his own life as getting better, as moving toward a better way in a better place.

What followed was the most sincere smile on Catti-brie's face in many, many months. She felt suddenly free, suddenly complete with her past, reconciled and able to move forward with her life.

She looked at the drow, wide-eyed, with a curiosity that seemed to surprise Drizzt. She could go on, but exactly what did that mean?

Slowly, Catti-brie began shaking her head, and Drizzt came to understand that the movement had something to do with him. He lifted a slender hand and brushed some stray hair back from her cheek, his ebony skin contrasting starkly with her light skin, even in the quiet light of night.

"I do love you," the drow admitted. The blunt statement did not catch Catti-brie by surprise, not at all. "As you love me," Drizzt went on, easily, confident that his words were on the mark. "And I, too, must look ahead now, must find my place among my friends, beside you, without Wulfgar."

"Perhaps in the future," Catti-brie said, her voice barely a whisper.

"Perhaps," Drizzt agreed. "But for now . . ."

"Friends," Catti-brie finished.

Drizzt moved his hand back from her cheek, held it in the air before her face, and she reached up and clasped it firmly.

Friends.

The moment lingered, the two staring, not talking, and it would have gone on much, much longer, except that there came a commotion from the trail behind them, and the sound of voices they both recognized.

"Stupid elf couldn't do this inside!" blustered Bruenor.

"The stars are more fitting for Guenhwyvar," huffed Regis breathlessly. Together they crashed through a bush not far behind the plateau and stumbled and skidded down to join their two friends.

"Stupid elf?" Catti-brie asked her father.

"Bah!" Bruenor snorted. "I'm not for saying . . ."

"Well, actually," Regis began to correct, but changed his mind when Bruenor turned his scarred visage the halfling's way and growled at him.

"So ye're right and I said stupid elf!" Bruenor admitted, speaking mostly to Drizzt, as close to an apology as he ever gave. "But I've got me work to do." He looked back up the trail, in the direction of Mithral Hall's eastern door. "Inside!" he finished.

Drizzt took out the onyx figurine and placed it on the ground, purposely right before the dwarf's heavy boots. "When Guenhwyvar is returned to us, I will explain how inconvenienced you were to come and witness her return," Drizzt said with a smirk.

"Stupid elf," Bruenor muttered under his breath, and he fully expected that Drizzt would have the cat sleep on him again, or something worse.

Catti-brie and Regis laughed, but their mirth was strained and nervous, as Drizzt called quietly for the panther. The pain they would have to bear if the magic of the figurine had not healed, if Guenhwyvar did not return to them, would be no less to the companions than the pain of losing Wulfgar.

They all knew it, even surly, blustery Bruenor, who to his grave would deny his affection for the magical panther. Silence grew around the figurine as the gray smoke came forth, swirled, and solidified.

Guenhwyvar seemed almost confused as she regarded the four companions standing around her, none of them daring to breathe.

Drizzt's grin was the first and the widest, as he saw that his trusted companion was whole again and healed, the black fur glistening in the starlight, the sleek muscles taut and strong.

He had brought Bruenor and Regis out to witness this moment. It was fitting that all four of them stood by when Guenhwyvar returned.

More fitting would it have been had the sixth companion, Wulfgar, son of Beornegar, joined them on that plateau, in the quiet night, under the stars, in the last hours of Mithral Hall's peace.

PART FOUR

I noticed something truly amazing, and truly heartwarming, as we, all the defenders of Mithral Hall and the immediate region, neared the end of preparations, neared the time when the drow would come.

I am drow. My skin proves that I am different. The ebony hue shows my heritage clearly and undeniably. And

THE DROW

MARCH

yet, not a glare was aimed my way, not a look of consternation from the Harpells and the Long-riders, not an angry word from volatile Berkthgar and his warrior people. And no dwarf, not even General Dagna, who did not like anyone who was not a dwarf, pointed an accusing finger at me.

We did not know why the drow had come, be it for me or for the promise of treasure from the rich dwarven complex. Whatever the cause, to the defenders, I was without blame. How wonderful that felt to me, who had worn the burden of self-imposed guilt for many months, guilt for the previous raid, guilt for Wulfgar, guilt that Catti-brie had been forced by friendship to chase me all the way to Menzoberranzan.

I had worn this heavy collar, and yet those around me who had as much to lose as I placed no burden on me.

You cannot understand how special that realization was to one of my past. It was a gesture of sincere friendship, and what made it all the more important is that it was an unintentional gesture, offered without thought or purpose. Too often in the past, my "friends" would make such gestures as if to prove something, more to themselves than to me. They could feel better about themselves because they could look beyond the obvious differences, such as the color of my skin.

Guenhwyvar never did that. Bruenor never did that. Neither did Catti-brie or Regis. Wulfgar at first despised me, openly and without excuse, simply because I was drow. They were honest, and thus, they were always my friends. But in the days of preparation for war, I saw that sphere of friendship expand many times over. I came to know that the dwarves of Mithral Hall, the men and women of Settlestone, and many, many more, truly accepted me.

That is the honest nature of friendship. That is when it becomes sincere, and not self-serving. So in those days, Drizzt Do'Urden came to understand, once and for all, that he was not of Menzoberranzan.

I threw off the collar of guilt. I smiled.

—Drizzt Do'Urden

BLINGDENSTONE

They were shadows among the shadows, flickering movements that disappeared before the eye could take them in. And there was no sound. Though three hundred dark elves moved in formation, right flank, left flank, center, there was no sound.

They had come to the west of Menzoberranzan, seeking the easier and wider tunnels that would swing them back toward the east and all the way to the surface, to Mithral Hall. Blingdenstone, the city of svirfnebli, whom the drow hated above all others, was not so far away, another benefit of this roundabout course.

Uthegental Armgo paused in one small, sheltered cubby. The tunnels were wide—uncomfortably so. Svirfnebli were tacticians and builders, and in a fight they would depend on formations, perhaps even on war machines, to compete with the more stealthy and individual-minded drow. The widening of these particular tunnels was no accident, Uthegental knew, and no result of nature. This battlefield had long ago been prepared by his enemies.

So where were they? Uthegental had come into their domain with three hundred drow, his group leading an army of eight thousand dark elves and thousands of humanoid slaves. And yet, though Blingdenstone itself could not be more than a twenty minute march from his position—and his scouts were even closer than that—there had been no sign of svirfnebli.

The wild patron of Barrison del'Armgo was not happy. Uthegental liked things predictable, at least as far as enemies were concerned, and had hoped that he and his warriors would have seen some action against the gnomes by now. It was no accident that his group, that he, was at the forefront of the drow army. That had been a concession by Baenre to Mez'Barris, an affirmation of the importance of the Second House. But with that concession came responsibility, which Matron Mez'Barris had promptly dropped on Uthegental's sturdy shoulders. House Barrison del'Armgo needed to come out of this war with high glory, particularly in light of Matron Baenre's incredible display in the destruction of House Oblodra. When this business with Mithral Hall was settled, the rearrangement of the pecking order in Menzoberranzan would likely begin. Interhouse wars seemed unavoidable, with the biggest holes to be filled those ranks directly behind Barrison del'Armgo.

Thus had Matron Mez'Barris promised full fealty to Baenre, in exchange for being personally excused from the expedition. She remained in Menzoberranzan, solidifying her House's position and working closely with Triel Baenre in forming a web of lies and allies to insulate House Baenre from further accusations. Baenre had agreed with Mez'Barris's offer, knowing that she, too, would be vulnerable if all did not go well in Mithral Hall.

With the matron mother of his House back in Menzoberranzan, the glory of House Barrison del'Armgo was Uthegental's to find. The fierce warrior was glad for the task, but he was edgy as well, filled with nervous energy, wanting a battle, any battle, that he might whet his appetite for what was to come, and might wet the end of his wicked trident with the blood of an enemy.

But where were the ugly little svirfnebli? he wondered. The marching plan called for no attack on Blingdenstone proper—not on the initial journey, at least. If there was to be an assault on the gnome city, it would come on the return from Mithral Hall, after the main objective had been realized. Uthegental had been given permission to test svirfneblin defenses, though, and to skirmish with any gnomes he and his warriors found out in the open tunnels.

Uthegental craved that, and had already determined that if he found and tested the gnome defenses and discovered sufficient holes in them, he would take the extra step, hoping to return to Baenre's side with the head of the svirfneblin king on the end of his trident.

All glory for Barrison del'Armgo.

One of the scouts slipped back past the guards, moved right up to the fierce warrior. Her fingers flashed in the silent drow code, explaining to her leader that she had gone closer, much closer, had even seen the stairway that led up to the level of Blingdenstone's massive front gates. But no sign had she seen of the svirfnebli.

It had to be an ambush. Every instinct within the seasoned weapons master told Uthegental that the svirfnebli were lying in wait, in full force. Almost any other dark elf, a race known for caution when dealing with others—mostly because the drow knew they could always win such encounters if they struck at the appropriate time—would have relented. In truth, Uthegental's mission, a scouting expedition, was now complete, and he could return to Matron Baenre with a full report that she would be pleased to hear.

But fierce Uthegental was not like other drow. He was less than relieved, was, in fact boiling with rage.

Take me there, his fingers flashed, to the surprise of the female scout.

You are too valuable, the female's hands replied.

"All of us!" Uthegental roared aloud, his volume surprising every one of the many dark elves around him. But Uthegental wasn't startled, and did not relent. "Send the word along every column," he went on, "to follow my lead to the very gates of Blingdenstone!"

More than a few drow soldiers turned nervous looks to each other. They numbered three hundred, a formidable force, but Blingdenstone held many times that number, and svirfnebli, full of tricks with the stone and often allied with powerful monsters from the Plane of Earth, were not easy foes. Still, not one of the dark elves would argue with Uthegental Armgo, especially since he alone knew what Matron Baenre expected of this point group.

And so they arrived in full, at the stairway and up it they climbed, to the very gates of Blingdenstone—gates that a drow engineer found devilishly trapped, with the entire ceiling above them rigged to fall if they were opened. Uthegental called to a priestess that had been assigned to his group.

You can get one of us past the barrier? his fingers asked her, to which she nodded.

Uthegental's stream of surprises continued when he indicated he would personally enter the svirfneblin city. It was an unheard-of request. No drow leader ever went in first. That's what commoners were for.

But again, who would argue with Uthegental? In truth, the priestess really didn't care if this arrogant male got torn apart. She began her casting at once, a spell that would make Uthegental as insubstantial as a wraith, would make his form melt away into something that could slip through the slightest cracks. When it was done, the brave Uthegental left without hesitation, without bothering to leave instructions in the event that he did not return.

Proud and supremely confident, Uthegental simply did not think that way.

A few minutes later, after passing through the empty guard chambers, crisscrossed with cunningly built trenches and fortifications, Uthegental became only the second drow, after Drizzt Do'Urden, to glance at the rounded, natural houses of the svirfnebli and the winding, unremarkable ways that composed their city. How different Blingdenstone was from Menzoberranzan, built in accord with what the gnomes had found in the natural caverns, rather than sculpted and reformed into an image that a dark elf would consider more pleasing.

Uthegental, who demanded control of everything around him, found the place repulsive. He also found it, this most ancient and hallowed of svirfneblin cities, deserted.

⚔ ⚔ ⚔ ⚔ ⚔

Belwar Dissengulp stared out from the lip of the deep chamber, far to the west of Blingdenstone, and wondered if he had done right in convincing King Schnicktick to abandon the gnomish city. The most honored burrow warden had reasoned that, with magic returned, the drow would surely march for Mithral Hall, and that course, Belwar knew, would take them dangerously close to Blingdenstone.

Though he had little difficulty in convincing his fellows that the dark elves would march, the thought of leaving Blingdenstone, of simply packing up their belongings and deserting their ancient home, had not settled well. For more than two thousand years the gnomes had lived in the ominous shadow of Menzoberranzan, and more than once had they believed the drow would come in full war against them.

This time was different, Belwar reasoned, and he had told them so, his speech full of passion and carrying the weight of his relationship with the renegade drow from that terrible city. Still, Belwar was far from convincing Schnicktick and the others until Councilor Firble piped in on the burrow warden's side.

It was indeed different this time, Firble had told them with all sincerity. This time, the whole of Menzoberranzan would band together, and any attack would not be the ambitious probing of a single House. This time the gnomes, and anyone else unfortunate enough to fall in the path of the drow march, could not depend on interhouse rivalries to save them. Firble had learned of House Oblodra's fall from Jarlaxle. An earth elemental sent secretly under Menzoberranzan and into the Clawrift by svirfneblin priests confirmed it and the utter destruction of the Third House. Thus, when, at their last meeting, Jarlaxle hinted "it would not be wise to harbor Drizzt Do'Urden," Firble, with his understanding of drow ways, reasoned that the dark elves would indeed march for Mithral Hall, in a force unified by the fear of the one who had so utterly crushed the Third House.

And so, on that ominous note, the svirfnebli had left Blingdenstone, and Belwar had played a critical role in the departure. That responsibility weighed heavily on the burrow warden now, made him second-guess the reasoning that had seemed so sound when he had thought danger imminent. Here to the west the tunnels were quiet, and not eerily so, as though enemy dark elves were slipping from shadow to shadow. The tunnels were quiet with peace; the war Belwar had anticipated seemed a thousand miles or a thousand years away.

The other gnomes felt it, too, and Belwar had overheard more than one complaining that the decision to leave Blingdenstone had been, at best, foolish.

Only when the last of the svirfnebli had left the city, when the long caravan had begun its march to the west, had Belwar realized the gravity of the departure, realized the emotional burden. In leaving, the gnomes were admitting to themselves that they were no match for the drow, that they could not protect themselves or their homes from the dark elves. More than a few svirfnebli, Belwar perhaps most among them, were sick about that fact. Their illusions of security, of the strength of their shamans, of their very god figure, had been shaken, without a single drop of spilled svirfneblin blood.

Belwar felt like a coward.

The most honored burrow warden took some comfort in the fact that eyes were still in place in Blingdenstone. A friendly elemental, blended with the stone, had been ordered to wait and watch, and to report back to the svirfneblin shamans who had summoned it. If the dark elves did come in, as Belwar expected, the gnomes would know of it.

But what if they didn't come? Belwar wondered. If he and Firble were wrong and the march did not come, then what loss had the svirfnebli suffered for the sake of caution?

Could any of them ever feel secure in Blingdenstone again?

⚔ ⚔ ⚔ ⚔

Matron Baenre was not pleased at Uthegental's report that the gnomish city was deserted. As sour as her expression was, though, it could not match the open wrath showing on the face of Berg'inyon, at her side. His eyes narrowed dangerously as he considered the powerful patron of the Second House, and Uthegental, seeing a challenge, more than matched that ominous stare.

Baenre understood the source of Berg'inyon's anger, and she, too, was not pleased by the fact that Uthegental had taken it upon himself to enter Blingdenstone. That act reflected clearly the desperation of Mez'Barris. Obviously Mez'Barris felt vulnerable in the shadows of Matron Baenre's display against Oblodra, and thus she had placed a great weight upon Uthegental's broad shoulders.

Uthegental marched for the glory of Barrison del'Armgo, Matron Baenre knew, marched fanatically, along with his force of more than three hundred drow warriors.

To Berg'inyon, that was not a good thing, for he, and not Matron Baenre, was in direct competition with the powerful weapons master.

Matron Baenre considered all the news in light of her son's expression, and in the end, she thought Uthegental's daring a good thing. The competition would push Berg'inyon to excellence. And if he failed, if Uthegental was the one who killed Drizzt Do'Urden—for that was obviously the prize both sought—even if Berg'inyon was killed by Uthegental, then so be it. This march was greater than House Baenre, greater than anyone's personal goals—except, of course, for Matron Baenre's own.

When Mithral Hall was conquered, whatever the cost to her son, she would be in the highest glory of the Spider Queen, and her House would be above the schemes of the others, if all the others combined their forces against her!

"You are dismissed," Baenre said to Uthegental. "Back to the forefront."

The spike-haired weapons master smiled wickedly and bowed, never taking his eyes from Berg'inyon. Then he spun on his heel to leave, but spun again immediately as Baenre addressed him once more.

"And if you chance to come upon the tracks of the fleeing svirfnebli," Baenre said, and she paused, looking from Uthegental to Berg'inyon, "do send an emissary to inform me of the chase."

Berg'inyon's shoulders slumped even as Uthegental's grin, showing those filed, pointy teeth, widened so much that it nearly took in his ears. He bowed again and ran off.

"The svirfnebli are mighty foes," Baenre said offhandedly, aiming the remark at Berg'inyon. "They will kill him and all of his party." She didn't really believe the claim, had made it only for Berg'inyon's sake. In looking at her wise son, though, she realized he didn't believe it either.

"And if not," Baenre said, looking the other way, to Quenthel, who stood by impassively, appearing quite bored, and to Methil, who always seemed quite bored, "the gnomes are not so great a prize." The matron mother's gaze snapped back over Berg'inyon. "We know the prize of this march," she said, her voice a feral snarl. She didn't bother to mention that her ultimate goal and Berg'inyon's goal were not the same.

The effect on the young weapons master was instantaneous. He snapped back to rigid attention, and rode off on his lizard as soon as his mother waved her hand to dismiss him.

Baenre turned to Quenthel. *See that spies are put among Uthegental's soldiers*, her fingers subtly flashed. Baenre paused a moment to consider the fierce weapons master, and to reflect on what he would do if such spies were discovered. *Males*, Baenre added to her daughter, and Quenthel agreed.

Males were expendable.

Sitting alone as her driftdisk floated amidst the army, Matron Baenre turned her thoughts to more important issues. The rivalry of Berg'inyon and Uthegental was of little consequence, as was Uthegental's apparent disregard for proper command. More disturbing was the svirfneblin absence. Might the wicked gnomes be planning an assault on Menzoberranzan even as Baenre and her force marched away?

It was a silly thought, one Matron Baenre quickly dismissed. More than half the dark elves remained in Menzoberranzan, under the watchful eyes of Mez'Barris Armgo, Triel, and Gromph. If the gnomes attacked, they would be utterly destroyed, more to the Spider Queen's glory.

But even as she considered those city defenses, the thought of a conspiracy against her nagged at the edges of Baenre's consciousness.

Triel is loyal and in control, came a telepathic assurance from Methil, who remained not so far away and was reading Baenre's every thought.

Baenre took some comfort in that. Before she had left Menzoberranzan, she had bade Methil to scour her daughter's reactions to her plans, and the illithid had come back with a completely positive report. Triel was not pleased by the decision to go to Mithral Hall. She feared her mother might be overstepping her bounds, but she was convinced, as most likely were all the others, that, in the face of the destruction of House Oblodra, Lolth had sanctioned this war. Thus, Triel would not head a coup for control of House Baenre in her mother's absence, would not, in any way, go against her mother at this time.

Baenre relaxed. All was going according to design, and it was not important that the cowardly gnomes had fled.

All was going even better than design, Baenre decided, for the rivalry between Uthegental and Berg'inyon would provide much entertainment. The possibilities were intriguing. Perhaps if Uthegental killed Drizzt, and killed Berg'inyon in the process, Matron Baenre would force the spike-haired savage into House Baenre to serve as her own weapons master. Mez'Barris would not dare protest, not after Mithral Hall was conquered.

18
UNEASY GATHERINGS

E ven now is Regweld, who shall lead us, meeting with Bruenor, who is king," said a rider, a knight wearing the most unusual of armor. There wasn't a smooth spot on the mail; it was ridged and buckled, with grillwork pointing out at various angles, its purpose to turn aside any blows, to deflect rather than absorb.

The man's fifty comrades—a strange-looking group indeed—were similarly outfitted, which could be readily explained by looking at their unusual pennant. It depicted a stick-man, his hair straight up on end and arms held high, standing atop a house and throwing lightning bolts to the sky—or perhaps he was catching lightning hurled down at him from the clouds—one could not be sure. This was the banner of Longsaddle and these were the Longriders, the soldiers of Longsaddle, a capable, if eccentric, group. They had come into Settlestone this cold and gloomy day, chasing the first flakes of the first snow.

"Regweld shall lead *you*," answered another rider, tall and sure on his saddle, carrying the scars of countless battles. He was more conventionally armored, as were his forty companions, riding under the horse-and-spear banner of Nesmé, the proud frontier town on the edge of the dreaded Trollmoors. "But not *us*. We are the Riders of Nesmé, who follow no lead but our own!"

"Just because you got here first doesn't mean you pick the rules!" whined the Longrider.

"Let us not forget our purpose," intervened a third rider, his horse trotting up, along with two companions, to greet the newest arrivals. When he came closer, the others saw from his angular features, shining golden hair, and similarly colored eyes that he was no man at all, but an elf, though tall for one of his race. "I am Besnell of Silverymoon, come with a hundred soldiers from Lady Alustriel. We shall each find our place when battle is joined, though if there is to be any leader among us, it shall be me, who speaks on behalf of Alustriel."

The man from Nesmé and the man from Longsaddle regarded each other helplessly. Their respective towns, particularly Nesmé, were surely under the shadow of Silverymoon, and their respective rulers would not challenge Alustriel's authority.

"But you are not in Silverymoon," came a roaring reply from Berkthgar, who had been standing in the shadows of a nearby doorway, listening to the argument, almost hoping it would erupt into something more fun than bandied words. "You are in Settlestone, where Berkthgar rules, and in Settlestone, you are ruled by Berkthgar!"

Everyone tensed, particularly the two Silverymoon soldiers flanking Besnell. The elven warrior sat quietly for a moment, eyeing the huge barbarian as Berkthgar, his gigantic sword strapped across his back, steadily and calmly approached. Besnell was not overly proud, and his rank alone in the Silverymoon detachment proved that he never let pride cloud good judgment.

"Well spoken, Berkthgar the Bold," he politely replied. "And true enough." He turned to the other two mounted leaders. "We have come from Silverymoon, and you from Nesmé, and you from Longsaddle, to serve in Berkthgar's cause, and in the cause of Bruenor Battlehammer."

"We came to Bruenor's call," grumbled the Longrider, "not Berkthgar's."

"Would you then take your horse into the dark tunnels beneath Mithral Hall?" reasoned Besnell, who understood from his meetings with Berkthgar and Catti-brie that the dwarves would handle the underground troubles, while the riders would join with the warriors of Settlestone to secure the outlying areas.

"His horse and he might be underground sooner than he expects," Berkthgar piped in, an open threat that shook the Longrider more than a little.

"Enough of this," Besnell was quick to interject. "We have all come together as allies, and allies we shall be, joined in a common cause."

"Joined by fear," the Nesmé soldier replied. "We in Nesmé once met Bruenor's . . ." He paused, looking to the faces of the other leaders, then to his own grim men for support, as he searched for the proper words. "We have met King Bruenor's dark-skinned friend," he said finally, his tone openly derisive. "What good might come from association with evil drow?"

The words had barely left his mouth before Berkthgar was upon him, reaching up to grab him by a crease in his armor and pull him low in the saddle, that he might look right into the barbarian's snarling visage. The nearby Nesmé soldiers had their weapons out and ready, but so, too, did Berkthgar's people, coming out of every stone house and around every corner.

Besnell groaned and the Longriders, every one, shook their heads in dismay.

"If ever again you speak ill of Drizzt Do'Urden," Berkthgar growled, caring nothing of the swords and spears poised not so far away, "you will offer me an interesting choice. Do I cut you in half and leave you dead on the field, or do I bring you in to Drizzt, that he might find the honor of severing your head himself?"

Besnell walked his horse right up to the barbarian and used its heavy press to force Berkthgar back from the stunned Nesmé soldier.

"Drizzt Do'Urden would not kill the man for his words," Besnell said with all confidence, for he had met Drizzt on many occasions during the dark elf's frequent visits to Silverymoon.

Berkthgar knew the elf spoke truly, and so the barbarian leader relented, backing off a few steps.

"Bruenor would kill him," Berkthgar did say, though.

"Agreed," said Besnell. "And many others would take up arms in the dark elf's defense. but as I have said, enough of this. All joined, we are a hundred and ninety calvary, come to aid in the cause." He looked all around as he spoke and seemed taller and more imposing than his elven frame would

normally allow. "A hundred and ninety come to join with Berkthgar and his proud warriors. Rarely have four such groups converged as allies. The Longriders, the Riders of Nesmé, the Knights in Silver, and the warriors of Settlestone, all joined in common cause. If the war does come—and looking at the allies I have discovered this day, I hope it does—our deeds shall be echoed throughout the Realms! And let the drow army beware!"

He had played perfectly on the pride of all of them, and so they took up the cheer together, and the moments of tension were passed. Besnell smiled and nodded as the shouts continued, but he understood that things were not as solid and friendly as they should be. Longsaddle had sent fifty soldiers, plus a handful of wizards, a very great sacrifice from the town that, in truth, had little stake in Bruenor's well-being. The Harpells looked more to the west, to Waterdeep, for trade and alliance, than to the east, and yet they had come to Bruenor's call, including their leader's own daughter.

Silverymoon was equally committed, both by friendship to Bruenor and Drizzt and because Alustriel was wise enough to understand that if the drow army did march to the surface, all the world would be a sadder place. Alustriel had dispatched a hundred knights to Berkthgar, and another hundred rode independently, skirting the eastern foothills below Mithral Hall, covering the more rugged trails that led around Fourthpeak's northern face, to Keeper's Dale in the west. All told, there were two hundred mounted warriors, fully two-fifths of the famed Knights in Silver, a great contingent and a great sacrifice, especially with the first winds of winter blowing cold in the air.

Nesmé's sacrifice was less, Besnell understood, and likely the Riders of Nesmé's commitment would be too. This was the town with the most to lose, except of course for Settlestone, and yet Nesmé had spared barely a tenth of its seasoned garrison. The strained relations between Mithral Hall and Nesmé were no secret, a brewing feud that had begun before Bruenor had ever found his homeland, when the dwarf and his fellow companions had passed near Nesmé. Bruenor and his friends had saved several riders from marauding bog blokes, only to have the riders turn on them when the battle had ended. Because of the color of Drizzt's skin and the reputation of his heritage, Bruenor's party had been turned away, and though the dwarf's outrage had been later tempered somewhat by the fact that soldiers from Nesmé had joined in the retaking of Mithral Hall, relations had remained somewhat strained.

This time the expected opponents were dark elves and no doubt, that fact alone had reminded the wary men of Nesmé of their distrust for Bruenor's closest friend. But at least they had come, and forty were better than none, Besnell told himself. The elf had openly proclaimed Berkthgar the leader of all four groups, and so it would be—though, if and when battle was joined, each contingent would likely fall into its own tactics, hopefully complementing each other—but Besnell saw a role for himself, less obvious, but no less important. He would be the peacemaker. He would keep the factions in line and in harmony.

If the dark elves did come, his job would be much easier, he knew, for in the face of so deadly an enemy, petty grievances would fast be forgotten.

⚔ ⚔ ⚔ ⚔ ⚔

Belwar didn't know whether to feel relief or fear when word came from the spying elemental that the drow, a single drow at least, had indeed gone into Blingdenstone, and that a drow army had marched past the deserted city, finding the tunnels back to the east, the route to Mithral Hall.

The most honored burrow warden sat again in his now customary perch, staring out at the empty tunnels. He thought of Drizzt, a dear friend, and of the place the dark elf now called home. Drizzt had told Belwar of Mithral Hall when he had passed through Blingdenstone on his way to Menzoberranzan several months earlier. How happy Drizzt had been when he spoke of his friends, this dwarf named Bruenor, and the human woman, Catti-brie, who had crossed through Blingdenstone on Drizzt's heels, and had, according to later reports, aided in Drizzt's wild escape from the drow city.

That very escape had facilitated this march, Belwar knew, and yet the gnome remained pleased that his friend had gotten free of Matron Baenre's clutches. Now Drizzt was home, but the dark elves were going to find him.

Belwar recalled the true sadness in Drizzt's lavender eyes when the drow had recounted the loss of one of his surface-found friends. What tears might

Drizzt know soon, the gnome wondered, with a drow army marching to destroy his new home?

"Decisions we have to make," came a voice behind the sturdy gnome. Belwar clapped his mithral "hands" together, more to clear his thoughts than anything else, and turned to face Firble.

One of the good things that had come from all of this confusion was the budding friendship between Firble and Belwar. As two of the older svirfnebli of Blingdenstone, they had known each other, or of each other, a very long time, but only when Belwar's eyes—because of his friendship with Drizzt—had turned to the world outside the gnomish city had Firble truly come into his life. At first the two seemed a complete mismatch, but both had found strength in what the other offered, and a bond had grown between them—though neither had as yet openly admitted it.

"Decisions?"

"The drow have passed," said Firble.

"Likely to return."

Firble nodded. "Obviously," the round-shouldered councilor agreed. "King Schnicktick must decide whether we are to return to Blingdenstone."

The notion hit Belwar like the slap of a cold, wet towel. Return to Blingdenstone? Of course they were to return to their homes! the most honored burrow warden's thoughts screamed out at him. Any other option was too ridiculous to entertain. But as he calmed and considered Firble's grim demeanor, Belwar began to see the truth of it all. The drow would be back, and if they had made a conquest near or at the surface, a conquest of Mithral Hall, as most believed was their intention, then there would likely remain an open route between Menzoberranzan and that distant place, a route that passed too close to Blingdenstone.

"Words, there are, and from many with influence, that we should go farther west, to find a new cavern, a new Blingdenstone," Firble said. From his tone it was obvious the little councilor was not thrilled at that prospect.

"Never," Belwar said unconvincingly.

"King Schnicktick will ask your opinion in this most important matter," Firble said. "Consider it well, Belwar Dissengulp. The lives of us all may hinge on your answer."

A long, quiet moment passed, and Firble gave a curt nod and turned to leave.

"What does Firble say?" Belwar asked before he could scurry off.

The councilor turned slowly, determinedly, staring Belwar straight in the eye. "Firble says there is only one Blingdenstone," he answered with more grit than Belwar had ever heard, or ever expected to hear, from him. "To leave as the drow pass by is one thing, a good thing. To stay out is not so good."

"Worth fighting for are some things," Belwar added.

"Worth dying for?" Firble was quick to put in, and the councilor did turn and leave.

Belwar sat alone with his thoughts for his home and for his friend.

19
IMPROVISING

Catti-brie knew as soon as she saw the dwarf courier's face, his features a mixture of anxiety and battle-lust. She knew, and so she ran off ahead of the messenger, down the winding ways of Mithral Hall, through the Undercity, seeming almost deserted now, the furnaces burning low. Many eyes regarded her, studied the urgency in her stride, and understood her purpose. She knew, and so they all knew.

The dark elves had come.

The dwarves guarding the heavy door leading out of Mithral Hall proper nodded to her as she came through. "Shoot straight, me girl!" one of them yelled at her back, and though she was terribly afraid, though it seemed as if her worst nightmare was about to come true, that brought a smile to her face.

She found Bruenor, Regis beside him, in a wide cavern, the same chamber where the dwarves had defeated a goblin tribe not so long ago. Now the place had been prepared as the dwarf king's command post, the central brain for the defense of the outer and lower tunnels. Nearly all tunnels leading to this chamber from the wilds of the Underdark had been thoroughly trapped or dropped altogether, or were now heavily guarded, leaving the chamber as secure a place as could be found outside Mithral Hall proper.

"Drizzt?" Catti-brie asked.

Bruenor looked across the cavern, to a large tunnel exiting into the deeper regions. "Out there," he said, "with the cat."

Catti-brie looked around. The preparations had been made; everything had been set into place as well as possible in the time allowed. Not so far away, Stumpet Rakingclaw and her fellow clerics crouched and knelt on the floor, lining up and sorting dozens of small potion bottles and preparing bandages, blankets, and herbal salves for the wounded. Catti-brie winced, for she knew that all those bandages and more would be needed before this was finished.

To the side of the clerics, three of the Harpells—Harkle, Bidderdoo, and Bella don DelRoy—conferred over a small, round table covered with dozens of maps and other parchments.

Bella looked up and motioned to Bruenor, and the dwarf king rushed to her side.

"Are we to sit and wait?" Catti-brie asked Regis.

"For the time," the halfling answered. "But soon Bruenor and I will lead a group out, along with one of the Harpells, to rendezvous with Drizzt and Pwent in Tunult's Cavern. I'm sure Bruenor means for you to come with us."

"Let him try to stop me," Catti-brie muttered under her breath. She silently considered the rendezvous. Tunult's Cavern was the largest chamber outside Mithral Hall, and if they were going to meet Drizzt there, instead of some out-of-the-way place—and if the dark elves were indeed in the tunnels near Mithral Hall—then the anticipated battle would come soon. Catti-brie took a deep breath and took up Taulmaril, her magical bow. She tested its pull, then checked her quiver to make sure it was full, even though the enchantment of the quiver ensured that it was always full.

We are ready, came a thought in her mind, a thought imparted by Khazid'hea, she knew. Catti-brie took comfort in her newest companion. She trusted the sword now, knew that it and she were of like mind. And they were indeed ready. They all were.

Still, when Bruenor and Bidderdoo walked away from the other Harpells, the dwarf motioning to his personal escorts and Regis and Catti-brie, the young woman's heart skipped a few beats.

⚔ ⚔ ⚔ ⚔ ⚔

The Gutbuster Brigade rambled and jostled, bouncing off walls and each other. Drow in the tunnels! They had spotted drow in the tunnels, and now they needed a catch or a kill.

To the few dark elves who were indeed so close to Mithral Hall, forward scouts for the wave that would follow, the thunder of Pwent's minions seemed almost deafening. The drow were a quiet race, as quiet as the Under-dark itself, and the bustle of surface-dwelling dwarves made them think that a thousand fierce warriors were giving chase. So the dark elves fell back, stretched their lines thin, with the more-important females taking the lead in the retreat and the males forced to hold the line and delay the enemy.

First contact was made in a narrow but high tunnel. The Gutbusters came in hard and fast from the east, and three drow, levitating among the stalactites, fired hand-crossbows, putting poison-tipped darts into Pwent and the two others flanking him in the front rank.

"What!" the battlerager roared, as did his companions, surprised by the sudden sting. The ever wary Pwent, cunning and comprehending, looked around, then he and the other two fell to the floor.

With a scream of surprise, the rest of the Gutbusters turned around and fled, not even thinking to recover their fallen comrades.

Kill two. Take one back for questioning, the most important of the three dark elves signaled as he and his companions began floating back to the floor.

They touched down lightly and drew out fine swords.

Up scrambled the three battleragers, their little legs pumping under them in a wild flurry. No poison, not even the famed drow sleeping poison, could get through the wicked concoctions this group had recently imbibed. Gutbuster was a drink, not just a brigade, and if a dwarf could survive the drink itself, he wouldn't have to worry much about being poisoned—or being cold—for some time.

Closest to the dark elves, Pwent lowered his head, with its long helmet spike, and impaled one elf through the chest, blasting through the fine mesh of drow armor easily and brutally.

The second drow managed to deflect the next battlerager's charge, turning the helmet spike aside with both his swords. But a mailed fist, the knuckles devilishly spiked with barbed points, caught the drow under the chin and

tore a gaping hole in his throat. Fighting for breath, the drow managed to score two nasty hits on his opponent's back, but those two strikes did little in the face of the flurry launched by the wild-eyed dwarf.

Only the third drow survived the initial assault. He leaped high in the air, enacting his levitation spell once more, and got just over the remaining dwarf's barreling charge—mostly because the dwarf slipped on the slick blood of Thibbledorf Pwent's quick kill.

Up went the drow, into the stalactite tangle, disappearing from sight.

Pwent straightened, shaking free of the dead drow. "That way!" he roared, pointing farther along the corridor. "Find an open area o' ceiling and take up a watch! We're not to let this one get away!"

Around the eastern bend came the rest of the Gutbusters, whooping and shouting, their armor clattering, the many creases and points on each suit grating and squealing like fingernails on slate.

"Take to lookin'!" Pwent bellowed, indicating the ceiling, and all the dwarves bobbed about eagerly.

One screeched, taking a hand-crossbow hit squarely in the face, but that shout of pain became a cry of joy, for the dwarf had only to back-track the angle to spot the floating drow. Immediately a globe of darkness engulfed that area of the stalactites, but the dwarves now knew where to find him.

"Lariat!" Pwent bellowed, and another dwarf pulled a rope from his belt and scrambled over to the battlerager. The end of the rope was looped and securely tied in a slip knot, and so the dwarf, misunderstanding Pwent's intent, put the lasso twirling over his head and looked to the darkened area, trying to discern his best shot.

Pwent grabbed him by the wrist and held fast, sending the rope limply to the floor. "Battlerager lariat," Pwent explained.

Other dwarves crowded around, not knowing what their leader had in mind. Smiles widened on every face as Pwent slipped the loop over his foot, tightened it around his ankle, and informed the others that it would take more than one of them to get this drow-catcher flying.

Every eager dwarf grabbed the rope and began tugging wildly, doing no more than to knock Pwent from his feet. Gradually, sobered by the threats of the vicious battlerager commander, they managed to find a rhythm, and soon had Pwent skipping around the floor.

Then they had him up in the air, flying wildly, round and round. But too much slack was given the rope, and Pwent scraped hard against one of the corridor walls, his helmet spike throwing a line of bright sparks.

This group learned fast, though—considering that they were dwarves who spent their days running headlong into steel-reinforced doors—and they soon had the timing of the spin and the length of the rope perfect.

Two turns, five turns, and off flew the battlerager, up into the air, to crash among the stalactites. Pwent grabbed onto one momentarily, but it broke away from the ceiling and down the dwarf and stone tumbled.

Pwent hit hard, then bounced right back to his feet.

"One less barrier to our enemy!" one dwarf roared, and before the dazed Pwent could protest, the others cheered and tugged, bringing the battlerager lariat to bear once more.

Up flew Pwent, to similar, painful results, then a third time, then a fourth, which proved the charm, for the poor drow, blind to the scene, finally dared to come out into the open, edging his way to the west.

He sensed the living lariat coming and managed to scramble behind a long, thin stalactite, but that hardly mattered, for Pwent took the stone out cleanly, wrapped his arms around it, and around the drow behind it, and drow, dwarf, and stone fell together, crashing hard to the floor. Before the drow could recover, half the brigade had fallen over him, battering him into unconsciousness.

It took them another five minutes to get the semiconscious Pwent to let go of the victim.

They were up and moving, Pwent included, soon after, having tied the drow, ankles and wrists to a long pole, supported on the shoulders of two of the group. They hadn't even cleared the corridor, though, when the dwarves farthest to the west, the two Pwent had sent to watch, took up a cry of "Drow!" and spun around at the ready.

Into the passage came a lone, trotting dark elf, and before Pwent could yell out "Not that one!" the two dwarves lowered their heads and roared in.

In a split second, the dark elf cut left, back to the right, spun a complete circuit to the right, then went wide around the end, and the two Gutbusters stumbled and slammed hard into the wall. They realized their foolishness when the great panther came by an instant later, following her drow companion.

Drizzt was back by the dwarves' side, helping them to their feet. "Run on," he whispered, and they paused at the warning long enough to hear the rumble of a not-so-distant charge.

Misunderstanding, the Gutbusters smiled widely and prepared to continue their own charge to the west, headlong into the approaching force, but Drizzt held them firmly.

"Our enemies are upon us in great numbers," he said. "You will get your fight, more than you ever hoped for, but not here."

By the time Drizzt, the two dwarves, and the panther caught up to Pwent, the noise of the coming army was clearly evident.

"I thought ye said the damned drow moved silent," Pwent remarked, double-stepping beside the swift ranger.

"Not drow," Drizzt replied. "Kobolds and goblins."

Pwent skidded to an abrupt halt. "We're runnin' from stinkin' kobolds?" he asked.

"Thousands of stinking kobolds," Drizzt replied evenly, "and bigger monsters, likely with thousands of drow behind them."

"Oh," answered the battlerager, suddenly out of bluster.

In the familiar tunnels, Drizzt and the Gutbusters had no trouble keeping ahead of the rushing army. Drizzt took no detours this time, but ran straight to the east, past the tunnels the dwarves had rigged to fall.

"Run on," the drow ordered the assigned trap-springers, a handful of dwarves standing ready beside cranks that would release the ropes supporting the tunnel structure. Each of them in turn stared blankly at the surprising command.

"They're coming," one remarked, for that is exactly why these dwarves were out in the tunnels.

"All you will catch is kobolds," Drizzt, understanding the drow tactics, informed them. "Run on, and let us see if we cannot catch a few drow as well."

"But none'll be here to spring the traps!" more than one dwarf, Pwent among them, piped in.

Drizzt's wicked grin was convincing, so the dwarves, who had learned many times to trust the ranger, shrugged and fell in line with the retreating Gutbusters.

"Where're we runnin' to?" Pwent wanted to know.

"Another hundred strides," Drizzt informed him. "Tunult's Cavern, where you will get your fight."

"Promises, promises," muttered the fierce Pwent.

Tunult's Cavern, the most open area this side of Mithral Hall, was really a series of seven caverns connected by wide, arching tunnels. Nowhere was the ground even; some chambers sat higher than others, and more than one deep fissure ran across the floors.

Here waited Bruenor and his escorts, along with nearly a thousand of Mithral Hall's finest fighters. The original plan had called for Tunult's Cavern to be set up as an outward command post, used as a send-off point to the remaining, though less direct, tunnels after the drow advance had been stopped cold by the dropped stone.

Drizzt had altered that plan, and he rushed to Bruenor's side, conferring with the dwarf king, and with Bidderdoo Harpell, a wizard that the drow was surely relieved to find.

"Ye gave up the trap-springing positions!" Bruenor bellowed at the ranger as soon as he understood that the tunnels beyond were still intact.

"Not so," Drizzt replied with all confidence. Even as his gaze led Bruenor's toward the eastern tunnel, the first of the kobold ranks rushed in, pouring like water behind a breaking dam into the waiting dwarves. "I merely got the fodder out of the way."

20

The Battle of Tunult's Cavern

The confusion was immediate and complete, kobolds swarming in by the dozens, and tough dwarves forming into tight battle groups and rushing fast to meet them.

Catti-brie put her magical bow up and fired arrow after arrow, aiming for the main entrance. Lightning flashed with each shot as the enchanted bolt sped off, crackling and sparking every time it skipped off a wall. Kobolds went down in a line, one arrow often killing several, but it hardly seemed to matter, so great was the invading throng.

Guenhwyvar leaped away, Drizzt quick-stepping behind. A score of kobolds had somehow wriggled past the initial fights and were bearing down on Bruenor's position. A shot from Catti-brie felled one; Guenhwyvar's plunge scattered the rest; and Drizzt, moving quicker than ever, slipped in, stabbed one, pivoted and spun to the left, launching the blue-glowing Twinkle against the attempted parry of another. Had Twinkle been a straight blade, the kobold's small sword would have deflected it high, but Drizzt deftly turned the curving weapon over in his hand and slightly altered the angle of his attack. Twinkle rolled over the kobold's sword and dived into its chest.

The drow had never stopped his run and now skittered back to the right and slid to one knee. Across came Twinkle, slapping against one kobold blade, driving it hard into a second. Stronger than both the creatures combined, and

with a better angle, Drizzt forced their swords and their defense high, and his second scimitar slashed across the other way, disemboweling one and taking the legs out from under the other.

"Damn drow's stealing all the fun," Bruenor muttered, running to catch up to the fray. Between Drizzt, the panther, and Catti-brie's continuing barrage, few of the twenty kobolds still stood by the time he got there, and those few had turned in full flight.

"Plenty more to kill," Drizzt said into Bruenor's scowl, recognizing the sour look.

A line of silver-streaking arrow cut between them as soon as the words had left the drow's mouth. When the spots cleared from before their eyes, the two turned and regarded the scorched and dead kobolds taken down by Catti-brie's latest shot.

Then she, too, was beside them, Khazid'hea in hand, and Regis, holding the little mace Bruenor had long ago forged for him, was beside her. Catti-brie shrugged as her friends regarded the change in weapon, and looking around, they understood her tactics. With more kobolds pouring in, and more dwarves coming out of the other chambers to meet the charge, it was simply too confusing and congested for the woman to safely continue with her bow.

"Run on," Catti-brie said, a wistful smile crossing her fair features.

Drizzt returned the look, and Bruenor, even Regis, had a sparkle in his eye. Suddenly it seemed like old times.

Guenhwyvar led their charge, Bruenor fighting hard to keep close to the panther's tail. Catti-brie and Regis flanked the dwarf, and Drizzt, speeding and spinning, flanked the group, first on the left, then on the right, seeming to be wherever battle was joined, running too fast to be believed.

⚔ ⚔ ⚔ ⚔ ⚔

Bidderdoo Harpell knew he had erred. Drizzt had asked him to get to the door, to wait for the first drow to show themselves inside the cavern and launch a fireball back down the tunnel, where the flames would burn through the supporting ropes and drop the stone.

"Not a difficult task," Bidderdoo had assured Drizzt, and so it should not have been. The wizard had memorized a spell that could put him in position, and knew others to keep him safely hidden until the blast was complete. So when all around him had run off to join in the fracas, they had gone reassured that the traps would be sprung, that the tunnels would be dropped, and that the tide of enemies would be stemmed.

Something went wrong. Bidderdoo had begun casting the spell to get him to the tunnel entrance, had even outlined the extradimensional portal that would reopen at the desired spot, but then the wizard had seen a group of kobolds, and they had seen him. This was not hard to do, for Bidderdoo, a human and not blessed with sight that could extend into the infrared spectrum, carried a shining gemstone. Kobolds were not stupid creatures, not when it came to battle, and they recognized this seemingly out-of-place human for what he was. Even the most inexperienced of kobold fighters understood the value of getting to a wizard, of forcing a dangerous spellcaster into melee combat, keeping his hands tied up with weapons rather than often explosive components.

Still, Bidderdoo could have beaten their charge, could have stepped through the dimensions to get to his appointed position.

For seven years, until the Time of Troubles, Bidderdoo Harpell had lived with the effects of a potion gone awry, had lived as the Harpell family dog. When magic went crazy, Bidderdoo had reverted to his human form—long enough, at least, to get the necessary ingredients together to counteract the wild potion. Soon after, Bidderdoo had gone back to his flea-bitten self, but he had helped his family find the means to get him out of the enchantment. A great debate had followed in the Ivy Mansion as to whether they should "cure" Bidderdoo or not. It seemed that many of the Harpells had grown quite fond of the dog, more so than they had ever loved Bidderdoo as a human.

Bidderdoo had even served as Harkle's seeing-eye dog on a long stretch of the journey to Mithral Hall, when Harkle had no eyes.

But then magic had straightened out, and the debate became moot, for the enchantment had simply gone away.

Or had it? Bidderdoo had held no doubts about the integrity of his cure until this very moment, until he saw the kobolds approaching. His upper lip

curled back in an open snarl. He felt the hair on the back of his neck bristling and felt his tailbone tighten—if he still had a tail, it would be straight out behind him!

He started down into a crouch, and noticed only then that he had not paws, but hands, hands that held no weapons. He groaned, for the kobolds were only ten feet away.

The wizard went for a spell instead. He put the tips of his thumbs together, hands out wide to each side, and chanted frantically.

The kobolds came in, straight ahead and flanking, and the closest of them had a sword high for a strike.

Bidderdoo's hands erupted in flame, jets of scorching, searing fire, arcing out in a semicircle.

Half a dozen kobolds lay dead, and several others blinked in amazement through singed eyelashes.

"Hah!" Bidderdoo cried, and snapped his fingers.

The kobolds blinked again and charged, and Bidderdoo had no spells quick enough to stop them.

⚔ ⚔ ⚔ ⚔ ⚔

At first the kobolds and goblins seemed a swarming, confused mass, and so it remained for many of the undisciplined brawlers. But several groups had trained for war extensively in the caverns beneath the complex of House Oblodra. One of these, fifty strong, formed into a tight wedge, three large kobolds at the tip and a tight line running back and wide to each side.

They entered the main chamber, avoided combat enough to form up, and headed straight to the left, toward the looming entrance of one of the side caverns. Mostly the dwarves avoided them, with so many other easier kills available, and the kobold group almost got to the side chamber unscathed.

Coming out of that chamber, though, was a group of a dozen dwarves. The bearded warriors hooted and roared and came on fiercely, but the kobold formation did not waver, worked to perfection as it split the dwarven line almost exactly in half, then widened the gap with the lead kobolds pressing to the very entrance of the side chamber. A couple of kobolds went down in that charge, and one dwarf died, but the kobold ranks tightened again immediately, and those dwarves caught along the inside line, caught between the kobolds and the main cavern's low sloping wall, found themselves in dire straights indeed.

Across the way, the "free" half of the dwarven group realized their error, that they had taken the kobolds too lightly and had not expected such intricate tactics. Their kin would be lost, and there was nothing they could do to get through this surprisingly tight, disciplined formation—made even tighter by the fact that, in going near the wall, the kobolds went under some low-hanging stalactites.

The dwarves attacked fiercely anyway, spurred on by the cries of their apparently doomed companions.

Guenhwyvar was low to the ground, low enough to skitter under any stalactites. The panther hit the back of the kobold formation in full stride, blasting two kobolds away and running over a third, claws digging in for a better hold as the cat crossed over.

Drizzt came in behind, sliding to one knee again and killing two kobolds in the first attack routine. Beside him charged Regis, no taller than a kobold and fighting straight up and even against one.

With his great, sweeping style of axe-fighting, Bruenor found the tight quarters uncomfortable at best. Even worse off was Catti-brie, not as agile or quick as Drizzt. If she went down to one knee, as had the drow, she would be at a huge disadvantage indeed.

But standing straight, a stalactite in her face, she wasn't much better off.

Khazid'hea gave her the answer.

It went against every instinct the woman had, was contrary to everything Bruenor—who had spent much of his life repairing damaged weapons—had taught her about fighting. but hardly thinking, Catti-brie clasped her sword hilt in both hands and brought the magnificent weapon streaking straight across, up high.

Khazid'hea's red line flashed angrily as the sword connected on the hanging stone. Catti-brie's momentum slowed, but only slightly, for Cutter lived up to its name, shearing through the rock. Catti-brie jerked to the side as the sword exited the stalactite, and she would have been vulnerable in that instant—except that the two kobolds in formation right before her were suddenly more concerned that the sky was falling.

One got crushed under the stalactite, and the other's death was just as quick, as Bruenor, seeing the opening, rushed in with an overhead chop that nearly took the wretched thing in half.

Those dwarves that had been separated on the outside rank took heart at the arrival of so powerful a group, and they pressed the kobold line fiercely, calling out to their trapped companions to "hold fast!" and promising that help would soon arrive.

Regis hated to fight, at least when his opponent could see him coming. He was needed now, though. He knew that, and would not shirk his responsibilities. Beside him, Drizzt fought from his knees. How could the halfling, who would have to get up on his tiptoes to bang his head on a stalactite, justify standing behind his drow friend this time?

Both hands on his mace handle, Regis went in fiercely. He smiled as he actually scored a hit, the well-forged weapon crumbling a kobold arm.

Even as that opponent fell away, though, another squeezed in and struck, its sword catching Regis under his upraised arm. Only fine dwarven armor saved him—he made a note to buy Buster Bracer a few large mugs of mead if he ever got out of this alive.

Tough was the dwarven armor, but the kobold's head was not as tough, as the halfling's mace proved a moment later.

"Well done," Drizzt congratulated, his battle ebbing enough for him to witness the halfling's strike.

Regis tried to smile, but winced instead at the pain of his bruised ribs.

Drizzt noted the look and skittered across in front of Regis, meeting the charge as the kobold formation shifted to compensate for the widening breach. The drow's scimitars went into a wild dance, slashing and chopping, often banging against the low-hanging stalactites, throwing sparks, but more often connecting on kobolds.

To the side, Catti-brie and Bruenor had formed up into an impromptu alliance, Bruenor holding back the enemy, while Catti-brie and Cutter continued to clear a higher path, dropping the hanging stones one at a time.

Across the way, though, the dwarves remained sorely pressed, with two down and the other five taking many hits. None of the friends could get to them in time, they knew, none could cross through the tight formation.

None except Guenhwyvar.

Flying like a black arrow, the panther bored on, running down kobold after kobold, shrugging off many wicked strikes. Blood streamed from the panther's flanks, but Guenhwyvar would not be deterred. She got to the dwarves and bolstered their line, and their cheer at her appearance was of pure delight and salvation.

A song on their lips, the dwarves fought on, the panther fought on, and the kobolds could not finish the task. With the press across the way, the formation soon crumbled, and the dwarven group was reunited, that the wounded could be taken from the cavern.

Drizzt and Catti-brie's concern for Guenhwyvar was stolen by the panther's roar, and its flight, as Guenhwyvar led the five friends off to the next place where they would be needed most.

⚔ ⚔ ⚔ ⚔ ⚔

Bidderdoo closed his eyes, wondering what mysteries death would reveal. He hoped there would be some, at least.

He heard a roar, then a clash of steel in front of him. Then came a grunt, and the sickening thud of a torn body slapping against the hard floor.

They are fighting over who gets to kill me, the mage thought.

More roars—dwarven roars!—and more grunts; more torn bodies falling to the stone.

Bidderdoo opened his eyes to see the kobold ranks decimated, to see a handful of the dirtiest, smelliest dwarves imaginable hopping up and down around him, pointing this way and that, as they of the Gutbuster Brigade tried to figure out where they might next cause the most havoc.

Bidderdoo took a moment to regard the kobolds, a dozen corpses that had been more than killed. "Shredded," he whispered, and he nodded, deciding that was a better word.

"Ye're all right now," said one of the dwarves—Bidderdoo thought he had heard this one's name as Thibbledorf Pwent or some such thing—not that anyone named Bidderdoo could toss insults regarding names. "And me and me own're off!" the wild battlerager huffed.

Bidderdoo nodded, then realized he still had a serious problem. He had only prepared for one spell that could open such a dimensional door, and that one was wasted, the enchantment expired as he had battled with the kobolds.

"Wait!" he screamed at Pwent, and he surprised himself, and the dwarf, for along with his words came out a caninelike yelp.

Pwent regarded the Harpell curiously. He hopped up right before Bidderdoo and cocked his head to the side, a movement exaggerated by the tilting helmet spike.

"Wait. Pray, do not run off, good and noble dwarf," Bidderdoo said sweetly, needing assistance.

Pwent looked around and behind, as if trying to figure out who this mage was talking to. The other Gutbusters were similarly confused, some standing and staring blankly, scratching their heads.

Pwent poked a stubby, dirty finger into his own chest, his expression showing that he hardly considered himself "good and noble."

"Do not leave me," Bidderdoo pleaded.

"Ye're still alive," Pwent countered. "And there's not much for killin' over here." As though that were explanation enough, the battlerager spun and took a stride away.

"But I've failed!" Bidderdoo wailed, and a howl escaped his lips at the end of the sentence.

"Ye've fail-doooo?" Pwent asked.

"Oh, we are all do-oooo-omed!" the howling mage went on dramatically. "It's too-oooo far."

All the battleragers were around Bidderdoo by this point, intrigued by the strange accent, or whatever it was. The closest enemies, a band of goblins, could have attacked then, but none wanted to go anywhere near this wild troupe, a point made especially clear with the last group of kobolds lying in bloody pieces around the area.

"Ye better be quick and to the point," Pwent, anxious to kill again, barked at Bidderdoo.

"Oooo."

"And stop the damned howlin'!" the battlerager demanded.

In truth, poor Bidderdoo wasn't howling on purpose. In the stress of the situation, the mage who had lived so long as a dog was unintentionally recalling the experience, discovering once more those primal canine instincts. He took a deep breath and pointedly reminded himself he was a man, not a dog. "I must get to the tunnel entrance," he said without a howl, yip, or yelp. "The drow ranger bade me to send a spell down the corridor."

"I'm not for carin' for wizard stuff," Pwent interrupted, and turned away once more.

"Are ye for droppin' the stinkin' tunnel on the stinkin' drow's 'eads?" Bidderdoo asked in his best battlerager imitation.

"Bah!" Pwent snorted, and all the dwarven heads were bobbing eagerly around him. "Me and me own'll get ye there!"

Bidderdoo took care to keep his visage stern, but silently thought himself quite clever for appealing to the wild dwarves' hunger for carnage.

In the blink of a dog's eye, Bidderdoo was swept up in the tide of running Gutbusters. The wizard suggested a roundabout route, skirting the left-hand, or northern, side of the cavern, where the fighting had become less intense.

Silly mage.

The Gutbuster Brigade ran straight through, ran down kobolds and the larger goblins who had come in behind the kobold ranks. They almost buried a couple of dwarves who weren't quick enough in diving aside; they bounced off stalagmites, ricocheting and rolling on. Before Bidderdoo could even begin to protest the tactic, he found himself nearing the appointed spot, the entrance to the tunnel.

He spent a brief moment wondering which was faster, a spell opening a dimensional door or a handful of battle-hungry battleragers. He even entertained the creation of a new spell, *Battlerager Escort,* but he shook that notion away as a more immediate problem, a pair of huge, bull-headed minotaurs and a dark elf behind them, entered the cavern.

"Defensive posture!" cried Bidderdoo. "You must hold them off! Defensive posture!"

Silly mage.

The closest two Gutbusters flew headlong, diving into the feet of the towering, eight-foot monsters. Before they even realized what had hit them, the minotaurs were falling forward. Neither made it unobstructed to the ground, though, as Pwent and another wild-eyed dwarf roared in, butting the minotaurs head-to-head.

A globe of darkness appeared behind the tumble, and the drow was nowhere to be seen.

Bidderdoo wisely began his spellcasting. The drow were here! Just as Drizzt had figured, the dark elves were coming in behind the kobold fodder. If he could get the fireball away now, if he could drop the tunnel . . .

He had to force the words through a guttural, instinctual growl coming from somewhere deep in his throat. He had the urge to join the Gutbusters, who were all clamoring over the fallen minotaurs, taking the brutes apart mercilessly. He had the urge to join in the feast.

"The feast?" he asked aloud.

Bidderdoo shook his head and began again, concentrating on the spell. Apparently hearing the wizard's rhythmic cadence, the drow came out of the darkness, hand-crossbow up and ready.

Bidderdoo closed his eyes, forced the words to flow as fast as possible. He felt the sting of the dart, right in the belly, but his concentration was complete and he did not flinch, did not interrupt the spell.

His legs went weak under him. He heard the drow coming, imagined a shining sword poised for a killing strike.

Bidderdoo's concentration held. He completed the dweomer, and a small, glowing ball of fire leaped out from his hand, soared through the darkness beyond, down the tunnel.

Bidderdoo teetered with weakness. He opened his eyes, but the cavern around him was blurry and wavering. Then he fell backward, felt as though the floor were rushing up to swallow him.

Somewhere in the back of his mind he expected to hit the stone hard, but then the fireball went off.

Then the tunnel fell.

21

ONE FOR THE GOOD GUYS

A heavy burden weighed on the most honored burrow warden's strong shoulders, but Belwar did not stoop as he marched through the long, winding tunnels. He had made the decision with a clear mind and definite purpose, and he simply refused to second-guess himself all the way to Mithral Hall.

His opponents in the debate had argued that Belwar was motivated by personal friendship, not the best interests of the svirfnebli. Firble had learned that Drizzt Do'Urden, Belwar's drow friend, had escaped Menzoberranzan, and the drow march, by all indications, was straight for Mithral Hall, no doubt motivated in part by Lolth's proclaimed hatred of the renegade.

Would Belwar lead Blingdenstone to war, then, for the sake of a single drow?

In the end, that vicious argument had been settled not by Belwar, but by Firble, another of the oldest svirfnebli, another of those who had felt the pain most keenly when Blingdenstone had been left behind.

"A clear choice we have," Firble had said. "Go now and see if we can aid the enemies of the dark elves, or a new home we must find, for the drow will surely return, and if we stand, we stand alone."

It was a terrible, difficult decision for the council and for King Schnicktick. If they followed the dark elves and found their suspicions confirmed, found

a war on the surface, could they even count on the alliance of the surface dwarves and the humans, races the deep gnomes did not know?

Belwar assured them they could. With all his heart, the most honored burrow warden believed that Drizzt, and any friends Drizzt had made, would not let him down. And Firble, who knew the outside world so well—but was, by his own admission, somewhat ignorant of the surface—agreed with Belwar, simply on the logic that any race, even not-so-intelligent goblins, would welcome allies against the dark elves.

So Schnicktick and the council had finally agreed, but like every other decision of the ultimately conservative svirfnebli, they would go only so far. Belwar could march in pursuit of the drow, and Firble with him, along with any gnomes who volunteered. They were scouts, Schnicktick had emphasized, and no marching army. The svirfneblin king and all those who had opposed Belwar's reasoning were surprised to find how many volunteered for the long, dangerous march. So many, in fact, that Schnicktick, for the simple sake of the city operation, had to limit the number to fifteen score.

Belwar knew why the other svirfnebli had come, and knew the truth of his own decision. If the dark elves went to the surface and overwhelmed Mithral Hall, they would not allow the gnomes back into Blingdenstone. Menzoberranzan did not conquer, then leave. No, it would enslave the dwarves and work the mines as its own, then pity Blingdenstone, for the svirfneblin city would be too close to the easiest routes to the conquered land.

So though all of these svirfnebli, Belwar and Firble included, were marching farther from Blingdenstone than they had ever gone before, they knew that they were, in effect, fighting for their homeland.

Belwar would not second-guess that decision, and keeping that in mind, his burden was lessened.

⚔ ⚔ ⚔ ⚔ ⚔

Bidderdoo put the fireball far down the tunnel, but the narrow ways could not contain the sheer volume of the blast. A line of fire rushed out of the tunnel, back into the cavern, like the breath of an angry red dragon, and Bidderdoo's own clothes lit up. The mage screamed—as did every dwarf and kobold near him, as did the next line of minotaurs, rushing down for the cavern, as did the skulking dark elves behind them.

In the moment of the wizard's fireball, all of them screamed, and just as quickly, the cries went away, extinguished, overwhelmed, by hundreds of tons of dropping stone.

Again the backlash swept into the cavern, a blast so strong that the gust of it blew away the fires licking at Bidderdoo's robes. He was flying suddenly, as were all those near him, flying and dazed, pelted with stone, and extremely lucky, for none of the dropping stalactites or the heavy stone displaced in the cavern squashed him.

The ground trembled and bucked. One of the cavern walls buckled, and one of the side chambers collapsed. Then it was done, and the tunnel was gone, just gone, as though it had never been there, and the chamber that had been named for the dwarf Tunult seemed much smaller.

Bidderdoo pulled himself up from the piled dust and debris shakily and brushed the dirt from his glowing gemstone. With all the dust in the air, the light from the enchanted stone seemed meager indeed. The wizard looked at himself, seeing more skin than clothing, seeing dozens of bruises and bright red on one arm, under the clinging dust, where the fires had gotten to his skin.

A helmet spike, bent slightly to the side, protruded from a pile not far away. Bidderdoo was about to speak a lament for the battlerager, who had gotten him to the spot, but Pwent suddenly burst up from the dust, spitting pebbles and smiling crazily.

"Well done!" the battlerager roared. "Do it again!"

Bidderdoo started to respond, but then he swooned, the insidious drow poison defeating the momentary jolt of adrenaline. The next thing the unfortunate wizard knew, Pwent was holding him up and he was gagging on the most foul-tasting concoction ever brewed. Foul but effective, for Bidderdoo's grogginess was no more.

"Gutbuster!" Pwent roared, patting the trusty flask on his broad belt.

As the dust settled, the bodies stirred, one by one. To a dwarf, the Gutbuster Brigade, tougher than the stone, remained, and the few kobolds that had survived were cut down before they could plead.

The way the cavern had collapsed, with the nearest side chamber gone, and the wall opposite that having buckled, this small group found itself cut off from the main force. They weren't trapped, though, for one narrow passage led to the left, back toward the heart of Tunult's Cavern. The fighting in there had resumed, so it seemed from the ring of metal and the calls of both dwarves and kobolds.

Unexpectedly, Thibbledorf Pwent did not lead his force headlong into the fray. The passage was narrow at this end, and seemed to narrow even more just a short way in, so much so that Pwent didn't even think they could squeeze through. Also, the battlerager spotted something over Bidderdoo's shoulder, a deep crack in the wall to the side of the dropped tunnel. As he neared the spot, Pwent felt the stiff breeze rushing out of the crack, as the air pressure in the tunnels beyond adjusted to the catastrophe.

Pwent hooted and slammed the wall below the crack with all his strength. The loose stone gave way and fell in, revealing a passageway angling into the deeper corridors beyond.

"We should go back and report to King Bruenor," Bidderdoo reasoned, "or go as far as the tunnel takes us, to let them know we are in here, that they might dig us out."

Pwent snorted. "Wouldn't be much at scoutin' if we let this tunnel pass," he argued. "If the drow find it, they'll be back quicker than Bruenor's expectin'. Now that's a report worth givin'!"

In truth, it was difficult for the outrageous dwarven warrior to ignore those tempting sounds of battle, but Pwent found his heart seeking the promise of greater enemies, of drow and minotaurs, in the open corridors the other way.

"And if we get stuck in that tunnel there," Pwent continued, pointing back toward what remained of Tunult's Cavern, "the damned drow'll walk right up our backs!"

The Gutbuster Brigade formed up behind their leader, but Bidderdoo shook his head and squeezed into the passage. His worst fears were quickly realized, for it did indeed narrow, and he could not get near the open area beyond, where the fighting continued, could not even get close enough to hope to attract attention above the tumult of battle.

Perhaps he had a spell that would aid him, Bidderdoo reasoned, and he reached into an impossibly deep pocket to retrieve his treasured spellbook. He pulled out a lump of ruffled pages, smeared and singed, many with ink blotched from the intense heat. The glue and stitches in the binding, too, had melted, and when Bidderdoo held the mess up, it fell apart.

The wizard, breathing hard suddenly, feeling as if the world were closing in on him, gathered together as many of the parchments as he could and scrambled back out of the passageway, to find, to his surprise and relief, Pwent and the others still waiting for him.

"Figgered ye'd change yer mind," the battlerager remarked, and he led the Gutbuster Brigade, plus one, away.

ⅩⅩⅩⅩⅩ

Fifty drow and an entire minotaur grouping, Quenthel Baenre's hands flashed, and from the sharp, jerking movements, her mother knew she was outraged.

Fool, Matron Baenre mused. She wondered then about her daughter's heart for this expedition. Quenthel was a powerful priestess, there could be no denying that, but only then did the withered old matron mother realize that young Quenthel had never really seen battle. House Baenre had not warred in many hundreds of years, and because of her accelerated education through the Academy, Quenthel had been spared the duties of escorting scouting patrols in the wild tunnels outside Menzoberranzan.

It struck Baenre then that her daughter had never even been outside the drow city.

The primary way to Mithral Hall is no more, Quenthel's hands went on. *And several paralleling passages have fallen as well. And worse,* Quenthel stopped abruptly, had to pause and take a deep breath to steady herself. When she began again, her face was locked in a mask of anger. *Many of the dead drow were females, several powerful priestesses and one a high priestess.*

Still the movements were exaggerated, too sharp and too quick. Did Quenthel really believe this conquest would be easy? Baenre wondered. Did she think no drow would be killed?

Baenre wondered, and not for the first time, whether she had erred in bringing Quenthel along. Perhaps she should have brought Triel, the most capable of priestesses.

Quenthel studied the hard look that was coming at her and understood that her mother was not pleased. It took her a moment to realize she was irritating Baenre more than the bad report would warrant.

"The lines are moving?" Baenre asked aloud.

Quenthel cleared her throat. "Bregan D'aerthe has discovered many other routes," she answered, "even corridors the dwarves do not know about, which come close to tunnels leading to Mithral Hall."

Matron Baenre closed her eyes and nodded, approving of her daughter's suddenly renewed optimism. There were indeed tunnels the dwarves did not know about, small passages beneath the lowest levels of Mithral Hall lost as the dwarves continued to shift their mining operations to richer veins. Old Gandalug knew those ancient, secret ways, though, and with Methil's intrusive interrogation, the drow knew them as well. These secret tunnels did not actually connect to the dwarven compound, but wizards could open doors where there were none, and illithids could walk through stone and could take drow warriors with them on their psionic journeys.

Baenre's eyes popped open. "Word from Berg'inyon?" she asked.

Quenthel shook her head. "He exited the tunnels, as commanded, but we have not heard since."

Baenre's features grew cross. She knew that Berg'inyon was outwardly pouting at being sent outside. He led the greatest cohesive unit of all, numerically speaking, nearly a thousand drow and five times that in goblins and kobolds, with many of the dark elves riding huge lizards. But Berg'inyon's duties, though vital to the conquest of Mithral Hall, put him on the mountainside outside the dwarven complex. Very likely, Drizzt Do'Urden would be inside, in the lowest tunnels, working in an environment more suited to a dark elf. Very likely, Uthegental Armgo, not Berg'inyon, would get first try at the renegade.

Baenre's scowl turned to a smile as she considered her son and his tantrum when she had given him his assignment. Of course he had to act angry, even outraged. Of course he had to protest that he, not Uthegental, should spearhead the assault through the tunnels. But Berg'inyon had been Drizzt's classmate and primary rival in their years at Melee-Magthere, the drow school for fighters. Berg'inyon knew Drizzt perhaps better than any living drow in Menzoberranzan. And Matron Baenre knew Berg'inyon.

The truth of it was, Berg'inyon didn't want anything to do with the dangerous renegade.

"Search out your brother with your magic," Baenre said suddenly, startling Quenthel. "If he continues his obstinacy, replace him."

Quenthel's eyes widened with horror. She had been with Berg'inyon when the force had exited the tunnels, crossing out onto a ledge on a mountain overlooking a deep ravine. The sight had overwhelmed her, had dizzied her, and many other drow as well. She felt lost out there, insignificant and vulnerable. This cavern that was the surface world, this great chamber whose black dome sparkled with pinpoints of unknown light, was too vast for her sensibilities.

Matron Baenre did not appreciate the horrified expression. "Go!" she snapped, and Quenthel quietly slipped away.

She was hardly out of sight before the next reporting drow stepped before Baenre's blue-glowing driftdisk.

Her report, of the progress of the force moving secretly in the lower tunnels, was better, but Baenre hardly listened. To her, these details were fast becoming tedious. The dwarves were good, and had many months to prepare, but in the end, Matron Baenre did not doubt the outcome, for she believed that Lolth herself had spoken to her. The drow would win, and Mithral Hall would fall.

She listened to the report, though, and to the next, and the next, and the next after that, a seemingly endless stream, and forced herself to look interested.

STAR LIGHT, STAR BRIGHT

F rom her high perch, her eyesight enhanced by magical dweomers, they seemed an army of ants, swarming over the eastern and steepest side of the mountain, filling every vale, clambering over every rock. Filtering behind in tight formations came the deeper blackness, the tight formations of drow warriors.

Never had the Lady of Silverymoon seen such a disconcerting sight, never had she been so filled with trepidation, though she had endured many wars and many perilous adventures. Alustriel's visage did not reflect those battles. She was as fair as any woman alive, her skin smooth and pale, almost translucent, and her hair long and silvery—not gray with age, though she was indeed very old, but lustrous and rich, the quiet light of night and the sparkling brightness of stars all mixed together. Indeed, the fair lady had endured many wars, and the sorrow of those conflicts was reflected in her eyes, as was the wisdom to despise war.

Across the way toward the southern face, around the bend of the conical mountain, Alustriel could see the banners of the gathered forces, most prominent among them the silver flag of her own knights. They were proud and anxious, Alustriel knew, because most of them were young and did not know grief.

The Lady of Silverymoon shook away the disconcerting thoughts and focused on what likely would transpire, what her role might be.

The bulk of the enemy force was kobolds, and she figured that the huge barbarians and armored riders should have little trouble in scattering them.

But how would they fare against the drow? Alustriel wondered. She brought her flying chariot in a wide loop, watching and waiting.

⚔ ⚔ ⚔ ⚔ ⚔

Skirmishes erupted along the point line, as human scouts met the advancing kobolds.

At the sound of battle, and with reports filtering back, Berkthgar was anxious to loose his forces, to charge off to fight and die with a song to Tempus on his lips.

Besnell, who led the Knights in Silver, was a tempered fighter, and more the strategist. "Hold your men in check," he bade the eager barbarian. "We will see more fighting this night than any of us, even Tempus, your god of battle, would enjoy. Better that we fight them on ground of our choosing." Indeed, the knight had been careful in selecting that very ground, and had argued against both Berkthgar and King Bruenor himself to win over their support for his plan. The forces had been broken into four groups, spaced along the south side of the mountain, Fourthpeak, which held both entrances to Mithral Hall. Northwest around the mountain lay Keeper's Dale, a wide, deep, rock-strewn, and mist-filled valley wherein lay the secret western door to the dwarven complex.

From the soldiers' positions northeast around the mountain, across wide expanses of open rock and narrow, crisscrossing trails, lay the longer, more commonly used path to Mithral Hall's eastern door.

Bruenor's emissaries had wanted the force to split, the riders going to defend Keeper's Dale and the men of Settlestone guarding the eastern trails. Besnell had held firm his position, though, and had enlisted Berkthgar by turning the situation back on the proud dwarves, by insisting that they should be able to conceal and defend their own entrances. "If the drow know where the entrances lie," he had argued, "then that is where they will expect resistance."

Thus, the south side of Fourthpeak was chosen. Below the positions of the defenders the trails were many, but above them the cliffs grew much steeper, so they expected no attack from that direction. The defenders' groups were mixed according to terrain, one position of narrow, broken trails exclusively barbarians, two having both barbarians and riders, and one, a plateau above a wide, smooth, gradually inclined rock face, comprised wholly of the Riders of Nesmé.

Besnell and Berkthgar watched and waited now from the second position. They knew the battle was imminent. The men around them could feel the hush, the crouch of the approaching army. The area lower on the mountain, to the east, exploded suddenly in bursts of shining light as a rain of enchanted pellets, gifts from dwarven clerics, came down from the barbarians of the first defense.

How the kobolds scrambled! As did the few dark elves among the diminutive creatures' front ranks. Those monsters highest on the face, near the secret position, were overwhelmed, a horde of mighty barbarians descending over them, splitting them in half with huge swords and battle-axes, or simply lifting the kobolds high over head and hurling them down the mountainside.

"We must go out and meet them!" Berkthgar roared, seeing his kin engaged. He raised huge Bankenfuere high into the air. "To the glory of Tempus!" he roared, a cry repeated by all those barbarians on the second position, and those on the third as well.

"So much for ambush," muttered Regweld Harpell, seated on his horsefrog, Puddlejumper. With a nod to Besnell, for the time drew near, Regweld gave a slight tug on Puddlejumper's rein and the weird beast croaked out a guttural whinny and leaped to the west, clearing thirty feet.

"Not yet," Besnell implored Berkthgar, the barbarian's hand cupping a dozen or so of the magic light-giving pellets. The knight pointed out the movements of the enemy force below, explained to Berkthgar that, while many climbed up to meet the defenders holding the easternmost position, many, many more continued to filter along the lower trails to the west. Also, the light was not so intense anymore, as dark elves used their innate abilities to counter the stingingly bright enchantments.

"What are you waiting for?" Berkthgar demanded.

Besnell continued to hold his hand in the air, continued to delay the charge.

To the east, a barbarian screamed as he saw that his form was outlined suddenly by blue flames, magical fires that did not burn. They weren't truly harmless, though, for in the night, they gave the man's position clearly away. The sound of many crossbows clicked from somewhere below, and the unfortunate barbarian cried out again and again, then he fell silent.

That was more than enough for Berkthgar, and he hurled out the pellets. His nearby kin did likewise, and this second section of the south face brightened with magic. Down charged the men of Settlestone, to Besnell's continuing dismay. The riders should have gone down first, but not yet, not until the bulk of the enemy force had passed.

"We must," whispered the knight behind the elven leader from Silverymoon, and Besnell quietly nodded. He surveyed the scene for just a moment. Berkthgar and his hundred were already engaged, straight down the face, with no hope of linking up with those brave men holding the high ground in the east. Despite his anger at the impetuous barbarian, Besnell marveled at Berkthgar's exploits. Mighty Bankenfuere took out three kobolds at a swipe, launching them, whole or in parts, high into the air.

"The light will not hold," the knight behind Besnell remarked.

"Between the two forces," Besnell replied, speaking loud enough so that all those riders around him could hear. "We must go down at an angle, between the two forces, so that the men in the east can escape behind us."

Not a word of complaint came back to him, though his chosen course was treacherous indeed. The original plan had called for the Knights in Silver to ride straight into the enemy, both from this position and the next position to the west, while Berkthgar and his men linked behind them, the whole of the defending force rolling gradually to the west. Now Berkthgar, in his bloodlust, had abandoned that plan, and the Knights in Silver might pay dearly for the act. But neither man nor elf complained.

"Keep fast your pellets," Besnell commanded, "until the drow counter what light is already available."

He reared his horse once, for effect.

"For the glory of Silverymoon!" he cried.

"And the good of all good folk!" came the unified response.

Their thunder shook the side of Fourthpeak, resonated deep into the dwarven tunnels below the stone. To the blare of horns, down they charged, a hundred riders, lances low, and when those long spears became entangled or snapped apart as they skewered the enemy, out came flashing swords.

More deadly were the sturdy mounts, crushing kobolds under pounding hooves, scattering and terrifying kobolds and goblins and drow alike, for these invaders from the deepest Underdark had never seen such a cavalry charge.

In mere minutes the enemy advance up the mountain was halted and reversed, with only a few of the defenders taken down. And as the dark elves continued to counter the light pellets, Besnell's men countered their spells with still more light pellets.

But the dark force continued its roll along the lower trails, evidenced by the blare of horns to the west, the calls to Tempus and to Longsaddle, and the renewed thunder as the Longriders followed the lead of the Knights in Silver.

The first real throw of magic led the charge from that third position, a lightning bolt from Regweld that split the darkness, causing more horror than destruction.

Surprisingly, there came no magical response from the drow, other than minor darkness spells or faerie fire limning selected defenders.

The remaining barbarian force did as the plan had demanded, angling between the Longriders and the area just below the second position, linking up, not with the Knights in Silver, as was originally planned, but with Berkthgar and his force.

⚔ ⚔ ⚔ ⚔ ⚔

High above the battle, Alustriel used all her discipline and restraint to hold herself in check. The defenders were, as expected, slicing the kobold and goblin ranks to pieces, killing the enemy in a ratio far in excess of fifty to one.

That number would have easily doubled had Alustriel loosed her magic, but she could not. The drow were waiting patiently, and she respected the powers of those evil elves enough to know that her first attack might be her only one.

She whispered to the enchanted horses pulling the aerial chariot and moved lower, nodding grimly as she confirmed that the battle was going as anticipated. The slaughter high on the south face was complete, but the dark mass continued to flow below the struggle to the west.

Alustriel understood that many drow were among the ranks of that lower group.

The chariot swooped to the east, swiftly left the battle behind, and the Lady of Silverymoon took some comfort in the realization that the enemy lines were not so long, not so far beyond the easternmost of the defensive positions.

She came to understand why when she heard yet another battle, around the mountain, to the east. The enemy had found Mithral Hall's eastern door, had entered the complex, and was battling the dwarves within!

Flashes of lightning and bursts of fire erupted within the shadows of that low door, and the creatures that entered were not diminutive kobolds or stupid goblins. They were dark elves, many, many dark elves.

She wanted to go down there, to rush over the enemy in a magical, explosive fury, but Alustriel had to trust in Bruenor's people. The tunnels had been prepared, she knew, and the attack from outside the mountain had been expected.

Her chariot flew on, around to the north, and Alustriel thought to complete the circuit, to cut low through Keeper's Dale in the east, where the other allies, another hundred of her Knights in Silver, waited.

What she saw did not settle well, did not comfort her.

The northern face of Fourthpeak was a treacherous, barren stretch of virtually unclimbable rock faces and broken ravines that no man could pass.

Virtually unclimbable, but not to the sticky feet of giant subterranean lizards.

Berg'inyon Baenre and his elite force, the four hundred famed lizard riders of House Baenre, scrambled across that northern facing, making swift progress to the west, toward Keeper's Dale.

The waiting knights had been positioned to shore up the final defenses against the force crossing the southern face. Their charge, if it came, would be to open up the last flank, to allow Besnell, the Longriders, and the men of Nesmé and Settlestone to get into the dale, which was accessible through only one narrow pass.

The lizard-riders would get there first, Alustriel knew, and they outnumbered the waiting knights—and they were drow.

✗ ✗ ✗ ✗ ✗

The easternmost position was surrendered. The barbarians, or what remained of their ranks, ran fast to the west, crossing behind the Knights in Silver to join Berkthgar.

After they had crossed, Besnell turned his force to the west as well, pushing Berkthgar's force, which had swelled to include nearly every living warrior from Settlestone, ahead.

The leader of the Knights in Silver began to think that Berkthgar's error would not be so devastating, that the retreat could proceed as planned. He found a high plateau and surveyed the area, nodding grimly as he noted that the enemy force below had rolled around the first three positions.

Besnell's eyes widened, and he gasped aloud as he realized the exact location of the leading edge of that dark cloud. The Riders of Nesmé had missed their call! They had to get down the mountainside quickly, to hold that flank, and yet, for some reason, they had hesitated and the leading edge of the enemy force seemed beyond the fourth, and last, position.

Now the Riders of Nesmé did come, and their full-out charge down the smoothest stone of the south face was indeed devastating, the forty horsemen trampling thrice that number of kobolds in mere moments.

But the enemy had that many to spare, Besnell knew, and many more beyond that. The plan had called for an organized retreat to the west, to Keeper's Dale, even in through Mithral Hall's western door if need be.

It was a good plan, but now the flank was lost and the way to the west was closed.

Besnell could only watch in horror.

Part Five

Old Kings and Old Queens

They came as an army, but not so. Eight thousand dark elves and a larger number of humanoid slaves, a mighty and massive force, swarmed toward Mithral Hall.

The descriptions are fitting in terms of sheer numbers and strength, and yet "army" and "force" imply something more, a sense of cohesion and collective purpose. Certainly the drow are among the finest warriors in the Realms, trained to fight from the youngest age, alone or in groups, and certainly the purpose seems clear when the war is racial, when it is drow battling dwarves. Yet, though their tactics are perfect, groups working in unison to support each other, that cohesion among drow ranks remains superficial.

Few, if any, dark elves of Lolth's army would give her or his life to save another, unless she or he was confident that the sacrifice would guarantee a place of honor in the afterlife at the Spider Queen's side. Only a fanatic among the dark elves would take a hit, however minor, to spare another's life, and only because that fanatic thought the act in her own best interest. The drow came crying for the glory of the Spider Queen, but in reality, they each were looking for a piece of her glory.

Personal gain was always the dark elves' primary precept.

That was the difference between the defenders of Mithral Hall and those who came to conquer. That was the one hope of our side when faced with such horrendous odds, outnumbered by skilled drow warriors!

If a single dwarf came to a battle in which his comrades were being overrun, he would roar in defiance and charge in headlong, however terrible the odds. Yet if we could catch a group of drow, a patrol, perhaps, in an ambush, those supporting groups flanking their unfortunate comrades would not join in unless they could be assured of victory.

We, not they, had true collective purpose. We, not they, understood cohesion, fought for a shared higher principle, and understood and accepted that any sacrifice we might make would be toward the greater good.

There is a chamber—many chambers, actually—in Mithral Hall, where the heroes of wars and past struggles are honored. Wulfgar's hammer is there; so was the bow—the bow of an elf—that Catti-brie put into service once more. Though she has used the bow for years, and has added considerably to its legend, Catti-brie refers to it still as "the bow of Anariel," that long-dead elf. If the bow is put into service again by a friend of Clan Battlehammer centuries hence, it will be called "the bow of Catti-brie, passed from Anariel."

There is in Mithral Hall another place, the Hall of Kings, where the busts of Clan Battlehammer's patrons, the eight kings, have been carved, gigantic and everlasting.

The drow have no such monuments. My mother, Malice, never spoke of the previous matron mother of House Do'Urden, likely because Malice played a hand in her mother's death. In the Academy, there are no plaques of former mistresses and masters. Indeed, as I consider it now, the only monuments in Menzoberranzan are the statues of those punished by Baenre, of those struck by Vendes and her wicked whip, their skin turned to ebony, that they might then be placed on display as testaments of disobedience on the plateau of Tier Breche outside the Academy.

That was the difference between the defenders of Mithral Hall and those who came to conquer. That was the one hope.

—Drizzt Do'Urden

23
POCKETS OF POWER

B idderdoo had never seen anything to match it. Literally, it was raining kobolds and pieces of kobolds all around the terrified Harpell as the Gutbuster Brigade went into full battle lust. They had come into a small, wide chamber and found a force of kobolds many times their own number. Before Bidderdoo could suggest a retreat—or a "tactical flanking maneuver," as he planned to call it, because he knew the word "retreat" was not in Thibbledorf Pwent's vocabulary—Pwent had led the forthright charge.

Poor Bidderdoo had been sucked up in the brigade's wake, the seven frenzied dwarves blindly, happily, following Pwent's seemingly suicidal lead right into the heart of the cavern. Now it was a frenzy, a massacre the likes of which the studious Harpell, who had lived all his life in the sheltered Ivy Mansion—and a good part of that as a family dog—could not believe.

Pwent darted by him, a dead kobold impaled on his helmet spike and flopping limply. Arms wide, the battlerager leaped into a group of kobolds and pulled as many in as possible, hugging them tightly. Then he began to shake, to convulse so violently that Bidderdoo wondered if some agonizing poison had found its way into the dwarf's veins.

Not so, for this was controlled insanity. Pwent shook, and the nasty ridges of his armor took the skin from his hugged enemies, ripped and tore them. He broke away—and three kobolds fell dying—with a left hook that brought his mailed, spiked gauntlet several inches into the forehead of the next unfortunate enemy.

Bidderdoo came to understand that the charge was not suicidal, that the Gutbusters would win easily by overwhelming the greater numbers with sheer fury. He also realized, suddenly, that the kobolds learned fast to avoid the furious dwarves. Six of them bypassed Pwent, giving the battlerager a respectfully wide berth. Six of them swung around and bore down on the one enemy they could hope to defeat.

Bidderdoo fumbled with the shattered remains of his spellbook, flipping to one page where the ink had not smeared so badly. Holding the parchment in one hand, his other hand straight out in front of him, he began a fast chant, waggling his fingers.

A burst of magical energy erupted from each of his fingertips, green bolts rushing out, each darting and weaving to unerringly strike a target.

Five of the kobolds fell dead, and the sixth came on with a shriek, its little sword rushing for Bidderdoo's belly.

The parchment fell from the terrified Harpell's hand. He screamed, thinking he was about to die, and reacted purely on instinct, falling forward over the blade, angling his chest down so that he buried the diminutive kobold beneath him. He felt a burning pain as the small creature's sword cut into his ribs, but there was no strength behind the blow and the sword did not dig in deeply.

Bidderdoo, so unused to combat, screamed in terror. And the pain, the pain . . .

Bidderdoo's screams became a howl. He looked down and saw the thrashing kobold, and saw more clearly the thrashing kobold's exposed throat.

Then he tasted warm blood and was not repulsed.

Growling, Bidderdoo closed his eyes and held on. The kobold stopped thrashing.

After some time, the poor Harpell noticed that the sounds of battle had ended around him. He gradually opened his eyes, turned his head slightly to look up at Thibbledorf Pwent, standing over him and nodding his head.

Only then did Bidderdoo realize he had killed the kobold, had bitten the thing's throat out.

"Good technique," Pwent offered, and started away.

⚔ ⚔ ⚔ ⚔ ⚔

While the Gutbuster Brigade's maneuvers were loud and straightforward, wholly dependent on savagery, another party's were a dance of stealth and ambush. Drizzt and Guenhwyvar, Catti-brie, Regis, and Bruenor moved silently from one tunnel to another, the drow and panther leading. Guenhwyvar was the first to detect an approaching enemy, and Drizzt quickly relayed the signals when the panther's ears went flat.

The five worked in unison, setting up so that Catti-brie, with her deadly bow, would strike first, followed by the panther's spring, the drow's impossibly fast rush into the fray, and Bruenor's typically dwarven roaring charge. Regis always found a way to get into the fight, usually moving in behind to slam a drow backside or a kobold's head with his mace when one of his friends became too closely pressed.

This time, though, Regis figured to stay out of the battle altogether. The group was in a wide, high corridor when Guenhwyvar, nearing a bend, fell into a crouch, ears flat. Drizzt slipped into the shadows of an alcove, as did Regis, while Bruenor stepped defensively in front of his archer daughter, so that Catti-brie could use the horns of his helmet to line up her shot.

Around the corner came the enemy, a group of minotaurs and drow, five of each, running swiftly in the general direction of Mithral Hall.

Catti-brie wisely went for the drow. There came a flash of silver, and one fell dead.

Guenhwyvar came out hard and fast, burying another dark elf, clawing and biting and rolling right away to bear down on a third drow.

A second flash came, and another elf fell dead.

But the minotaurs came on hard, and Catti-brie would get no third shot. She went for her sword as Bruenor roared and rushed out to meet the closest monster.

The minotaur lowered its bull-like head, and Bruenor dropped his notched

battle-axe right behind him over his head, holding the handle tightly in both hands.

In came the minotaur, and over came the axe. The crack sounded like the snapping of a gigantic tree.

Bruenor didn't know what hit him. Suddenly he was flying backward, bowled over by six hundred pounds of minotaur.

× × × × ×

Drizzt came out spinning and darting. He hit the first minotaur from the side, a scimitar cutting deep into the back of the creature's thigh, stopping its charge. The ranger spun away and went down to one knee, jabbing straight ahead with Twinkle, hooking the tip of the blue-glowing scimitar over the next monster's kneecap.

The minotaur howled and half-fell, half-dived right for Drizzt, but the drow's feet were already under him, already moving, and the brute slammed hard into the stone.

Drizzt turned back for Catti-brie and Bruenor and the two remaining brutes bearing down on his friends. With incredible speed, he caught up to them almost immediately and his scimitars went to work on one, again going for the legs, stopping the charge.

But the last minotaur caught up to Catti-brie. Its huge club, made of hardened mushroom stalk, came flying around, and Catti-brie ducked fast, whipping her sword above her head.

Khazid'hea sliced right through the club, and as the minotaur stared at the remaining piece dumbfoundedly, Catti-brie countered with a slashing backhand.

The minotaur looked at her curiously. She could not believe she had missed.

× × × × ×

Regis watched from the shadows, knowing he was overmatched by any enemy in this fight. He tried to gauge his companions, though, wanting to be ready if needed. Mostly he watched Drizzt, mesmerized by the sheer speed of the drow's charges and dodges. Drizzt had always been quick afoot, but this display was simply amazing, the ranger's feet moving so swiftly that Regis could hardly distinguish them. More than once, Regis tried to anticipate Drizzt's path, only to find himself looking where the drow was not.

For Drizzt had cut to the side, or reversed direction altogether, more quickly than the halfling would have believed possible.

Regis finally just shook his head and filed his questions away for another time, reminding himself that there were other, more important considerations. He glanced around and noticed the last of the enemy drow slipping to the side, out of the way of the panther.

⚔ ⚔ ⚔ ⚔ ⚔

The last drow wanted no part of Guenhwyvar, and was glad indeed that the woman with the killing bow was engaged in close combat. Two of his dark elf companions lay dead from arrows, a third squirmed around on the floor, half her face torn away by the panther's claws, and all five minotaurs were down or engaged. The fourth drow had run off, back around the bend, but that wicked panther was only a couple of strides behind, and the hiding dark elf knew his companion would be down in a matter of moments.

Still, the drow hardly cared, for he saw Drizzt Do'Urden, the renegade, the most hated. The ranger was fully engaged and vulnerable, working furiously to finish the three minotaurs he had wounded. If this drow could seize the opportunity and get Drizzt, then his place of glory, and his House's glory, would be sealed. Even if he was killed by Drizzt's friends, he would have a seat of honor beside Lolth, the Spider Queen.

He loaded his most potent dart, a bolt enchanted with runes of fire and lightning, onto his heavy, two-handed crossbow, an unusual weapon indeed for dark elves, and brought the sights in line.

Something hit the crossbow hard from the side. The drow pulled the trigger instinctively, but the bolt, knocked loose, went nowhere but down, exploding at his feet. The jolt sent him flying, and the puff of flame singed his hair and momentarily blinded him.

He rolled over on the floor and managed to get out of his burning *piwafwi*. Dazed, he noticed a small mace lying on the floor, then saw a small, plump hand reaching down to pick it up. The drow tried to react as the bare feet, hairy on top—something the Underdark drow had never seen before—steadily approached.

Then all went dark.

⚔ ⚔ ⚔ ⚔ ⚔

Catti-brie cried out and leaped back, but the minotaur did not charge. Rather, the brute stood perfectly still, eyeing her curiously.

"I didn't miss," Catti-brie said, as if her denial of what seemed obvious would change her predicament. To her surprise, she found she was right.

The minotaur's left leg, severed cleanly by Khazid'hea's passing, caved in under it, and the brute fell sidelong to the floor, its lifeblood pouring out unchecked.

Catti-brie looked to the side to see Bruenor, grumbling and groaning, crawling out from under the minotaur he had killed. The dwarf hopped to his feet, shook his head briskly to clear away the stars, then stared at his axe, hands on hips, head shaking in dismay. The mighty weapon was embedded nearly a foot deep in the minotaur's thick skull.

"How in the Nine Hells am I going to get the damned thing out?" Bruenor asked, looking at his daughter.

Drizzt was done, as was Regis, and Guenhwyvar came back around the corner, dragging the last of the dark elves by the scruff of his broken neck.

"Another win for our side," Regis remarked as the friends regrouped.

Drizzt nodded his agreement but seemed not so pleased. It was a small thing they were doing, he knew, barely scratching at the surface of the force that had come to Mithral Hall. And despite the quickness of this latest encounter, and of the three before it, the friends had been, ultimately, lucky. What would have happened had another group of drow or minotaurs, or even kobolds, come around the corner while the fight was raging?

They had won quickly and cleanly, but their margin of victory was a finer line and a more tentative thing than the rout would indicate.

"Ye're not so pleased," Catti-brie said quietly to the ranger as they started off once more.

"In two hours we have killed a dozen drow, a handful of minotaurs and a score of kobold fodder," Drizzt replied.

"With thousands more to go," the woman added, understanding Drizzt's dismay.

Drizzt said nothing. His only hope, Mithral Hall's only hope, was that they and other groups like them would kill enough drow to take the heart from their enemy. Dark elves were a chaotic and supremely disloyal bunch, and only if the defenders of Mithral Hall could defeat the drow army's will for the war did they have a chance.

Guenhwyvar's ears went flat again, and the panther slipped silently into the darkness. The friends, feeling suddenly weary of it all, moved into position and were relieved indeed when the newest group rambled into sight. No drow this time, no kobolds or minotaurs. A column of dwarves, more than a score, hailed them and approached. This group, too, had seen battle since the fight in Tunult's Cavern. Many showed fresh wounds, and every dwarven weapon was stained with enemy blood.

"How fare we?" Bruenor asked, stepping to the front.

The leader of the dwarven column winced, and Bruenor had his answer. "They're fightin' in the Undercity, me king," said the dwarf. "How they got into the place, we're not for knowin'! And fightin' too, in the upper levels, by all reports. The eastern door's been breached."

Bruenor's shoulders visibly slumped.

"But we're holdin' at Garumn's Gorge!" the dwarf said with more determination.

"Where're ye from and where're ye going?" Bruenor wanted to know.

"From the last guard room," the dwarf explained. "Come out in a short circuit to find yerself, me king. Tunnels're thick with drow scum, and glad we be to see ye standing!" He pointed behind Bruenor, then jabbed his finger to the left. "We're not so far, and the way's still clear to the last guard room . . ."

"But it won't be for long," another dwarf piped in glumly.

"And clear all the way to the Undercity from there," the leader finished.

Drizzt pulled Bruenor to the side and began a whispered conversation. Catti-brie and Regis waited patiently, as did the dwarves.

" . . . keep searching," they heard Drizzt say.

"Me place is with me people!" Bruenor roughly replied. "And yer own is with me!"

Drizzt cut him short with a long stream of words. Catti-brie and the others heard snatches such as "hunting the head" and "roundabout route," and they knew Drizzt was trying to convince Bruenor to let him continue his hunt through the outer, lower tunnels.

Catti-brie decided then and there that if Drizzt and Guenhwyvar were to go on, she, with her Cat's Eye circlet, which Alustriel had given her to allow her to see in the dark, would go with him. Regis, feeling unusually brave and useful, silently came to the same conclusion.

Still, the two were surprised when Drizzt and Bruenor walked back to the group.

"Get ye to the last guard room, and all the way to the Undercity if need be," Bruenor commanded the column leader.

The dwarf's jaw dropped with amazement. "But, me king," he sputtered.

"Get ye!" Bruenor growled.

"And leave yerself alone out here?" the stunned dwarf asked.

Bruenor's smile was wide and wicked as he looked from the dwarf to Drizzt, to Catti-brie, to Regis, and to Guenhwyvar, then finally, back to the dwarf.

"Alone?" Bruenor replied, and the other dwarf, knowing the prowess of his king's companions, conceded the point.

"Get ye back and win," Bruenor said to him. "Me and me friends got some huntin' to do."

The two groups split apart once more, both grimly determined, but neither overly optimistic.

Drizzt whispered something to the panther, and Guenhwyvar took up the lead as before. To this point, the companions had been lying in wait for every enemy group that came their way, but now, with the grim news from the Undercity and the eastern door, Drizzt changed that tactic. If they could not avoid the small groups of drow and other monsters, then they would fight, but otherwise, their path now was more direct. Drizzt wanted to find the priestesses—and he knew it had to be priestesses—who had led this march. The dwarves' only chance was to decapitate the enemy force.

And so the companions were now, as Drizzt had quietly put it to Bruenor, "hunting the head."

Regis, last in line, shook his head and looked more than once back the way the dwarven column had marched. "How do I always get myself into this?" the halfling whispered. Then, looking at the backs of his hearty, sometimes reckless friends, he knew he had his answer.

Catti-brie heard the halfling's resigned sigh, understood its source, and managed to hide her smile.

24

FIERY FURY

Alustriel watched from her high perch as the southern face of Fourthpeak flickered with light that seemed to be blinking like the stars above. The exchange of enchanted pellets from the defenders and countering dark magic from the invaders was furious. As she brought her chariot around the southwestern cliffs, the Lady of Silverymoon grew terribly afraid, for the defenders had been pushed into a U formation, surrounded on all sides by goblins, kobolds, and fierce drow warriors.

Still, the forces of the four armies fought well, practically back to back, and their line was strong. No great number could strike at them from the gap at the top of the U, the logical weak spot, because of the almost sheer cliffs, and the defenders were tightly packed enough along the entire line to hold against any concentrated assaults.

Even as Alustriel fostered that thought, her hopes were put to the test. A group of goblins, led by huge bugbears, seven-foot, hairy versions of goblins, formed into a tight diamond and spearheaded into the defenders' eastern flank.

The line wavered, and Alustriel almost revealed herself with a flurry of explosive magic.

But amidst the chaos and the press rose one sword above all others, one song above all others.

Berkthgar the Bold, his wild hair flying, sang to Tempus with all his heart, and Bankenfuere hummed as it swept through the air. Berkthgar ignored the lesser goblins and charged straight for the bugbears, and each mighty swipe cut one of them down. The leader of Settlestone took a vicious hit, and another, but no hint of pain crossed his stern visage or slowed his determined march.

Those bugbears who escaped the first furious moments of the huge man's assault fled from him thereafter, and with their leaders so terrified, the goblins quickly lost heart for the press and the diamond disintegrated into a fleeing mob.

Many would be the songs to celebrate Berkthgar, Alustriel knew, but only if the defenders won. If the dark elves succeeded in their conquest, then all such heroics would be lost to the ages, all the songs would be buried beneath a black veil of oppression. That could not happen, the Lady of Silverymoon decided. Even if Mithral Hall were to fall this night, or the next, the war would not be lost. All of Silverymoon would mobilize against the drow, and she would go to Sundabar, in the east, to Citadel Adbar, stronghold of King Harbromme and his dwarves, and all the way to Waterdeep, on the Sword Coast, to muster the necessary forces to push the drow back to Menzoberranzan!

This war was not lost, she reminded herself, and she looked down at the determined defenders, holding against the swarm, fighting and dying.

Then came the tragedy she had expected and feared all along: the magical barrage, bursts of fireballs and lightning, lines of consuming magical energy and spinning bolts of destruction.

The assault focused on the southwestern corner of the U, blew apart the ranks of the Riders of Nesmé, consuming horse and man alike. Many humanoid slaves fell as well, mere fodder and of no concern to the wicked drow wizards.

Tears streamed down Alustriel's face as she watched that catastrophe, as she heard the agonized cries of man and beast and saw that corner of the mountain become charred under the sheer power of the barrage. She berated herself for not foreseeing this war, for underestimating the intensity of the drow march, for not having her army fully entrenched, warriors, wizards, and priests alike, in the defense of Mithral Hall.

The massacre went on for many seconds, seeming like hours to the horrified defenders. It went on and on, the explosions and the cries.

Alustriel found her heart again and looked for the source, and when she saw it, she came to realize that the dark elf wizards, in their ignorance of the surface world, had erred.

They were concentrated within a copse of thick trees, under cover and hurling out their deadly volley of spells.

Alustriel's features brightened into a wicked smile, a smile of vengeance, and she cut her chariot across at a sharp angle, swooping down the mountainside from on high, flying like an arrow for the heart of her enemies.

The drow had erred; they were in the trees.

As she crossed the northern edge of the battlefield, Alustriel cried out a command, and her chariot, and the team of enchanted horses that pulled it, ignited into bright flames.

Below her she heard the cries of fear, from friend and enemy alike, and she heard the trumpets from the Knights in Silver, who recognized the chariot and understood that their leader had come.

Down she streaked, a tremendous fireball leading the way, exploding in the heart of the copse. Alustriel sped right to the trees' edge, then banked sharply and rushed along the thick line, the flames of her chariot igniting branches wherever she passed.

The drow wizards had erred!

She knew the dark elves had likely set up wards against countering magic—perhaps even over themselves—that would defeat even the most intense fires, but they did not understand the flammable nature of trees. Even if the fire did not consume them, the flames would blind them and effectively put them out of the fighting.

And the smoke! The thick copse was damp from previous rains and frost, and billowing black clouds thickened the air. Even worse for the drow, the wizards countered as they had always countered fire, with spells creating water. So great was their response, that the flames would have been quenched, except that Alustriel did not relent, continued to rush around the copse, even cut into the copse wherever she found a break. No water, not the ocean itself, could extinguish the fires of her enchanted chariot. As

she continued to fuel the flames, the drenching spells by the wizards added steam to the smoke, thickened the air so that the dark elves could not see at all and could not breathe.

Alustriel trusted in her horses, extensions of her will, to understand her intent and keep the chariot on course, and she watched, her spells ready, for she knew the enemy could not remain within the copse. As she expected, a drow floated up through the trees, rising above the inferno, levitating into the air and trying to orient himself to the scene beyond the copse.

Alustriel's lightning bolt hit him in the back of the head and sent him spinning over and over, and he hung, upside down and dead, until his own spell expired, dropping him back into the trees.

Even as she killed that wizard, though, a ball of flame puffed in the air right before the chariot, and the speeding thing, and Alustriel with it, plunged right through. The Lady of Silverymoon was protected from the flames of her own spell, but not so from the fireball, and she cried out and came through pained, her face bright from burn.

⚔ ⚔ ⚔ ⚔ ⚔

Higher up the mountainside, Besnell and his soldiers witnessed the attack against Alustriel. The elf steeled his golden eyes, and his men cried out in outrage. If their earlier exploits had been furious, they were purely savage now, and Berkthgar's men, fighting beside them, needed no prodding.

Goblins and kobolds, bugbears and orcs, even huge minotaurs and skilled drow, died by the score in the next moments of battle.

It hardly seemed to matter. Whenever one died, two took its place, and though the knights and the barbarians could have cut through the enemy lines, there was nowhere for them to go.

Farther to the west, his own Longriders similarly pressed, Regweld understood their only hope. He leaped Puddlejumper to a place where there were no enemies and cast a spell to send a message to Besnell.

To the west! the wizard implored the knight leader.

Then Regweld took up the new lead and turned his men and the barbarians closest to them westward, toward Keeper's Dale, as the original plan had demanded. The drow wizards had been silenced, momentarily at least, and now was the only chance Regweld would have.

A lightning bolt split the darkening air. A fireball followed, and Regweld followed that, leaping Puddlejumper over the ranks of his enemies and loosing a barrage of magical missiles below him as he flew.

Confusion hit the enemy ranks, enough so that the Longriders, men who had fought beside the Harpells for all their lives and understood Regweld's tactics, were able to slice through, opening a gap.

Beside them came many of the Settlestone warriors and the few remaining horsemen from Nesmé. Behind them came the rest of the barbarian force and the Knights in Silver, mighty Berkthgar bringing up the rear, almost single-handedly keeping the pursuing monsters at bay.

The defenders punched through quickly, but found their momentum halted as another force, mostly drow, cut across in front, forming thick ranks.

Regweld continued his magical barrage, charged ahead with Puddlejumper, expecting to die.

And so he would have, except that Alustriel, forced away from the copse by the increasingly effective counters of the drow wizards, rushed back up the mountainside, right along the dark elf line, low enough so that the drow who did not flee were trampled and burned by her fiery passing.

Besnell and his men galloped to the front of the fleeing force, cried out to Alustriel and for the good of all goodly folk, and plunged into the confusion of the drow ranks, right into the flaming chariot's charred wake.

Many more men died in those few moments of hellish fighting, many men and many drow, but the defenders broke free to the west, ran and rode on, and found the path into Keeper's Dale before the enemy could block it.

Above the battle once more, Alustriel slumped with exhaustion. She had not launched so concentrated a barrage of magic in many, many years, and had not engaged so closely in any conflict since the days before she had come to rule Silverymoon. Now she was tired and wounded, burned and singed, and she had taken several hits by sword and by quarrel as she had rushed along the drow ranks. She knew the disapproval she would find when she returned to Silverymoon, knew that her advisors, and the city's council, and

colleagues from other cities, would think her rash, even stupid. Mithral Hall was a minor kingdom not worth her life, her detractors would say. To take such risks against so deadly an enemy was foolish.

So they would say, but Alustriel knew better, knew that the freedoms and rights that applied to Silverymoon were not there simply because of her city's size and strength. They applied to all, to Silverymoon, to Waterdeep, and to the smallest of kingdoms that so desired them, because otherwise the values they promoted were meaningless and selfish.

Now she was wounded, had nearly been killed, and she called off her chariot's flames as she rose high into the sky. To show herself so openly would invite a continuing magical attack that would likely destroy her. She was sorely wounded, she knew, but Alustriel was smiling. Even if she died this night, the Lady of Silverymoon would die smiling, because she was following her heart. She was fighting for something bigger than her life, for values that were eternal and ultimately right.

She watched with satisfaction as the force, led by Besnell and her own knights, broke free and sped for Keeper's Dale, then she climbed higher into the cold sky, angling for the west.

The enemy would pursue, and more enemies were coming fast around the north, and the battle had only just begun.

※ ※ ※ ※ ※

The Undercity, where two thousand dwarves often labored hard at their most beloved profession, had never seen such bustle and tumult as this day. Not even when the shadow dragon, Shimmergloom, and its host of evil gray dwarves had invaded, when Bruenor's grandfather had been king, had the Undercity been engulfed in such a battle.

Goblins and minotaurs, kobolds and wicked monsters that the dwarves could not name flooded in from the lower tunnels and through the floor itself, areas that had been breached by the magic of the illithids. And the drow, scores of dark elves, struggled and battled along every step and across the wide floor, their dance a macabre mix of swirling shadows in the glow of the many low-burning furnaces.

Still, the main tunnels to the lower levels had not been breached, and the greatest concentration of enemies, particularly the drow force, remained outside Mithral Hall proper. Now the dark elves who had gained the Undercity meant to open that way, to link up with the forces of Uthegental and Matron Baenre.

And the dwarves meant to stop them, knowing that if that joining came to pass, then Mithral Hall would be lost.

Lightning flashed, green and red and sizzling black bolts from below, from the drow, and it was answered from above by Harkle and Bella don DelRoy.

The lowest levels began to grow darker as the drow worked their magic to gain a favorable battlefield.

The fall of light pellets upon the floor sounded like a gentle rain as Stumpet Rakingclaw and her host of dwarven priests countered the magic, brightening the area, loading spell after spell, stealing every shadow from every corner. Dwarves could fight in the dark, but they could fight in the light as well, and the drow and other creatures from the Underdark were not so fond of brightness.

One group of twenty dwarves formed a tight formation on the wide floor and rolled over a band of fleeing goblins. Their boots sounded like a heavy, rolling wheel, a general din, mowing over whatever monster dared to stay in their path.

A handful of dark elves fired stinging crossbow quarrels, but the dwarves shook off the hits—and, since their blood ran thick with potions to counter any poisons, they shook off the infamous drow sleeping drug as well.

Seeing that their attack was ineffective, the drow scattered, and the dwarven wedge rolled toward the next obstacle, two strange-looking creatures that the bearded folk did not know, two ugly creatures with slimy heads that waved tentacles where the mouths should have been, and with milky white eyes that showed no pupils.

The dwarven wedge seemed unstoppable, but when the illithids turned their way and loosed their devastating mental barrage, the wedge wobbled and fell apart, stunned dwarves staggering aimlessly.

"Oh, there they are!" Harkle squealed from the third tier of the Undercity, more than sixty feet from the floor.

Bella don DelRoy's face crinkled with disgust as she looked at mind flayers for the first time. She and Harkle had expected the creatures. Drizzt had told them about Matron Baenre's "pet." Despite her disgust, Bella, like all Harpells, was more curious than afraid. The illithids had been expected—she just hadn't expected them to be so damned ugly!

"Are you sure of this?" the diminutive woman asked Harkle, who had devised the strategy for fighting the squishy-headed things. Her good eye revealed her true hopes, though, for while she talked to Harkle, it remained fixated on the ugly illithids.

"Would I have gone to all the trouble of learning to cast from the different perspective?" Harkle answered, seeming wounded by her doubts.

"Of course," Bella replied. "Well, those dwarves do need our help."

"Indeed."

A quick chant by the daughter of DelRoy brought a shimmering blue, door-shaped field right before the two wizards.

"After you," Bella said politely.

"Oh, rank before beauty," Harkle answered, waving his hand toward the door, indicating that Bella should lead.

"No time for wasting!" came a clear voice behind them, and surprisingly strong hands pressed against both Bella and Harkle's hips, heaving them both for the door. They went through together, and Fret, the tidy dwarf, pushed in right behind them.

The second door appeared on the floor, between the illithids and their stunned dwarven prey, and out popped the three dimensional travelers. Fret skidded to the side, trying to round up the vulnerable dwarves, while Harkle and Bella don DelRoy mustered their nerve and faced the octopus-headed creatures.

"I understand your anger," Harkle began, and he and his companion shuddered as a wave of mental energy rolled across their chests and shoulders and heads, leaving a wake of tingles.

"If I were as ugly as you . . ." Harkle continued, and a second wave came through.

". . . I would be mean, too!" Harkle finished, and a third blast of energy came forth, followed closely by the illithids. Bella screamed and Harkle nearly fainted as the monstrous things pushed in close, tentacles latching onto cheeks and chins. One went straight up Harkle's nose, in search of brain matter to devour.

"You are sure?" Bella cried out.

But Harkle, deep in the throes of his latest spell, didn't hear her. He didn't struggle against the illithid, for he didn't want the thing to jostle him too severely. It was hard enough to concentrate with wriggling tentacles burrowing under the skin of his face!

Those tentacles swelled now, extracting their prize.

An unmistakably sour look crossed the normally expressionless features of both the creatures.

Harkle's hands came up slowly, palms down, his thumbs touching and his other fingers spread wide. A flash of fire erupted from his hands, searing the confused illithid, burning its robes. It tried to pull away, and Harkle's facial skin bulged weirdly as the tentacles began to slide free.

Harkle was already moving with his next spell. He reached into his robes and extracted a dart, a leaf that had been mushed to powder, and a stringy, slimy thing, a snake's intestine, and squashed them all together as he completed the chant.

From that hand came forth a small bolt, shooting across the two feet to stick into the still-burning illithid's belly.

The creature gurgled something indecipherable and finally fell away, stumbling, grasping at its newest wound, for while the fires still nipped at it in places, this newest attack hurt more.

The enchanted bolt pumped acid into its victim.

Down went the illithid, still clutching at the leaking bolt. It had underestimated its enemy, and it telepathically sent that very message to its immediate companion, who already understood their error, and to Methil, deep in the caverns beside Matron Baenre.

Bella couldn't concentrate. Though her spell of polymorph had been perfect, her brain safely tucked away where the illithid could not find it, she simply couldn't concentrate with the squiggly tentacles probing around her skull. She berated herself, told herself that the daughter of DelRoy should be more in control.

She heard a rumbling sound, a cart rolling near, and opened her eyes to see Fret push the cart right up behind the illithid, a host of drow in pursuit. Holding his nerve, the tidy dwarf leaped atop the cart and drew out a tiny silver hammer.

"Let her go!" Fret cried, bringing the nasty little weapon to bear. To the dwarf's surprise, and disgust, his hammer sank into the engaged illithid's bulbous head and ichor spewed forth, spraying the dwarf and staining his white robes.

Fret knew the drow were bearing down on him. He had resolved to make one attack on the illithid, then turn in defense against the dark elves. But all plans flew away in the face of that gory mess, the one thing that could bring the tidy dwarf into full battle rage.

No woodpecker ever hit a log as rapidly. Fret's hammer worked so as to seem a blur, and each hit sent more of the illithid's brain matter spraying, which only heightened the tidy dwarf's frenzy.

Still, that would have been the end of Fret, of all of them, had not Harkle quickly enacted his next spell. He focused on the area in front of the charging drow, threw a bit of lard into the air, and called out his next dweomer.

The floor became slick with grease, and the charge came to a stumbling, tumbling end.

Its head smashed to dripping pulp, the illithid slumped before Bella, the still-clinging tentacles bringing her low as well. She grabbed frantically at those tentacles and yanked them free, then stood straight and shuddered with pure revulsion.

"I told you that was the way to fight mind flayers!" Harkle said happily, for it had been his plan every step of the way.

"Shut up," Bella said to him, her stomach churning. She looked all around, seeing enemies closing in from many directions. "And get us out of here!" she said.

Harkle looked at her, confused and a bit wounded by her disdain. The plan had worked, after all!

A moment later, Harkle, too, became more than a little frightened, as he came to realize that he had forgotten that last little detail, and had no spells left that would transport them back to the higher tiers.

"Ummm," he stammered, trying to find the words to best explain their dilemma.

Relieved he was, and Bella, too, when the dwarven wedge reformed around them, Fret joining the ranks.

"We'll get ye back up," the leader of the grateful dwarves promised, and on they rolled, once more burying everything in their path.

Even more destructive now was their march, for every so often a blast of lightning or a line of searing fire shot out from their ranks as Harkle and Bella joined in the fun.

Still, Bella remained uncomfortable and wanted this all to end so that she could return to her normal physiology. Harkle had studied illithids intently, and knew as much about them as perhaps any wizard in all the Realms. Their mentally debilitating blasts were conical, he had assured her, and so, if he and she could get close, only the top half of their bodies would be affected.

Thus they had enacted the physical transformation enchantment, wherein Harkle and Bella appeared the same, yet had transfigured two areas of their makeup, their brains and their buttocks.

Harkle smiled at his cleverness as the wedge rolled on. Such a transformation had been a delicate thing, requiring many hours of study and preparation. But it had been worth the trouble, every second, the Harpell believed, recalling the sour looks on the ugly illithid faces!

⚔ ⚔ ⚔ ⚔ ⚔

The rumbles from the collapse of the bridges, and of all the antechambers near Garumn's Gorge, were felt in the lowest tunnels of Mithral Hall, even beyond, in the upper passages of the wild Underdark itself. How much work Bruenor's people would have if ever they tried to open the eastern door again!

But the drow advance had been stopped, and was well worth the price. For now General Dagna and his force of defenders were free to go.

But where? the tough, battle-hardened dwarf wondered. Reports came to him that the Undercity was under full attack, but he also realized that the western door, near Keeper's Dale, was vulnerable, with only a few hundred dwarves guarding the many winding tunnels and with no provisions for such catastrophic measures as had been taken here in the east. The tunnels in the west could not be completely dropped; there had not been time to rig them so.

Dagna looked around at his thousand troops, many of them wounded, but all of them eager for more battle, eager to defend their sacred homeland.

"The Undercity," the general announced a moment later. If the western door was breached, the invaders would have to find their way through, no easy task considering the myriad choices they would face. The fighting had already come to the Undercity, so that was where Dagna belonged.

Normally it would have taken many minutes, a half hour or more, for the dwarves to get down to the fighting, even if they went the whole way at a full charge. But this, too, had been foreseen, so Dagna led his charges to the appointed spot, new doors that had been cut into the walls connecting to chimneys running up from the great furnaces. As soon as those doors were opened, Dagna and his soldiers heard the battle, so they went without delay, one after another, onto the heavy ropes that had been set in place.

Down they slid, fearlessly, singing songs to Clanggedon. Down they went, hitting the floor at a full run, rushing out of the warm furnaces and right into the fray, streaming endlessly, it seemed, as were the drow coming in from the lower tunnels.

The fighting in the Undercity grew ever furious.

KEEPER'S DALE

B erg'inyon's force swept into Keeper's Dale, the sticky-footed lizards making trails where none could be found. They came down the northern wall like a sheet of water, into the misty valley, ominous shadows slipping past tall pillars of stone.

Though it was warmer here than on the open northern face, the drow were uncomfortable. There were no formations like this in the Underdark, no misty valleys, except those filled with the toxic fumes of unseen volcanoes. Scouting reports had been complete, though, and had specifically outlined this very spot, the doorstep of Mithral Hall's western door, as safe for passage. Thus, the Baenre lizard riders went into the valley without question, fearing their own volatile matron mother more than any possible toxic fumes.

As they entered the vale, they heard the fighting on the southern side of the mountain. Berg'inyon nodded when he took the moment to notice that the battle was coming closer—all was going as planned. The enemy was in retreat, no doubt, being herded like stupid rothé into the valley, where the slaughter would begin in full.

The moving shadows that were Berg'inyon's force slipped quietly through the mist, past the stone sentinels, trying to get a lay of the valley, trying to find the optimum ambush areas.

Above the mist, a line of fire broke the general darkness of the night sky,

streaking fast and angling into the vale. Berg'inyon watched it, as did so many, not knowing what it might be.

As she crossed above the force, Alustriel loosed the last barrage of her magic, a blast of lightning, a rain of greenish pulses of searing energy, and a shower of explosive fireballs that liquified stone.

The alert dark elves responded before the chariot crossed over the northern lip of the vale, hit back with enchanted crossbow quarrels and similar spells of destruction.

The flames of the chariot flared wider, caught in the midst of a fireball, and the whole of the cart jerked violently to the side as a line of lightning blasted against its base.

Alustriel's magic had killed more than a few, and taken the mounts out from under many others, but the real purpose in the wizard's passing had been the part of decoy, for every drow eye was turned heavenward when the second battalion of the Knights in Silver joined the fray, charging through Keeper's Dale, horseshoes clacking deafeningly on the hard stone.

Lances lowered, the knights barreled through the initial ranks of drow, running them down with their larger mounts.

But these were the Baenre lizard riders, the most elite force in all of Menzo-berranzan, a complement of warriors and wizards that did not know fear.

Silent commands went out from Berg'inyon, passed from waggling fingers to waggling fingers. Even after the surprise barrage from the sky and the sudden charge of the force that the drow did not know were in Keeper's Dale, the dark elf ranks outnumbered the Knights in Silver by more than three to one. Had those odds been one-to-one, the Knights in Silver still would have had no chance.

The tide turned quickly, with the knights, those who were not taken down, inevitably falling back and regrouping into tight formations. Only the mist and the unfamiliar terrain prevented the slaughter from being wholesale; only the fact that the overwhelming drow force could not find all the targets allowed the valiant knights to continue to resist.

Near the rear of the dark elf ranks, Berg'inyon heard the commotion as one unfortunate human got separated and confused, galloping his mount unintentionally toward the north, away from his comrades.

The Baenre son signaled for his personal guards to follow him, but to stay behind, and took up the chase, his great lizard slinking and angling to intercept. He saw the shadowy figure—and what a magnificent thing Berg'inyon thought the rider to be, so high and tall on his powerful steed.

That image did not deter the weapons master of Menzoberranzan's First House. He came around a pillar of stone, just to the side of the knight, and called out to the man.

The great horse skidded and stopped, the knight wheeling it around to face Berg'inyon. He said something Berg'inyon could not understand, some proclamation of defiance, no doubt, then lowered his long lance and kicked his horse into a charge.

Berg'inyon leveled his own mottled lance and drove his heels into the lizard's flanks, prodding the beast on. He couldn't match the speed of the knight's horse, but the horse couldn't match the lizard's agility. As the opponents neared, Berg'inyon swerved aside, brought his lizard right up the side of a thick stone pillar.

The knight, surprised by the quickness of the evasion, couldn't bring his lance out fast enough for an effective strike, but as the two passed, Berg'inyon managed to prod the running horse in the flank. It wasn't a severe hit, barely a scratch, but this was no ordinary lance. The ten-foot pole that Berg'inyon carried was a devilish death lance, among the most cunning and wicked of drow weapons. As the lance tip connected on the horseflesh, cutting through the metal armor the beast wore as though it were mere cloth, dark, writhing tentacles of black light crawled down its length.

The horse whinnied pitifully, kicked and jumped and came to a skidding stop. Somehow the knight managed to hold his seat.

"Run on!" he cried to his shivering mount, not understanding. "Run on!"

The knight suddenly felt as though the horse was somehow less substantial beneath him, felt the beast's ribs against his calves.

The horse threw its head back and whinnied again, an unearthly, undead cry, and the knight blanched when he looked into the thing's eyes, orbs that burned red with some evil enchantment.

The death lance had stolen the creature's life-force, had turned the proud, strong stallion into a gaunt, skeletal thing, an undead, evil thing. Thinking quickly, the knight dropped his lance, drew his huge sword, and sheared off the monster's head with a single swipe. He rolled aside as the horse collapsed beneath him, and came to his feet, hopping around in confusion.

Dark shapes encircled him, and he heard the hiss of nearby lizards, sucking sounds as sticky feet came free of stone.

Berg'inyon Baenre approached slowly. He, too, lowered his lance. A flick of his wrist freed him from his binding saddle, and he slid off his mount, determined to test one of these surface men in single combat, determined to show those drow nearby the skill of their leader.

Out came the weapons master's twin swords, sharp and enchanted, among the very finest of drow weapons.

The knight, nearly a foot taller than this adversary, but knowing the reputation of dark elves, was rightfully afraid. He swallowed that fear, though, and met Berg'inyon head-on, sword against sword.

The knight was good, had trained hard for all of his adult life, but if he trained for all of his remaining years as well, they would not total the decades the longer-living Berg'inyon had spent with the sword.

The knight was good. He lived for almost five minutes.

⚔ ⚔ ⚔ ⚔ ⚔

Alustriel felt the chill, moist air of a low cloud brush her face, and it brought her back to consciousness. She moved quickly, trying to right the chariot, and felt the bite of pain all along her side.

She had been hit by spell and by weapon, and her burned and torn robes were wet with her own blood.

What would the world think if she, the Lady of Silverymoon, died here? she wondered. To her haughty colleagues, this was a minor war, a battle that had no real bearing on the events of the world, a battle, in their eyes, that Alustriel of Silverymoon should have avoided.

Alustriel brushed her long, silvery hair—hair that was also matted with blood—back from her beautiful face. Anger welled within her as she thought of the arguments she had fought over King Bruenor's request for aid. Not a single advisor or councilor in Silverymoon, with the exception of Fret, wanted to answer that call, and Alustriel had to wage a long, tiresome battle of words to get even the two hundred Knights in Silver released to Mithral Hall.

What was happening to her own city? the lady wondered now, floating high above the disaster of Fourthpeak. Silverymoon had earned a reputation as the most generous of places, as a defender of the oppressed, champion of goodness. The knights had gone off to war eagerly, but they weren't the problem, and had never been.

The problem, the wounded Alustriel came to realize, was the comfortably entrenched bureaucratic class, the political leaders who had become too secure in the quality of their own lives. That seemed crystal clear to Alustriel now, wounded and fighting hard to control her enchanted chariot in the cold night sky above the battle.

She knew the heart of Bruenor and his people; she knew the goodness of Drizzt, and the value of the hearty men of Settlestone. They were worth defending, Alustriel believed. Even if all of Silverymoon were consumed in the war, these people were worth defending, because, in the end, in the annals future historians would pen, that would be the measure of Silverymoon. That generosity would be the greatness of the place, would be what set Silverymoon apart from so many other petty kingdoms.

But what was happening to her city? Alustriel wondered, and she came to understand the cancer that was growing amidst her own ranks. She would go back to Silverymoon and purge that disease, she determined, but not now.

Now she needed rest. She had done her part, to the best of her abilities, and perhaps at the price of her own life, she realized as another pain shot through her wounded side.

Her colleagues would lament her death, would call it a waste, considering the minor scale of this war for Mithral Hall.

Alustriel knew better, knew how she, like her city, would be ultimately judged.

She managed to bring the chariot crashing down to a wide ledge, and she tumbled out as the fiery dweomer dissipated into nothingness.

The Lady of Silverymoon sat there against the stone, in the cold, looking down on the distant scramble far below her. She was out of the fight, but she had done her part.

She knew she could die with no guilt weighing on her heart.

※ ※ ※ ※ ※

Berg'inyon Baenre rode through the ranks of lizard-mounted drow, holding high his twin bloodstained swords. The dark elves rallied behind their leader, filtered from obelisk to obelisk, cutting the battlefield in half and more. The mobility and speed of the larger horses favored the knights, but the dark elves' cunning tactics were quick to steal that advantage.

To their credit, the knights were killing drow at a ratio of one to one, a remarkable feat considering the larger drow numbers and the skill of their enemies. Even so, the ranks of knights were being diminished.

Hope came in the form of a fat wizard riding a half-horse, half-frog beastie and leading the remnants of the defenders of the southern face, hundreds of men, riding and running—from battle and into battle.

Berg'inyon's force was fast pushed across the breadth of Keeper's Dale, back toward the northern wall, and the defending knights rode free once more.

But in came the pursuit from the south, the vast force of drow and humanoid monsters. In came those dark elf wizards who had survived Alustriel's conflagration in the thick copse.

The ranks of the defenders quickly sorted out, with Berkthgar's hearty warriors rallying behind their mighty leader and Besnell's knights linking with the force that had stood firm in Keeper's Dale. Likewise did the Longriders fall into line behind Regweld, and the Riders of Nesmé—both of the survivors—joined their brethren from the west.

Magic flashed and metal clanged and man and beast screamed in agony. The mist thickened with sweat, and the stone floor of the valley darkened with blood.

The defenders would have liked to form a solid line of defense, but to do so would leave them terribly vulnerable to the wizards, so they had followed savage Berkthgar's lead, had plunged into the enemy force headlong, accepting the sheer chaos.

Berg'inyon ran his mount halfway up the northern wall, high above the valley, to survey the glorious carnage. The weapons master cared nothing for his dead comrades, including many dark elves, whose broken bodies littered the valley floor.

This fight would be won easily, Berg'inyon thought, and the western door to Mithral Hall would be his.

All glory for House Baenre.

⚔ ⚔ ⚔ ⚔ ⚔

When Stumpet Rakingclaw came up from the Undercity to Mithral Hall's western door, she was dismayed—not by the reports of the vicious fighting out in Keeper's Dale, but by the fact that the dwarven guards had not gone out to aid the valiant defenders.

Their orders had been explicit: they were to remain inside the complex, to defend the tighter tunnels, and if the secret door was found by the enemy and the defenders were pushed back, the dwarves were prepared to drop those tunnels near the door. Those orders, given by General Dagna, Bruenor's second in command, had not foreseen the battle of Keeper's Dale.

Bruenor had appointed Stumpet as High Cleric of Mithral Hall, and had done so publicly and with much fanfare, so that there would be no confusion concerning rank once battle was joined. That decision, that public ceremony, gave Stumpet the power she needed now, allowed her to change the orders, and the five hundred dwarves assigned to guard the western door, who had watched with horror the carnage from afar, were all too happy to hear the new command.

There came a rumbling beneath the ground in all of Keeper's Dale, the grating of stone against stone. On the northern side of the valley, Berg'inyon held tight to his sticky-footed mount and hoped the thing wouldn't be shaken from the wall. He listened closely to the echoes, discerning the pattern, then looked to the southeastern corner of the valley.

A glorious, stinging light flashed there as the western door of Mithral Hall slid open.

Berg'inyon's heart skipped a beat. The dwarves had opened the way!

Out they came, hundreds of bearded folk, rushing to their allies' aid, singing and banging their axes and hammers against their shining shields, pouring from the door that was secret no more. They came up to, and beyond, Berkthgar's line, their tight battle groups slicing holes in the ranks of goblin and kobold and drow alike, pushing deeper into the throng.

"Fools!" the Baenre weapons master whispered, for even if a thousand, or two thousand dwarves came into Keeper's Dale, the course of the battle would not be changed. They had come out because their morals demanded it, Berg'inyon knew. They had opened their door and abandoned their best defenses because their ears could not tolerate the screams of men dying in their defense.

How weak these surface dwellers were, the sinister drow thought, for in Menzoberranzan courage and compassion were never confused.

The furious dwarves came into the battle hard, driving through drow and goblins with abandon. Stumpet Rakingclaw, fresh from her exploits in the Undercity, led their charge. She was out of light pellets but called to her god now, enacting enchantments to brighten Keeper's Dale. The dark elves quickly countered every spell, as the dwarf expected, but Stumpet figured that every drow concentrating on a globe of darkness was out of the fight, at least momentarily. The magic of Moradin, Dumathoin, and Clanggedon flowed freely through the priestess. She felt as though she was a pure conduit, the connection to the surface for the dwarven gods.

The dwarves rallied around her loud prayers as she screamed to her gods with all her heart. Other defenders rallied around the dwarves, and suddenly they were gaining back lost ground. Suddenly the idea of a single line of defense was not so ridiculous.

High on the wall across the way, Berg'inyon chuckled at the futility of it all. This was a temporary surge, he knew, and the defenders of the western door had come together in one final, futile push. All the defense and all the defenders, and Berg'inyon's force still outnumbered them several times over.

The weapons master coaxed his mount back down the wall, gathered his elite troops around him, and determined how to turn back the momentum. When Keeper's Dale fell, so, too, would the western door.

And Keeper's Dale would fall, Berg'inyon assured his companions with all confidence, within the hour.

26

Snarl Against Snarl

The main corridors leading to the lower door of Mithral Hall had been dropped and sealed, but that had been expected by the invading army. Even with the largest concentration of drow slowed to a crawl out in the tunnels beyond the door, the dwarven complex was hard pressed. And though no reports had come to Uthegental about the fighting outside the mountain, the mighty weapons master could well imagine the carnage on the slopes, with dwarves and weakling humans dying by the score. Both doors of Mithral Hall were likely breached by now, Uthegental believed, with Berg'inyon's lizard riders flooding the higher tunnels.

That notion bothered the weapons master of Barrison del'Armgo more than a little. If Berg'inyon was in Mithral Hall, and Drizzt Do'Urden was there, the renegade might fall to the son of House Baenre. Thus Uthegental and the small band of a half-dozen elite warriors he took in tow now sought the narrow ways that would get them to the lowest gate of Mithral Hall proper. Those tunnels should be open, with the dark elves filtering out from the Undercity to clear the way.

The weapons master and his escort came into the cavern that had previously served as Bruenor's command post. It was deserted now, with only a few parchments and scraps from clerical preparations to show that anyone had been in the place. After the fall of the tunnels and the collapse of portions of Tunult's Cavern—and many side tunnels, including the main one that led back to this chamber—Bruenor's lower groups apparently had been scattered, without any central command.

Uthegental passed through the place, hardly giving it a thought. The drow band moved swiftly down the corridors, staying generally east, silently following the weapons master's urgent lead. They came to a wide fork in the trail and noticed the very old bones of a two-headed giant lying against the wall—ironically, a kill Bruenor Battlehammer had made centuries before. Of more concern, though, was the fork in the tunnel.

Frustrated at yet another delay, Uthegental sent scouts left and right, then he and the rest of his group went right, the more easterly course.

Uthegental sighed, relieved that they had at last found the lower door, when his scout and another drow, a priestess, met him a few moments later.

"Greetings, Weapons master of the Second House," the priestess greeted, affording mighty Uthegental more respect than was normally given to mere males.

"Why are you out in the tunnels?" Uthegental wanted to know. "We are still far from the Undercity."

"Farther than you think," the priestess replied, looking disdainfully back toward the east, down the long tunnel that ended at the lower door. "The way is not clear."

Uthegental issued a low growl. Those dark elves should have taken the Undercity by now, and should have opened the passages. He stepped by the female, his pace revealing his anger.

"You'll not break through," the priestess assured him, and he spun around, scowling as though she had slapped him in the face.

"We have been striking at the door for an hour," the priestess explained. "And we shall spend another tenday before we get past that barricade. The dwarves defend it well."

"*Ultrin sargtlin!*" Uthegental roared, his favorite title, to remind the priestess of his reputation. Still, despite the fact that Uthegental had earned that banner of "Supreme Warrior," the female did not seem impressed.

"A hundred drow, five wizards, and ten priestesses have not breached the door," she said evenly. "The dwarves strike back against our magic with great spears and balls of flaming pitch. And the tunnel leading to the door is narrow and filled with traps, as well defended as House Baenre itself. Twenty minotaurs went down there, and those dozen that stumbled past the traps found hearty dwarves waiting for them, coming out of concealment from small, secret cubbies. Twenty minotaurs were slain in the span of a few minutes.

"You'll not break through," the priestess said again, her tone matter-of-fact and in no way insulting. "None of us will unless those who have entered the dwarven complex strike at the defenders of the door from behind."

Uthegental wanted to lash out at the female, mostly because he believed her claim.

"Why would you wish to enter the complex?" the female asked unexpectedly, slyly.

Uthegental eyed her with suspicion, wondering if she was questioning his bravery. Why wouldn't he want to find the fighting, after all?

"Whispers say your intended prey is Drizzt Do'Urden," the priestess went on.

Uthegental's expression shifted from suspicion to intrigue.

"Other whispers say the renegade is in the tunnels outside Mithral Hall," she explained, "hunting with his panther and killing quite a few drow."

Uthegental ran a hand through his spiked hair and looked back to the west, to the wild maze of tunnels he had left behind. He felt a surge of adrenaline course through his body, a tingling that tightened his muscles and set his features in a grim lock. He knew that many groups of enemies were operating in the tunnels outside the dwarven complex, scattered bands fleeing the seven-chambered cavern where the first battle had been fought. Uthegental and his companions had met and slain one such group of dwarves on their journey to this point.

Now that he thought about it, it made sense to Uthegental that Drizzt would be out here as well. It was very likely the renegade had been in the battle in the seven-chambered cavern, and if that was true, then why would Drizzt flee back into Mithral Hall?

Drizzt was a hunter, a former patrol leader, a warrior that had survived a decade alone with his magical panther in the wild Underdark—no small feat, and one that even Uthegental respected.

Yes, now that the priestess had told him the rumor, it made perfect sense to Uthegental that Drizzt Do'Urden would be out there, somewhere back in the tunnels to the west, roaming and killing. The weapons master laughed loudly and started back the way he had come, offering no explanation.

None was needed, to the priestess or to Uthegental's companions, who fell into line behind him.

The weapons master of the Second House was hunting.

⚔ ⚔ ⚔ ⚔ ⚔

"We are winning," Matron Baenre declared.

None of those around her—not Methil or Jarlaxle, not Matron Zeerith Q'Xorlarrin, of the Fourth House, or Auro'pol Dyrr, matron mother of House Agrach Dyrr, now the Fifth House, not Bladen'Kerst or Quenthel Baenre—argued the blunt statement.

Gandalug Battlehammer, dirty and beaten, his wrists bound tightly by slender shackles so strongly enchanted that a giant could not break them, cleared his throat, a noise that sounded positively gloating. There was more bluster than truth in the dwarf's attitude, for Gandalug carried with him a heavy weight. Even if his folk were putting up a tremendous fight, dark elves had gotten into the Undercity. And they had come to that place because of Gandalug, because of his knowledge of the secret ways. The old dwarf understood that no one could withstand the intrusions of an illithid, but the guilt remained, the notion that he, somehow, had not been strong enough.

Quenthel moved before Bladen'Kerst could react, smacking the obstinate prisoner hard across the back, her fingernails drawing lines of blood.

Gandalug snorted again, and this time Bladen'Kerst whacked him with her five-tonged snake-headed whip, a blow that sent the sturdy dwarf to his knees.

"Enough!" Matron Baenre growled at her daughters, a hint of her underlying frustration showing through.

They all knew—and it seemed Baenre did as well, despite her proclamation—that the war was not going according to plan. Jarlaxle's scouts had informed them of the bottleneck near Mithral Hall's lowest door, and that the eastern door from the surface had been blocked soon after it was breached, at a cost of many drow lives. Quenthel's magical communications with her brother told her that the fighting was still furious on the southern and western slopes of Fourthpeak, and that the western door from the surface had not yet been approached. And Methil, who had lost his two illithid companions, had telepathically assured Matron Baenre that the fight for the Undercity was not yet won, not at all.

Still, there was a measure of truth in Baenre's prediction of victory, they all knew, and her confidence was not completely superficial. The battle outside the mountain was not finished, but Berg'inyon had assured Quenthel that it soon would be—and given the power of the force that had gone out beside Berg'inyon, Quenthel had no reason to doubt his claim.

Many had died in these lower tunnels, but most of the losses had been humanoid slaves, not dark elves. Now those dwarves who had been caught outside their complex after the tunnel collapse had been forced into tactics of hunt and evade, a type of warfare that surely favored the stealthy dark elves.

"All the lower tunnels will soon be secured," Matron Baenre elaborated, a statement made obvious by the simple fact that this group, which would risk no encounters, was on the move once more. The elite force surrounding Baenre was responsible for guiding and guarding the first matron mother. They would not allow Baenre any advancement unless the area in front of them was declared secure.

"The region above the ground around Mithral Hall will also be secured," Baenre added, "with both surface doors to the complex breached."

"And likely dropped," Jarlaxle dared to put in.

"Sealing the dwarves in their hole," Matron Baenre was quick to respond. "We will fight through this lower door, and our wizards and priestesses will find and open new ways into the tunnels of the complex, that we might filter among our enemy's ranks."

Jarlaxle conceded the point, as did the others, but what Baenre was talking about would take quite a bit of time, and a drawn out siege had not been part of the plan. The prospect did not sit well with any of those around

Matron Baenre, particularly the other two matron mothers. Baenre had pressured them to come out, so they had, though their Houses, and all the city, was in a critical power flux. In exchange for the personal attendance of the matron mothers in the long march, House Xorlarrin and House Agrach Dyrr had been allowed to keep most of their soldiers at home, while the other Houses, particularly the other ruling Houses, had sent as much as half their complement of dark elves. For the few months that the army was expected to be away, the fourth and fifth Houses seemed secure.

But Zeerith and Auro'pol had other concerns, worries of power struggles within their families. The hierarchy of any drow House, except perhaps for Baenre, was always tentative, and the two matron mothers knew that if they were away for too long, they might return to find they had been replaced.

They exchanged concerned looks now, doubting expressions that ever observant Jarlaxle did not miss.

Baenre's battle group moved along on its slow and determined way, the three matron mothers floating atop their driftdisks, flanked by Baenre's two daughters—dragging the dwarf—and the illithid, who seemed to glide rather than walk, his feet hidden under his long, heavy robes. A short while later, Matron Baenre informed them that they would find an appropriate cavern and set up a central throne room, from which she could direct the continuing fight.

It was another indication that the war would be a long one, and again Zeerith and Auro'pol exchanged disconcerted looks.

Bladen'Kerst Baenre narrowed her eyes at both of them, silently threatening.

Jarlaxle caught it all, every connotation, every hint of where Matron Baenre might find her greatest troubles.

The mercenary leader bowed low and excused himself, explaining that he would join up with his band and try to garner more timely information.

Baenre waved her hand, dismissing him without a second thought. One of her escorts was not so casual.

You and your mercenaries will flee, came an unexpected message in Jarlaxle's mind.

The mercenary's own thoughts whirled in a jumble, and caught off guard, he couldn't avoid sending the telepathic reply that the notion of deserting the war had indeed crossed his mind. As close to desperation as he had ever been, Jarlaxle looked back over his shoulder at the expressionless face of the intruding illithid.

Beware of Baenre should she return, Methil imparted casually, and he continued on his way with Baenre and the others.

Jarlaxle paused for a long while when the group moved out of sight, scrutinizing the emphasis of the illithid's last communication. He came to realize that Methil would not inform Baenre of his wavering loyalty. Somehow, from the way the message had been given, Jarlaxle knew that.

The mercenary leaned against a stone wall, thinking hard about what his next move should be. If the drow army stayed together, Baenre would eventually win—that much he did not doubt. The losses would be greater than anticipated—they already had been—but that would be of little concern once Mithral Hall was taken, along with all its promised riches.

What, then, was Jarlaxle to do? The disturbing question was still bouncing around the mercenary's thoughts when he found some of his Bregan D'aerthe lieutenants, all bearing news of the continuing bottleneck near the lower door, and information that even more dark elves and slaves were being killed in the outer tunnels, falling prey to roving bands of dwarves and their allies.

The dwarves were defending, and fighting, well.

Jarlaxle made his decision and relayed it silently to his lieutenants in the intricate hand code. Bregan D'aerthe would not desert, not yet. But neither would they continue to spearhead the attack, risking their forward scouts.

Avoid all fights, Jarlaxle's fingers flashed, and the gathered soldiers nodded their accord. *We stay out of the way, and we watch, nothing more.*

Until Mithral Hall is breached, one of the lieutenants reasoned back.

Jarlaxle nodded. *Or until the war becomes futile*, his fingers replied, and from his expression, it was obvious the mercenary leader did not think his last words ridiculous.

✕ ✕ ✕ ✕ ✕

Pwent and his band rambled through tunnel after tunnel, growing frustrated, for they found no drow, or even kobolds, to slam.

"Where in the Nine Hells are we?" the battlerager demanded. No answer came in reply, and when he thought about it, Pwent really couldn't expect one. He knew these tunnels better than any in his troupe, and if he had no idea where they were, then certainly the others were lost.

That didn't bother Pwent so much. He and his furious band really didn't care where they were as long as they had something to fight. Lack of enemies was the real problem.

"Start to bangin'!" Pwent roared, and the Gutbusters ran to the walls in the narrow corridor and began slamming hammers against the stone, causing such a commotion that every creature within two hundred yards would easily be able to figure out where they were.

Poor Bidderdoo Harpell, swept up in the wake of the craziest band of suicidal dwarves, stood in the middle of the tunnel, using his glowing gem to try to sort through the few remaining parchments from his blasted spellbook, looking for a spell, any spell—though preferably one that would get him out of this place!

The racket went on for several minutes, and frustrated, Pwent ordered his dwarves to form up, and off they stormed. They went under a natural archway, around a couple of bends in the passage, then came upon a wider and squarer way, a tunnel with worked stone along its walls and an even floor. Pwent snapped his fingers, realizing that they had struck out to the west and south of Mithral Hall. He knew this place, and knew that he would find a dwarven defensive position around the next corner. He bobbed around in the lead, and scrambled over a barricade that reached nearly to the ceiling, hoping to find some more allies to "enlist" into his terror group. As he crested the wall, Pwent stopped short, his smile erased.

Ten dwarves lay dead on the stone floor, amidst a pile of torn goblins and orcs.

Pwent fell over the wall, landed hard, but bounced right back to his feet. He shook his head as he walked among the carnage. This position was strongly fortified, with the high wall behind, and a lower wall in front, where the corridor turned a sharp corner to the left.

Mounted against that left-hand wall, just before the side tunnel, was a curious contraption, a deadly dwarven side-slinger catapult, with a short, strong arm that whipped around to the side, not over the top, as with conventional catapults. The arm was pulled back now, ready to fire, but Pwent noticed immediately that all the ammunition was gone, that the valiant dwarves had held out to the last.

Pwent could smell the remnants of that catapult's missiles and could see flickering shadows from the small fires. He knew before he peeked around the bend that many, many dead enemies would line the corridor beyond.

"They died well," the battlerager said to his minions as they and Bidderdoo crossed the back wall and walked among the bodies.

The charge around the corner came fast and silent, a handful of dark elves rushing out, swords drawn.

Had Bidderdoo Harpell not been on the alert—and had he not found the last remaining usable page of his spellbook—that would have been the swift end of the Gutbuster Brigade, but the wizard got his spell off, enacting a blinding—to the drow—globe of brilliant light.

The surprised dark elves hesitated just an instant, but long enough for the Gutbusters to fall into battle posture. Suddenly it was seven dwarves against five dark elves, the element of surprise gone. Seven battleragers against five dark elves, and what was worse for the drow, these battleragers happened to be standing among the bodies of dead kin.

They punched, kicked, jumped, squealed, and head-butted with abandon, ignoring any hits, fighting to make their most wild leader proud. They plowed under two of the drow, and one dwarf broke free, roaring as he charged around the bend.

Pwent got one drow off to the side, caught the dark elf's swinging sword in one metal gauntlet and punched straight out with the other before the drow could bring his second sword to bear.

The drow's head verily exploded under the weight of the spiked gauntlet, furious Pwent driving his fist right through the doomed creature's skull.

He hit the drow again, and a third time, then tossed the broken body beside the other four dead dark elves. Pwent looked around at his freshly bloodied troops, noticed at once that one was missing, and noticed, too, that Bidderdoo was trembling wildly, his jowls flapping noisily. The battlerager would have asked the wizard about it, but then the cry of agony from down the side corridor chilled the marrow in even sturdy Thibbledorf Pwent's bones. He leaped to the corner and looked around.

The carnage along the length of the fifty-foot corridor was even more tremendous than Pwent had expected. Scores of humanoids lay dead, and several small fires still burned, so thick was the pitch from the catapult missiles along the floor and walls.

Pwent watched as a large form entered the other end of the passage, a shadowy form, but the battlerager knew it was a dark elf, though certainly the biggest he had ever seen. The drow carried a large trident, and on the end of the trident, still wriggling in the last moments of his life, was Pwent's skewered Gutbuster. Another drow came out behind the huge weapons master, but Pwent hardly noticed the second form, and hardly cared if a hundred more were to follow.

The battlerager roared in protest, but did not charge. In a rare moment where cleverness outweighed rage, Pwent hopped back around the corner.

"What is it, Most Wild Battlerager?" three of the Gutbusters yelled together.

Pwent didn't answer. He jumped into the basket of the side-slinger and slashed his spiked gauntlet across the trigger rope, cutting it cleanly.

Uthegental Armgo had just shaken free the troublesome kill when the side-slinger went off, shooting the missile Pwent down the corridor. The weapons master's eyes went wide; he screamed as Pwent screamed. Suddenly Uthegental wished he still had the dead dwarf handy, that he might use the body as a shield. Purely on instinct, the warrior drow did the next best thing. He grabbed his drow companion by the collar of his *piwafwi* and yanked him in front.

Pwent's helmet spike, and half his head, blasted the unfortunate dark elf, came through cleanly enough to score a hit on Uthegental as well.

The mighty weapons master extracted himself from the tumble as Pwent tore free of the destroyed drow. They came together in a fit of fury, rage against rage, snarl against snarl, Pwent scoring several hits, but Uthegental, so strong and skilled, countering fiercely.

The butt of the trident slammed Pwent's face, and his eyes crossed. He staggered backward and realized, to his horror, that he had just given this mighty foe enough room to skewer him.

A silver beast, a great wolf running on its hind legs, barreled into Uthegental from the side, knocking him back to the floor.

Pwent shook his head vigorously, clearing his mind, and regarded the newest monster with more than a little apprehension. He glanced back up the corridor to see his Gutbusters approaching fast, all of them pointing to the wolf and howling with glee.

"Bidderdoo," Pwent mumbled, figuring it out.

Uthegental tossed the werewolf Harpell aside and leaped back to his feet. Before he had fully regained his balance, though, Pwent sprang atop him.

A second dwarf leaped atop him, followed by a third, a fourth, the whole of the Gutbuster Brigade.

Uthegental roared savagely, and suddenly, the drow possessed the strength of a giant. He stood tall, dwarves hanging all over him, and threw his arms out wide, plucking dwarves and hurling them as though they were mere rodents.

Pwent slammed him in the chest, a blow that would have killed a fair-sized cow.

Uthegental snarled and gave the battlerager a backhand slap that launched Pwent a dozen feet.

"Ye're good," a shaky Pwent admitted, coming up to one knee as Uthegental stalked in.

For the first time in his insane life—except, perhaps, for when he had inadvertently battled Drizzt—Thibbledorf Pwent knew he was out-matched—knew that his whole brigade was outmatched!—and thought he was dead. Dwarves lay around groaning and none would be able to intercept the impossibly strong drow.

Instead of trying to stand, Pwent cried out and hurled himself forward, scrambling on his knees. He came up at the last second, throwing all of his weight into a right hook.

Uthegental caught the hand in midswing and fully halted Pwent's momentum. The mighty drow's free hand closed over Pwent's face, and Uthegental began bending the poor battlerager over backward.

Pwent could see the snarling visage through the wide-spread fingers. He somehow found the strength to lash out with his free left, and scored a solid hit on the drow's forearm.

Uthegental seemed not to care.

Pwent whimpered.

The weapons master threw his head back suddenly.

Pwent thought the drow meant to issue a roar of victory, but no sound came from Uthegental's mouth, no noise at all, until a moment later when he gurgled incoherently.

Pwent felt the drow's grip relax, and the battlerager quickly pulled away. As he straightened, Pwent came to understand. The silver werewolf had come up behind Uthegental and had bitten the drow on the back of the neck. Bidderdoo held on still, all the pressure of his great maw crushing the vertebrae and the nerves.

The two held the macabre pose for many heartbeats, and all the conscious Gutbusters gathered around them marveled at the strength of Bidderdoo's mouth, and at the fact that this tremendous drow warrior was still holding his feet.

There came a loud crack, and Uthegental jerked suddenly, violently. Down he fell, the wolf atop him, holding fast.

Pwent pointed to Bidderdoo. "I got to get him to show me how he did that," the awe-stricken battlerager remarked.

Bidderdoo, clamped tightly on his kill, didn't hear.

27

THE LONGEST NIGHT

B elwar heard the echoes, subtle vibrations in the thick stone that no surface dweller could ever have noticed. The other three hundred svirfnebli
heard them as well. This was the way of the deep gnomes—in the deeper tunnels of the Underdark, they often communicated by sending quiet vibrations
through the rock. They heard the echoes now, constant echoes, not like the
one huge explosion they had heard a couple of hours before, the rumbling of
an entire network of tunnels being dropped. The seasoned svirfnebli fighters considered the newest sound, a peculiar rhythm, and they knew what it
meant. Battle had been joined, a great battle, and not so far away.

Belwar conferred with his commanders many times as they inched
through the unfamiliar terrain, trying to follow the strongest vibrations.
Often one of the svirfnebli on the perimeter, or at the point of the group,
would tap his hammer slightly on the stone, trying to get a feel for the density
of the rock. Echo hunting was tricky because the density of the stone was
never uniform, and vibrations were often distorted. Thus, the svirfnebli,
arguably the finest echo followers in all the world, found themselves more
than once going the wrong way down a fork in the trail.

A determined and patient bunch, though, they stayed with it, and after
many frustrating minutes, a priest named Suntunavick bobbed up to Belwar
and Firble and announced with all confidence that this was as close to the
sound as these tunnels would allow them to get.

The two followed the priest to the exact spot, alternately putting their ears against the stone. Indeed the noise beyond was loud, relatively speaking.

And constant, Belwar noted with some confusion, for this was not the echoing of give-and-take battle, not the echoes they had heard earlier, or at least, there was more to the sound than that.

Suntunavick assured the burrow warden this was the correct place. Mixed in with this more constant sound was the familiar rhythm of battle joined.

Belwar looked to Firble, who nodded, then to Suntunavick. The burrow warden poked his finger at the spot on the wall, then backed away, so Suntunavick and the other priests could crowd in.

They began their chanting, a grating, rumbling, and apparently wordless sound, and every once in a while one of the priests would throw a handful of some mudlike substance against the stone.

The chanting hit a crescendo. Suntunavick rushed up to the wall, his hands straight out in front of him, palms pressed tightly together. With a cry of ecstacy, the little gnome thrust his fingers straight into the stone. Then he groaned, his arm and shoulder muscles flexing as he pulled the wall apart, opened it as though it were no more solid than a curtain of heavy fabric.

The priest jumped back, and so did all the others, as the echo became a roar and a fine spray, the mist of a waterfall, came in on them.

"The surface, it is," Firble muttered, barely able to find his breath.

And so it was, but this deluge of water was nothing like any of the gnomes had pictured the surface world, was nothing like the descriptions in the many tales they had heard of the strange place. Many in the group harbored thoughts of turning back then and there, but Belwar, who had spoken with Drizzt not so long ago, knew something here was out of the ordinary.

The burrow warden hooked a rope from his belt with his pick-axe hand and held it out to Firble, indicating that the councilor should tie it around his waist. Firble did so and took up the other end, bracing himself securely.

With only the slightest of hesitation, the brave Belwar squeezed through the wall, through the veil of mist. He found the waterfall, and a ledge that led him around it, and Belwar gazed upon stars.

Thousands of stars!

The gnome's heart soared. He was awed and frightened all at once. This was the surface world, that greatest of caverns, under a dome that could not be reached.

The moment of pondering, of awe, was short-lived, defeated by the clear sounds of battle. Belwar was not in Keeper's Dale, but he could see the light of the fight, flames from torches and magical enchantments, and he could hear the ring of metal against metal and the familiar screams of the dying.

With Belwar in their lead, the three hundred svirfnebli filtered out of the caverns and began a quiet march to the east. They came upon many areas that seemed impassable, but a friendly elemental, summoned by gnomish priests, opened the way. In but a few minutes, the battle was in sight, the scramble within the misty vale, of armor-clad horsemen and lizard-riding drow, of wretched goblins and kobolds and huge humans more than twice the height of the tallest svirfneblin.

Now Belwar did hesitate, realizing fully that his force of three hundred would plunge into a battle of thousands, a battle in which the gnomes had no way of discerning who was winning.

"It is why we have come," Firble whispered into the burrow warden's ear.

Belwar looked hard at his uncharacteristically brave companion.

"For Blingdenstone," Firble said.

Belwar led the way.

⚔ ⚔ ⚔ ⚔

Drizzt held his breath, they all did, and even Guenhwyvar was wise enough to stifle an instinctive snarl.

The five companions huddled on a narrow ledge in a high, wide corridor, while a column of drow, many drow, marched past, a line that went on and on and seemed as if it would never end.

Two thousand? Drizzt wondered. Five thousand? He had no way of guessing. There were too many, and he couldn't rightly stick his head out and begin a count. What Drizzt did understand was that the bulk of the drow force had linked together and was marching with a singular purpose. That could mean only that the way had been cleared, at least to Mithral Hall's lower door. Drizzt took heart when he thought of that door, of the many cunning defenses that had been rigged in that region. Even this mighty force would be hard-pressed to get through the portal; the tunnels near the lower door would pile high with bodies, drow and dwarf alike.

Drizzt dared to slowly shift his head, to look past Guenhwyvar, tight against the wall beside him, to Bruenor, stuck uncomfortably between the panther's rear end and the wall. Drizzt almost managed a smile at the sight, and at the thought that he had better move quickly once the drow column passed, for Bruenor would likely heave the panther right over the lip of the ledge, taking Drizzt with her.

But that smile did not come to Drizzt, not in the face of his doubts. Had he done right in leading Bruenor out here? he wondered, not for the first time. They could have gone back to the lower door with the dwarves they had met hours before; the king of Mithral Hall could be in place among his army. Drizzt did not underestimate how greatly Bruenor's fiery presence would bolster the defense of that lower door, and the defense of the Undercity. Every dwarf of Mithral Hall would sing a little louder and fight with a bit more heart in the knowledge that King Bruenor Battlehammer was nearby, joining in the cause, his mighty axe leading the way.

Drizzt's reasoning had kept Bruenor out, and now the drow wondered if his action had been selfish. Could they even find the enemy leaders? Likely the priestesses who had led this army would be well hidden, using magic from afar, directing their forces with no more compassion than if the soldiers were pawns on a gigantic chess board.

The matron mother, or whoever was leading this force, would take no personal risks, because that was the drow way.

Suddenly, up there and crouched on that ledge, Drizzt Do'Urden felt very foolish. They were hunting the head, as he had explained to Bruenor, but that head would not be easy to find. and given the size of the force that was marching along below them, toward Mithral Hall, Drizzt and Bruenor and their other companions would not likely get anywhere near the dwarven complex anytime soon.

The ranger put his head down and blew a deep, silent breath, composing himself, reminding himself he had taken the only possible route to winning the day, that though that lower door would not be easily breached, it would eventually come down, whether or not Bruenor Battlehammer was among the defenders. But out here now, with so many drow and so many tunnels, Drizzt began to appreciate the enormity of the task before him. How could he ever hope to find the leaders of the drow army?

What Drizzt did not know was that he was not the only one on a purposeful hunt.

⚔ ⚔ ⚔ ⚔

"No word from Bregan D'aerthe."

Matron Baenre sat atop her driftdisk, digesting the words and the meaning behind them. Quenthel started to repeat them, but a threatening scowl from her mother stopped her short.

Still the phrase echoed in Matron Baenre's mind. "No word from Bregan D'aerthe."

Jarlaxle was lying low, Baenre realized. For all his bravado, the mercenary leader was, in fact, a conservative one, very cautious of any risks to the band he had spent centuries putting together. Jarlaxle hadn't been overly eager to march to Mithral Hall, and had, in fact, come along only because he hadn't really been given a choice in the matter.

Like Triel, Baenre's own daughter and closest advisor, the mercenary had hoped for a quick and easy conquest and a fast return to Menzoberranzan, where so many questions were still to be answered. The fact that no word had come lately from the Bregan D'aerthe scouts could be coincidence, but Baenre suspected differently. Jarlaxle was lying low, and that could mean only that he, with the reports that he was constantly receiving from the sly scouts of his network, believed the momentum halted, that he, like Baenre herself, had come to the conclusion that Mithral Hall would not be easily swept away.

The withered old matron mother accepted the news stoically, with confidence that Jarlaxle would be back in the fold once the tide turned again in the dark elves' favor. She would have to come up with a creative punishment for the mercenary leader, of course, one that would let Jarlaxle know the depth of her dismay without costing her a valuable ally.

A short while later, the air in the small chamber Baenre had come to use as her throne room began to tingle with the budding energy of an enchantment. All in the room glanced nervously around and breathed easier when Methil stepped out of thin air into the midst of the drow priestesses.

His expression revealed nothing, just the same passive, observant stare that always came from one of Methil's otherworldly race. Baenre considered that always unreadable face the most frustrating facet of dealing with the illithids. Never did they give even the subtlest clue of their true intentions.

Uthegental Armgo is dead, came a thought in Baenre's mind, a blunt report from Methil.

Now it was Baenre's turn to put on a stoic, unrevealing facade. Methil had given the disturbing thought to her and to her alone, she knew. The others, particularly Zeerith and Auro'pol, who were becoming more and more skittish, did not need to know the news was bad, very bad.

The march to Mithral Hall goes well, came Methil's next telepathic message. The illithid shared it with all in the room, which Matron Baenre realized by the suddenly brightening expressions. *The tunnels are clear all the way to the lower door, where the army gathers and prepares.*

Many nods and smiles came back at the illithid, and Matron Baenre did not have any more trouble than Methil in reading the thoughts behind those expressions. The illithid was working hard to bolster morale—always a tentative thing in dealing with dark elves. but like Quenthel's report, or lack of report, from Bregan D'aerthe, the first message the illithid had given echoed in Baenre's thoughts disconcertingly. Uthegental Armgo was dead! What might the soldiers of Barrison del'Armgo, a significant force vital to the cause, do when they discovered their leader had been slain?

And what of Jarlaxle? Baenre wondered. If he had learned of the brutish weapons master's fall, that would certainly explain the silence of Bregan D'aerthe. Jarlaxle might be fearing the loss of the Barrison del'Armgo garrison, a desertion that would shake the ranks of the army to its core.

Jarlaxle does not know, nor do the soldiers of the Second House, Methil answered her telepathically, obviously reading her thoughts.

Still Baenre managed to keep up the cheery—relatively speaking—front, seeming thrilled at the news of the army's approach to the lower door. She clearly saw a potential cancer growing within her ranks, though, a series of events that could destroy the already shaky integrity of her army and her alliances, and could cost her everything. She felt as though she were falling back to that time of ultimate chaos in Menzoberranzan just before the march, when K'yorl seemed to have the upper hand.

The destruction of House Oblodra had solidified the situation then, and Matron Baenre felt she needed something akin to that now, some dramatic victory that would leave no doubts in the minds of the rank and file. Foster loyalty with fear. She thought of House Oblodra again and toyed with the idea of a similar display against Mithral Hall's lower door. Baenre quickly dismissed it, realizing that what had happened in Menzoberranzan had been a one-time event. Never before—and likely never again—and certainly not so soon afterward!—had Lolth come so gloriously and so fully to the Material Plane. On the occasion of House Oblodra's fall, Matron Baenre had been the pure conduit of the Spider Queen's godly power.

That would not happen again.

Baenre's thoughts swirled in a different direction, a more feasible trail to follow. *Who killed Uthegental?* she thought, knowing that Methil would "hear" her.

The illithid had no answer, but understood what Baenre was implying. Baenre knew what Uthegental had sought, knew the only prize that really mattered to the mighty weapons master. Perhaps he had found Drizzt Do'Urden.

If so, that would mean Drizzt Do'Urden was in the lower tunnels, not behind Mithral Hall's barricades.

You follow a dangerous course, Methil privately warned, before Baenre could even begin to plot out the spells that would let her find the renegade.

Matron Baenre dismissed that notion with hardly a care. She was the first matron mother of Menzoberranzan, the conduit of Lolth, possessed of powers that could snuff the life out of any drow in the city, any matron mother, any

wizard, any weapons master, with hardly an effort. Baenre's course now was indeed dangerous, she agreed—dangerous for Drizzt Do'Urden.

⚔ ⚔ ⚔ ⚔ ⚔

Most devastating was the dwarven force and the center of the blocking line, a great mass of pounding, singing warriors, mulching goblins and orcs under their heavy hammers and axes, leaping in packs atop towering minotaurs, their sheer weight of numbers bringing the brutes down.

But all along the eastern end of Keeper's Dale, the press was too great from every side. Mounted knights rushed back and forth across the barbarian line, bolstering the ranks wherever the enemy seemed to be breaking through, and with their timely support, the line held. Even so, Berkthgar's people found themselves inevitably pushed back.

The bodies of kobolds and goblins piled high in Keeper's Dale; a score dying for every defender. But the drow could afford those losses, had expected them, and Berg'inyon, sitting astride his lizard, calmly watching the continuing battle from afar along with the rest of the Baenre riders, knew that the time for slaughter grew near. The defenders were growing weary, he realized. The minutes had turned into an hour, and that into two, and the assault did not diminish.

Back went the defending line, and the towering eastern walls of Keeper's Dale were not so far behind them. When those walls halted the retreat, the drow wizards would strike hard. Then Berg'inyon would lead the charge, and Keeper's Dale would run even thicker with the blood of humans.

⚔ ⚔ ⚔ ⚔ ⚔

Besnell knew they were losing, knew that a dozen dead goblins were not worth the price of an inch of ground. A resignation began to grow within the elf, tempered only by the fact that never had he seen his knights in finer form. Their tight battle groups rushed to and fro, trampling enemies, and though every man was breathing so hard he could barely sing out a war song, and every horse was lathered in thick sweat, they did not relent, did not pause.

Grimly satisfied, and yet terribly worried—and not just for his own men, for Alustriel had made no further appearance on the field—the elf turned his attention to Berkthgar, then he was truly amazed. The huge flamberge, Bankenfuere, hummed as it swept through the air, each cut obliterating any enemies foolish enough to stand close to the huge man. Blood, much of it his own, covered the barbarian from head to toe, but if Berkthgar felt any pain, he did not show it. His song and his dance were to Tempus, the god of battle, and so he sang, and so he danced, and so his enemies died.

In Besnell's mind, if the drow won here and conquered Mithral Hall, one of the most tragic consequences would be that the tale of the exploits of mighty Berkthgar the Bold would not leave Keeper's Dale.

A tremendous flash to the side brought the elf from his contemplations. He looked down the line to see Regweld Harpell surrounded by a dozen dead or dying, flaming goblins. Regweld and Puddlejumper were also engulfed by the magical flames, dancing licks of green and red, but the wizard and his extraordinary mount did not seem bothered and continued to fight without regard for the fires. Indeed, those fires engulfing the duo became a weapon, an extension of Regweld's fury when the wizard leaped Puddlejumper nearly a dozen yards, to land at the feet of two towering minotaurs. Red and green flames became white hot and leaped out from the wizard's torso, engulfing the towering brutes. Puddlejumper hopped straight up, bringing Regweld even with the screaming minotaurs' ugly faces. Out came a wand, and green blasts of energy tore into the monsters.

Then Regweld was gone, leaping to the next fight, leaving the minotaurs staggering, flames consuming them.

"For the good of all goodly folk!" Besnell cried, holding his sword high. His battle group formed beside him, and the thunder of the charge began anew, this time barreling full stride through a mass of kobolds. They scattered the beasts and came into a thicker throng of larger enemies, where the charge was stopped. Still atop their mounts, the Knights in Silver hacked through the morass, bright swords slaughtering enemies.

Besnell was happy. He felt a satisfaction coursing through his body, a sensation of accomplishment and righteousness. The elf believed in

Silverymoon with all his heart, believed in the precept he yelled out at every opportunity.

He was not sad when a goblin spear found a crease at the side of his breastplate, rushed in through his ribs, and collapsed a lung. He swayed in his saddle and somehow managed to knock the spear from his side.

"For the good of all goodly folk!" he said with all the strength he could muster. A goblin was beside his mount, sword coming in.

Besnell winced with pain as he brought his own sword across to block. He felt weak and suddenly cold. He hardly registered the loss as his sword slipped from his hand to clang to the ground.

The goblin's next strike cut solidly against the knight's thigh, the drow-made weapon tearing through Besnell's armor and drawing a line of bright blood.

The goblin hooted, then went flying away, broken apart by the mighty sweep of Bankenfuere.

Berkthgar caught Besnell in his free hand as the knight slid off his mount. The barbarian felt somehow removed from the battle at that moment, as though he and the noble elf were alone, in their own private place. Around them, not so far away, the knights continued the slaughter and no monsters approached.

Berkthgar gently lowered Besnell to the ground. The elf looked up, his golden eyes seeming hollow.

"For the good of all goodly folk," Besnell said, his voice barely a whisper, but by the grace of Tempus, or whatever god was looking over the battle of Keeper's Dale, Berkthgar heard every syllable.

The barbarian nodded and silently laid the dead elf's head on the stone.

Then Berkthgar was up again, his rage multiplied, and he charged head-long into the enemy ranks, his great sword cutting a wide swath.

⚔ ⚔ ⚔ ⚔ ⚔

Regweld Harpell had never known such excitement. Still in flames that did not harm him or his horse-frog, but attacked any that came near, the wizard single-handedly bolstered the southern end of the defending line. He was quickly running out of spells, but Regweld didn't care, knew that he would find some way to make himself useful, some way to destroy the wretches that had come to conquer Mithral Hall.

A group of minotaurs converged on him, their great spears far out in front to prevent the fires from getting at them.

Regweld smiled and coaxed Puddlejumper into another flying leap, straight up between the circling monsters, higher than even minotaurs and their long spears could reach.

The Harpell let out a shout of victory, then a lightning bolt silenced him.

Suddenly Regweld was free-flying, spinning in the air, and Puddlejumper was spinning the other way just below him.

A second thundering bolt came in from a different angle, and a third, forking so that it hit both the wizard and his strange mount.

They were each hit again, and again after that as they tumbled, falling very still upon the stone.

The drow wizards had joined the battle.

The invaders roared and pressed on, and even Berkthgar, outraged by the valiant elf's death, could not rally his men to hold the line. Drow lizard riders filtered in through the humanoid ranks, their long lances pushing the mounted knights inevitably back, back toward the blocking wall.

⚔ ⚔ ⚔ ⚔ ⚔

Berg'inyon was among the first to see the next turn of the battle. He ordered a rider up the side of a rock pillar, to gain a better vantage point, then turned his attention to a group nearby, pointing to the northern wall of the valley.

Go up high, the weapons master's fingers signaled to them. *Up high and around the enemy ranks, to rain death on them from above when they are pushed back against the wall.*

Evil smiles accompanied the agreeing nods, but a cry from the other side, from the soldier Berg'inyon had sent up high, stole the moment.

The rock pillar had come to life as a great elemental monster. Berg'inyon and the others looked on helplessly as the stone behemoth clapped together great rock arms, splattering the drow and his lizard.

There came a great clamor from behind the drow lines, from the west, and above the thunder of the svirfneblin charge was heard a cry of "Bivrip!" the word Belwar Dissengulp used to activate the magic in his crafted hands.

✕ ✕ ✕ ✕ ✕

It was a long time before Berkthgar and the other defenders at the eastern end of Keeper's Dale even understood that allies had come from the west. Those rumors eventually filtered through the tumult of battle, though, heartening defender and striking fear into invader. The goblins and dark elves engaged near that eastern wall began to look back the other way, wondering if disaster approached.

Now Berkthgar did rally what remained of the non-dwarven defenders: two-third of his barbarians, less than a hundred Knights in Silver, a score of Longriders, and only two of the men from Nesmé. Their ranks were depleted, but their spirit returned, and the line held again, even made progress in following the dwarven mass back out toward the middle of Keeper's Dale.

Soon after, all semblance of order was lost in the valley. No longer did lines of soldiers define enemies. In the west, the svirfneblin priests battled drow wizards, and Belwar's warriors charged hard into drow ranks. They were the bitterest of enemies, ancient enemies, drow and svirfnebli. No less could be said on the eastern side of the valley, where dwarves and goblins hacked away at each other with abandon.

It went on through the night, a wild and horrible night. Berg'inyon Baenre engaged in little combat and kept the bulk of his elite lizard riders back as well, using his monstrous fodder to weary the defense. Even with the unexpected arrival of the small but powerful svirfneblin force, the drow soon turned the tide back their way.

"We will win," the young Baenre promised those soldiers closest to him. "And what defense might be left in place beyond the western door of the dwarven complex?

DIVINATION

Quenthel Baenre sat facing a cubby of the small chamber's wall, staring down into a pool of calm water. She squinted as the pool, a scrying pool, brightened, as the dawn broke on the outside world, not so far to the east of Fourthpeak.

Quenthel held her breath, though she wanted to cry out in despair.

Across the small chamber, Matron Baenre was similarly divining. She had used her spells to create a rough map of the area, and to enchant a single tiny feather. Chanting again, Baenre tossed the feather into the air above the spread parchment and blew softly.

"Drizzt Do'Urden," she whispered in that breath, and she puffed again as the feather flopped and flitted down to the map. A wide, evil grin spread across Baenre's face when the feather, the magical pointer, touched down, its tip indicating a group of tunnels not far away.

It was true, Baenre knew then. Drizzt Do'Urden was indeed in the tunnels outside Mithral Hall.

"We leave," the matron mother said suddenly, startling all in the quiet chamber.

Quenthel looked back nervously over her shoulder, afraid that her mother had somehow seen what was in her scrying pool. The Baenre daughter found that she couldn't see across the room, though, for the view was blocked by a scowling Bladen'Kerst, glaring down at her, and past her, at the approaching spectacle.

"Where are we to go?" Zeerith, near the middle of the room, asked aloud, and from her tone, it was obvious she was hoping Matron Baenre's scrying had found a break in the apparent stalemate.

Matron Baenre considered that tone and the sour expression on the other matron mother's face. She wasn't sure whether Zeerith, and Auro'pol, who was similarly scowling, would have preferred to hear that the way was clear into Mithral Hall, or that the attack had been called off. Looking at the two of them, among the very highest-ranking commanders of the drow army, Baenre couldn't tell whether they preferred victory or retreat.

That obvious reminder of how tentative her alliance was angered Baenre. She would have liked to dismiss both of them, or, better, to have them executed then and there. But Baenre could not, she realized. The morale of her army would never survive that. Besides, she wanted them, or at least one of them, to witness her glory, to see Drizzt Do'Urden given to Lolth.

"You shall go to the lower door, to coordinate and strengthen the attack," Baenre said sharply to Zeerith, deciding that the two of them standing together were becoming too dangerous. "And Auro'pol shall go with me."

Auro'pol didn't dare ask the obvious question, but Baenre saw it clearly anyway from her expression.

"We have business in the outer tunnels," was all Matron Baenre would offer.

Berg'inyon will soon see the dawn, Quenthel's fingers motioned to her sister.

Bladen'Kerst, always angry, but now boiling with rage, turned away from Quenthel and the unwanted images in the scrying pool and looked back to her mother.

Before she could speak, though, a telepathic intrusion came into her mind, and into Quenthel's. *Do not speak ill of other battles,* Methil imparted to them both. *Already, Zeerith and Auro'pol consider desertion.*

Bladen'Kerst considered the message and the implications and wisely held her information.

The command group split apart, then, with Zeerith and a contingent of the elite soldiers going east, toward Mithral Hall, and Matron Baenre leading Quenthel, Bladen'Kerst, Methil, half a dozen skilled Baenre female warriors, and the chained Gandalug off to the south, in the direction of the spot indicated by her divining feather.

✕ ✕ ✕ ✕ ✕

On another plane, the gray mists and sludge and terrible stench of the Abyss, Errtu watched the proceedings in the glassy mirror Lolth had created on the side of the mushroom opposite his throne.

The great balor was not pleased. Matron Baenre was hunting Drizzt Do'Urden, Errtu knew, and he knew, too, that Baenre would likely find the renegade and easily destroy him.

A thousand curses erupted from the tanar'ri's doglike maw, all aimed at Lolth, who had promised him freedom—freedom that only a living Drizzt Do'Urden could bestow.

To make matters even worse, a few moments later, Matron Baenre was casting yet another spell, opening a planar gate to the Abyss, calling forth a mighty glabrezu to help in her hunting. In his twisted, always suspicious mind, Errtu came to believe that this summoning was enacted only to torment him, to take one of his own kind and use the beast to facilitate the end of the pact. That was the way with tanar'ri, and with all the wretches of the Abyss, Lolth included. These creatures were without trust for others, since they, themselves, could not be trusted by any but a fool. And they were an ultimately selfish lot, every one. In Errtu's eyes, every action revolved around him, because nothing else mattered, and thus, Baenre summoning a glabrezu now was not coincidence, but a dagger jabbed by Lolth into Errtu's black heart.

Errtu was the first to the opening gate. Even if he was not bound to the Abyss by banishment, he could not have gone through, because Baenre, so skilled in this type of summoning, was careful to word the enchantment for a specific tanar'ri only. But Errtu was waiting when the glabrezu appeared through the swirling mists, heading for the opened, flaming portal.

The balor leaped out and lashed out with his whip, catching the glabrezu by the arm. No minor fiend, the glabrezu moved to strike back, but stopped, seeing that Errtu did not mean to continue the attack.

"It is a deception!" Errtu roared.

The glabrezu, its twelve-foot frame hunched low, great pincers nipping anxiously at the air, paused to listen.

"I was to come forth on the Material Plane," Errtu went on.

"You are banished," the glabrezu said matter-of-factly.

"Lolth promised an end!" Errtu retorted, and the glabrezu crouched lower, as if expecting the volatile fiend to leap upon him.

But Errtu calmed quickly. "An end, that I might return, and bring forth behind me an army of tanar'ri." Again Errtu paused. He was improvising now, but a plan was beginning to form in his wicked mind.

Baenre's call came again, and it took all the glabrezu's considerable will-power to keep it from leaping through the flaring portal.

"She will allow you only one kill," Errtu said quickly, seeing the glabrezu's hesitance.

"One is better than none," the glabrezu answered.

"Even if that one prevents my freedom on the Material Plane?" Errtu asked. "Even if it prevents me from going forth, and bringing you forth as my general, that we might wreak carnage on the weakling races?"

Baenre called yet again, and this time it was not so difficult for the glabrezu to ignore her.

Errtu held up his great hands, indicating that the glabrezu should wait here a few moments longer, then the balor sped off, into the swirl, to retrieve something a lesser fiend had given him not so long ago, a remnant of the Time of Troubles. He returned shortly with a metal coffer and gently opened it, producing a shining black sapphire. As soon as Errtu held it up, the flames of the magical portal diminished, and almost went out altogether. Errtu was quick to put the thing back in its case.

"When the time is right, reveal this," the balor instructed, "my general."

He tossed the coffer to the glabrezu, unsure, as was the other fiend, of how this would all play out. Errtu's great shoulders ruffled in a shrug then, for there was nothing else he could do. He could prevent this fiend from going to Baenre's aid, but to what end? Baenre hardly needed a glabrezu to deal with Drizzt Do'Urden, a mere warrior.

The call from the Material Plane came yet again, and this time the glabrezu answered, stepping through the portal to join Matron Baenre's hunting party.

Errtu watched in frustration as the portal closed, another gate lost to the Material Plane, another gate that he could not pass through. Now the balor had done all he could, though he had no way of knowing if it would be enough, and he had so much riding on the outcome. He went back to his mushroom throne then, to watch and wait.

And hope.

✖ ✖ ✖ ✖ ✖

Bruenor remembered. In the quiet ways of the tunnels, no enemies to be seen, the eighth king of Mithral Hall paused and reflected. Likely the dawn was soon to come on the outside, another crisp, cold day. But would it be the last day of Clan Battlehammer?

Bruenor looked to his four friends as they took a quick meal and a short rest. Not one of them was a dwarf, not one.

And yet, Bruenor Battlehammer could not name any other friends above these four: Drizzt, Catti-brie, Regis, and even Guenhwyvar. For the first time, that truth struck the dwarf king as curious. Dwarves, though not xenophobic, usually stayed to their own kind. Witness General Dagna, who, if given his way, would kick Drizzt out of Mithral Hall and would take Taulmaril away from Catti-brie, to hang the bow once more in the Hall of Dumathoin. Dagna didn't trust anyone who was not a dwarf.

But here they were, Bruenor and his four non-dwarven companions, in perhaps the most critical and dangerous struggle of all for the defense of Mithral Hall.

Surely their friendship warmed the old dwarf king's heart, but reflecting on that now did something else as well.

It made Bruenor think of Wulfgar, the barbarian who had been like his own son, and who would have married Catti-brie and become his son-in-law, the unlikely seven-foot prince of Mithral Hall. Bruenor had never known such grief as that which bowed his strong shoulders after Wulfgar's

fall. Though he should live for more than another century, Bruenor had felt close to death in those tendays of grieving, and had felt as if death would be a welcome thing.

No longer. He missed Wulfgar still—forever would his gray eye mist up at the thought of the noble warrior—but he was the eighth king, the leader of his proud, strong clan. Bruenor's grief had passed the point of resignation and had shifted into the realm of anger. The dark elves were back, the same dark elves who had killed Wulfgar. They were the followers of Lolth, evil Lolth, and now they meant to kill Drizzt and destroy all of Mithral Hall, it seemed.

Bruenor had wetted his axe on drow blood many times during the night, but his rage was far from sated. Indeed, it was mounting, a slow but determined boil. Drizzt had promised they would hunt the head of their enemy, would find the leader, the priestess behind this assault. It was a promise Bruenor needed to see the drow ranger keep.

He had been quiet through much of the fighting, even in preparing for the war. Bruenor was quiet now, too, letting Drizzt and the panther lead, finding his place among the friends whenever battle was joined.

In the few moments of peace and rest, Bruenor saw a wary glance come his way more than once and knew that his friends feared he was brooding again, that his heart was not in the fight. Nothing could have been farther from the truth. Those minor skirmishes didn't matter much to Bruenor. He could kill a hundred—a thousand!—drow soldiers, and his pain and anger would not relent. If he could get to the priestess behind it all, though, chop her down and decapitate the drow invading force . . .

Bruenor might know peace.

The eighth king of Mithral Hall was not brooding. He was biding his time and his energy, coming to a slow boil. He was waiting for the moment when revenge would be most sweet.

⚔ ⚔ ⚔ ⚔ ⚔

Baenre's group, the giant glabrezu in tow, had just begun moving again, the matron mother guiding them in the direction her scrying had indicated, when Methil telepathically informed her that matrons Auro'pol and Zeerith had been continually entertaining thoughts of her demise. If Zeerith couldn't find a way through Mithral Hall's lower door, she would simply organize a withdrawal. Even now, Auro'pol was considering the potential for swinging the whole army around and leaving Matron Baenre dead behind them, according to Methil.

Do they plot against me? Baenre wanted to know.

No, Methil honestly replied, *but if you are killed, they will be thrilled to turn back for Menzoberranzan without you, that a new hierarchy might arise.*

In truth, Methil's information was not unexpected. One did not have to read minds to see the discomfort and quiet rage on the faces of the matron mothers of Menzoberranzan's fourth and Fifth Houses. Besides, Baenre had suffered such hatred from her lessers, even from supposed allies such as Mez'Barris Armgo, even from her own daughters, for all her long life. That was an expected cost of being the first matron mother of chaotic and jealous Menzoberranzan, a city continually at war with itself.

Auro'pol's thoughts were to be expected, but the confirmation from the illithid outraged the already nervous Matron Baenre. In her twisted mind, this was no ordinary war, after all. This was the will of Lolth, as Baenre was the Spider Queen's agent. This was the pinnacle of Matron Baenre's power, the height of Lolth-given glory. How dare Auro'pol and Zeerith entertain such blasphemous thoughts? the first matron mother fumed.

She snapped an angry glare over Auro'pol, who simply snorted and looked away—possibly the very worst thing she could have done.

Baenre issued telepathic orders to Methil, who in turn relayed them to the glabrezu. The driftdisks, side by side, were just following Baenre's daughters around a bend in the tunnel when great pincers closed around Auro'pol's slender waist and yanked her from her driftdisk, the powerful glabrezu easily holding her in midair.

"What is this?" Auro'pol demanded, squirming to no avail.

"You wish me dead," Baenre answered.

Quenthel and Bladen'Kerst rushed back to their mother's side, and both were stunned that Baenre had openly moved against Auro'pol.

"She wishes me dead," Baenre informed her daughters. "She and Zeerith believe Menzoberranzan would be a better place without Matron Baenre."

Auro'pol looked to the illithid, obviously the one who had betrayed her. Baenre's daughters, who had entertained similar treasonous thoughts on more than one occasion during this long, troublesome march, looked to Methil as well.

"Matron Auro'pol bears witness to your glory," Quenthel put in. "She will witness the death of the renegade and will know that Lolth is with us."

Auro'pol's features calmed at that statement, and she squirmed again, trying to loosen the tanar'ri's viselike grip.

Baenre eyed her adversary dangerously, and Auro'pol, cocky to the end, matched the intensity of her stare. Quenthel was right, Auro'pol believed. Baenre needed her to bear witness. Bringing her into line behind the war would solidify Zeerith's loyalty as well, so the drow army would be much stronger. Baenre was a wicked old thing, but she had always been a calculating one, not ready to sacrifice an inch of power for the sake of emotional satisfaction. Witness Gandalug Battlehammer, still alive, though Baenre certainly would have enjoyed tearing the heart from his chest many times during the long centuries of his imprisonment.

"Matron Zeerith will be glad to hear of Drizzt Do'Urden's death," Auro'pol said, and lowered her eyes respectfully. The submissive gesture would suffice, she believed.

"The head of Drizzt Do'Urden will be all the proof Matron Zeerith requires," Baenre replied.

Auro'pol's gaze shot up, and Baenre's daughters, too, looked upon their surprising mother.

Baenre ignored them all. She sent a message to Methil, who again relayed it to the glabrezu, and the great pincers began to squeeze around Auro'pol's waist.

"You cannot do this!" Auro'pol objected, gasping for every word. "Lolth is with me! You weaken your own campaign!"

Quenthel wholeheartedly agreed, but kept silent, realizing the glabrezu still had an empty pincer.

"You cannot do this!" Auro'pol shrieked. "Zeerith will . . ." Her words were lost to pain.

"Drizzt Do'Urden killed you before I killed Drizzt Do'Urden," Matron

Baenre explained to Auro'pol. "Perfectly believable, and it makes the renegade's death all the sweeter." Baenre nodded to the glabrezu, and the pincers closed, tearing through flesh and bone.

Quenthel looked away, but wicked Bladen'Kerst watched the spectacle with a wide smile.

Auro'pol tried to call out once more, tried to hurl a dying curse Baenre's way, but her backbone snapped and all her strength washed away. The pincers snapped shut, and Auro'pol Dyrr's body fell apart to the floor.

Bladen'Kerst cried out in glee, thrilled by her mother's display of control and power. Quenthel, though, was outraged. Baenre had stepped over a dangerous line. She had killed a matron mother, and had done so to the detriment of the march to Mithral Hall, purely for personal gain. Wholeheartedly devoted to Lolth, Quenthel could not abide such stupidity, and her thoughts were similar indeed to those that had gotten Auro'pol Dyrr chopped in half.

Quenthel snapped a dangerous glare over Methil, realizing the illithid was reading her thoughts. Would Methil betray her next?

She narrowed her thoughts into a tight focus. *It is not Lolth's will!* her mind screamed at Methil. *No longer is the Spider Queen behind my mother's actions.*

That notion held more implications for Methil, the illithid emissary to Menzoberranzan, not to Matron Baenre, than Quenthel could guess, and her relief was great indeed when Methil did not betray her.

⚔ ⚔ ⚔ ⚔ ⚔

Guenhwyvar's ears flattened, and Drizzt, too, thought he heard a slight, distant scream. They had seen no one, enemies or friends, for several hours, and the ranger believed that any group of dark elves they now encountered would likely include the high priestess leading the army.

He motioned for the others to move with all caution, and the small band crept along, Guenhwyvar leading the way. Drizzt fell into his Underdark instincts now. He was the hunter again, the survivor who had lived alone for a decade in the wilds of the Underdark. He looked back at Bruenor, Regis, and Catti-brie often, for, though they were moving with all the stealth they could manage, they sounded like a marching army of armored soldiers to Drizzt's keen ears. That worried the drow, for he knew their enemies would be far quieter. He considered going a long way ahead with Guenhwyvar, taking up the hunt alone.

It was a passing thought. These were his friends, and no one could ever ask for finer allies.

They slipped down a narrow, unremarkable tunnel and into a chamber that opened wide to the left and right, though the smooth wall directly opposite the tunnel was not far away. The ceiling here was higher than in the tunnel, but stalactites hung down in several areas, nearly to the floor in many places.

Guenhwyvar's ears flattened again, and the panther paused at the entrance. Drizzt came beside her and felt the same tingling sensation.

The enemy was near, very near. That warrior instinct, beyond the normal senses, told the drow ranger the enemy was practically upon them. He signaled back to the three trailing, then he and the panther moved slowly and cautiously into the chamber, along the wall to the right.

Catti-brie came to the entrance next and fell to one knee, bending back her bow. Her eyes, aided by the Cat's Eye circlet, which made even the darkest tunnels seem bathed in bright starlight, scanned the chamber, searching among the stalactite clusters.

Bruenor was soon beside her, and Regis came past her on the left. The halfling spotted a cubby a few feet along the wall. He pointed to himself, then to the cubby, and he inched off toward the spot.

A green light appeared on the wall opposite the door, stealing the darkness. It spiraled out, opening a hole in the wall, and Matron Baenre floated through, her daughters and their prisoner coming in behind her, along with the illithid.

Drizzt recognized the withered old drow and realized his worst fears, knew immediately that he and his friends were badly overmatched. He thought to go straight for Baenre, but realized that he and Guenhwyvar were not alone on this side of the chamber. From the corner of his wary eye Drizzt caught some movement up among the stalactites.

Catti-brie fired a silver-streaking arrow, practically point-blank. The arrow exploded into a shower of multicolored, harmless sparks, unable to penetrate the first matron mother's magical shields.

Regis went into the cubby then and cried out in sudden pain as a ward exploded. Electricity sparked around the halfling, sending him jerking this way and that, then dropping him to the floor, his curly brown hair standing straight on end.

Guenhwyvar sprang to the right, burying a drow soldier as she floated down from the stalactites. Drizzt again considered going straight for Baenre, but found himself suddenly engaged as three more elite Baenre guards rushed out of hiding to surround him. Drizzt shook his head in denial. Surprise now worked against him and his friends, not for them. The enemy had expected them, he knew, had hunted them even as they had hunted the enemy. And this was Matron Baenre herself!

"Run!" Drizzt cried to his friends. "Flee this place!"

29
KING AGAINST QUEEN

The long night drifted into morning, with the dark elves once again claiming the upper hand in the battle for Keeper's Dale. Berg'inyon's assessment of the futility of the defense, even with the dwarven and svirfneblin reinforcements, seemed correct as the drow ranks gradually engulfed the svirfnebli, then pushed the line in the east back toward the wall once more.

But then it happened.

After an entire night of fighting, after hours of shaping the battle, holding back the wizards, using the lizard riders at precise moments and never fully committing them to the conflict, all the best laid plans of the powerful drow force fell apart.

The rim of the mountains east of Keeper's Dale brightened, a silvery edge that signaled the coming dawn. For the drow and the other monsters of the Underdark, that was no small event.

One drow wizard, intent on a lightning bolt that would defeat the nearest enemies, interrupted his spell and enacted a globe of darkness instead, aiming it at the tip of the sun as it peeked over the horizon, thinking to blot out the light. The spell went off and did nothing more than a put a black dot in the air a long way off, and as the wizard squinted against the glare, wondering what he might try next, those defenders closest charged in and cut him down.

Another drow battling a dwarf had his opponent all but beaten. So intent was he on the kill that he hardly noticed the coming dawn—until the tip of the sun broke the horizon, sending a line of light, a line of agony, to sensitive drow eyes. Blinded and horrified, the dark elf whipped his weapons in a frenzy, but he never got close to hitting the mark.

Then he felt a hot explosion across his ribs.

All these dark elves had seen things in the normal spectrum of light before, but not so clearly, not in such intense light, not with colors so rich and vivid. They had heard of the terrible sunshine—Berg'inyon had witnessed a dawn many years before, had watched it over his shoulder as he and his drow raiding party fled back for the safe darkness of the lower tunnels. Now the weapons master and his charges did not know what to expect. Would the infernal sun burn them as it blinded them? They had been told by their elders that it would not, but had been warned they would be more vulnerable in the sunlight, that their enemies would be bolstered by the brightness.

Berg'inyon called his forces into tight battle formations and tried to regroup. They could still win, the weapons master knew, though this latest development would cost many drow lives. Dark elves could fight blindly, but what Berg'inyon feared here was more than a loss of vision. It was a loss of heart. The rays slanting down from the mountains were beyond his and his troops' experience. And as frightening as it had been to walk under the canopy of unreachable stars, this event, this sunrise, was purely terrifying.

Berg'inyon quickly conferred with his wizards, tried to see if there was some way they could counteract the dawn. What he learned instead distressed him as much as the infernal light. The drow wizards in Keeper's Dale had eyes also in other places, and from those far-seeing mages came the initial whispers that dark elves were deserting in the lower tunnels, that those drow who had been stopped in the tunnels near the eastern door had retreated from Mithral Hall and had fled to the deeper passages on the eastern side of Fourthpeak. Berg'inyon understood that information easily enough; those drow were already on the trails leading back to Menzoberranzan.

Berg'inyon could not ignore the reports' implications. Any alliance between dark elves was tentative, and the weapons master could only guess at how widespread the desertion might be. Despite the dawn, Berg'inyon believed his force would win in Keeper's Dale and would breach the western door, but suddenly he had to wonder what they would find in Mithral Hall once they got there.

Matron Baenre and their allies? King Bruenor and the renegade, Drizzt, and a host of dwarves ready to fight? The thought did not sit well with the worried weapons master.

Thus, it was not greater numbers that won the day in Keeper's Dale. It was not the courage of Berkthgar or Besnell, or the ferocity of Belwar and his gnomes, or the wisdom of Stumpet Rakingclaw. It was the dawn and the distrust among the enemy ranks, the lack of cohesion and the very real fear that supporting forces would not arrive, for every drow soldier, from Berg'inyon to the lowest commoner, understood that their allies would think nothing of leaving them behind to be slaughtered.

Berg'inyon Baenre was not questioned by any of his soldiers when he gave the order to leave Keeper's Dale. The lizard riders, still more than three hundred strong, rode out to the rough terrain of the north, their sticky-footed mounts leaving enemies and allies alike far behind.

The very air of Keeper's Dale tingled from the tragedy and the excitement, but the sounds of battle died away to an eerie stillness, shattered occasionally by a cry of agony. Berkthgar the Bold stood tall and firm, with Stumpet Rakingclaw and Terrien Doucard, the new leader of the Knights in Silver, flanking him, and their victorious soldiers waiting, tensed, behind them.

Ten feet away, Belwar Dissengulp stood point for the depleted svirfneblin ranks. The most honored burrow warden held his strong arms out before him, cradling the body of noble Firble, one of many svirfnebli who had died this day, so far from, but in defense of, their home.

They did not know what to make of each other, this almost-seven-foot barbarian, and the gnome who was barely half his height. They could not talk to each other, and had no comprehensible signs of friendship to offer.

They found their only common ground among the bodies of hated enemies and beloved friends, piled thick in Keeper's Dale.

⚔ ⚔ ⚔ ⚔ ⚔

Faerie fire erupted along Drizzt's arms and legs, outlining him as a better target. He countered by dropping a globe of darkness over himself, an attempt to steal the enemy's advantage of three-to-one odds.

Out snapped the ranger's scimitars, and he felt a strange urge from one, not from Twinkle, but from the other blade, the one Drizzt had found in the lair of the dragon Dracos Icingdeath, the blade that had been forged as a bane to creatures of fire.

The scimitar was hungry. Drizzt had not felt an urge from it since . . .

He parried the first attack and groaned, remembering the other time his scimitar had revealed its hunger, when he had battled the balor Errtu. Drizzt knew what this meant.

Baenre had brought friends.

⚔ ⚔ ⚔ ⚔ ⚔

Catti-brie fired another arrow, straight at the withered old matron mother's laughing visage. Again the enchanted arrow merely erupted into a pretty display of useless sparks. The young woman turned to flee, as Drizzt had ordered. She grabbed her father, meaning to pull him along.

Bruenor wouldn't budge. He looked to Baenre and knew she was the source. He looked at Baenre and convinced himself that she had personally killed his boy. Then Bruenor looked past Baenre, to the old dwarf. Somehow Bruenor knew that dwarf. In his heart, the eighth king of Mithral Hall recognized the patron of his clan, though he could not consciously make the connection.

"Run!" Catti-brie yelled at him, taking him temporarily from his thoughts. Bruenor glanced at her, then looked behind, back down the tunnel.

He heard fighting in the distance, from somewhere behind them.

Quenthel's spell went off then, and a wall of fire sprang up in the narrow tunnel, cutting off retreat. That didn't bother determined Bruenor much, not now. He shrugged himself free of Catti-brie's hold and turned back to face Baenre—in his own mind, to face the evil dark elf who had killed his boy.

He took a step forward.

Baenre laughed at him.

✘ ✘ ✘ ✘ ✘

Drizzt parried and struck, then, using the cover of the darkness globe, quick-stepped to the side, too quickly for the dark elf coming in at his back to realize the shift. She bored in and struck hard, hitting the same drow that Drizzt had just wounded, finishing her.

Hearing the movement, Drizzt came right back, both his blades whirling. To the female's credit, she registered the countering move in time to parry the first attack, the second and the third, even the fourth.

But Drizzt did not relent. He knew his fury was a dangerous thing. There remained one more enemy in the darkness globe, and for Drizzt to press against a single opponent so forcefully left him vulnerable to the other. But the ranger knew, too, that his friends sorely needed him, that every moment he spent engaged with these warriors gave the powerful priestesses time to destroy them all.

The ranger's fifth attack, a wide-arcing left, was cleanly picked off, as was the sixth, a straightforward right thrust. Drizzt pressed hard, would not relinquish the offensive. He knew, and the female knew, that her only hope would be in her lone remaining ally.

A stifled scream, followed by the growl of a panther ended that hope.

Drizzt's fury increased, and the female continued to fall back, stumbling now in the darkness, suddenly afraid. And in that moment of fear, she banged her head hard against a low stalactite, an obstacle her keen drow senses should have detected. She shook off the blow and managed to straighten her posture, throwing one sword out in front to block another of the ranger's furious thrusts.

She missed.

Drizzt didn't, and Twinkle split the fine drow armor and dived deep into the female's lung.

Drizzt yanked the blade free and spun around.

His darkness globe went away abruptly, dispelled by the magic of the waiting tanar'ri.

✘ ✘ ✘ ✘ ✘

Bruenor took another step, then broke into a run. Catti-brie screamed, thinking him dead, as a line of fire came down on him.

Furious, frustrated, the young woman fired her bow again, and more harmless sparks exploded in the air. Through the tears of outrage that welled in her blue eyes she hardly noticed that Bruenor had shrugged off the stinging hit and broke into a full charge again.

Bladen'Kerst stopped the dwarf, enacting a spell that surrounded Bruenor in a huge block of magical, translucent goo. Bruenor continued to move, but so slowly as to be barely perceptible, while the three drow priestesses laughed at him.

Catti-brie fired again, and this time her arrow hit the block of goo, diving in several feet before stopping and hanging uselessly in place above her father's head.

Catti-brie looked to Bruenor, to Drizzt and the horrid, twelve-foot fiend that had appeared to the right, and to Regis, groaning and trying to crawl at her left. She felt the heat as fires raged in the tunnel behind her, heard the continuing battle back, that way which she did not understand.

They needed a break, a turn in the tide, and Catti-brie thought she saw it then, and a moment of hope came to her. Finished with the kill, Guenhwyvar growled and crouched, ready to spring upon the tanar'ri.

That moment of hope for Catti-brie was short-lived, for as the panther sprang out, one of the priestesses casually tossed something into the air, Guenhwyvar's way. The panther dissipated into gray mist in midleap and was gone, sent back to the Astral Plane.

"And so we die," Catti-brie whispered, for this enemy was too strong. She dropped Taulmaril to the floor and drew Khazid'hea. A deep breath steadied her, reminded her that she had run close to death's door for most of her adult life. She looked to her father and prepared to charge, prepared to die.

A shape wavered in front of the block of goo, between Catti-brie and Bruenor, and the look of determination on the young woman's face turned to one of disgust as a gruesome, octopus-headed monster materialized on this side of the magical block, calmly walking—no, floating—toward her.

Catti-brie raised her sword, then stopped, overwhelmed suddenly by a psionic blast, the likes of which she had never known.

Methil waded in.

✖ ✖ ✖ ✖ ✖

Berg'inyon's force pulled up and regrouped when they had cleared Keeper's Dale completely, had left the din of battle far behind and were near the last run for the tunnels back to the Underdark. Dimensional doors opened near the lizard riders, and drow wizards—and those other dark elves fortunate enough to have been near the wizards when the spells were enacted—stepped through. Stragglers, infantry drow and a scattering of humanoid allies, struggled to catch up, but they could not navigate the impossible terrain on this sign of the mountain. And they were of no concern to the Baenre weapons master.

All those who had escaped Keeper's Dale looked to Berg'inyon for guidance as the day brightened around them.

"My mother was wrong," Berg'inyon said bluntly, an act of blasphemy in drow society, where the word of any matron mother was Lolth-given law.

Not a drow pointed it out, though, or raised a word of disagreement. Berg'inyon motioned to the east, and the force lumbered on, into the rising sun, miserable and defeated.

"The surface is for surface-dwellers," Berg'inyon remarked to one of his advisors when she walked her mount beside his. "I shall never return."

"What of Drizzt Do'Urden?" the female asked, for it was no secret that Matron Baenre wanted her son to slay the renegade.

Berg'inyon laughed at her, for not once since he had witnessed Drizzt's exploits at the Academy had he entertained any serious thoughts of fighting the renegade.

✖ ✖ ✖ ✖ ✖

Drizzt could see little beyond the gigantic glabrezu, and that spectacle was enough, for the ranger knew he was not prepared for such a foe, knew that the mighty creature would likely destroy him.

Even if it didn't defeat him, the glabrezu would surely hold him up long enough for Matron Baenre to kill them all!

Drizzt felt the savage hunger of his scimitar, a blade forged to kill such beasts, but he fought off the urge to charge, knew that he had to find a way around those devilish pincers.

He noted Guenhwyvar's futile leap and disappearance. Another ally lost.

The fight was over before it had begun, Drizzt realized. They had killed a couple of elite guards and nothing more. They had walked headlong into the pinnacle of Menzoberranzan's power, the most high priestesses of the Spider Queen, and they had lost. Waves of guilt washed over Drizzt, but he dismissed them, refused to accept them. He had come out, and his friends had come beside him, because this had been Mithral Hall's only chance. Even if Drizzt had known that Matron Baenre herself was leading this march, he would have come out here, and would not have denied Bruenor, Regis, and Catti-brie the opportunity to accompany him.

They had lost, but Drizzt meant to make their enemy hurt.

"Fight on, demon spawn," he snarled at the glabrezu, and he fell into a crouch, waving his blades, eager to give his scimitar the meal it so greatly desired.

The tanar'ri straightened and held out a curious metal coffer.

Drizzt didn't wait for an explanation, and almost unintentionally destroyed the only chance he and his friends had, for as the tanar'ri moved to open the coffer, Drizzt, with the enchanted ankle bracers speeding his rush, yelled and charged, right past the lowered pincers, thrusting his scimitar into the fiend's belly.

He felt the surge of power as the scimitar fed.

❌ ❌ ❌ ❌ ❌

Catti-brie was too confused to strike, too overwhelmed to even cry out in protest as Methil came right up to her and the wretched tentacles licked her face. Then, through the confusion, a single voice, the voice of Khazid'hea, her sword, called out in her head.

Strike!

She did, and though her aim was not perfect, Khazid'hea's wicked edge hit Methil on the shoulder, nearly severing the illithid's arm.

Out of her daze, Catti-brie swept the tentacles from her face with her free hand.

Another psionic wave blasted her, crippling her once more, stealing her strength and buckling her legs. Before she went down, she saw the illithid jerk weirdly, then fall away, and saw Regis, staggering, his hair still dancing wildly. The halfling's mace was covered in blood, and he fell sidelong, over the stumbling Methil.

That would have been the end of the illithid, especially when Catti-brie regained her senses enough to join in, except that Methil had anticipated such a disaster and had stored enough psionic energy to get out of the fight. Regis lifted his mace for another strike, but felt himself sinking as the illithid dissipated beneath him. The halfling cried out in confusion, in terror, and swung anyway, but his mace clanged loudly as it hit only the empty stone floor beneath him.

⚔ ⚔ ⚔ ⚔ ⚔

It all happened in a mere instant, a flicker of time in which poor Bruenor had not gained an inch toward his taunting foes.

The glabrezu, in pain greater than anything it had ever known, could have killed Drizzt then. Every instinct within the wicked creature urged it to snap this impertinent drow in half. Every instinct except one: the fear of Errtu's reprisal once the tanar'ri got back to the Abyss—and with that vile scimitar chewing away at its belly, the tanar'ri knew it would soon make that trip.

It wanted so much to snap Drizzt in half, but the fiend had been sent here for a different reason, and evil Errtu would accept no explanations for failure. Growling at the renegade Do'Urden, taking pleasure only in the knowledge that Errtu would soon return to punish this one personally, the glabrezu reached across and tore open the shielding coffer, producing the shining black sapphire.

SIEGE OF DARKNESS

The hunger disappeared from Drizzt's scimitar. Suddenly, the ranger's feet weren't moving so quickly.

Across the Realms, the most poignant reminder of the Time of Troubles were the areas known as dead zones, wherein all magic ceased to exist. This sapphire contained within it the negative energy of such a zone, possessed the antimagic to steal magical energy, and not Drizzt's scimitars or his bracers, not Khazid'hea or the magic of the drow priestesses, could overcome that negative force.

It happened for only an instant, for a consequence of revealing that sapphire was the release of the summoned tanar'ri from the Material Plane, and the departing glabrezu took with it the sapphire.

For only an instant, the fires stopped in the tunnel behind Catti-brie. For only an instant, the shackles binding Gandalug lost their enchantment. For only an instant, the block of goo surrounding Bruenor was no more.

For only an instant, but that was long enough for Gandalug, teeming with centuries of rage, to tear his suddenly feeble shackles apart, and for Bruenor to surge ahead, so that when the block of goo reappeared, he was beyond its influence, charging hard and screaming with all his strength.

Matron Baenre had fallen unceremoniously to the floor, and her driftdisk reappeared when magic returned, hovering above her head.

Gandalug launched a backhand punch to the left, smacking Quenthel in the face and knocking her back against the wall. Then he jumped to the right and caught Bladen'Kerst's five-headed snake whip in his hand, taking more than one numbing bite.

The old dwarf ignored the pain and pressed on, barreling over the surprised Baenre daughter. He reached around her other shoulder and caught the handle of her whip in his free hand, then pulled the thing tightly against her neck, strangling her with her own wicked weapon.

They fell in a clinch.

✕ ✕ ✕ ✕ ✕

In all the Realms there was no creature more protected by magic than Matron Baenre, no creature shielded from blows more effectively, not even a

322

thick-scaled ancient dragon. But most of those wards were gone now, taken from her in the moment of antimagic. And in all the Realms there was no creature more consumed by rage than Bruenor Battlehammer, enraged at the sight of the old, tormented dwarf he knew he should recognize. Enraged at the realization that his friends, that his dear daughter, were dead, or soon would be. Enraged at the withered drow priestess, in his mind the personification of the evil that had taken his boy.

He chopped his axe straight overhead, the many-notched blade diving down, shattering the blue light of the driftdisk, blowing the enchantment into nothingness. Bruenor felt the burn as the blade hit one of the few remaining magical shields, energy instantly coursing up the weapon's head and handle, into the furious king.

The axe went from green to orange to blue as it tore through magical defense after magical defense, rage pitted against powerful dweomers. Bruenor felt agony, but would admit none.

The axe drove through the feeble arm that Baenre lifted to block, through Baenre's skull, through her jawbone and neck, and deep into her frail chest.

⚔ ⚔ ⚔ ⚔ ⚔

Quenthel shook off Gandalug's heavy blow and instinctively moved for her sister. Then, suddenly, her mother was dead and the priestess rushed back toward the wall instead, through the green-edged portal, back into the corridor beyond. She dropped some silvery dust as she passed through, enchanted dust that would dispel the portal and make the wall smooth and solid once again.

The stone spiraled in, fast transforming back into a solid barrier.

Only Drizzt Do'Urden, moving with the speed of the enchanted anklets, got through that opening before it snapped shut.

⚔ ⚔ ⚔ ⚔ ⚔

Jarlaxle and his lieutenants were not far away. They knew that a group of wild dwarves and a wolfman had met Baenre's other elite guards in the

tunnels across the way, and that the dwarves and their ally had overwhelmed the dark elves and were fast bearing down on the chamber.

From a high vantage point, looking out from a cubby on the tunnel behind that chamber, Jarlaxle knew the approaching band of furious dwarves had already missed the action. Quenthel's appearance, and Drizzt's right behind her, told the watching mercenary leader the conquest of Mithral Hall had come to an abrupt end.

The lieutenant at Jarlaxle's side lifted a hand-crossbow toward Drizzt, and seemed to have a perfect opportunity, for Drizzt's focus was solely on the fleeing Baenre daughter. The ranger would never know what hit him.

Jarlaxle grabbed the lieutenant's wrist and forced the arm down. Jarlaxle motioned to the tunnels behind, and he and his somewhat confused, but ultimately loyal, band slipped silently away.

As they departed, Jarlaxle heard Quenthel's dying scream, a cry of "Sacrilege!" She was yelling out a denial, of course, in Drizzt Do'Urden's—her killer's—face, but Jarlaxle realized she could just as easily, and just as accurately, have been referring to him.

So be it.

✕ ✕ ✕ ✕ ✕

The dawn was bright but cold, and it grew colder still as Stumpet and Terrien Doucard, of the Knights in Silver, made their way up the difficult side of Keeper's Dale, climbing hand over hand along the almost vertical wall.

"Ye're certain?" Stumpet asked Terrien, a half-elf with lustrous brown hair and features too fair to be dimmed by even the tragedy of the last night.

The knight didn't bother to reply, other than with a quick nod, for Stumpet had asked the question more than a dozen times in the last twenty minutes.

"This is the right wall?" Stumpet asked, yet another of her redundant questions.

Terrien nodded. "Close," he assured the dwarf.

Stumpet came up on a small ledge and slid over, putting her back against the wall, her feet hanging over the two-hundred-foot drop to the valley floor.

She felt she should be down there in the valley, helping tend to the many, many wounded, but if what the knight had told her was true, if Lady Alustriel of Silverymoon had fallen up here, then this trip might be the most important task Stumpet Rakingclaw ever completed in her life.

She heard Terrien struggling below her and bent over, reaching down to hook the half-elf under the shoulder. Stumpet's powerful muscles corded, and she easily hoisted the slender knight over the ledge, guiding him into position beside her against the wall. Both the half-elf and the dwarf breathed heavily, puffs of steam filling the air before them.

"We held the dale," Stumpet said cheerily, trying to coax the agonized expression from the half-elf's face.

"Would the victory have been worth it if you had watched Bruenor Battlehammer die?" the half-elf replied, his teeth chattering a bit from the frigid air.

"Ye're not for knowing that Alustriel died!" Stumpet shot back, and she pulled the pack from her back, fumbling around inside. She had wanted to wait a while before doing this, hopefully to get closer to the spot where Alustriel's chariot had reportedly gone down.

She took out a small bowl shaped of silvery mithral and pulled a bulging waterskin over her head.

"It is probably frozen," the dejected half-elf remarked, indicating the skin.

Stumpet snorted. Dwarven holy water didn't freeze, at least not the kind Stumpet had brewed, dropping in a little ninety-proof to sweeten the mix. She popped the cork from the waterskin and began a rhythmic chant as she poured the golden liquid into the mithral bowl. She was lucky—she knew that—for though the image her spells brought forth was fuzzy and brief, an area some distance away, she knew this region, and knew where to find the indicated ledge.

They started off immediately at a furious and reckless pace, Stumpet not even bothering to collect her bowl and skin. The half-elf slipped more than once, only to be caught by the wrist by Stumpet's strong grasp, and more than once Stumpet found herself falling, and only the quick hands of Terrien Doucard, deftly planting pitons to secure the rope between them, saved her.

Finally, they got to the ledge and found Alustriel lying still and cold. The only indication that her magical chariot had ever been there was a scorch mark where the thing had crashed, on the floor of the ledge and against the mountain wall. Not even debris remained, for the chariot had been wholly a creation of magic.

The half-elf rushed to his fallen leader and gently cradled Alustriel's head in one arm. Stumpet whipped out a small mirror from her belt pouch and stuck it in front of the lady's mouth.

"She's alive!" the dwarf announced, tossing her pack to Terrien. The words seemed to ignite the half-elf. He gently laid Alustriel's head to the ledge, then fumbled in the pack, tearing out several thick blankets, and wrapped his lady warmly, then began briskly rubbing Alustriel's bare, cold hands. All the while, Stumpet called upon her gods for spells of healing and warmth, and gave every ounce of her own energy to this wondrous leader of Silverymoon.

Five minutes later, Lady Alustriel opened her beautiful eyes. She took a deep breath and shuddered, then whispered something neither Stumpet nor the knight could hear, so the half-elf leaned closer, put his ear right up to her mouth.

"Did we hold?"

Terrien Doucard straightened and smiled widely. "Keeper's Dale is ours!" he announced, and Alustriel's eyes sparkled. Then she slept, peacefully, confident that this furiously working dwarven priestess would keep her warm and well, and she was confident that, whatever her own fate, the greater good had been served.

For the good of all goodly folk.

EPILOGUE

B erg'inyon Baenre was not surprised to find Jarlaxle and the soldiers of Bregan D'aerthe waiting for him far below the surface, far from Mithral Hall. As soon as he had heard reports of desertion, Berg'inyon realized that the pragmatic mercenary was probably among those ranks of drow fleeing the war.

Methil had informed Jarlaxle of Berg'inyon's approach, and the mercenary leader was indeed surprised to find that Berg'inyon, the son of Matron Baenre, the weapons master of the First House, had also run off in desertion. The mercenary had figured that Berg'inyon would fight his way into Mithral Hall and die as his mother had died.

Stupidly.

"The war is lost," Berg'inyon remarked. Unsure of himself, he looked to Methil, for he hadn't anticipated that the illithid would be out here, away from the matriarch. The illithid's obvious wounds, one arm hanging limply and a large hole on the side of his octopus head, grotesque brain matter oozing out, caught Berg'inyon off guard as well, for he never expected that anyone could catch up to Methil and harm him so.

"Your mother is dead," Jarlaxle replied bluntly, drawing the young Baenre's attention from the wounded illithid. "As are your two sisters and Auro'pol Dyrr."

Berg'inyon nodded, seeming hardly surprised.

Jarlaxle wondered whether he should mention that Matron Baenre was the one who had murdered the latter. He held the thought in check, figuring he might be able to use that little bit of information against Berg'inyon at a later time.

"Matron Zeerith Q'Xorlarrin led the retreat from Mithral Hall's lower door," the mercenary went on.

"And my own force caught up to those drow who tried, and failed, to get in the eastern door," Berg'inyon added.

"And you punished them?" Jarlaxle wanted to know, for he was still unsure of Berg'inyon's feelings about all of this, still unsure if he and his band were about to fight yet another battle down here in the tunnels.

Berg'inyon scoffed at the notion of punishment, and Jarlaxle breathed a little easier.

Together, they marched on, back for the dark and more comfortable ways of Menzoberranzan. They linked with Zeerith and her force soon after, and many other groups of dark elves and humanoids fell into line as the days wore on. In all, more than two thousand drow, a fourth of them Baenre soldiers, had died in the assault on Mithral Hall, and twice that number of humanoid slaves had been killed, most outside the mountain, on Fourthpeak's southern slopes and in Keeper's Dale. And a like number of humanoids had run off after the battles, fleeing to the surface or down other corridors, taking their chances in the unknown world above or in the wild Underdark rather than return to the tortured life as a slave of the drow.

Things had not gone as Matron Baenre had planned.

Berg'inyon fell into line as the quiet force moved away, letting Zeerith control the procession.

"Menzoberranzan will be many years in healing from the folly of Matron Baenre," Jarlaxle remarked to Berg'inyon later that day, when he came upon the young weapons master alone in a side chamber as the army camped in a region of broken caves and short, connecting tunnels.

Berg'inyon didn't disagree with the statement and showed no anger at all. He understood the truth of Jarlaxle's words, and knew that much trouble would befall House Baenre in the days ahead. Matron Zeerith was outraged, and Mez'Barris Armgo and all the other matron mothers would be, too, when they learned of the disaster.

"The offer remains," Jarlaxle said, and he left the chamber, left Berg'inyon alone with his thoughts.

House Baenre would likely survive, Berg'inyon believed. Triel would assume its rulership, and though they had lost five hundred skilled soldiers, nearly two thousand remained, including more than three hundred of the famed lizard riders. Matron Baenre had built a huge network of allies outside the House as well, and even this disaster, and the death of Baenre, would not likely topple the First House.

There would indeed be trouble, though. Matron Baenre was the solidifying force. What might House Baenre expect from troublesome Gromph with her gone?

And what of Triel? Berg'inyon wondered. Where would he fit into his sister's designs? Now she would be free to raise children of her own and bring them into power. The first son born to her would either be groomed as the House wizard or as a candidate for Berg'inyon's position as weapons master.

How long, then, did Berg'inyon have? Fifty years? A hundred? Not long in the life span of a dark elf.

Berg'inyon looked to the archway, to the back of the departing mercenary, and considered carefully Jarlaxle's offer for him to join Bregan D'aerthe.

⚔ ⚔ ⚔ ⚔ ⚔

Mithral Hall was a place of mixed emotions: tears for the dead and cheers for the victory. All mourned Besnell and Firble, Regweld Harpell and so many others who had died valiantly. And all cheered for King Bruenor and his mighty friends, for Berkthgar the Bold, for Lady Alustriel, still nursing her grievous wounds, and for Stumpet Rakingclaw, hero of both the Undercity and Keeper's Dale.

And all cheered most of all for Gandalug Battlehammer, the patron of Clan Battlehammer, returned from the grave, it seemed. How strange it was for Bruenor to face his own ancestor, to see the first bust in the Hall of Kings come to life!

The two dwarves sat side by side in the throne room on the upper levels of the dwarven complex, flanked by Alustriel—with Stumpet kneeling beside the Lady of Silverymoon's chair, nagging her to rest!—on the right and Berkthgar on the left.

The celebration was general throughout the dwarven complex, from the Undercity to the throne room, a time of gathering, and of parting, a time when Belwar Dissengulp and Bruenor Battlehammer finally met. Through the magic of Alustriel, an enchantment that sorted out the language problems, the two were able to forge an alliance between Blingdenstone and Mithral Hall that would live for centuries, and they were able to swap tales of their common drow friend, particularly when Drizzt was wandering around, just far enough away to realize they were talking about him.

"It's the damned cat that bothers me," Bruenor huffed on one occasion, loud enough so that Drizzt would hear.

The drow sauntered over, put a foot on the raised dais that held the thrones, and leaned forward on his knee, very close to Belwar. "Guenhwyvar humbles Bruenor," Drizzt said in the Drow tongue, a language Belwar somewhat understood, but which was not translated by Alustriel's spell for Bruenor. "She often uses the dwarf for bedding."

Bruenor, knowing they were talking about him, but unable to understand a word, hooted in protest—and protested louder when Gandalug, who also knew a bit of the Drow tongue, joined in the conversation and the mirth.

"But suren the cat's not fer using me son's son's son's son's son's son's son's 'ead fer a piller!" the old dwarf howled. "Too hard it be. Too, too!"

"By Moradin, I should've left with the damned dark elves," a defeated Bruenor grumbled.

That notion sobered old Gandalug, took the cheer from his face in the blink of an eye.

Such was the celebration in Mithral Hall, a time of strong emotions, both good and bad.

Catti-brie watched it all from the side, feeling removed and strangely out of place. Surely she was thrilled at the victory, intrigued by the svirfnebli, whom she had met once before, and even more intrigued that the patron of her father's clan had been miraculously returned to the dwarven complex he had founded. Along with those exciting feelings, though, the young woman felt a sense of completion. The drow threat to Mithral Hall was ended this time, and new and stronger alliances would be forged between Mithral Hall and all its neighbors, even Nesmé. Bruenor and Berkthgar seemed old friends now—Bruenor had even hinted on several occasions that he might be willing to let the barbarian wield Aegis-fang.

Catti-brie hoped that would not come to pass, and didn't think it would. Bruenor had hinted at the generous offer mostly because he knew it wouldn't really cost him anything, Catti-brie suspected. After Berkthgar's exploits in Keeper's Dale, his own weapon, Bankenfuere, was well on its way as a legend among the warriors of Settlestone.

No matter what Berkthgar's exploits might be, Bankenfuere would never rival Aegis-fang, in Catti-brie's mind.

Though she was quiet and reflective, Catti-brie was not grim, not maudlin. Like everyone else in Mithral Hall, she had lost some friends in the war. But like everyone else, she was battle-hardened, accepting the ways of the world and able to see the greater good that had come from the battle. She laughed when a group of svirfnebli practically pulled out what little hair they had, so frustrated were they in trying to teach a group of drunken dwarves how to hear vibrations in the stone. She laughed louder when Regis bopped into the throne room, pounds of food tucked under each arm and already so stuffed that the buttons on his waistcoat were near bursting.

And she laughed loudest of all when Bidderdoo Harpell raced past her, Thibbledorf Pwent scrambling on his knees behind the wizard, begging Bidderdoo to bite him!

But there remained a reflective solitude behind that laughter, that nagging sense of completion that didn't sit well on the shoulders of a woman who had just begun to open her eyes to the wide world.

✕ ✕ ✕ ✕ ✕

In the smoky filth of the Abyss, the balor Errtu held his breath as the shapely drow, the delicate disaster, approached his mushroom throne.

Errtu didn't know what to expect from Lolth; they had both witnessed the disaster.

The balor watched as the drow came through the mist, the prisoner, the promised gift, in tow. She was smiling, but on the face of the Lady of Chaos, one could never hope to guess what that meant.

Errtu sat tall and proud, confident he had done as instructed. If Lolth tried to blame him for the disaster, he would argue, he determined, though if she had somehow found out about the antimagic stone he had sent along with the glabrezu . . .

"You have brought my payment?" the balor boomed, trying to sound imposing.

"Of course, Errtu," the Spider Queen replied.

Errtu cocked his tremendous, horned head. There seemed no deception in either her tone or her movements as she pushed the prisoner toward the gigantic, seated balor.

"You seem pleased," Errtu dared to remark.

Lolth's smile nearly took in her ears, and Errtu understood. She was pleased! The old wretch, the most wicked of the wicked, was glad of the outcome. Matron Baenre was gone, as was all order in Menzoberranzan. The drow city would know its greatest chaos now, thrilling interhouse warfare and a veritable spiderweb of intrigue, layer upon layer of lies and treachery, through each of the ruling Houses.

"You knew this would happen from the beginning!" the balor accused.

Lolth laughed aloud. "I did not anticipate the outcome," she assured Errtu. "I did not know Errtu would be so resourceful in protecting the one who might end his banishment."

The balor's eyes widened, and his great leathery wings folded close around him, a symbolic, if ineffective, movement of defense.

"Fear not, my fiendish ally," Lolth cooed. "I will give you a chance to redeem yourself in my eyes."

Errtu growled low. What favor did the Spider Queen now want from him?

"I will be busy these next decades, I fear," Lolth went on, "in trying to end the confusion in Menzoberranzan."

Errtu scoffed. "Never would you desire such a thing," he replied.

"I will be busy watching the confusion then," Lolth was willing to admit. Almost as an afterthought, she added, "And watching what it is you must do for me."

Again came that demonic growl.

"When you are free, Errtu," Lolth said evenly, "when you have Drizzt Do'Urden entangled in the tongs of your merciless whip, do kill him slowly, painfully, that I might hear his every cry!" The Spider Queen swept hers arms up then and disappeared with a flurry of crackling black energy.

Errtu's lip curled up in an evil smile. He looked to the pitiful prisoner, the key to breaking the will and the heart of Drizzt Do'Urden. Sometimes, it seemed, the Spider Queen did not ask for much.

⚔ ⚔ ⚔ ⚔

It had been two tendays since the victory, and in Mithral Hall the celebration continued. Many had left—first the two remaining men from Nesmé and the Longriders, along with Harkle and Bella don DelRoy—though Pwent finally convinced Bidderdoo to stick around for a while. Then Alustriel and her remaining Knights in Silver, seventy-five warriors, began their journey back to Silverymoon with their heads held high, the lady ready to meet the challenges of her political rivals head-on, confident that she had done right in coming to King Bruenor's aid.

The svirfnebli were in no hurry to leave, though, enjoying the company of Clan Battlehammer, and the men of Settlestone vowed to stay until the last of Mithral Hall's mead was drained away.

Far down the mountain from the dwarven complex, on a cold, windy plain, Catti-brie sat atop a fine roan—one of the horses that had belonged to a slain Silverymoon knight. She sat quietly and confidently, but the sting in her heart as she looked up to Mithral Hall was no less acute. Her eyes scanned the trails to the rocky exit from the mountains, and she smiled, not surprised, in seeing a rider coming down.

"I knew ye'd follow me down here," she said to Drizzt Do'Urden when the ranger approached.

"We all have our place," Drizzt replied.

"And mine's not now in Mithral Hall," Catti-brie said sternly. "Ye'll not change me mind!"

Drizzt paused for a long while, studying the determined young woman. "You've talked with Bruenor?" he asked.

"Of course," Catti-brie retorted. "Ye think I'd leave me father's house without his blessings?"

"Blessings he gave grudgingly, no doubt," Drizzt remarked.

Catti-brie straightened in her saddle and locked her jaw firmly. "Bruenor's got much to do," she said. "And he's got Regis and yerself . . ." She paused and held that thought, noticing the heavy pack strapped behind Drizzt's saddle. "And Gandalug and Berkthgar beside him," she finished. "They've not even figured which is to rule and which is to watch, though I'm thinking Gandalug's to let Bruenor remain king."

"That would be the wiser course," Drizzt agreed.

A long moment of silence passed between them.

"Berkthgar talks of leaving," Drizzt said suddenly, "of returning to Icewind Dale and the ancient ways of his people."

Catti-brie nodded. She had heard such rumors.

Again came that uncomfortable silence. Catti-brie finally turned her eyes away from the drow, thinking he was judging her, thinking, in her moment of doubt, that she was being a terrible daughter to Bruenor, terrible and selfish. "Me father didn't try to stop me," she blurted with a tone of finality, "and yerself cannot!"

"I never said I came out to try to stop you," Drizzt calmly replied.

Catti-brie paused, not really surprised. When she had first told Bruenor she was leaving, that she had to go out from Mithral Hall for a while and witness the wonders of the world, the crusty dwarf had bellowed so loudly that Catti-brie thought the stone walls would tumble in on both of them.

They had met again two days later, when Bruenor was not so full of dwarven holy water, and to Catti-brie's surprise and relief, her father was much more reasonable. He understood her heart, he had assured her, though his gruff voice cracked as he delivered the words, and he realized she had to follow it, had to go off and learn who she was and where she fit in the world. Catti-brie had thought the words uncharacteristically understanding and philosophical of Bruenor, and now, facing Drizzt, she was certain of their source. Now she knew who Bruenor had spoken to between their meetings.

"He sent ye," she accused Drizzt.

"You were leaving and so was I," Drizzt replied casually.

"I just could not spend the rest o' me days in the tunnels," Catti-brie said, suddenly feeling as if she had to explain herself, revealing the guilt that had weighed heavily on her since her decision to leave home. She looked all around, her eyes scanning the distant horizon. "There's just so much more for me. I'm knowing that in me heart. I've known it since Wulfgar . . ."

She paused and sighed and looked to Drizzt helplessly.

"And more for me," the drow said with a mischievous grin, "much more."

Catti-brie glanced back over her shoulder, back to the west, where the sun was already beginning its descent.

"The days are short," she remarked, "and the road is long."

"Only as long as you make it," Drizzt said to her, drawing her gaze back to him. "And the days are only as short as you allow them to be."

Catti-brie eyed him curiously, not understanding that last statement.

Drizzt was grinning widely as he explained, as full of anticipation as was Catti-brie. "A friend of mine, a blind old ranger, once told me that if you ride hard and fast enough to the west, the sun will never set for you."

By the time he had finished the statement, Catti-brie had wheeled her roan and was in full gallop across the frozen plain toward the west, toward Nesmé and Longsaddle beyond that, toward mighty Waterdeep and the Sword Coast. She bent low in the saddle, her mount running hard, her cloak billowing and snapping in the wind behind her, her thick auburn hair flying wildly.

Drizzt opened a belt pouch and looked at the onyx panther figurine. No one could ask for better companions, he mused, and with a final look to the mountains, to Mithral Hall, where his friend was king, the ranger kicked his stallion into a gallop and chased after Catti-brie.

To the west and the adventures of the wide world.

The Legend of Drizzt

Continues in

Passage to Dawn

Available in Hardcover
from Wizards of the Coast
March 2007